I0594610

KEEPING FAITH

BEVERLEY OAKLEY

SANI
PUBLISHING

Copyright © 2019 by Beverley Oakley

All rights reserved.

No part of this book may be reproduced in any form or by any electronic or mechanical means, including information storage and retrieval systems, without written permission from the author, except for the use of brief quotations in a book review.

KEEPING FAITH

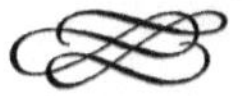

CHAPTER 1

"What did you learn last night?"

"A gentleman must always believe he knows best."

Confident that her answer was pleasing, Faith reached across the table to help herself to a macaroon, but a sharp slap across the back of the hand stopped her progress by the silver teapot.

Her smile of feigned contrition was rewarded with the briefest of nods from Madame Chambon. Not an invitation to partake of a macaroon though. The table laden with eclairs and petit fours in Madame's private sitting room was merely for show.

"Greedy girl, Faith! You can eat at Claridges Hotel tomorrow, and I daresay you won't even spare a thought for the other girls who are justified in being somewhat jealous of your cosseted life."

Madame sniffed as she patted one of the grizzled orange curls of her elaborate coiffure. Faith suspected a squirrel's pelt had made its contribution. "I'm sure they wonder every day why you never have to stir yourself, or anyone else for that matter, to get your fine clothes or a roof over your head." Madame Chambon piled three macaroons onto her already laden plate, before making a sweeping gesture that encompassed the furnishings of her surprisingly decorous private sitting room with its gold-tasselled, green-velvet curtains and flock wallpaper. "What have you told them, Faith? About why you are here, I mean."

Faith's stomach rumbled as she gazed from the prints of the famous artists that lined the walls to the fine fare in front of her, ordered from Fortnum and Mason. These monthly sessions in table manners were supposed to give Faith the practise she needed to deport herself like a lady when eating in public, though, under Madame's guardianship, Faith never actually got to try the specialties.

"Answer me, Faith. In all the three years that you've been here, you've had to do precisely nothing to justify your existence. Surely the girls have questioned you? I have my own version of the truth for them, as you know, but I'd be interested to hear what you have to say."

Faith didn't answer. She already knew how lucky she was, but Madame was not ready to drop the subject, despite having just crammed an entire chocolate éclair into her mouth. Faith just managed to make out the muffled words, "Every night you lie peacefully in your bed while the other girls have to earn their livings."

Lying *peacefully* in her bed was not how Faith would describe the restfulness of her slumber. She was kept awake every night by the grunts and cries of ecstasy that penetrated the thin walls of her attic chamber.

Still, she'd finally learned when it was wise to respond meekly, so she bowed her head and stared at her neat kid gloves while dreaming of the delicacies Mrs Gedge would order for them when Faith really was dining with her at Claridges Hotel the following afternoon. The Sacher-torte

Mrs Gedge had *ummed* and *aahed* over before finally choosing the baked Alaska from the sweets trolley last month still haunted her. However, since part of Faith's tutoring included how to win over reluctant gentlemen 'and make them wild with wanting' which is how Madame phrased it, then surely Faith could persuade her American benefactress to order the Austrian chocolate specialty?

She was so busy rehearsing her words for tomorrow that she almost missed Madame's prophetic and appalling statement.

"Well, Faith, the time has come for you to start earning your way now."

It seemed the ground fell away from under her as Faith gripped the table edge. For so long, she'd known the reckoning would come. Yes, and with three years preparing for it, she'd believed she could meet it head-on with the necessary fortitude.

But there'd been no warning.

She began to shake, biting into her bottom lip and clasping her hands beneath the table to try and keep secret the manifestations of her terror from Madame, who'd only be spurred into gloating and make her suffer even more.

"Mrs Gedge reported last month that she wasn't entirely happy you were ready for what she has in store for you when she took you to tea, Faith." Madame chewed noisily, unperturbed, it seemed, by the crumbs that landed on her gaudy vermillion skirts.

Faith didn't suggest that Mrs Gedge's dissatisfaction was perhaps the fault of Faith's tutor, the one sitting in front of her, who knew nothing about deporting oneself as a lady.

With a dainty gesture using only her forefingers, Madame Chambon raised her plate and licked at the crumbs that had not been dislodged by her fat fingers before saying, "Fortunately, Lady Vernon is recovered at last from her long indisposition and has agreed to forget your rudeness to her from six months ago. In fact, she'll be here shortly. Yes, she'll soon have you passing the scrutiny of the most discerning duchess." Madame gobbled down another macaroon with as much finesse as the dogs Faith's father used to goad into fighting each other for the scraps from the scrubbed wooden table at the farm. Not that there'd been many scraps with ten children to feed.

"Should we not have waited for Lady Vernon?" Faith suggested, daringly. But she had to say *something* to stop herself from launching into a volley of querulous questions about exactly what form this 'having to earn her own way' might take.

Madame Chambon pushed aside an untouched plate of bread and butter to reach for another chocolate éclair and sighed. "There was just so much food on the table it seemed unnecessary to wait if her ladyship was going to be late. Ah! And here she is." Madame's orange-painted mouth turned up at a knock on the door. "Shoulders back, Faith! And make sure you don't talk with your mouth full."

Since this was not a danger, Faith supposed there might be some compensation in having to face her former nemesis, who surely must subscribe to the belief that learning table manners required one having to *eat*.

Madame threw her arms wide in a welcome as the door opened to admit the new arrival. "Good evening, Lady Vernon. We're so glad you've recovered from your chest ailment," she gushed. "A good rest has done you the world of good. Why, you look ten years younger. Just as you do every time I see you in fact. And we're indeed humbled that you've consented to return." Madame simpered at the elderly woman dressed all in black who looked, Faith thought, even more wraith-like than usual as she pinned up the veil of her bonnet and took the seat at the table proffered by Madame, who went on, "I'm sure you'll feel even better once you've heard Faith's heartfelt apology."

Faith blushed under the scrutiny of the two pairs of expectant, unforgiving eyes, and glanced longingly at the remaining macaroon.

Yes, there were times when it was worth being abject. She mightn't mean what she said, but if the last three years under Madame Chambon's roof had taught her one thing, it was how to sound heartfelt and sincere when she felt anything but.

"I'm sorry for my rude comments about…" Faith hesitated. Perhaps it was best not to stir up old memories. While it must be perfectly obvious to anyone who met Lady Vernon as to why an earl's daughter could remain a spinster into her sixtieth year, it hadn't been in anyone's interest—Faith's least of all, it turned out—for Faith to have gone into quite such specific and extensive detail regarding her thoughts on the likely reasons. "I behaved like a child, though it's such a long time ago now, I can barely remember what was going through my head at the time. I *was* only seventeen and, in those days, prone to losing my temper, but now I'm eighteen and thanks to all your efforts in teaching me how to act like a lady, Lady Vernon, I'm so far from the rude and impulsive young thing I was before, you'd not recognise me today. Thanks to your thorough tutelage, I am determined that I will never speak out of turn to you, or anyone. Indeed, I have changed! I truly believe that confronted by a table of delicacies like this, for example, I would certainly not embarrass you or Mrs Gedge or any lovely young man or his mother who might take me out to tea by any show of greediness or lack of restraint."

Lady Vernon's eyes remained fixed firmly on Faith for the duration of this speech with no indication of how forgiving, or otherwise, she might prove to be.

After a long silence, she spoke. "Restraint?" She sniffed. "Restraint is the most important requirement of any young lady, Faith. I've told you this many times, so I'm glad it's a lesson you claim to have finally learned."

Still with her eyes fixed on Faith, she reached towards the remaining macaroon that sat lonely on its plate just in front of them both, her long-fingered hand hovering just above. "Please pass that to me, Faith. I can't seem to reach it."

Wordlessly, Faith complied, schooling her features into impassivity while she railed inside, *I hate you! I hate you!* Outwardly, she gave nothing away as she watched Lady Vernon transport the coconut confection to her thin, bloodless lips.

"Delicious," murmured Lady Vernon. "In fact, I believe it is the best macaroon I have ever tasted. You must surely agree, Faith, since the plate is now empty."

She looked pointedly at the two remaining crumbs that clung to the edge, as if to imply that Faith had eaten the rest. Then she indicated the plate of bread and butter near Madame Chambon. "Please eat, Faith. Madame Chambon and I have a leisurely afternoon at our disposal. She and I will partake of the remaining chocolate eclairs..." Her pointed chin wobbled slightly, whether from the suppression of mirth, or the swallowing of bile, Faith could only guess, "while you make good work of the bread and butter with all the ladylike restraint you're so anxious to prove."

CHAPTER 2

Faith had learned to suffer in silence and to keep her thoughts to herself, long before she'd been brought to Madame Chambon's. Madame might have been gloating the day before over her silly little bit of power play but in a few hours Faith would be sitting at a proper grand table laden with even nicer delicacies. Ones she could eat.

Furthermore, she'd be free of Madame's cloying presence for an afternoon, admired in public by women who would sweep past in fashionable gowns adorned with cascades of bows and swathes of silk and satin who would see that she was every bit their equal.

Faith could barely suppress her excitement as Charity, from the room below hers, pinned up her hair the following afternoon.

"I'll bring a macaroon home for you, Charity," Faith promised, sitting as still as she could while Charity arranged a small jewelled comb amongst Faith's fair curls.

"I doubt your Mrs Gedge would take kindly to that. Wouldn't she call it stealing?"

Faith took a quick, surprised breath and glanced at Charity. Her best friend at Madame Chambon's had never before resorted to unkind digs. But perhaps Charity was simply reminding Faith of the very real dangers of taking what Faith honestly believed had been promised; only to have it called stealing. It's how Faith had found herself deposited at Madame Chambon's, instead of before a magistrate.

"You *will* get your macaroon, Charity. And it won't be stealing. I shall simply be practising what Mrs Gedge has instructed I be taught these past three years." Faith smiled sweetly. "Deception. Taking what I want without the other party realising they've surrendered what they had not intended giving. Inveigling my way into their good offices." Immediately, she felt overwhelmed by the unknown. "Do you think I'm up to the task, Charity?"

"Lord, Faith, I'm not used to hearing you talk like that, and it's unnerving." Charity stepped in front of Faith, her eyes skimming the length of her ensemble, from the demure neckline to the simple and depressingly plain skirt. Faith had expected to be dressed with all the flamboyance exhibited by Charity's black and scarlet polonaise with its daringly low neckline and whisper of a sleeve. "You always sound like you know exactly how to get what you want."

"It's what I pretend. To Madame and the other girls." Faith squeezed her eyes shut briefly and flicked away a tear. "Well, she might think I'm beholden to her because I have nowhere else to go and because Mrs Gedge pays her to keep me, but I swear to you that there are some things I won't stoop to, regardless of whether it's in Mrs Gedge's grand scheme for me."

Charity looked at her enquiringly.

It had seemed foolishly naïve to voice this determination in a bawdy house and to a friend who, every night, suffered what Faith was about to declare she'd never do.

"I will never go with a man I do not love. Yes! You might

smile, Charity, but I have learning, and I have fine clothes, and I know how to behave like a lady. I'm cleverer than Madame Chambon thinks, and I am not afraid of Mrs Gedge anymore." Her bosom heaved. Now that she was voicing her most fervently held innermost thoughts, there was no turning back. "No Charity, I swear it! I will not be taken by a man I do not love."

"Ah Faith, now sit down again and let me repin that errant curl at the back." Charity's tone was as light as her hands were on Faith's shoulders as she resettled Faith upon the stool of her dressing table. "I believe that's what Anastasia said too, which got the fire up Madame's backside and all but condemned Anastasia to the very worst next gentleman. You be careful who you say such things to."

Faith glanced at the keyhole. They'd been foolish words and too loudly declared. What Charity said was true.

"How is Anastasia now?" she asked, biting her lip. "I haven't seen her for a few days."

"That's because she's not here anymore. Didn't you know?" Gently, Charity began to massage Faith's neck. "Once her bruises had faded, Madame said she couldn't risk Anastasia ruining the reputation of a house to which gentlemen came expecting the loving comfort for which Madame Chambon's is renowned. Now, you look beautiful, Faith. And I'm sure Mrs Gedge will think so too." She smiled and touched Faith's cheek, saying with genuine kindness, "And so too will the handsome gentleman Mrs Gedge has lined up for you. Indeed, I believe he'll be so kind and gallant that you'll fall instantly in love with him, and he with you, and soon you'll be galloping into the sunset together to some gilded castle where you'll enjoy a life of ease and domestic joy for the rest of your days." She sighed wistfully. "And I will never hear from you again, but I will go peacefully to my grave knowing that at least *you* found happiness, Faith."

CHAPTER 3

"A good thing you know how to balance your appetite for the good things in life without spoiling your pretty figure, Faith." Mrs Gedge's American accent seemed more pronounced when she was in fine spirits. She smiled at Faith across the damask-covered dining table, before taking a sip of Rhenish. Her violet ostrich feathers, coloured to match the silk polonaise she wore, reminded Faith of bowing acolytes. Like the other women in the room, she exuded wealth and privilege. Faith felt dowdy in comparison. She'd truly believed Mrs Gedge was going to dress her up to the nines to show off her protégé. "I was a beauty in my day," Mrs Gedge went on. "I worked hard at it, and I had many marriage offers."

A stroll through Hyde Park and an exhibition had followed their afternoon tea at Claridges, and now they were seated in a restaurant with hand-painted ceilings, attended by obsequious waiters while an orchestra played, partly visible through the sumptuous palm fronds that screened their table.

Mrs Gedge put down her knife and fork and sent a

considered look about her. "The power and wealth of the gentlemen in this room could tilt the world's axis if they only knew how to work together." Her nostrils flared. "If they only harnessed it for good rather than expended their energies on satisfying their personal desires. I brought you here for a reason, you know. Because someone of interest was going to be dining here. Do you recognise anyone?"

Faith blinked at the abruptness of the question. She also put down her knife and fork and looked carefully at the faces of the dozen or so gentlemen dining with other men or, occasionally, a woman.

"Several," she said, returning to her food. The sole with chive sauce was delicious and not the kind of fare she generally enjoyed. The expense and effort to which Madame went to ensure the trappings of her sumptuous establishment and the outward appearance of the girls who represented it were only skin deep. Therefore, dining on something other than potatoes and gravy with the occasional piece of gristle made it worth pandering to Mrs Gedge.

"I trust you would not be recognised?" There was steel behind the question, but Faith knew that being kept hidden from the gentlemen who visited Madame Chambon's girls was an important clause in the contract Mrs Gedge had with the brothel keeper.

"Of course not." Faith dabbed delicately at her lips with her napkin and smiled again at her benefactress. "I recognise a great many people here in fact. That gentlemen dining with his mother over there is one of Charity's most regular clients—"

"How do you know she's his mother?"

"Because I used to clean the grate and make up the fire in her bedchamber when she was a guest at Wildwood Lodge. She's a friend of Lady Carmody's. That red hair is hard to miss." Faith hesitated. "Do you think she'll come over and say hello to you?"

Mrs Gedge shuddered. "Lord, I've worked too hard to ensure I'll not be recognised these past few years. Like you. No, I no longer care to recall those days at Wildwood Lodge." She picked at her food, sad and no longer the hard, determined woman Faith had always known. "Tell me, Faith, do you miss your friends from Wildwood Lodge?" Mrs Gedge's laboured breathing seemed due to more than just the stress put on her corset by the large quantity of food and wine she'd just consumed. Her mouth trembled. "Do you resent me for taking you away from there? I trust you've had no communication with anyone from your old life. If you have, now is the time to tell me."

"You know my only friends are the girls at Madame Chambon's." Faith resented the intrusion and the suspicion in her benefactress's voice, but she spoke the truth. "You made sure of that," she added, spearing a Brussels sprout.

"For your own good, Faith. I made you a lady. I think some sacrifices have been worth the position in which you now find yourself."

Faith offered the requisite smile, tilting her head to regard Mrs Gedge with a level stare and, in the process, intercepted the interested glance of a young man across the room through the fronds of the Kentish palm to her right. He was dining with an older gentleman and a woman. Parents, perhaps, in the way they communicated an expectation of filial obedience as they now rose, gathering gloves and cane.

The young gentleman got to his feet more slowly, his eyes lingering on Faith. Though surprised, and somewhat unnerved, she did not look away as he brushed back the heavy hair that flopped over his brow, all the while keeping his eyes firmly on her. His lips curved slightly as he made some signal to his companions that he was about to follow them.

Faith returned his level stare. *Give nothing away.* That's what she'd been taught. *Yet show that you have noticed him.*

She was brought back to the present by Mrs Gedge's thoughtful tone. "My, my, I did not expect *this.*"

"I don't know what you mean." Faith clasped her hands in her lap and returned Mrs Gedge's look with unusual defiance across the table.

Surprise still lurked in the other woman's expression before Mrs Gedge laughed softly. "My dear Faith, you were magnificent." She sat back, her bosom heaving. "That young man...you don't know him surely?"

"I've never seen him in my life."

"Did you think him handsome?"

"Very."

"Why, pray?"

Faith shrugged. "I like an athletic physique. And he had nice eyes. He looked...kind."

"Kind?!" The word snapped like a whip across the table, and Faith felt her mouth drop open.

Before another beat had passed, Mrs Gedge had recovered herself. A slow smile curved her lips as she said slowly, "Why, Faith, this is a miracle. I cannot believe how easy this is going to be. You did not even try." She took another sip of wine, then announced, "Tomorrow night you are going to your first soiree."

Faith jerked her head up.

"I had not thought you ready, but it's important to strike while the iron is hot, as they say." Faith sent her a narrow look and wondered if Mrs Gedge had drunk too much. "I will not accompany you, Faith, of course. No, Lady Vernon will do that. A good thing she's recovered her health for it'll be a busy few weeks." Businesslike, Mrs Gedge went on, "She will accompany you to a great many functions: balls, soirees, picnics – and she will report back to me, you understand?"

Mrs Gedge finished her wine and put her knife and fork together. Faith waited. This was not some reward, she knew. She was expected to perform, though she wasn't sure, exactly, how. Surprisingly, tingles in the tips of her fingers were echoed by a prickling sensation on the backs of her legs, and her breath was suddenly shallow. Fear? Anticipation? Excitement?

Hope.

In the end, she had to ask. "Is this…to be my purpose, Mrs Gedge?"

A flash of triumph brightened the other woman's eye. "Yes, Faith. For three years, you've been trained to behave like a young lady, and I've asked nothing in return." Mrs Gedge had positioned herself so that she could not be observed by the company currently leaving; however, she could clearly see that the young man had stopped at the double doors for a final look over his shoulder at Faith.

Looking from the handsome young man with the athletic physique and the kind eyes to Faith, she said softly, "I have waited a long time for this but…tomorrow you will begin to repay me."

$\mathcal{A}$ strong smell of boiled cabbage permeated Lady Vernon's musty lodgings.

The hackney carriage had dropped her off in the cobbled street in front of the narrow terrace house, and having been ushered into an unused bedchamber, Faith's earlier excitement was being sorely tested.

She stared with dismay at the simple gown Lady Vernon held up.

She was hardly going to make the grand entrance she'd envisaged in this plain, pale-cream silk ensemble trimmed with pink bows.

"Very virginal, isn't it, Faith? Not what you're used to regarding as up to the mark in the household you inhabit." Lady Vernon's fingers pinched Faith's flesh as she turned her around and, without ceremony, began to unbutton the back of her dress. "No, you fancy the tawdry, I daresay, because even if you've not yet had the pleasure of a man, you're still no better than those other girls you live with."

"Lady Vernon, don't you look just the thing!" Mrs Gedge, who'd just been admitted by the parlourmaid, interrupted the unwise response Faith was about to deliver. The American woman looked, in contrast to Lady Vernon, quite animated as she took in the gown that clothed the noblewoman's frail frame. Perhaps it had been up to the mark a decade previously, but it had been obviously refashioned into a poor copy of the day's fashions. The feathers in Lady Vernon's headdress looked as tired as the grey-faced old woman who wore them.

"And Faith, you know what is expected of you, don't you?"

Faith nodded as Lady Vernon peeled her blue day dress over her shoulders and down her hips, then began to button up the cream silk once Faith had stepped into it. She was so disappointed she thought she might cry. The previous week, when the dressmaker had fitted her with the calico toile, Faith had been led to believe the figure-hugging ensemble was going to be in bold, eye-catching colours.

"And you, Lady Vernon?" Mrs Gedge began to circle.

"I know exactly what is expected, Madam." Lady Vernon's tone was grim. "I will not let Faith out of my sight."

"And she is to come back here tonight. I don't want to run the risk of her being followed. In fact…" Mrs Gedge sent them both a considering look. "Faith will stay here for the next few weeks. Lady Vernon, you will arrange for her belongings to be brought around and you, Faith, are to have nothing to do with any of the girls at Madame Chambon's from now on." She rubbed her hands as if in anticipation of something very pleasurable while Faith reassessed her idea of success. In the short term, success simply meant extricating herself from the smell of mould and boiled cabbage that pervaded Lady Vernon's premises. She didn't think she could bear it a moment longer.

"Whatever you wish, Mrs Gedge."

Meanwhile, Mrs Gedge was reaching forward to take a

tendril of Faith's golden hair. "You were blessed, child," she murmured. "Blessed like few others of your squalid upbringing. I wish you to turn expectation on its head. That's what I wish for you tonight."

"And…who am I to play?"

The question lingered in the damp air, clearly a source of amusement to Mrs Gedge.

"Who are you to play?" Mrs Gedge laughed softly and turned to Lady Vernon. "Who is this shy beauty, Lady Vernon? Show me how well you know your part."

Lady Vernon inclined her head and intoned in a dry, unemotional voice, "I'd like to introduce my impoverished goddaughter rescued from an untenable situation in the north of the country. Well connected by birth but penniless." She looked at Faith almost with dislike. "A penniless beauty."

Faith ran her hands down the princess-line gown and glanced again at her reflection. She had to admit that there was an elegant simplicity to the unadorned cream silk. A tiny row of pink bows down the front of her gown and one large pink bow at the back of the swathed bustle would make her stand out from the crowd, she knew. A simple cross on a chain at her throat completed the ensemble.

~

It was the society event Faith had imagined but certainly not the grand debut.

She and Lady Vernon stood out for the very fact that they stepped across the threshold into the dazzling ballroom and richly garbed crowd as, clearly, the poor relations.

"Welcome, Lady Vernon. And who is the young lady?"

Their hostess for the evening, Lady Griffin, seemed pleasant and welcoming. Even sympathetic when Lady

Vernon explained she was taking her goddaughter to a few places during her first visit to the metropolis.

"I agreed to sponsor the girl to the extent my limited resources will allow." Lady Vernon sighed as if Faith were the greatest cross to bear. But then Lady Vernon seemed to regard any effort on her part as an imposition. "She's the eldest of ten." She sniffed. "Daughters, mainly, so I'm doing what I can for the family. If Faith is not successful in the few weeks she has in the metropolis, I'll be sending her to Yorkshire where she's to take up a post as governess." She sniffed again. "It does seem a shame to see her wasted. Such a biddable girl, too." Her brow creased as she added, almost in wonder, "Not the slightest bit vain. She'd suit a young clerk with prospects, perhaps." Lady Vernon smiled hopefully at her hostess.

ON THE OTHER SIDE OF THE ROOM, CRISPIN WESTAWAY WAS trying hard to attend to his aunt, who was waxing lyrical on the play she'd attended the previous night. However, his gaze kept straying to the unusual pair speaking to their hostess beneath the Goya painting. He'd barely been able to believe his eyes when they'd alighted on the vision from the restaurant the night before.

Now he couldn't wait for an opportunity to address her in person.

"The Prince of Wales is causing his poor mother headaches again," he heard his aunt confide in her nasal manner to her friend, Lady Braxsted. "Have you heard, Crispin? What a trial one's children can be."

Crispin didn't care what the Prince of Wales was up to, but he was happy to corroborate his aunt, Lady Pymble's mild outrage at the latest scandal while his gaze drifted to the humpbacked dowager in the far corner who seemed to be shielding her charge.

The girl's hair was like a halo of sensuous golden light, cascading down her back in fashionable ringlets, her small fringe highlighting her elfin face. He'd never seen anyone so lovely, and his fingers itched to grasp his paintbrush. It would be a challenge to capture the wistful half smile the girl directed at the woman when her companion made some remark.

"Excuse me, who is that young woman over there?" he interrupted, causing his gossiping aunt and her friend to stop midsentence and look at him in surprise. They squinted in the direction in which he pointed and shook their heads.

"Never seen her in my life," Lady Braxted said, "though it looks like Lady Vernon is sponsoring her tonight." She gave a snide laugh. "Probably did it for money."

Crispin narrowed his eyes. "Money? It doesn't look like the girl is blessed with a family who can expend much on the outward adornments."

His aunt made a tutting noise. "What a thing to say, Crispin. Most young men would not make observations about the plainness of her dress. They'd have eyes only for the beauty of the young woman. I have to say, she is rather exceptional. Shall I make some investigations on your behalf?" She sent Crispin a sly look.

He nodded. "I would appreciate that, Aunt."

His aunt looked on the point of happily announcing some scheme to facilitate Crispin's wishes, for she was a woman who adored schemes and plots, before she was nearly knocked over by an enthusiastic young lady cutting a swathe through the crowd.

"I am so sorry!" came the mortified, immediately identifiable mid-Atlantic tones of the young lady who'd inadvertently bumped into Lady Pymble. "I really have no idea how to behave, do I?" She put her hand to her mouth as she hiccupped. "Off the boat from New York last week and unleashed this evening for my first London soiree, and already I'm scandalising my English relatives. I'm Miss Amy Eaves, by the way. Pleased to meet you!"

Crispin smiled inwardly as he witnessed the aversion his aunt had in taking the hand thrust into her face. He wondered if she'd go so far as to tell Miss Eaves that young ladies did not introduce themselves in such a manner in *this* country.

To his surprise, she merely said, "You clearly have much to learn about English ways, Miss Eaves, but I daresay one has to start somewhere. I'm Lady Pymble, and this is my nephew, Mr Westaway."

"Oh, my! Lady Pymble, is it? My apologies again." Now Miss Eaves was curtseying. Crispin didn't know whether to be embarrassed or amused. He chose the latter.

"Welcome to London, Miss Eaves. And what are your plans while you are in our fair city?" Miss Eaves was not a beauty in any conventional sense, but there was an enthusiasm about her that set her apart from the coy, well-mannered debutantes of his acquaintance.

Miss Eaves replied with unsurprising directness, "Well, my father wants a title. That is, he wants *me* to snare one since he's got everything else. Including the world's biggest yacht which he's sailing around the world."

"Indeed." Lady Pymble seemed not to know what to say.

Miss Eaves rubbed her little snub nose and frowned. "So, why are you a lady and your nephew is only a Mr?"

Crispin and his aunt exchanged a glance. At least she looked more amused than scandalised now.

"My nephew is in line for a title. Once his father dies. But let's talk of other things, shall we?" She sent a searching look about the room and added, "I'm sure someone must be looking for you, Miss Eaves."

She took this for dismissal and nodded. "Well, I don't know how well you know my uncle, Sir Albion McKinley, but everyone here seems to know everyone else, and if you can persuade him to let me get a job, I'll be mighty grateful."

"A job."

Crispin wasn't surprised his aunt sounded so scandalised.

"Not for money, surely?" Lady Pymble went on.

Miss Eaves nodded again. "I've asked my uncle if I can write about the artists who exhibit for him, and he says I might dip my ink in the inkwell if I choose, but that he won't pay me a penny for my trouble and scandalise my father."

"I should think not," murmured Lady Pymble.

"Oh, I know ladies don't get paid, of course. But I don't want to be a lady." Miss Eaves sent Crispin a considered look. "So, you needn't worry you'll hear from me when you land that title. Anyway..." She took a step away. "If you hear of some newspaper job going, please keep me in mind, only don't get the message to me through my uncle."

"Your uncle is Sir Albion McKinley?" Crispin tried to see anything to connect the highly esteemed patron of the London Society of Artists with this brash young woman. "Not the greatest proponent of women's suffrage I would have thought." He envisioned the tight-lipped, balding and slightly stooped gentleman he'd met on the many occasions he'd ventured into the hallowed precincts of the Royal Society of Artists. Not that that had been for a while. Crispin's passion for art had been effectively strangled by his father's insistence he apply himself to following in the family tradition by entering the world of politics. It had been a long time since he'd picked up a paintbrush.

"No, he is not. I might have earned a way into his good

books if I'd had an ounce of artistic talent in my little finger, but I do not." Miss Eaves shrugged. "No, I like to write, and I think I'm good at it. I also think it's a mighty fine way for a woman to earn a respectable income but..." she sighed. "There you go!"

"Yes, there you go," Crispin repeated, stepping aside in order to facilitate a satisfactory end to the conversation, for it appeared Miss Eaves was ready to settle in for the night, and he was growing increasingly impatient to meet the vision of loveliness still alone with her chaperone on the other side of the room.

With Miss Eaves finally despatched, Crispin was halfway towards Lady Vernon and her unknown charge when his father clapped him on the shoulder with a demand for an inventory on Crispin's activities for the past week.

Dutifully, Crispin outlined the tedium with which he'd occupied mind and body, surprised when Lord Maxwell remarked, "Your Aunt Alice thinks you look weary. Says she spied you across the street when she alighted from a hackney at Marble Arch, and she commented on your grey pallor and hunched shoulders, which she put down to the work in the satchel you carried." Lord Maxwell's craggy face grew more lined as he frowned, though Crispin recognised this as the ghost of a smile. "You'll be doing well if you've inherited half her persuasive talents, for by the end of the conversation, I'd promised that I'd give you a fortnight off. Yes, a week to amuse yourself before you return to the studies required by your new position."

Crispin couldn't have been more surprised.

"A fortnight, Father?"

"Possibly three, in fact, and funds enough to take yourself off to the South of France if you so wish." His brows knitted. "Just make sure you're ready to throw yourself back into work when you return and don't get enticed away by some Frenchie vixen, mind."

Crispin grinned, and content with this out of character interview, was about to buoyantly head off in Lady Vernon's direction when he saw that lady deep in conversation with Miss Eaves, who appeared to have wandered into their enclave with the same abandon she had when she'd met Crispin and his aunt.

Better to wait, he thought, so he could have the field uncluttered. Meanwhile, visions of his week of pure pleasure floated enticingly about his head. Where would he go? What would he do?

His friend Roger Jolimont had a boat. Perhaps they'd sail to the French Riviera. That could be jolly good fun at this time of year. If his father were in such an indulgent mood, perhaps he'd grant Crispin a month.

FAITH WAS BORED. TONIGHT WAS PROVING A DISMAL FAILURE. No one had come up to speak to them except for a talkative American young woman whom Lady Vernon had collared, no doubt to extrapolate information about her earlier conversation with the young man she'd noticed glancing at Faith all evening.

Faith now knew exactly how things were to play out. First, Mrs Gedge had known the young man she'd seen at the restaurant would be there. And now he was here again. Clearly, he had been selected, for reasons that Faith would find out in due course. Faith's job, of course, would be to entice him, seduce him, make him fall in love with her, and then break his heart.

She was almost one hundred percent sure that this was Lady Gedge's plan. It seemed the obvious reason for calling Faith her 'beautiful revenge' for all these years.

And yet, *why*?

The young man chosen was certainly a very handsome specimen, so of course that made Faith's task so much easier. Her heart had even given a little jolt when she'd locked eyes with him through the Kentish palm at the restaurant the previous night. It was true that she'd declared she'd rather die than offer her body to a man she didn't love, but what if she simply found him attractive enough not to be repulsed by what Mrs Gedge wanted her to do? That would surely be within her code?

And she did need to eat. She had precious few alternatives other than the one Mrs Gedge intended for her.

Faith studied the young man closely through lowered eyelashes while she sipped from her champagne flute. He was tall, with dependable shoulders, and when he spoke, there was an animation about him absent from so many of the bored gentlemen about town who frequented Madame Chambon's.

That was certainly in his favour.

Faith decided she liked the way his mouth quirked when he was clearly amused, which, it seemed, he frequently was, and his quick, impatient gestures in raking his floppy fringe back from his face.

She couldn't decide whether he was of an artistic temperament or just filled with energy that needed to find an outlet. Part of her lessons at Madame's had been in how to read a man. Not only had Faith attended sessions where young men willingly revealed themselves to a dozen or so of Madame Chambon's girls for a practical demonstration of how easily they were aroused, and by what, but she'd had to listen endlessly to Madame discussing man's many temperaments and how to pander to them for the greatest return.

An artistic temperament required feeding a man's passion by suggesting that one, alone, had what was required to unleash his genius.

"There he is, Faith. What do you think?"

As Lady Vernon had asked the question, Faith was less inclined to answer truthfully. And yet there were benefits since it would be reported back to Mrs Gedge and, in truth, Faith had hoped very much that she'd be able to please her benefactress. It made life so much easier.

"He's very handsome," Faith conceded.

"And you'll be five hundred pounds richer once he seduces you."

Faith gasped and glanced about her, but they were within no one's hearing. Surprised at her reaction, when she'd lived so long in a house of ill repute, she said, staring stonily ahead, "That will be between the gentleman, whose name I don't even know, and myself." She offered Lady Vernon her haughtiest expression. "I'll thank you to keep your nose out of my personal affairs."

"It's what I'm being paid for, and I am just as keen to earn *my* five hundred pounds and be rid of *you*, my girl." Lady Vernon stared down her thin nose at Faith. "The sooner you complete the business, the better." She hesitated. "Though there is a little more to the transaction."

"Yes, of course there is. Don't I have to make him fall in love with me, then break his heart?" Faith thought the acid in her tone was justified.

"Don't pride yourself on being too clever. That was plain for anyone in your position to know."

"And why does Mrs Gedge wish her revenge on this man, in particular?"

Lady Vernon shrugged, and the rise and fall of her bony shoulders accentuated her flat chest. Faith stared at the woman, unloved and bitter, but whose nature had perhaps never invited friendship, and decided she'd never be like Lady Vernon with a title and living a celibate life on a diet of boiled cabbage. No, Faith would make the most of her youth and beauty to find an escape from the evil house that confined her until she'd expedited Mrs Gedge's plans for revenge. She'd find a rich and handsome man who'd love her despite her secrets and sordid past, and who'd marry her and give her a life of comfort and security.

She sent her prospective gentleman another assessing glance. Perhaps he actually might be the one who would do all this for her.

"Mrs Gedge is a woman who jumps to conclusions. I think you know that, Faith. She also harbours grudges. Grudges that are never laid to rest until she's satisfied her requirements have been conquered." Lady Vernon rummaged in her reticule and produced a lace handkerchief. "That American woman has too much time on her hands to brood and too much money, but if she wants to throw it in our direction, I'm not going to stop her." She blew her nose. "Who knows why she wants revenge on him. Perhaps he's the sacrificial lamb substituting for someone else? His father, perhaps. I really don't care. I just want my five hundred pounds, as do you, I'm sure." She gave Faith a warning glance. "Just don't lose your own heart in all this."

"I'm surprised you care enough to warn me, Lady Vernon."

"Oh, I don't care a jot. I'm just stating the obvious to fill in a little time and to find something to say while this young man makes his leisurely way over here."

Faith now saw that Lady Vernon was using her handkerchief as cover for a very close scrutiny of the gentleman who was perhaps ten feet away, when the old woman took Faith by the elbow and started leading her towards the door, not pausing as they passed by him.

"Where are we going?" Faith asked. "It's so early and...he was just about to speak to us!" She felt ridiculously disappointed all of a sudden. Was Lady Vernon suddenly deciding she needed to protect Faith from herself, or the young man, or Mrs Gedge?

"Yes, I'm afraid we must go home now, Faith. My poor old back is hurting and I'm longing for my bed, but don't make the mistake of thinking Mrs Gedge will be displeased." Her lined face softened beneath a rare smile as they reached the double doors which were opened in unison by a pair of footmen. The cool night air hit them like a slap in Faith's face. "Tomorrow or the next your work will begin in earnest. Soon, Mrs Gedge will understand I'm worth so much more than the paltry allowance she pays me."

CHAPTER 5

Crispin opened the book that teetered near the top of the pile his father had given him, and tried to focus his attention on its account of British and Prussian diplomatic relations in the past decade.

An ornate gilt clock loudly proclaimed the passing of time, while the crackle of the small fire in the study grate on this unseasonably chilly day was even more distracting.

Last night had been a bore. And a sore disappointment. There'd been no lively conversation; no interesting revelations. And the young lady he'd wanted to speak to had simply disappeared in front of his nose.

He could picture her now, the golden hair that rippled down her back, the intricately coiffured curls complementing her fashionable hairstyle and contrasting with her spectacularly plain dress. Would she look more beautiful in bolder colours or did a more austere presentation highlight her beauty?

His father had promised him three weeks of freedom and, of course, Crispin was itching to be gone from his books and the stifling timetable his father demanded.

Yet, it would have been diverting to have made the girl's acquaintance. It had been such a long time since he'd confronted such a vision that made him so ready to whip out his paintbrush and paints and set to work.

After another half an hour of diligent study, Crispin was more than ready to entertain the interruption that came from one of the housemaids, who put her head around the door half an hour later to tell him he had visitors and should she show them in?

It was more shock than surprise that tore through him when they were announced.

"Lady Vernon?" he repeated. She was not someone with whom his parents were on any level of intimacy, though he knew of her. Her father had been a nobleman fallen from grace on account of some very shady dealings which his untimely death had fortunately meant were not fully investigated.

Not that that was of any interest when the lovely creature in her shadow was materialising upon the threshold.

Attempting to mask his delight, Crispin directed them to take a seat on the Chesterfield sofa positioned at right angles to the fire.

"To what do I owe the pleasure?" he asked, as he lowered himself into a leather wingback chair opposite.

Lady Vernon clasped her black-gloved hands in her lap with the look of someone who has something very particular to say.

Crispin glanced from her bony fingers to the interested expression on the face of the girl on the sofa beside her, and felt the heat rise in his cheeks and his body respond. He leaned forward and looked at the pair expectantly as Lady Vernon cleared her throat.

"My charge, Miss Montague, is well practised at achieving the utmost stillness required of an artist's model, though naturally I would be in attendance at all times, Mr Westaway." She cleared her throat again. "That is, if you believe she is suitable."

Crispin drew back in surprise, but even before Lady Vernon finished, he was conjuring up exactly what hue he would pick to achieve the soft peach colour of the girl's cheeks and the red of her Cupid's bow. Her hair was an altogether thrilling proposition.

Then common sense returned. In the next day or so he'd be heading for the French Riviera. After that, he'd be heading for Germany where he'd take up the life of diplomacy just as his father had done and his grandfather before that.

Regretfully he said, "I believe there's been a misunderstanding, Lady Vernon. I no longer paint, and I don't know who gave you the impression that I would consider a painting commission."

The pucker between the old woman's grey, bristly eyebrows indicated the disappointment he was at pains to hide.

Crispin leaned back in his chair and steepled his fingers. "I am preparing to take up a posting as British Third Secretary to the British Ambassador to Germany. My intended departure is a little over a month from now."

"I saw the portrait of Madame Lascelles. A beautiful and faithful rendition so true to life, for I know the young lady. *You* painted that, Mr Westaway." There was the hint of aggression in her tone.

"I did, but that was two years ago, and my career was not decided then. I was following my inclinations only."

"You wanted to be a great artist, I heard, Mr Westaway, and there were many who believed you could be. Sir Albion considered you the finest talent of your generation."

The jolt Crispin felt was not altogether pleasant. Sir Albion had found plenty to criticise in Crispin's efforts. He was not a man to praise lightly. And yet he had always been encouraging. Crispin wondered with the vaguest tinge of regret, whether a more pointed word from the Patron of the Royal Society of Artists might have swayed him when his father was so intent that Crispin turn his back on his art in order to pursue a more serious path.

He was about to respond when Lady Vernon went on, "It is why I assumed you'd be looking for a model when I learned of this newly announced and extremely prestigious art prize under the auspices of the Society. I hoped, in turn, that a painting by you might improve the marital prospects of my goddaughter, Miss Montague."

Crispin directed a surprised stare at the young lady whose cheeks were a far rosier hue than they had been. She'd not said a word, but she clearly was invested in the conversation.

Lady Vernon's crisp tones reverberated through the silence. "I want Faith to be noticed, Mr Westaway, and I thought that through your talents, she would be."

Crispin refrained from saying that he thought she needed no one's talents to be noticed. Miss Montague was one of the most exquisite-looking young women he had ever encountered.

"Mr Westaway, I have taken it upon myself to do what I can for dear Faith. It may well be a futile and thankless task for she is the youngest of ten with nothing to offer anyone except a pliant nature."

"And her beauty." He swallowed. Had he actually said that?

"Precisely. Some gentlemen would overlook her lack of dowry because of her beauty, which is why I want you to paint her and show her to society. To the world. It is the only plan I have. Otherwise, she must return to her disappointed family in a few weeks, before taking up a position as governess to a family in Yorkshire that has evinced interest in Faith's keen grasp of politics and her interest in philosophy."

Crispin looked at the girl with even greater interest. "You have an interest in politics?"

She nodded as she dropped her gaze from his. She seemed nervous, and suddenly he wanted to reassure her. He smiled encouragingly, and she murmured, "The young boy whom I shall tutor has a desire to become a diplomat. It was after I was engaged in conversation with his father that I was provisionally employed…" She hesitated before saying with what Crispin perceived as a touch of embarrassment. "That is, if my London debut is not a success."

"How can it not be, Miss Montague?" Crispin smiled warmly at her and was delighted at the reappearance of the rosy hue in her cheeks. "I predict you will take society by storm entirely through your own talents. You need no help from me."

He offered them tea and carefully steered the talk to other matters after they declined and he led them to the door.

He said how deeply disappointed he was that he could not humour Lady Vernon, and refrained from saying that he was even more disappointed he'd see no more of Miss Montague.

But he knew that with his departure so imminent, he could afford no distractions. Succumbing to his desire to paint would be dangerous.

Succumbing to his desire to further his acquaintance with Miss Montague could prove fatal.

FAITH STOOD ON THE DOORSTEP OF MR WESTAWAY'S townhouse and plucked at the neckline of her blue cotton figure-hugging, but plainly adorned, polonaise, while she summoned the courage to do what Lady Vernon had insisted was their next step.

It was true that she was more than just a little excited to see Mr Westaway again, but she wished she could do so wearing a more lavishly embellished and modish gown. However, now that Mrs Gedge had endorsed Lady Vernon's plan of offering up Faith as a charity case, Faith had no choice but to adopt the role assigned to her.

In the hall, she heard muted footsteps before the door was opened and the butler stared at her with astonishment.

"I am so terribly sorry to disturb you, but my companion in the park just across the road has succumbed to a dizzy spell and begs for a glass of water," Faith preempted him to explain her unchaperoned state.

She was counting on the fact the butler would not leave her on the doorstep while he attended to her request so was relieved when he conducted her into the drawing room to wait.

Lady Vernon was indeed in the park, and Faith had a few moments to carry out the other woman's plan for Mr Westaway had been seen entering the house some minutes before. To Faith's intense relief, it was Mr Westaway who happened upon her before she'd been spurred into snooping about in the hopes of somehow stumbling upon him.

"Good heavens, Miss Montague!" he cried upon stepping into the drawing room, apparently deep in thought, before glancing up to see Faith gripping the back of the sofa.

Almost giddy with relief, she said, smiling, "You remembered my name, Mr Westaway. I am so very pleased, for you can't imagine how ashamed I was to enter your house unaccompanied by Lady Vernon. She's in the park and not well, and so I came here as I recognised the area we were in yesterday."

Mr Westaway's smile broadened before he quickly schooled his features into an expression more appropriate. "Your godmother is indisposed? I'm sorry to hear it. I passed my butler in the corridor who said he was fetching water for someone which I thought rather odd at the time. Now I understand. Please, take a seat while I go myself to ensure she's all right."

Faith moved forward as if to halt him then stopped. "There's really no need to do that. Lady Vernon regularly has dizzy spells. She'll be up to the mark as soon as she's rested a little and had some water." She heard the nervousness in her voice and counselled herself to be more contained. "The truth is, I wanted to speak to you, alone, Mr Westaway."

He stopped and waited. He certainly didn't seem as susceptible as she might have liked to the idea that she was alone in his home.

Yet.

Faith plucked at the fingers of one glove and avoided his eyes, before fixing him with a heartfelt look and launching into her hurried speech. "Please, Mr Westaway, are you certain you don't want to enter the art competition? The prize money is unprecedented, and Sir Albion has proclaimed it a call to arms for the country's greatest new generation of talents, of whom he numbers you amongst them. It's true." She tried for her most disarming smile, aware her mouth was trembling.

In the silence, she could hear the maids talking somewhere in the corridor and the ticking of the clock. Now she was truly nervous. So much hinged upon her success in making him yield. Mrs Gedge had thought it would be easy. Lady Vernon thought it was no contest at all, given that painting was all he'd ever wanted to do, apparently.

But now Faith's future hinged upon Mr Westaway reneging.

She gave a little sob as she sank against the heavy curtains in the window embrasure. "Please consider taking up the painting challenge, though I now beg you for purely selfish reasons." She put her hands to her eyes. "Everything Lady Vernon said yesterday is true. If I do not have a marriage offer by the end of July, I shall be sent to a remote household in Yorkshire against my will."

"A marriage offer?" He raised one eyebrow, smiling as he repeated the words. "I take it you mean a marriage offer from some *other* gentleman who might be made…aware of you through the interest a painting by me of you will inevitably garner when it's displayed amongst the competing entries at the Royal Society. An anonymously sponsored competition, which, I gather, has added to the sensation surrounding it."

She could see him wavering. Was it because of *her* or that the thought of wielding a paintbrush was so enticing?

Faith was silent as she waited. He would have to make some kind of response, even if it were to regretfully inform her that her request was, after all, out of the question. But his silence did not mean she missed the way his eyes roamed over her.

His awareness of her was thrilling. This was power. Yes, her first experience of holding the interest of a man. She was beautiful. She'd been told that, and although she hadn't actually met any of the clients of Madame Chambon, when she compared herself to the girls who were the paramours of dukes and princes, she knew she was every bit their equal.

What did it matter that Mrs Gedge was using her for some underhand purpose? That she called Faith her 'beautiful revenge'? Faith's greatest, perhaps only, power was in the allure she exerted over the male species, and now she was proving just how adept she was at her calling. Not her chosen calling but her calling by default. Succeeding in this arena was the only way she could survive, and the fact she liked this man gave her mission a life-and-death quality.

He gripped the back of the sofa too, his hands only inches from hers, his body angled half towards her. She could feel his tenseness; his desire. He was intrigued. Her beauty was a gift to the painter, her vulnerability hard to ignore. In a moment, he would waver. She could see it happening already. Mr Westaway would be all hers, and Faith would notch up her first conquest in the elaborate dance that would bind him to her and make him her slave, just as Mrs Gedge required.

"I believe my butler has taken your godmother a glass of water, Miss Montague." His voice broke the spell, his body relaxing, the tension dissipating. With a polite indication of the door he said with genuine regret, "I'm sorry to disappoint you, but the truth is that as much as I would love nothing more than to idle away many pleasant hours doing justice to your beauty and wielding a paintbrush, I will be leaving the country in a couple of short months to take up a position in Germany. I have too much to learn about my duties there to be able to accede to your request." His smile was kind. "As much as I would desire it."

Her mouth dropped open. She suddenly felt a fool. This was not how it was supposed to go. Failure? On her first attempt? Faith took a step towards the door and straightened her shoulders with as much dignity as she could manage.

"I am familiar with the political situation that exists between the two countries," she managed. "Great Britain and Germany. I could tell you about it while you painted me."

He laughed outright at that and Faith stepped across the threshold, defeated. "I did not mean to amuse you, sir," she said stiffly. "Thank you for considering it, nevertheless."

"Please, Miss Montague, it was not my intention to embarrass you." He extended his hand towards her, his kind eyes looking concerned, whereas she'd seen the amusement in his dismissiveness just before and it wounded her to the quick.

"Good day to you, Mr Westaway," she said, ignoring his overtures. "I wish you well for your new posting."

She avoided his attempt to stay her, gliding to the front door which the butler was holding open. Across the cobbled street, she could see the outline of Lady Vernon behind the railings of the park, no doubt congratulating herself prematurely on her success in sending Faith to personally petition for the dreams she was certain the young man would be unable to resist.

But Faith had failed.

Faith was unused to the feelings that beset her as she sat alone in a small curtained alcove in one of the empty reception rooms at Madame Chambon's later that evening.

The velvet sofa was comfortable and the gold tasselled curtains opulent and concealing. She was very conscious of the heavy perfume that overlaid the air and looked down at her dress, so unusually plain in contrast.

Perhaps the Failure of Lady Vernon's latest gambit in thrusting Faith under Mr Westaway's nose would have Mrs Gedge adopting a new strategy that included dressing Faith a little more fashionably due to the failure of Lady Vernon's gambit. She'd changed out of her demure blue gown and was wearing one of the other girl's more tawdry cast-offs. The purple and gold striped dress with its tight skirt, heavily adorned bustle and low neckline would have been perfect had it been in more restrained colouring and made of a better fabric.

"What are you doing here, Faith?"

Faith glanced up as Charity stopped in passing. Her hair

was uncoiled and hung in a thick dark curtain over one shoulder. In the dim light her cheeks were flushed and her gown was askew.

Embarrassed, suddenly, Charity straightened her dress. Faith knew Madame Chambon's ire was easily whipped up by untidiness. She would not house slatterns, Faith had heard her say on many an occasion.

"I fell asleep wearing this and then woke up and couldn't sleep again. It was too noisy to remain in my room," she said.

Faith nodded. Daisy who slept next door to Charity and below Faith had been entertaining a very noisy gentleman which was why Faith had retreated to the quietest part of the house.

Charity gave a snide laugh and ran her fingers through her hair. She didn't look as composed as she usually did. "You should have stayed out longer for I don't think there's a room unoccupied that isn't doing a roaring trade tonight. It must be the full moon." She closed her eyes and but her lip which Faith now saw was trembling. "Consider yourself lucky, Faith, if noise is the extent of your troubles. You're soon going to be leaving this place and it won't be a moment too soon."

Faith ran the tip of her tongue over her lips and hunched forward. "I shall be here longer than I'd hoped. Mr Westaway declined to paint me." With a few hours to think over the ramifications of her failure she'd become truly afraid. Her belief in her allure had been overblown. She'd misread Mr Westaway, for all he'd been apparently regretful, and now her future was a terrifying void.

"And I don't mind about the noise." She knew she was a source of conjecture amongst the other girls. Faith was so privileged, Faith never had to see customers. Faith was kept out of their sight, in fact. She never had to accede to the desire of anyone prepared to pay. Why? To attract a prince, perhaps?

Well, Mr Westaway was far from a prince. He was a privileged, handsome young man, in line for a title but far from the rich bounty that might have been imagined considering her three years of training.

"Charity! Come! Oh, and Faith, you too!" Red haired Mabel appeared in the entrance, her eyes bright with excitement – brandy, too, Faith thought – and beckoned to them, before darting forward to take their hands and pull them after her. "I've got something to show you. Well, Mr Schofield has and he's going to let me work the contraption."

Mabel was already hustling them towards a small group already positioned for what Faith saw was a posing for a photograph, the hooded camera unmanned before the young man who was apparently Mr Schofield, darted back to his place.

Three of Madame Chambon's girls giggled in a group while a single elderly gentleman stood just behind them, stroking the hair of a slim dark-haired girl in a green dress. Nell. Faith wondered if this was the gentleman Nell had been so excited might set her up. He looked much older than Faith had been led to believe.

Mr Schofield regarded the scene from his post, frowning, before clapping his hands suddenly and welcoming a new arrival who'd just stepped through the curtain as he pushed Mabel towards the camera.

"Aha, I think we have the numbers. Everybody, assume the waltz position!" He rushed forward, pushing Nell into the arms of the grey haired gentleman, Faith into the arms of the new arrival while he positioned himself with Charity.

"Now, remain very still until I tell you."

Obediently, Faith remained frozen like a statue while she

thought of how Madame Chambon and Mrs Gedge were going to react to her failure.

Mr Westaway was not susceptible at all. Yes, he'd been interested. Clearly. But she'd failed to reel him in.

Why? After all her training.

Training. She shuddered at the term but it was true. She'd attended lessons and, in theory, she knew how to smile and simper at a gentleman. How to entrance them, make them a slave.

Well, this was how it had been described.

Yet, she'd never tried it in real life until now and she'd been patently lacklustre, apparently.

She forced herself back to the present as she became conscious of the light pressure on her waist and holding her hand, while in the background Mr Schofield exhorted them all, "Imagine you're on the dance floor. Look at your partner. Smile now and don't move until I give you leave."

Smile. Maybe Faith had been *too* restrained, thinking that her silent beauty and enigmatic presence would pique Mr Westaway's interest when in fact she'd simply failed to register in his consciousness sufficiently.

She blinked away the tears. Madame deplored weakness. She'd make Faith suffer even more if Faith displayed her fear and disappointment. Well, Faith knew how to shine. She tilted her chin, pursed her lips and unleashed her most devastating smile upon the gentleman with whom she was supposedly dancing while she heard Mr Schofield count down the seconds.

Staring at him was a novelty. She'd never stared at a gentleman in such a staged setting for so long and it was interesting to take account of the nuances of the face before her. He was tall and blonde and in his middle to late thirties, with a lean jaw and noticeably blue eyes which bored appreciatively into her.

More appreciatively than Mr Westaway's had, she thought resentfully. Yet the same speculative gleam had been in both gentlemen's eyes. Faith had just failed to lure Mr Westaway towards making the next step.

"Girls! Gentlemen! What a picture!" Madame Chambon's interruption broke the mood and as she pushed aside the curtain and entered the room, clapping her hands together, Faith, too, stepped back; but with a sudden sinking feeling, for she realised she'd made a grave miscalculation. She was not supposed to be seen with the other girls or by the gentlemen.

What had she been thinking? Well, she hadn't.

She felt Madame's eyes resting on her and felt ill before her shoulders slumped and she turned away from the gentleman who'd continued to gaze so appreciatively at her. Still, what did any of it matter? She'd leave this place. Perhaps she could go back to the country and beg her family to take her back until she found a position.

Any would do.

"Lord Harkom, I hope you've enjoyed yourself this evening."

Madame was addressing the blonde gentleman, her voice oozing obsequiousness but her hand was now resting heavily on Faith's shoulder. With ominous pressure.

"As always, Madame." He bowed deeply

"We are always honoured by your visits. Don't forget that there are always fresh girls to give satisfaction."

Faith exhaled in fright and pulled away but Madame held her so that she had to suffer the touch of Lord Harkom's hand upon her cheek as he said, "Indeed, and I see you have another one I've not laid eyes upon. What a beauty. Perhaps I won't leave so early, after all."

The air died in Faith's lungs. She thought she would faint upon the spot.

But then Madame was drawing her back from the brink, a protective arm about Faith's shoulders as she said, "Alas, this one is very new and quite untried. She needs more training."

"I am very good at that, you know." He was pawing her again, his fingertips brushing her face as he looked hungrily at her décolletage. "My, but she is strikingly lovely. Yes, I am definitely interested." His smile was for Madame Chambon, now, and Faith could see Madame yielding as he purred, "We've always come to an agreement, before, Madame. I'm sure this will be no exception."

"I'm not ready!" Faith pulled away, her bosom heaving, and felt the eyes of everyone in the room upon her.

She couldn't bear it a moment longer. Standing upon the threshold, she clutched at her neckline but found no comforting sheathing fabric, only bare skin. Bare skin that Lord Harkom, a stranger, soon would run his hands over as he sampled her wares at Madame Chambon's behest.

Had Madame given up on her so quickly?

"You can't make me, Madame!" she cried, her voice shaking. "I'm saving myself for Mr Westaway!"

"Mr Westaway doesn't want you, Faith." There was a low, warning note in Madame's tone which Faith knew she should heed. Madame would not thank her to make a scene in front of everyone but perhaps Madame had drunk too much brandy and forgotten that Faith was 'special'.

"If Mr Westaway doesn't want you, Faith, then you're no longer any use to Mrs Gedge." Madame stepped close to Faith and gripped her chin as she said, lowering her voice "Which means you're mine now."

Faith wrenched herself backwards. She felt Charity's hands upon her shoulders to steady her. "I won't be sold like … an animal!" Her voice was shrill. She'd never heard the note before. For so long she'd taken for granted the fact that she did not have to sell her body like the other girls did. Seducing only one man would be her allotted task. A young, handsome man. A young man whom she thought she could like meaning she could fulfil her role with ease and no conscience.

But now her fate was like that of all the girls here.

"And where will you go, Faith?" There was a note of relish in Madame Chambon's. Perhaps she was now enjoying the fact that there were others to witness Faith being pulled down to their level. The fact that Madame Chambon did not distinguish, after all. A girl was only useful – and therefore would be housed and fed – if she brought gain to the ruthless brothel owner.

A terrible blackness consumed Faith's ability to think more than cursorily about the truth. There was nowhere else she could go. She was deluding herself to think there would be a welcome for her in the brutish household in which she'd grown up, the dilapidated cottage that housed her family in lieu of her father's obligation to the farmer for whom he worked.

She had no friends. No relatives. Well, none upon whose mercy she could throw herself.

"Perhaps I should hand you over to the magistrate or the police as Mrs Gedge wanted to do before she brought you here."

"I am *not* a thief." Faith enunciated the words carefully but with more bitterness than the fear with which she'd imbued the words when Mrs Gedge had found her in Miss Constancia's room admiring the young woman's bracelet the young woman had promised her.

She brought her hands up to cover her face, to block out the terrible images and whereas her fourteen-year-old self had wept piteously as she'd defended herself, Faith now intoned, bleakly, "I was given the bracelet, Madame."

"Well, that's not what Mrs Gedge told me and unless you want to go to the police or out onto the streets where it's dark and raining, I think Charity should take you upstairs to prepare yourself while Lord Harkom and I have a little chat."

Numb with shock, Faith allowed herself to be led to her bedchamber.

She'd assumed Charity would silently do Madame's bidding and find appropriate clothing, dress her hair, but once the door had closed behind them, Charity leaned against the edge of Faith's dressing table and just stared, white-faced, at Faith who sat on the bed.

"I don't know what you can do," she whispered.

Faith bowed her and stared at her shoes that peeped from beneath the satin folds of her skirts. She felt dirty and shameful in her tawdry gown and wished she could be back in her simple, unadorned polonaise feeling special and full of hope and... *almost* free.

"I'll run away!" Faith raised her head and saw her hopelessness reflected in Charity's eyes. "What else can I do?"

"It's dark and dangerous out there, Faith." Charity pressed her lips together. "Where would you find shelter? I don't know anyone who could help you. Otherwise I'd be there, myself. No, stop!"

For Faith had risen as if about to carry out her determination.

"You don't know how vulnerable you are, alone on the streets. Someone will get to you and it'll be a lot worse than...staying here."

Faith sat down again. She saw the hopeless slump of Charity's shoulders in the looking glass and asked, "What can I expect?"

Charity was silent a moment, as if preparing her answer. "The gentlemen are all different. Just hope Lord Harkom will be gentle tonight. Knowing that you're a virgin, that is."

"So they're not all the same?"

Charity laughed. "Of course not! Lord, Faith, you really do know nothing! Some come here looking to cure their loneliness. They're the ones you want."

"And the others? What's the *worst* …so I'm prepared?"

"Those that come looking here looking someone to blame for their disappointments. They want to feel powerful and so they use us. A shadow crossed Charity's face. "But then there are the surprises." For a moment she was animated, and a look of such youthful hope crossed her face that Faith forgot her own terrors for a moment as she asked, "What are you saying, Charity?"

"Just that I've met a young man and…I'm in love." Her smile broadened. "*We're* in love."

"Faith! Are you ready?"

The girls jumped at the sound of Madame's voice from behind the door and leapt to their feet as she thrust herself unceremoniously into the room, furious when she saw that Faith was still in her old dress.

"Lord Harkom has agreed to far more than I'd expected and he'll not take kindly to being kept waiting!" she snarled, gripping Faith's shoulder and shaking her. "Get out of this room, Charity, and tend to your customers if you want a roof over your head and food in your belly."

For that's what have it boiled down to. Life's barest necessities in return for the only labour the girls at Madame Chambon's were trained in.

LORD HARKOM WAS VISIBLY IMPATIENT BY THE TIME FAITH appeared.

Her hopes that he might deal more kindly to her on account of her inexperience were swept away when he began to circle her like a dog, sniffing out his next adventure, the moment she entered the room.

"Madame swears you're a virgin and I'll find out soon enough if she's lying." He put out one pale-fingered, long thin hand and toyed with the ringlet that lay upon Faith's shoulder. "Well, that's real enough," he commented when Faith gave a soft cry of pain and indignation after he tugged it. "It'll be interesting to see if all of you is real. Madame knows I'm not one for artifice. It makes me very ill-tempered."

He had the petulant look of an indulged, overgrown schoolboy. His fair hair flopped over his forehead and he had a habit of tossing back his head as if he were a prime piece of horseflesh showing off his prowess amongst a herd of mares.

Faith could suffer this kind of pawing for only so long and when he cupped her face in his hands as if he might kiss her, she leapt backwards. "What are you doing, my lord?"

"I've bought you for the night. I can do whatever I want." His nostrils flared.

Faith's back was against the wall while the door was behind Lord Harkom. She was trapped. She shook her head. "No, my lord, you can *not*! You are rude and full of deceit if you think that!"

She got no further for suddenly his face was thrust towards her, mottled with anger, his hands on her shoulders. Her throat was dry and she suddenly felt entirely unable to move. Would anyone come if she screamed?

Not Madame, that was certain.

"No one speaks to me like that, you little strumpet! No one! Certainly not someone whom I'm paying for a night of pleasure." He fisted his hand as he insinuated it into her bodice, pummelling the tender flesh of her breasts pushed up above her corset.

Faith winced.

"Do you realise how fortunate you are that I of all people should have the breaking in of you?"

"I'd rather die!"

Her defiance seemed only to inflame him more. With a sharp tug, he ripped the silk of her cuirasse, pulling her towards him as he seized a hank of her hair.

Faith wept with pain as she lashed out with both hands, her fingernails scoring his stubble dusted cheeks.

"Harlot!" Whore!" His words blasted into her head as he threw himself on top of her, the bed behind her breaking her fall. A minor comfort she thought disjointedly as he hiked up her skirts.

CHAPTER 7

For so long had Crispin been staring at the open book in front of him, or rather, the honey bees hovering above the honeysuckle outside his study window, that he'd entered a different time zone. A more pleasant time zone. He'd swapped politics and diplomacy for a panorama featuring a beautiful sunset, which had him deliberating on the palette for the pale pinks that splashed through the darkening blue. Except that the blue kept metamorphosing into the blue of a neat, simple, figure-hugging dress worn by an exquisitely beautiful young girl with rippling golden hair.

A young woman bringing beauty to life in all its guises. A young woman he was itching to paint. That was, in truth, what was making him feel alive at this moment. Not two weeks on the French Riviera.

"I'm glad to see you applying yourself so diligently, Crispin."

He turned at the sound of his father's voice, gravelly and now, unusually, softened by approval. Crispin had long sought to win his pater's regard. Since Crispin had been appointed third secretary with his diplomatic prospects

51

now all but assured, provided he didn't disgrace himself, the relationship between the two of them had greatly improved.

"With less than four weeks before I leave, I want to be as well versed in continental politics as possible." Crispin smiled, looking up from his books and gesturing for his father to take a seat upon the leather sofa at right angles to him. "I think I shall enjoy it though I'll miss you and Boxer, naturally."

"Is that all you'll miss? Your father and your dog? There's not a young lady who has captured your interest?" Without waiting for a reply, he went on, "I'm glad to hear it, Crispin, for you must focus your time and energies on your career for at least the next two years."

Crispin grimaced. "Is that a suggestion or a stricture, Papa? That I do not marry for two years?"

His father's expression softened to amusement as he idly picked up a book that was lying on the side table. "I'm not suggesting you deny yourself pleasure, my boy. Pleasure and marriage are not exclusive of each other." He tapped the book, which happened to be on portraiture. "Once you've established your career you can paint as much as you like. I'm only guiding you, my boy. I've trodden the path you're on now, and I have wisdom and experience which you do not have."

Crispin avoided his father's look to stare over the potted palms through the window. When his father insisted on continuing his monologue in the same vein, he groaned inwardly. "Designing females who throw themselves at you in the hopes of a title are a different kettle of fish to females who are in the market for pleasure; happy with a transaction that'll keep them in pretty clothes while you can let off some steam. It's the way of the world, my boy." He hesitated, caught Crispin's eye for but a moment, then stared out of the window. "Whatever happened in the past, Crispin…you were not to blame."

"Perhaps not entirely, Father."

Lord Maxwell swung round. "How quickly society would have judged had the wrong information been…reported."

Crispin was not about to be drawn. "You made sure of that, Papa," he muttered, rifling through the papers on his desk to distract himself and wishing his father would leave.

"Would you have expected me to do other than what I did?" his father returned sharply, his craggy face stern. "See my only son's name splashed across the newspapers together with whispers that you were a…" He shuddered, unable to say the word. "It would have ruined your career."

"I would have been cleared in an investigation, Father."

"Mud sticks, Crispin."

Crispin gave a taut smile. "But thanks to you, Father, my reputation remained pristine."

"By God, boy, I did what any father would do under the circumstances. A girl died. Tragic, of course. But the fault was hers. Alone!" His father made an effort to keep his anger in check. "So, tell me, Crispin, how will you spend the next three weeks preparing?"

"Preparing to leave my homeland? I shall do little different to what I have been doing. I shall study hard."

"You need diversion."

"Perhaps I should pick up my paintbrushes again."

Lord Maxwell sighed. "And get drawn into a world from which you can only extricate yourself with the utmost effort when time is of the essence?" He sighed. "No, Crispin. Establish your career and then you can dabble in your paints if that's what you wish. It's not for me to ban you forever from an artistic pursuit I'd happily condone if you could control it, but…it's an addiction with you, my boy. As dangerous as any bubble pipe, I fear."

"It's a diversion. One I find enormously fulfilling. Isn't that what you were advocating, Papa? A little diversion?"

"I was thinking along the lines of the female variety." Lord Maxwell cleared his throat. "A woman who can take away your cares for just a short while before you leave. If you need help in this area, I can recommend—"

Crispin cut him off curtly. "I don't need a woman, thank you." He might have added that the last thing he'd enjoy was a woman he suspected of being in any degree intimate with his father. Crispin respected his father in so many regards, just not when it came to the way he relegated women to varying degrees of usefulness; Crispin's late mother having been one of these: consort in public, mother of his children, and bearer of his heir. But when his father required pleasure, he consorted with an altogether different type of woman.

It was not the way Crispin intended to live his life.

With a sigh, Lord Maxwell made a move towards the door, his tone testy as if reading his son's thoughts, "If plans for the French Riviera came to nothing, I certainly don't advocate you mouldering here, in this musty townhouse, entirely alone with your books."

Crispin straightened, suddenly alive as a thread of possibility pierced his brain. "I don't intend to, Father. You're right. I've taken your words to heart, and I think I will head off to the country for a few days. Perhaps for some duck shooting. Perhaps to walk the peaks. Or, perhaps I'll visit Aunt Angela and Uncle Barnabus for the next ten days. They said I was always welcome."

"They are away, although the house is yours, if you wish it for a change of scene, of course. They've always said that. And, if you have a predilection for horsey women or career spinsters and country Assembly balls, for I'm sure nothing has changed in that part of the Cotswolds in fifty years, then I'm sure it'll do very nicely."

Crispin didn't care that his father considered the idea with as much enthusiasm as a plate of cold porridge. If there was little probability of being visited there by him, then all to the good.

His father farewelled him upon the threshold. "Not too much more studying tonight, Crispin. The light is poor and you need exercise. Perhaps a turn about Hyde Park would do you good."

Crispin shook his head. "No, there are a couple of other errands I need to do and the walk will do me good."

He joined his father on the front portico and stood for a moment upon the top step, staring at the setting sun. What palette could do justice to the pinks and golds that melded into each other? No longer did the French Riviera or a week of duck shooting hold any enticement for him.

As he watched his father's carriage disappear into the sunset, he frowned, wondering if his aunt who lived only two streets away, might know the address of Lady Vernon.

CHAPTER 8

*H*ow had it come to this?

Faith's terrified scream was muffled by Lord Harkom's cynical laughter as he straddled her, pinning her arms above her head with one strong hand while the other gripped her thigh.

He pinched her and she yelped; the wooden floor hard beneath her tailbone.

"You don't suppose your gracious madame is going to come to your aid when I've paid her such a hefty sum for the breaking in of you, do you?" He chuckled, clearly enjoying himself now that he had mastery over her.

His fingers crept higher up her thigh. Faith thought she was going to be ill. Was this what the sex act was all about? Mastery? Brutality? Power? The other girls were clear enough about their disdain for what was required of them. Some of them made a joke of the feigned pleasure gasps they'd perfected for earning themselves a tip.

Faith squeezed her eyes shut and forced her body to go slack. If a struggle was what he wanted, then she wasn't going to humour this man in any way. She opened her eyes, and it was the devil staring down at her.

It galvanised her to action. Meekly taking what was coming to her so as to lessen the pain was not how she'd play things. She'd not spent three years being turned into a lady only to be cast to the wolves and consumed like a sacrificial lamb the moment she fell short of Mrs Gedge's expectations of her.

She'd kill him. That's what she'd do. And then she'd run. She might have to jump out of the window first, but she'd not whore herself out to any man off the street willing to pay for her. She'd not whore herself for anyone except…

Yes, there was one exception. She could do it for Mr Westaway. *With* Mr Westaway. One man. Mrs Gedge's revenge. That was the mission for which Faith had been groomed, and she'd been prepared to compromise herself with *only* one man in order to earn her freedom.

"Lord Harkom!"

A furious pounding on the door was met by his lordship's horror.

"What is the meaning of this?" he shouted as Madame burst into the room.

"You've not spoiled her?" Madame demanded breathlessly. "Thank God!" she added as she ran her gaze across his still-buttoned breeches. With heaving bosom, and heels clicking across the floorboards, she arrived at Faith's side and, seizing her arm, yanked her to her feet. "Beg pardon but there's been a terrible mistake, my lord. Naturally, you'll be adequately compensated. I've any number…"

But Madame did not finish, for as Lord Harkom straightened his clothing as he stalked to the door, he was well into his threats against her house, issued from the threshold, that her business would suffer for the terrible insult he'd just endured.

Dazed, Faith stumbled into the passage as Madame led her past young women lounging with or without gentlemen consorts, who all eyed her curiously as she was pushed into Madame's private sitting room.

"You're to say nothing of this, do you hear?" Madame's voice was a low hiss, her body trembling with suppressed emotion as she pointed to the red-velvet upholstered sofa, indicating for Faith to sit.

To Faith's astonishment, a brandy was thrust into her hand with the order that she drink it all.

Madame sat down opposite her and fixed her with a beady stare.

"Nothing! Do you hear?"

Faith was trembling so much she could barely manage a reply. She nodded dumbly. What choice did she have but to agree? She'd been spared, and she had a roof over her head. She could count herself lucky.

Madame's fingers shook as she fixed the squirrel pelt with a pin to her coiffure. "Tomorrow, I'll see to your wardrobe, and the next day you'll be heading north to spend a week in a cottage in the country."

"With Lord Harkom?" It was all Faith could think to say.

"Don't be ridiculous. What do you suppose all that business just now was about? No, you're going to the Cotswolds."

True to her word, it was Madame herself who, the next day, personally oversaw the petticoats, stockings, shoes, bonnets, and gowns Faith would take with her to her unusual destination.

And, all brand new.

"Am I going to see Mr Westaway?" Faith asked. "Did *he* request that I come?"

"Mrs Gedge will tell you what you need to know."

Madame did not speak with her usual aplomb, and Faith suspected the previous evening's events had discomposed her, too.

Her friend Charity confirmed it as she took over the more menial task of folding ribbons and seeing that Faith's jewellery, simple pieces, were properly secured in their velvet boxes.

"Serves her ladyship right for selling you to the biggest brute that's ever crossed this threshold. And for your first time, too!" Her scorn was apparent, and when Faith stared, open-mouthed, she went on, "There's nothing that woman won't do if enough coin crosses her palm. It wasn't just Anastasia he hurt, though I couldn't say it to you last night. Lydia and Ruby had bruises for days after their sessions with the beast, and while Madame banned him for a month, I suppose she couldn't refuse him when he offered her such a bounty for supposedly the newest and loveliest virgin in town."

Faith sat heavily on the bed. "He must have come offering just moments after Mrs Gedge said she no longer wanted me."

"Oh, it was Lady Vernon who told Madame that you were no longer any use to Mrs Gedge. I think the old cat thought she could make a pretty penny on the side by selling you out."

"Lady Vernon?" Faith gasped, clenching her fists. "By God, I'll scratch her eyes out."

"It was Lady Vernon who came hurrying over just an hour later to say there'd been a new development, and that you were suddenly required by Mrs Gedge to go to the Cotswolds," Charity said. "Perhaps she only wanted to frighten you."

"How could Lady Vernon do such a thing? She's so...old and...poor."

"She needs money. Exactly. And she's ruthless, and you are nothing but a means of keeping food in that skinny belly of hers and a roof over her head. So, when you spend your enchanted week with Mr Westaway, I'd be far more distrustful of Lady Vernon than your young man who seems quite harmless." Charity folded another petticoat and dropped it on top of a pile of folded underwear lying in Faith's carpetbag. Seeing Faith's look of concern, she smiled. "Don't worry, Faith, Mr Westaway will think you're quite delightful; I'm sure of it. I've seen him, and he has a pleasant manner. He's not the kind who pushes his weight around to prove he's better than his peers and want to show the likes of us just how important he is. I think he'll be kind to you."

"He's been here?"

"Lord, no!" Charity laughed. "I've asked around and he doesn't frequent establishments such as ours. In fact, he's not been associated with any young woman whom anyone knows about so perhaps Mrs Gedge will be disappointed in her grand designs by finding his tastes run more to the Greek."

Faith put her hand to her mouth. "He doesn't fancy women?"

Charity shrugged. "I don't know. Perhaps he likes both. Perhaps he's a virgin, and you'll have to be the one to show him what to do."

Faith stared at her shoes. Her encounter with Lord Harkom, so fresh and horrifying, had made her feel vulnerable and powerless in a way that being Mrs Gedge's pawn never had. Ever since she'd come under Mrs Gedge's thumb, Faith had been quietly confident she would one day outwit the older woman. Yet in only a few minutes, Lord Harkom had used his brute strength to subdue her. Not only would he be able to subdue her, physically, any time he wanted, the frightening reality was that in the world in which Faith lived, his money sanctioned any amount of brutality.

"How will I do that when I don't know what to do?" she asked.

Charity laughed as she sat on the bed beside Faith and hugged her briefly. "What a question when you've lived in this place so long," she said. "You've seen the living displays. Besides, haven't you ever put your eye to a peephole in all these years?"

"Of course not! And I block my ears if I have to." Faith shuddered, and Charity put her hand to Faith's chin and turned her head so she could look into her eyes, saying quite seriously now, "Have you really been able to live at London's most notorious, high-class brothel for three years and block out everything that goes on here?"

"I know what happens…physically. But that's very different from everything else."

"Don't let your encounter with Lord Harkom colour your feelings." Charity was matter of fact now. "He's a well-known brute and granted, there are a few like him. But mostly, the men are respectful, even if they're self-absorbed and think only of their own pleasure." Her smile broadened. "Sometimes it's even possible to fall in love with a kind regular. That is, when he brings you gifts, and fills your ears with sweet ones, telling you you're the only one. Making you believe him when he says that one day he'll take you away to a new life."

"Do you really believe that, Charity?" Faith felt sad for her friend. Glad that she could enjoy the brief pleasure of being in love, but sad that her love was doomed.

"Of course, I know not to believe it," Charity added quickly. "It's words only. But it makes the act tolerable. No, it makes it a pleasure."

"A pleasure? For a woman? But what pleasure *is* there?"

Faith was now more troubled by the possibility that she might have some feeling unleashed in her than by the mechanics of what she'd long resigned herself to. Tonight had made everything a sudden, horrible reality.

Charity rose. "You'll have to leave that to Mr Westaway. Make him desire you, encourage him with your shy but eager responses. You've learned how to do *that* during your apprenticeship here. And those other classes Lady Vernon took you off in your carriage to attend?"

"Philosophy, politics and art and classics with Professor Monk?"

"Professor Monk!" Charity let out a scream of laughter. "And was he? We girls used to speculate his reception of you was far from monkish."

"Professor Monk is at least sixty, no, seventy! With hair growing out of his ears and nose and, obviously, no interest in women at all." Faith considered the gentleman who'd opened her mind to the wonders of the wider world through the uncensored education he'd given her, teaching her the same curriculum he taught all the boys who came to him for similar instruction. "But he was always kind to me."

"So he taught you nothing about the workings of the body? How to prevent conception, how to feign pleasure?" Charity gave a sly smile. "How to give and receive pleasure?"

Faith imagined her wizened old tutor being involved in any such instruction and laughed for the first time.

"Oh Faith, you are so pretty when you're not so serious!" Charity exclaimed. "But, of course, Madame has taught you these things? She has, I know it, for all we girls must attend the instruction Madame conducts here."

"I know the basics," Faith admitted. "But for you girls, it's all so real and necessary because it's all about the things you do every day. For me, I never dreamed the day would come when I really had to..." she swallowed "...sell my body."

Charity rose with a shrug as she headed towards the door. She had to leave, Faith knew, as she had a customer waiting for her. Daisy, the tweeny, had just called through the keyhole to tell her.

"It's not so bad when you get used to it," Charity said bolsteringly, as she let herself into the passage. "As long as you have a plan to escape. Even if that plan is just in your head."

With quiet resolve, Faith said, "I plan to escape the moment I've done all the damage to Mr Westaway that Mrs Gedge wants me to. I've signed a contract giving me five hundred pounds if I can get from him an agreement to set me up as his mistress which I will decline. If he makes me an offer of marriage, then she'll double that."

"A marriage offer is worth a great deal more than a thousand pounds, Faith! What a strange contract. You surely didn't sign that, did you? I mean, sign to say you'd reject him and break his heart in order to get yourself a thousand pounds?"

"I did sign it, because when I first came here, the alternative was that or be handed over to the magistrate." Faith felt uncomfortable. "And then I just did my lessons, and I had a place to live, and I didn't give it much thought. Now, though…"

"Well, if you can make him fall in love with you, maybe you can fall in love with him, Faith. Maybe, out of all of us, you can be the one to get your marriage offer and live happily ever after."

Faith saw that although she smiled, she looked worried. "It's a legal contract," she said. "I know it is."

Charity sighed. "I just worry that if Mrs Gedge is anything like Madame, you'll never be free."

"But if I can truly make Mr Westaway fall in love with me, then maybe I can be."

CHAPTER 9

Faith hadn't left London since she'd arrived a little over three years before as an innocent country girl from Dorset. Now her transformation was complete, and no one from her village or perhaps even her family, would recognise the poised young woman who swayed from side to side in the train carriage beside her chaperone.

Not that she felt poised. Faith was a jumble of nerves inside.

She and Lady Vernon had not spoken in two hours since their initial brittle greeting before being transported to the station.

Lady Vernon had immediately opened a book once the conductor had led them to their seats and slammed the door on their compartment.

Faith had tried to read, but after an hour, the anger bubbling inside her could no longer be suppressed. Lady Vernon wasn't some brutal dominator who could reduce Faith to a quivering mass of tearful powerlessness, and yet that's what the frail old woman hunched in the corner had effectively done to the 'goddaughter' she was supposed to protect.

Finally, she could bear the silence no longer. "How much did Madame pay you to release me to the first high-paying customer who happened to fancy using strength and violence to break in a virgin?"

There! The words should have made the old woman turn from her usual grey parchment colour to a sickly off-white.

Lady Vernon put her book down. She swayed from side to side as the train rounded several bends. "Madame Chambon told me she arrived just in time." But there was fear in her tone. Obviously, she trusted Madame to tell her the truth as little as Faith did.

Faith stared at her. "How long does it take for a big, strong, arrogant man to rip the clothes off a lady and have his way with her? I don't suppose you know, Lady Vernon, though I see the thought is unpalatable to you. And yet you were willing for that to happen to me as long as you got enough gold coins in your pocket."

Lady Vernon's nostrils flared, and the lashes over her rheumy eyes fluttered. "You are…intact, Faith. Madame assured me you were."

Faith banged her hand onto her book in frustration. "Do you ask because you're filled with remorse and truly hope I am unscathed out of concern for me? Or because I'm worth more to you if I *am*… intact?"

"Regardless of what did or didn't happen, you'd do well to preserve the fiction you're a virgin if you wish to keep Mrs Gedge as a benefactress." Lady Vernon sounded bolder now. "If you're not, and word gets out, then you're no good to anyone. And if you're no good to anyone, you'll starve, my girl, so consider yourself lucky that you're here with me."

Faith looked out of the window at the passing countryside. It looked green and lovely, the air fresh and clean now they were out of London. "As if anyone would know or care to wonder if I was a virgin if they knew where I've spent the last three years," she muttered. Lady Vernon looked so harmless, so utterly inconsequential, sitting in the corner like a bundle of rags, except that the gown that covered her bones was silk. Very old silk, now dusty with age. But perhaps she was even more ruthless than Madame. Or Mrs Gedge? Faith would have to remember that as she embarked upon the next part of her journey.

"Now, I understand that you are aware of the requirement that you're to enslave this young man's heart, but don't be too eager," Lady Vernon said, changing the subject. As if she knew anything about enticing a young man—or any man.

Faith sent her the filthiest look she could but said nothing.

"We both know that your future, and mine, hinge upon your success."

"How do you know his heart isn't already engaged?" Faith asked. "How do you know he'll even like me?"

"His heart is not engaged, and you are just the kind of young lady to appeal to this young man. Appeal to his chivalrous nature; his protective instincts. Don't be too eager for intimacy or it won't ring true. Reel him in, slowly."

"Have you had much success using this strategy yourself, Lady Vernon?" Faith enquired politely and was rewarded with a bitter smile. Good, she'd touched a nerve.

"What if I feel sorry for him and don't wish to ruin him?" Faith added. "I'm not cruel by nature. Not like you and Mrs Gedge." She gave a short laugh. "If he falls in love with me, then I may think it more worthwhile to run away with him than accept Mrs Gedge's fee with my freedom."

"My dear girl, I certainly don't think you're quite so stupid." Lady Vernon pulled out her wire-rimmed spectacles to examine Faith as if she honestly believed the girl could be mentally deficient. "You surely must realise that Mrs Gedge will reveal everything about you to him if you were to do that. And then what future could there be for you? Do you think his father would allow him to marry a prostitute, even if you both were madly in love with one another? No, break the boy's heart, wait for further instructions, and when you've fulfilled your duty to Mrs Gedge's satisfaction, you will be given your freedom and assured that your prospects for making a respectable match with some other worthy gentleman will be fostered by the woman who has been so good to you all these years."

Faith sighed. The prospect of her journey into Mr Westaway's arms and into his bed didn't particularly move her, though she supposed anything was preferable to being pounded into submission like Lord Harkom had nearly done.

But at least Mr Westaway seemed pleasant enough.

Though falling in love was not something Faith intended doing for a long time.

CHAPTER 10

Crispin couldn't remember the last time he'd whiled away a few hours in a hammock. He should have done this a long time ago—had a few days' break from London and his father's scrutiny.

He raised the book resting over his face by a few inches and waved it in the air to shoo away the bee or fly that threatened to settle on his chin. For the moment, the enjoyment of simply doing nothing was almost more enticing than picking up a paintbrush. Perhaps his father's strictures that he give up his art until he was well entrenched in his new position was not such a bad one.

He wondered now at the wisdom of asking Miss Montague to be his model for the painting he intended entering into the prestigious art competition that had so stirred his blood a few short days ago.

For today, languid in the sun, he had no urge to do anything very much except rest completely. His brain was tired; his body was tired. In the three short weeks before he was due to board a packet to France and begin his journey to the country that would be his home for the next few years, perhaps he should simply rest.

He'd have to compensate Miss Montague for her time, of course. He'd been fired up by the idea of furthering her acquaintance, but over the past few days, her image had dimmed. And over the past day and a half spent lazing in the lovely cottage garden of the small manor house that had been given over to his use by his aunt and uncle, all his desires and ambitions had quite drained away.

He was drifting off when he heard a clear voice say, "*The History of a Crime*. I enjoyed Victor Hugo's essay about Napoleon III's takeover of France, though I did find it heavy in parts."

He opened his eyes, astonished to find himself staring at Miss Montague, dressed simply in white and flanked by the funereal-looking Lady Vernon.

"When did you read that?" he was startled into asking, before good manners came to the fore, and he removed himself from the hammock and ushered the ladies to a garden bench nearby.

"As soon as it was published. I love anything by Victor Hugo though my papa feels he's unsuitable."

"Unsuitable?"

"Yes. Do you think it's unsuitable for a young lady to read Victor Hugo? And if so, why?"

He hadn't expected she'd be so direct when given the chance to converse with her beyond the confines of the ballroom.

"Unexpected, perhaps, is a better term. It was recommended reading by my papa in view of my imminent posting. I must admit I find it heavy going too. If you gleaned anything from it, you'll have to impart your insights when you pose for me." He studied her covertly while pretending to arrange the cushions in the chair upon which he sat opposite her. Her hair had the look of newly threshed corn. There was a golden glow about the rippling tresses that immediately had him envisioning his palette of oils.

"It would be a pleasure. I'm very good at keeping still, but the time passes more quickly if we're discussing something interesting. That's if your concentration is up to it."

Crispin smiled. Her transformation was astonishing. She looked much more at home in the colourful summer garden in the country discussing an intellectual topic than when she'd been so obviously on display in a public arena.

And, the more he thought about it, the way the sun glistened on her beautiful hair made him long to run his fingers through the ringlets that fell over her right shoulder in preference to painting it.

The thought startled him, and he made a mental note to beware of any similar urges.

Miss Montague was a penniless girl sent here to model for him, and he was off to the Continent in just under a month for a posting of many years. He had a career that couldn't include dowerless potential brides, no matter how entertaining and easy on the eye, while she was on the lookout for a husband. Her godmother had already admitted that Miss Montague could not afford to be discerning if she were to escape her fate as a governess.

No, Crispin was expected to do much better than Miss Montague when the time came.

Nevertheless, the interested way she was looking at him now was having a rather tumultuous effect on him.

"I'll enjoy testing your knowledge and reporting back to your tutor," Crispin said with a levity he did not feel for, in truth, his fingers were just itching to seize a paintbrush and stand in front of a canvas while his senses directed him from there.

That's what he loved so much about being a painter. The

ability to let his mind wander at will. It was something his father had deplored in his dreamy young son, insisting that learning and application led to a future based on merit.

Lady Vernon cleared her throat. "We are putting up at the White Swan for this week. It's convenient as it's only a short walk, and the weather looks set to be good for the next few days. When will you want Faith for her first sitting? And what should she wear?"

Crispin laughed and immediately apologised. He was not used to being asked for his advice on a lady's attire. Suddenly, the situation in which he'd been thrust seemed ludicrous. And yes, as the sun fell across Miss Montague's sweet, smiling face, quite delicious.

At his hesitation, Lady Vernon went on, "The title of the work that is to be painted is *Lady at Sunset*, if you recall, Mr Westaway. How would you like to direct Faith? Do you have a location in mind? Or will you paint her in a studio and do the setting later?"

Good lord, this woman, oh yes, the girl's godmother, knew what she was about. Crispin hadn't given a proper thought to the requirements of the piece. He didn't expect to win. Perhaps he wouldn't even enter the work. However, as an opportunity for a week or two of idleness, or rather indulgence, doing what he loved most, he was not about to look a gift horse in the mouth. As long as his father had no idea what he was actually doing, Crispin could look upon this week as a necessary holiday before the hard work of his career began.

"Whatever Miss Montague wishes," he said, remembering she had little in the way of a wardrobe. And as Miss Montague would look lovely in whatever she chose, he didn't want to embarrass her over her impecuniousness.

"And when would you like us to return?"

Crispin felt like a ten-year-old, the way he was being

spoken to. He hoped Lady Vernon didn't always insist on being present, though he supposed it was necessary. He certainly didn't want to be responsible for anyone casting aspersions on Miss Montague's good character. In fact, he rather liked the idea of aiding her in her quest to find herself a better match through his painting. A painting that would advertise her beauty to the world. A noble cause.

This would be a week of wicked indulgence for him when painting had been long forbidden. But it would be a means to elevate Miss Montague's chances in the world.

An image flashed through his mind of the dead girl. Miss Montague would be his chance to atone for the past. He could improve her future prospects, and hopefully, because of him, see her enjoy prosperity and happiness rather than a cruel and impoverished destiny.

"Tomorrow." He flexed his fingers, remembering how deft his hands were when he had a project that fired him up. "At noon." He closed his eyes briefly and imagined the leisurely morning he would have constructing the scene in his head that he would paint. "And bring something warm. It might be a long evening."

He would have to scout out a suitable spot by the lake in which to paint her. He'd have her in position when the sun went down, burnishing her hair with gold, while the long shadows turned her skin to toasted alabaster.

CHAPTER 11

The White Swan was a comfortable and respectable country inn. Fortunately Faith had her own bed chamber and had slept surprisingly well before she was disturbed by the knock on the door that heralded the start of her mission.

However, she was suitably docile as Lady Vernon selected her wardrobe. In fact, she barely troubled herself with any of the decisions associated with her sojourn as she sat up in bed reading the final of Victor Hugo's essays. She'd found them instructive, even compelling reading, and was rather looking forward to discussing them with Mr Westaway. That is, if he'd really read them. Many times she'd caught out a gentleman in a lie. In her younger days at Madame Chambon's when she'd served the girls refreshments as they'd entertained gentlemen in the drawing room, she'd overhear some pink of the ton boast of a literary accomplishment, only to discover, upon listening further, that it was likely he'd never truly read the book.

She tried to stifle her fears for the future. For any possibility of failure.

Now that she'd progressed to the stage where Mr Westaway wanted to paint her, and she'd be in his company for at least a week, she had to play her cards right.

Overcoming any physical barriers on her part would not be a problem. She was confident she liked him enough to do what she needed to.

Overcoming any gentlemanly restraint on his part would be the challenge.

Yes, she'd seen the admiration in his eyes that she was confident could be attributed to enthusiasm for his project on a number of fronts. But would he be easily persuaded to kiss her?

If she could manage just that, then she hoped matters would progress as Mrs Gedge required.

Her ugly encounter with Lord Harkom had put things into perspective. He was a violent brute.

Therefore losing her virginity to Mr Westaway didn't trouble Faith too much if it meant she gained her freedom.

Having heard the primal grunts and cries of release through the thin walls at Madame Chambon's for so many years, the sexual act held little interest and certainly no appeal. It was simply a means to an end.

A way for Faith to gain her independence and be free of Mrs Gedge and Madame Chambon.

And that detestable cockroach, Lady Vernon.

"The blue, I think."

She could hear Lady Vernon muttering under her breath as if the decision were of the utmost importance. "The colour of forget-me-nots. An innocent colour; a simple yet alluring gown. Ah, my dear, he won't be able to keep his hands off you."

This brought Faith's head up with a jerk. When Lady Vernon turned back to her, her minder was all innocence herself, as if she'd never spoken of Faith in such terms.

"Are you ready? No, ten minutes longer, I think. We need to keep him waiting. Increase his impatience because you need to trade on every advantage. You are the supplicant, after all. The penniless creature who needs his good offices, yet you need to shore up your power. Impatience is the way to play the game, my dear, though I've no doubt Madame Chambon has taught you all the tricks of the trade."

Faith stretched and put her feet on the floor but made no answer. The less she told Lady Vernon the better, and besides, she was hardly about to divulge such matters of a personal nature. That yes, for years Madame Chambon had included Faith in the regular sessions that acquainted her girls with a myriad of ways to whip up a man's desire. Innocent things like the feather-light touch of fingertips grazing exposed flesh, a flare of promise at odds with demurely lowered lashes.

Once, Faith had been required to sit in on a lecture-like session involving a handsome, well-built young man, who'd reclined on a bed and exhibited to the newest and most innocent of Madame Chambon's recruits the astonishing ways in which a man's body reacted to certain stimuli.

Intrigued and horrified in equal measure, Faith, fortunately, never had to return to a similar lesson after she'd communicated her disgust to Mrs Gedge one afternoon tea at Claridges. Clearly, Mrs Gedge considered she was behaving with proper moral rectitude by simply housing Faith without requiring her to be a participant in the less savoury dealings of the household.

Mrs Gedge was biding her time for when she needed Faith and Faith's pristine innocence to do her bidding.

Finally, it was time to go, Faith feeling like an obedient little lapdog, beautifully brushed and prepared for her afternoon encounter.

They found Mr Westaway in the garden, all impatience as

he grasped his paintbrush and paced back and forth by the rhododendron bushes staring at the sky.

"Lady Vernon, Miss Montague." He swept them a bow and then led Faith to an arbour amidst the trees and bushes where he invited her to sit. She could sense his urgency for something which he believed was purer than it was. She saw, also, Lady Vernon's secret smile of satisfaction, but all Faith could recognise in Mr Westaway's manner was his desire to fulfil an artistic challenge. Nothing more.

Concerning. She'd have to use everything she had at her disposal to change that.

"I've laid out a blanket and a cushion for your comfort though I'll paint them out in the final rendition."

Faith shrugged. "I don't mind doing without such comforts if it'll make your life easier." Easy to please. She'd start with that.

"You may need to remain still for up to three hours." His brows arched as if surprised by a thought that hadn't occurred to him. "I've been told you're practised at keeping still for long periods of time, Miss Montague?"

"Three hours is a trifle," she assured him though secretly horrified at the prospect. But if this was necessary to please Mr Westaway, she'd gladly start with three hours of boredom.

Except that it wasn't the kind of boredom or discomfort she'd expected. Yes, bees buzzed a little too close sometimes, and the odd beetle crossed her flesh and made her cry out in surprise, but that just lightened the mood unexpectedly. And soon she and Mr Westaway were laughing companionably as Lady Vernon snored gently in a chair beneath the over-hanging branches of an ancient elm tree.

"Stay! Just like that!" The sudden imperative was out of keeping with the earlier tone, but Faith recognised artistic passion when she heard it. She also proved adept at complying just as her benefactor had obviously wished judging by the gleam in his eye. Faith lay prone, relaxed upon the grass, her head resting on her arm and supported by her elbow, her expression enigmatic. Yes, enigmatic was what he wanted and apparently Faith did it well.

"Keep looking like that," he murmured, moving away from his easel and kneeling at her side to tweak a fold of her forget-me-not skirts that the breeze had moved slightly. His expression was intense, his frown of concentration when he got closer suggesting that what he was about to do was of the greatest import.

To touch a fold of forget-me-not cotton twill?

A surge of pique made her shift position though she hid her frown.

He was not looking at her. She was an object. Not an object of lustful desire as Mrs Gedge would have her but upholding the same degree of value to him as if she were inanimate. A Sèvres vase, perhaps?

She was more discomposed by the realisation than she'd expected. After all, it wasn't as if she desired to be desired. She didn't. Yet, nor could she fail at her task.

Her task to make him fall in love with her.

But there was *nothing* in his eyes to suggest she might even come close.

As his fingers smoothed a fold of her skirt, she gasped, as if stung, and rolled onto her back and away from his hand while he blinked in surprise and said, "I suppose I should have warned you I was going to touch you." He reddened. "I mean, touch your dress. Make it look exactly as it did before the breeze disturbed it. I beg your pardon, Miss Montague. I meant no disrespect."

"None taken," she murmured, reddening also. How interesting that she could simulate these innocent responses when she didn't feel embarrassed in the slightest. Merely a little frustrated that she was taking so long to elicit from him any kind of interest. She pressed her lips together. He was still on his knees beside her as he tried to explain. "I truly am sorry. Something happens to me when I paint. And it's been so long I'd forgotten how intense I can be."

His laugh sounded forced as he rose and returned to the easel where he spent a long time mixing paints and staring at the result, as if he couldn't bring himself to look at her. Finally, he glanced at her from around the canvas. "It's probably why my father detests my passion. He sees I can have no sensible thought in my mind when I am so preoccupied."

"What does he consider sensible?"

"The security of England. The possibility of a threat from Germany. Assessing that threat. Mitigating it. Diplomacy." Now his laugh was more genuine, though self-effacing. "None of the kinds of things a young lady like you would trouble herself about."

Faith closed her eyes and raised her face to the sun while all the book learning she'd acquired floated through her mind. She'd been surprised to discover how much she loved history. Her tutor had loved politics, and the result was that she was often engaged in a series of spirited discussions on various topics in the old man's musty little study in Maida Vale. Including the increasing threat posed by Germany.

"Your father was a diplomat, wasn't he?" Faith didn't want to look at Mr Westaway while she formulated her words. If she couldn't impress him with her beauty, Mrs Gedge's hope was that Faith would interest him with her mind.

"He was, and I am to follow in his footsteps."

"He wants you to be just like him?"

There was a silence, and Faith opened her eyes to see him looking intently at her. "Yes." He nodded slowly. "He does."

Clearly, Mr Westaway wasn't enamoured by the idea.

"I daresay you discuss these matters with him," Faith went

on innocently. "France's shattering defeat by Prussia a few years ago, for example. Do *you* think that means that France has been supplanted as a threat by a new potential enemy? Should we be worried?" She gazed at Mr Westaway with her most disarming half smile. Some men couldn't resist the combination of a young girl's innocent desire to impress, at the same time as be educated, she had learned.

He opened his mouth to reply but she wanted to push her advantage while she had it, going on quickly, "Germany is efficient, militaristic, ruthless, and ambitious. Of course, we should be worried, shouldn't we, Mr Westaway? Your job is to reduce the risk to our country through gathering information, but of course you have to be discreet. Your father would want you to be as vigilant in your attention to detail as a diplomat as you clearly are as an artist."

CRISPIN NEARLY DROPPED HIS PAINTBRUSH. WAS THIS THE same young woman whose quiet, artistic posture had first attracted his interest? She'd stood out from the many other debutantes that night on account of the plainness of her attire, which contrasted with her beauty. She had been unleashed upon society in the hopes of finding a husband who might see her looks as compensating for her material deficiencies, and Crispin had taken pity on her for no other reason than that she made a good model when he suddenly had the opportunity to paint.

A clandestine activity because it bore no relation to his work. His all-important work for which he'd been groomed since childhood—to follow his father into the diplomatic service.

Yet in a few sentences, she'd succinctly summarised the

situation with which he and his father had grappled during long dinner conversations these past months.

He wished his father could have heard Miss Montague speak just now.

And then remembered his father must never know of Miss Montague's existence or the fact that Crispin was painting.

"You have a remarkable grasp on the situation, Miss Montague," he allowed. "Where did you pick up such information?"

"I read a lot."

Her face was turned up to the sun, and her lids had drifted sleepily closed while a contented smile played about her lips. In her hands, she held a small posy of flowers he'd placed there for artistic value. Now, as he gazed at her, he was struck by a sensation he was completely unable to identify. He frowned as his eyes roamed the length of her. She was a beauty, and she seemed entirely unaware of the fact.

What else was in that mind of hers? He could wonder for it went without saying that any other part of her was out of bounds.

Into the lengthening silence, she volunteered on a small sigh, "There's not much a girl like me *can* do except read… and do other people's bidding." She blinked open her eyes suddenly and smiled. It was like a shadow giving way to the sun. Her eyes were pools of crystal water; her skin dew-brushed petals.

"Don't move!" he cried again, dipping his paintbrush into a blob of colour on the palette. "Keep smiling. You don't smile enough. Yes, that was the problem before."

Feverishly he returned to work. He'd thought a pensive creature suited the mood of what he sought to recreate. But that was before her lightness had transformed his work. His world. She was all vibrancy and life, not a half-dead creature lying languidly amongst the grass. Not a girl living a half life, burdened by a destiny that would not be of her choosing. He'd not thought any of this, but it flashed through his mind in a blinding maelstrom of insight—replacing in the vacuum left behind only the fear that he hadn't the talent to capture the exquisite purity, the joyful radiance of a young woman, in that moment, uninhibited and alive.

She gave him a few minutes to satisfy the call of genius and then said lightly, "Ah, but I thought the problem was that *you* were too serious, Mr Westaway. I was afraid I'd fall in your estimation if I allowed my frivolous nature to reveal itself."

She was teasing him. The chit of a girl so beneath him in age, station, and everything else was smiling her amusement with all the consummate confidence of a dowager holding forth in a salon.

And he was entranced.

He returned her smile, but beneath the veneer of a sudden shared camaraderie, lurked an uncomfortable realisation that she was becoming just a little too interesting.

He'd have to bring the session to an early finish.

"Thank you, Miss Montague."

Her mouth dropped open as he nodded, suddenly brisk as he began to clean his brushes. He was sorry his words sounded unaccountably clipped and tried to ameliorate with a smile any sense she might have that he was displeased with her.

"You have been a wonderful subject."

"Surely, you've not finished the painting, Mr Westaway? May I look?" Once she'd got over her surprise, her good nature seemed to have returned, and he was grateful. Relations between them must be utterly proper, verging on formal even—if he were to do what he had to do. Paint the picture that would satisfy his artistic urges, so he could do his father's bidding and concentrate on more important matters in the world.

"Of course, though it is very raw in its current form."

He was too conscious of her closeness when she came to stand beside him, pointing out various flourishes she liked, admiring the work that fed his desperate need to be recognised for what was most important to him in the world —his art.

He stepped away slightly and glanced from the beautiful, smiling girl whose head came up just above his shoulder, to the withered, sleeping woman in the wicker chair beneath the apple tree. The contrast between the two suddenly overwhelmed him with possibilities, and without thinking, he put his hands on her shoulders to move her into a position in the foreground where her youthful bloom would shine as the subject, and the old woman in the background, surrounded by fallen apples, would be the juxtaposition.

Fuelled by artistic excitement, he cupped her cheek. Smooth. The essence of eternal youth. Her halo of golden hair would complete the picture. It would be better than anything he'd done. His head throbbed with excitement, and unconsciously, he stroked the beautifully rendered contours of her brow, nose, and cheek. Her lips. Yes...this was the angle.

And then, as his fragmented vision for what could be coalesced into what *was*, he saw that she'd closed her eyes and raised her face to his.

She was anticipating a kiss? A plethora of emotions slammed through him. First and foremost was the desire to respond, but fast on its heels was the realisation that succumbing to such desire would doom them both. He swallowed, and she opened her eyes in time to catch his confusion.

Quickly, he said, "I want to paint you exactly as you are

and in just that position…that alignment with your chaperone just behind, still sleeping, is perfect. Please indulge me a few minutes longer, Miss Montague?"

"Of course." She pressed her lips together, and as the hot blush spread from her bosom upwards, he cursed himself for putting either of them in such a position.

Channelling his frustrated desire into artistic energy he worked quickly, teasing out the expressions with a few accurate strokes, throwing the entire mood he'd wanted to create right onto the canvas.

It was done in a flash of time, a blur of colour, and he was breathing quickly when he put down his paintbrush and was ready to…

Dismiss her?

Yes, that's what he had to do if he was to get through this unscathed.

"You've been marvellous, Miss Montague," he declared with false bonhomie. "I've never had a better model. So still, so…"

"So obedient?" She was smiling that artless smile of hers, and he wondered if she had any inkling of the trauma he'd just been through.

But of course she would have no idea. She was very young but, yes, very obedient. Well trained would perhaps be apt, for once she'd recovered from the moment of awkwardness over the nearly kiss, she was as perfectly composed and well behaved as any demure debutante needed to be in order to prosper in society.

"Very obedient!" he said on a laugh which broke the ice and woke Lady Vernon, who now called out peevishly for her charge to fetch her sticks and help her to her feet.

"Will you require another sitting, Mr Westaway?" Lady Vernon asked as they prepared to leave. "I trust she was everything for which you'd hoped. She's not very experienced, but she wanted very much to please, didn't you, Faith?"

"With nine brothers and sisters, that's my primary duty, Lady Vernon. To please." She speared him with a look of amusement that insinuated itself more than it should. Was she sharing a secret joke with him? If she were older, more experienced in the ways of the world, he'd have *known* that's what she was doing.

"A great trial you obviously bear very well, Miss Montague," he managed as the safest response he could come up with. "And I'm delighted with today's progress. Thank you for your consummate professionalism for I have managed to get down everything I need and can work on the rest at my leisure. No, I won't require another sitting."

She nodded and gave a half curtsey. "Glad to have obliged, Mr Westaway. In that case, I daresay we shall return to London in the morning." She glanced at Lady Vernon for corroboration, but the old woman shook her head.

"We've booked the room for a few more days, and these weary old bones of mine aren't up to a return trip to the hustle and bustle of the city just yet. Where would you suggest we go for a short sightseeing trip, Mr Westaway? You know the area."

FAITH HAD GROWN UP A COUNTRY GIRL. UNTIL THE AGE OF twelve, the cramped cottage she shared with her nine siblings and parents in the Welsh Borderlands had epitomised all she wanted to escape. At thirteen, she'd gone into service and learned the ways of the gentry. She'd learned how they spoke and watched how they behaved.

Now, the rolling countryside of the West-Midland Vales with its elm-fringed water meadows of the Severn and Avon, and orchards laden with damson, cherry, apple, and pear, represented freedom.

Even if just for a day or two.

That morning, they'd traipsed through the town of Stratford-Upon-Avon, imbibing the history of the Great Bard, William Shakespeare and, later, learned of efforts expended by the actor David Garrick whose Shakespeare Jubilee the previous century had contributed to turning it into a tourist town.

This was the kind of safe, prescribed sightseeing Lady Vernon preferred. Faith would have preferred to delay their journey amidst the lush green fields and go for a meandering walk in the woods. This, of course, was out of the question due to Lady Vernon's infirmity, though she'd proved nimble enough in town until clearly worn out in the Guild Chapel where she now sank into a pew to gaze at the medieval paintings in the nave.

"Five minutes, and no longer, and then we must have lunch at the teahouse at the end of the road," she announced between wheezes. The sunlight that streamed through the stained-glass windows was not kind to her, highlighting the sagging bags of wrinkles under her eyes and the energetic spouting of hairs from the fleshy mole on her chin.

"We can rest longer if you like," Faith said, determined to be amenable and charitable. She knew Lady Vernon would be reporting back to Mrs Gedge on Faith's success which, to date, had been negligible. Staring at the old woman, she wondered if Lady Vernon had ever had a modicum of good looks before her mouth had caved in and age had stuck its claws into her.

The reflection sent fear like a frisson of electricity up her spine, reminding her that she only had a handful of years, herself, in which to cement her own future. A future which, she'd assumed, would be assured by the conclusion of her visit to the Cotswolds. Mr Westaway should have been eating out of her hands by now.

"We need to be at Mrs Bromley's Corner Teahouse by one o' clock," Lady Vernon announced, consulting her watch, and the way she said it made it clear there was a very good reason for this. Something to do with Mr Westaway, Faith presumed.

Correctly, it transpired, when Lady Vernon fixed a pair of beetling eyes upon her and said, "You could at least pretend interest in the young man. I thought you were as anxious as your benefactress to expedite this little matter and claim your reward."

She made it sound so sordid.

Which, Faith supposed, it was.

"I like him very much, and I've hinted so, obliquely, which is all a well-brought-up girl like myself can do. With all due respect, you've been asleep most of the time, Lady Vernon."

"Well-brought-up…" Lady Vernon repeated on a decidedly ill-bred snort, thought Faith as she resisted the urge to offer a tart rejoinder. Too much hinged on Lady Vernon's good offices and while, before she'd sat for Mr Westaway, she could afford to talk back, her current failure could only be laid at her door. What was Mrs Gedge going to say?

Her earlier frisson of fear for her future paid a return visit and settled about her like a cloak 'which old men huddle about their love, as if to keep it warm.' Since they were in the town of the old bard, it seemed appropriate to borrow his quote for personal use. Faith had read much of Shakespeare and King Lear was her favourite.

"Yes, this old church is as cold as the grave and it's time we settled ourselves for lunch," Lady Vernon announced, mistaking Faith's shiver of fearful foreboding.

"So, Mr Westaway knows we'll be at Mrs Bromley's Teahouse then?"

Lady Vernon sent her an arch look over her shoulder as they trod the thin red carpet down the nave towards the open double doors. "Of course he does. Someone has to keep you on the right path if you're to succeed in this venture. I'd have hoped Mr Westaway would be eating out of your hands by now."

"There's not been much time." Faith gritted her teeth as she obediently followed Lady Vernon's wraith-like shadow down the nave. "I can't let him think I'm fast."

"No, a girl brought up in a brothel could hardly let a gentleman think that, could she?"

Faith wasn't sure she'd heard correctly for the muffled words were indistinct and partly swallowed up by the ringing of their shoes upon the stone steps.

Furious, she hurried to keep up. "I might wish my circumstances were different, and believe me, there's no love lost between Mrs Gedge and me, but I am better educated than any of the debutantes who have no doubt been paraded in front of Mr Westaway's nose *and* more beautiful, and regardless of where I rest my head at night, my virtue is unblemished. And will remain so!" Faith descended the steps beside her chaperone into the street. "So don't you make false aspersions about my good character." If ever there was proof that Lady Vernon cared little for Faith and had taken her on purely for the money, this was it.

"Ah, now, my dear, only a short walk and then we can rest our weary bones and see if Mr Westaway has taken the bait." Lady Vernon spoke as if she hadn't heard Faith, her smile cloying, her tone dripping with false pleasure at the journey ahead.

"You make me feel like a…dog or a…rat caught in a trap," Faith muttered. The more she spent time with this abominable woman the less able she was to hold her tongue. She and Lady Vernon were partners in a grubby intrigue of which no one else must be the wiser. Sadly, it meant Lady Vernon was the only person she could speak honestly to.

Lady Vernon swung around, and as her eyes met Faith's, her slack jaw snapped shut, giving her the look of a lazy bloodhound at rest transforming instantly into a pointer, alert and on the hunt.

"We are both rats caught in a trap, and you'd do well to remember that, young lady," she said, taking Faith's arm to lean on as if the pair were grandmother and granddaughter enjoying a gentle stroll. "That's what poverty does to a woman!" She sniffed. "At least I have good breeding as my insurance."

"And I have beauty as mine," Faith snapped back, tipping up her chin and wishing her searing gaze could reduce Lady Vernon to a pile of cinders.

Unscathed, and unconcerned, apparently, Lady Vernon cast Faith a dismissive look before her eyes settled for a second too long, lower down the girl's body. "Yes, it's *all* you have to trade on, girl, so don't make a mess out of this one opportunity to secure your future, and make mine more comfortable until my next call-out to chaperone some horsey-looking blue blood whose mama can't summon the energy." A look of triumph wiped away her peevishness, and the fingers of her left hand dug more deeply into Faith's arm as she raised her right to hail a gentleman hovering by the front entrance of Mrs Bromley's Corner Teahouse.

"Goodness, Mr Westaway! What a surprise to see you here!"

Suddenly, Lady Vernon looked like a sweet old lady with not a venomous thought in her age-ravaged, ugly old head, Faith thought as she was borne along upon a tide of hopefulness; the tide of hopefulness being on Lady Vernon's account that she would be paid for notching up a triumphant success.

As for Faith, she didn't know what she felt. There was so

much riding on this next meeting with Mr Westaway. She didn't want to trade on her beauty and have to do things with a line-up of men that didn't involve her heart.

Yet, as Faith intercepted, then analysed, the look he sent in her direction, the foundation of the three women's collective plan suddenly seemed as rackety and shoddy as the multiple theatres they'd visited to honour the town's great bard that had either been swept away or dismantled to be utilised for something newer and better.

"Miss Montague." He rose from a gallant bow and there was genuine pleasure in his smile. Faith's earlier doubts dissipated. She had managed to conquer. Enough to get things underway, at any rate. Why else had he come in search of her after dismissing her the previous afternoon? "I hoped I'd find you in town."

"You did?" Faith tried to look coy, when in fact she was overcome by an unexpected wave of desperation. *Please, make him amenable and easy to manage from hereon in.*

"Yes, I did want to see you again because I...I can't do justice to your eyes, Miss Montague." He looked anxious as he tried to express himself. Right now, he was the artist, tortured by his creativity, not the diplomat. He tried again, using his hands as if that might make his meaning clearer. "The painting is so close to being finished. I'm nearly happy with it but—" He broke off and sent her a beseeching look. "Would you come back and sit for me one last time?"

Faith glanced at Lady Vernon then back at Mr Montague. He did look very appealing, hanging upon her acceptance.

With a slight shrug, she deferred to her chaperone. "I'm afraid that only Lady Vernon can make that decision. I know she's set on the idea of returning to London on tomorrow's early train, but if she can be persuaded, I don't mind."

I don't mind.

Was that the right thing to say? Would her lack of enthusiasm strike the right note with both Lady Vernon and Mr Westaway? She had to appear pliable; a girl who knew her place. Not too eager yet also hint at a flicker of interest. To bolster this last, she fluttered her eyelashes and looked demurely at her hands as if suddenly shy. That should be a nice finish to the whole charade before Lady Vernon fixed the time for tomorrow.

Yet her intake of satisfaction was expelled on resignation. She didn't feel true to herself to be taking manipulation to such extremes.

Still, she thought, the moment she had her cheque for five hundred pounds from Mrs Gedge she could do as she pleased. She'd never again have to worry about pretending or about what anyone else thought. How pleasing that would be.

"Tomorrow then. At ten o' clock?" He smiled, and Faith thought what pleasant grey eyes he had. "In the garden where the light is good. It'll be a fine day, I believe."

HE SHOULDN'T HAVE ASKED HER TO COME BACK. WITH sparkling morning light streaming from an azure blue sky imbuing the scene with a magical sense of hope and promise, it hadn't taken more than ten minutes with brush and paints and the girl lying amidst the daisy-strewn grass before Crispin knew this.

Still, what was the harm in the simple pleasure of transferring her exceptional beauty onto the canvas in front of him? He hadn't painted in two years, and there was fever in his fingers to create and do justice to his subject.

He felt alive.

That was all this feeling was. A desire to do his best work

knowing that the girl in front of him offered him the means to do that.

"Would you put aside what you're holding please, Miss Montague?" She'd broken the ennui of her dull, wearying task to make a daisy chain. Now he needed her to be still. "Sorry to sound like the grim voice of authority." He tried to inject levity into his tone, though he was tense with the need to get his painting right. What *was* required to get the light in her eyes just so? He'd nearly had it yesterday. Now it eluded him. A pinprick of white, perhaps? "You'll be comparing me to your pater in his grumpiest frame of mind," he muttered, half attending to the need to put her at ease while he loaded his paintbrush.

"Oh, that tone is very mild compared with my father's temper." Obediently, she put down the daisy chain and stared up at the sky, and as he studied his work, pleased with the effect, he wondered for the first time about her large family.

"I'm sure he's only concerned for the happiness of you all. That's how my pater excuses his lapses of good humour." Crispin smiled across at her, but instead of meeting happy collusion or agreement, her expression was closed. And dark.

Of course, it was no business of his to pry, but he suddenly wanted to get a sense of Miss Montague's position in the world. Not that it would matter to him after today from a personal sense, but if he could aid her in any way in what he supposed was her primary duty, to succeed in the marital market, it would be helpful to know a little about her father.

"You have sisters, don't you, Miss Montague?"

"Six, Mr Westaway, and only one married. We are a great trial to our father."

"I'm sure if they're all as lovely as you, it won't be long before your father can bask in the collective success of his seven daughters who'll have made his family so well connected. I presume your married sister is older?"

"Twelve months older than me and married to a man who is to turn sixty in a few months. Not a love match."

That stopped him in his tracks. Crispin wasn't easily shocked, but this didn't reflect well on Mr Montague. He racked his brains to come up with what he knew of Miss Montague's family and realised he knew nothing.

"So, Mr Westaway, are you pleased with your painting?" She was turning the topic to lighten the mood, for now she was all smiles as she raised herself onto her elbows. "I hope I've been a good subject. Despite what Lady Vernon told you, I do find it hard to stay still unless there is a great deal at stake."

"My painting?" He felt ill at ease. Not only was there the self-imposed pressure of painting his best work, but that of producing a painting that promised this young woman a better future.

"Yes, I want you to recommend me to your artist friends as a model. My father knows nothing of what I'm doing here and would be shocked, but this is better than a great deal of other ways to save himself the expense of keeping me than the ones he has in mind." She rose and came over to stand at his shoulder, her admiring gasp sending desire washing over him like a hot wave. He stepped back quickly, masking his awkwardness with a smile as he said, "I could never do justice to your beauty, Miss Montague, but I believe it is a fair likeness."

Her surprise and admiration seemed genuine. "It's…it's truly brilliant! Oh, Mr Westaway, you'll win the competition; indeed, you will! And you'll show your father what talent you have, and he'll let you do what you want to be happy. I'm so proud of you."

"I only wish it were so simple." He thought of his father's

fury should he learn that Crispin had been wasting his time on artistic pursuits, when he should be attending to the delicate strategic relations between England and her allies and potential enemies.

"But your talent is prodigious. It mustn't be wasted. You must tell him it's what you want." She took his hand and squeezed it, her eyes shining. "I knew you were good, but I didn't realise how good. You truly have made me the happiest girl."

"You enjoy admiration? Well, you shall have it in spade loads." *I just can't lavish it on you, personally, as I would wish.* Gently, he disengaged his hands and sent a glance up at the house. "Lady Vernon was hoping to catch the morning train to London, and there's still time, Miss Montague." He swallowed down his disappointment that he could not respond to her as he wished, and gave her what he hoped was a paternal pat on her shoulder. "Now, let me walk you to the house. I'll see you in London at the unveiling."

"Why so glum, Faith? I think it was a poor plan of Mrs Gedge's to see you clothed like a parson's daughter when you're to be competing with duchesses." Charity was curled up on Faith's bed like a cat, her long hair undressed and pooling about her. She sent Faith a bolstering smile. "Don't be afraid. Tonight, it will all work out."

Faith nibbled her nail and nodded. She couldn't trust herself to answer.

Her vulnerability was like a gaping wound and the future like a black, angry, dangerous void waiting to hungrily devour her. She'd be like all the other girls at Madame Chambon's, with closed heart and open legs, submitting to a line-up of meaningless sexual encounters just so she could keep body and soul together. And then the moment she was no longer giving value, if she got sick or her looks were marred or faded, she'd be thrown into the gutter to fend for herself.

All because she'd not managed to do one simple thing— entice Mr Westaway enough to at least give the appearance to Mrs Gedge that he'd fallen in love with her.

She dusted her décolletage with a rabbit's foot loaded with fine powder while her brain whirled feverishly. Perhaps she could win him over using honesty. That would be novel?

"I know you're disappointed he didn't fall in love with you, Faith, but is he nice, this Mr Westaway?"

"He's lovely." Faith had no hesitation in answering. "I like him very much, and if it wasn't so vital to…everything…that I make him fall in love with me, I'd say I liked him too much to *want* to make him fall in love with me, if that makes sense."

"It doesn't make sense at all." Charity shook her head. "But then, nothing much makes sense."

With a sigh, Faith rose. "How do I look?"

"Like an angel, truly! You don't need bows and furbelows. In fact, you're more striking without, and I can now see exactly what was in Mrs Gedge's mind. Oh, but I do hope it works tonight. If Mr Westaway doesn't fall in love with you just by looking at you, he'll never fall in love with anyone!"

With this bolstering pronouncement ringing in her ears, Faith prepared to make her grand entrance at the Grand London Art Exhibition, arriving in Lady Vernon's hired carriage, which was waiting for her discreetly a little distance up the road.

SHE HADN'T THOUGHT SHE'D BE EXCITED AT THE OUTCOME. There was no outcome that promised what she needed without some compromise, and the fact she'd simply sat for a painting meant nothing when the real purpose behind the whole charade had come to naught.

Yet, as the double doors opened to the hallowed precincts of the Royal Society of Artists, a frisson of very real expectation skittered up the back of Faith's knees and lodged in her stomach. Mr Westaway's talent was undeniable. The painting had been exceptional. He deserved recognition.

And when across a crowded floor of patrons, mostly whiskered older men in sombre evening attire, Faith caught a glimpse of Mr Westaway, she was suddenly a jumble of nerves. He was in conversation with a lady and a gentleman, and he was laughing, a drink in his hand, and all eyes seemed to be on him. She noticed people around her indicating him with nods and veiled gestures, and her excitement grew.

People knew already that Mr Westaway was good. That they had a fine artist in their midst. She wasn't imagining all this.

While the crowd pulsed around her, she couldn't take her eyes off him. He looked so handsome, so self-assured. So right at home in his domain and Faith felt so proud of him.

As Lady Vernon gave her a little prod to keep her moving, she was addressed by a small, forceful young woman with a jaunty little feathered hat holding a notepad whom she recognised before the strong American accent gave her away.

"Miss Montague, I'm going to make you famous!" The confidence and enthusiasm in Miss Eaves's tone were in striking contrast to the way Faith felt.

"I don't want to be famous. I'm English," she said, making the young woman throw back her head and give an unlady-like guffaw.

"Uncle, Miss Montague says she doesn't want to be famous. But I tell you, she's going to be after Mr Westaway wins this show hands down, and I write her story."

The gentleman with a long white beard and sombre, impressive bearing—which belied any relationship to the young lady who'd just addressed Faith—nodded at Faith as he introduced himself as Sir Albion, the patron of the Society. "Write your story, Amy, but don't tell anyone it's going to make them famous. It's a vulgar notion, I might add."

"Indeed, most vulgar," Lady Vernon muttered, her nose twitching as if she actually did have a barometer for what was morally acceptable. It was difficult for Faith to keep her own nostrils from flaring in disdain. Instead, she inclined her head and said with her most demure smile, "Notoriety is for those who seek it, and I certainly do not. If Mr Westaway is to be commended for his painting, I am simply happy that I assisted in some small way."

Sir Albion looked at her with approval. "I marked him out as a great talent many years ago, but I feared he'd lost his passion. Clearly you, Miss Montague, have reawakened it. Ah, here comes the gentleman in question now."

"My ears are burning." Mr Westaway looked a touch self-conscious as his gaze flickered from Faith's face to his esteemed patron as he acknowledged the ladies with a small bow. "But I'd not expected to have such strong competition when the time frame was so limited. Some of the finest are competing for the grand prize."

"The challenge of a time frame and the inducement of such a grand sum of money makes their enthusiasm not so surprising, for all that we like to think ourselves above such considerations."

"We all need to eat, Sir Albion."

"Indeed we do, Miss Montague," Sir Albion said, raising his eyes, before glancing at his niece. "Amy here thinks she owes it to herself to do that through her own merits. A very progressive thought indeed. Clearly, things are different in America."

"Things are changing, Uncle, both here and across the Atlantic where less and less is it considered vulgar for a woman to advance herself through honest toil and her own endeavours." Miss Eaves puffed out her chest importantly, and the little bird on top of her jaunty hat did a trembling dance of agreement. Faith stifled the urge to laugh, which was prompted more by her nervousness in being in such close proximity to such influential people. Influential because her fate lay in their hands more than they could know.

"There is no competition; we do know that, Mr Westaway," Miss Eaves said with conviction, and everyone looked at her in surprise causing the young lady to shake her head. "I don't know the outcome, if that's what you think, though my uncle does. The patron of the competition—who is anonymous, by the way, though word has it that she's an extremely wealthy American—has already judged the entries. In my opinion, though, there is no competition. Mr Westaway is going to become a famous artist, and Miss Montague is...." She looked enquiringly at Faith. "What do you hope to achieve out of all this?"

Sir Albion gave a gruff laugh. "Too direct by half, as you'd say yourself, Amy. One doesn't ask young ladies such things. Certainly not in company."

"Why, because their intentions can only be one thing? And it's vulgar to express that we all know what that is? Surely, we all want to succeed and profit, and get ahead. And what's the harm in that? It's human nature! So why should we not be allowed to voice such things aloud?" Undeterred by her uncle, she looked enquiringly at Faith, demanding it would seem, an answer.

Faith glanced at Lady Vernon for inspiration, but Lady Vernon appeared as caught off balance as she herself.

"Miss Montague is about to take London by storm." Faith was saved by Mr Westaway's gallant pronouncement. "When I am in Germany and reading the English newspapers, I shall no doubt come upon an announcement that she's either become the muse of a great painter or the wife of a great nobleman." He smiled at Faith. "I believe either would be the pinnacle of Miss Montague's ambitions."

Miss Eaves looked dubious but then conceded, "I suppose that would be a great advancement for a parson's daughter with nine brothers and sisters, I hope I have that number right, and yes, I have been doing my homework." She hadn't finished making her point though, and she strung out her response with a pointed look at everyone in turn. Faith wasn't sure if she liked the young woman or not. While she could concur with some of her sentiments, her manner was too brash and confronting for her comfort.

Miss Eaves sniffed. "Indeed, I look forward to the time when a woman is allowed to make her own way in the world without having to rely on any man; however, I will allow that Miss Montague has shown talent and strategy."

Sir Albion sent a pointed look in his niece's direction. "A demure, discreet demeanour will still get a young woman a great deal further than…otherwise," he finished with raised eyebrows. Miss Eaves was not put in her place. Faith decided she was not the kind who would ever be silenced by criticism.

However, she was glad when the collective attention of the crowd was stirred by something taking place at the far end of the room, and when Faith looked, it was to see that three paintings had been separated from the rest of the exhibits and were now lined up beside each other under lights upon the dais.

Miss Eaves gave a murmur of excitement; Lady Vernon gripped Faith's arm, and a great silence descended upon the room. The moment was nearly upon them.

Faith exchanged a quick, nervous look with Mr Westaway, her mouth dry.

He stepped close to her. "I don't know whether I'll be relieved or disappointed by the outcome," he admitted.

"You surely want to win, don't you, Mr Westaway?" Faith whispered. "Every great talent craves recognition, even if they are unwilling to admit as much." As a gentle hum went through the crowd, and as conversation resumed in the delay before an announcement, Faith told him, "My sister, the eldest and, seemingly, the most modest and retiring of all of us, worked twice as hard for the crumbs of praise that were few and far between in our household. But her zealousness, or martyrdom, came from the desire for recognition, purely, though she was the last to admit that she did what she did to be noticed. I know you love painting, but do you really do it only for the love of it?"

His surprise was obvious. After a moment, he confessed in a low voice, "I'll give you the truth, Miss Montague, and this is only between you and me because we have been part of something…more important than simply creating a painting. Yes, I crave to be recognised as a great talent. But I also crave the continued love and respect of my father. That, and my desire to be a great painter, are incompatible. And so, tonight I confess to secretly wishing I might be declared the winner to bolster my own vanity in my abilities. But perhaps more than that, I wish the prize might go to someone else as it would enable me to accept more easily that this is *not* my calling." He looked at her carefully, and Faith felt sure she read longing in the depths of his gaze. "You know I go to Germany in before the end of the month, Miss Montague. Nothing will make my father prouder than to see me take up this important position. I've been groomed to follow in his footsteps for my whole life."

Faith felt a stab of something between pain and disappointment. Not for seeing her own dreams and ambitions go up in smoke, but for the bond between this man and his father. In all her young life, she'd never felt the kind of love and respect for anyone that would make her sacrifice her own ambitions. Granted, her scope had been limited, and she'd been at the mercy of those stronger than herself, but for these short moments talking to Mr Westaway, she wished she had an affiliation of the heart with someone that was greater than her own vanity, desires, and all those other foibles that made human beings so... fallible.

Mr Westaway's life was built on a foundation of love and filial duty, honour and nobility.

Faith's was built on a lie.

But if Faith only had the chance to prove to someone the inner core of nobility she was sure existed somewhere, she'd gladly make such a sacrifice for love.

She hadn't realised her feelings showed on her face and was surprised by his sudden concern. "Are you all right, Miss Montague?"

Faith took a sip of her champagne and tried to cleanse her smile of all bitterness and disappointment. "I was just thinking how nice it would be to love and respect one's father as you clearly do, Mr Westaway. Oh, my goodness!" She broke off suddenly as the first of the paintings on stage had its concealing sheet whipped away, and the audience gasped.

How strange it was to see herself lying in the grass amidst a field of daisies, her expression animated, her hair spread like a halo about her, the beautiful countryside as her backdrop. It was a picture of lovely innocence—even she could see that before the corroborating comment from a nearby dowager.

The next painting was good, also. A young woman was sitting on a swing holding a bouquet of flowers while a young fawn grazed nearby. It was a gladdening scene, but it had not quite the expertise as Mr Westaway's painting, of that Faith was certain.

When the three paintings were revealed, side by side, having been selected from a field of twenty-five, Faith had expected a clear winner was inevitable. But to her surprise, and obviously the surprise of everyone else, Sir Albion stood on stage and announced the unexpected news that these three painters would be pitted against each other in a run-off. A theme had been chosen; the deadline was tight, one week only, after which a clear winner would be announced and would receive an astonishing amount of prize money.

A great deal of murmuring and a few disgruntled mumblings followed this pronouncement. Mr Westaway looked distinctly discomposed.

Faith could only stare as she felt her heart pounding in her ears.

She'd been given a second chance. Mrs Gedge was the anonymous benefactor of this extremely handsome prize, and she'd manufactured a means by which Faith could spend another week in Mr Westaway's company.

That is, if Mr Westaway was prepared to risk the tenuous relationship of balancing his desire for recognition in the world of art with managing his father's respect and expectations.

She sent him a furtive glance beneath lowered lashes. He was not overjoyed at the prospect of having to produce another painting if he wanted to remain a contender. The tightly pressed lips highlighted the planes of his cheekbones. He looked like a handsome ascetic deliberating over a weighty matter that had repercussions for the world.

Before they were interrupted by the advancing well-wishers, Faith locked eyes with him, and it was as if the spear of his own agony communicated itself to her for the crucial second it needed for her to subsume her own desires for the justice of his.

"Don't accept on my account—if that has any bearing on your decision," she said quickly. "You have your father and your career to consider."

"Mr Westaway, you are a prodigious talent indeed! And

this is the young lady? But of course, for you have indeed been faithful to the original, to such superlative beauty."

Two whiskered gentlemen and a lady bore down upon them. "The field is narrow, but you will outshine your competitors. I remember your first unveiling, why, five years ago it must have been. And then you disappeared?" It soon became clear to Faith that the lady, who was introduced as Mrs Cannington, the wife of the tallest of the whiskered gentlemen, was an authority and leading force in the organisation. It seemed she also was more than capable of achieving Faith's purpose, all on her own. "You are concerned you might discompose your father if you follow up on this incredible opportunity?" she paraphrased, or rather, interpreted from Mr Westaway's brief response. "Why, I understand that Lord Maxwell is not a great patron of the arts, but he is not a philistine. And only a philistine would place such an obstacle in the way of the nurturing of a truly great talent."

Faith was amused to see Mr Westaway blush. "Please, Mrs Cannington, don't blame my father. I'm about to realise his greatest ambition and take up a diplomatic post in Germany. In fact, I sail in less than three weeks, so you can understand the conflict."

"But part of the challenge is that the painting must be completed in one." She looked triumphant, as did the two gentlemen flanking her. As did Lady Vernon, who'd not had to utter one word to see the progression of Mrs Gedge's plan.

"It's not only that the prize itself is considerable, unusually and surprisingly so, but the recognition would be invaluable."

"Excuse me, but who is sponsoring the prize?"

Everyone turned, surprised, to Faith. "Are they known in art circles? A great artist, themselves, perhaps?" She needed to draw out what public knowledge there might be about Mrs Gedge, the kind of person she was and, perhaps even her motives.

"A wealthy American woman who wishes to remain anonymous," said Mr Cannington. "A woman who selected these three paintings herself," he indicated the three canvases with a flourish, "and who'd be exceedingly disappointed if one of her selections did not pursue the challenge into the final round. Now, please reconsider, Mr Westaway. All that's required is seven days in a pursuit that you have already admitted would give you great satisfaction. Surely there is no obstacle other than your reluctance to apprise your father that you are engaged in activities that do not actively further your imminent career posting." He checked himself. "I take it the young lady is available to sit for the painting? It is one of the stipulations that the original muse is to be featured in the second painting."

Faith nodded.

"Is it indeed, and is that the only stipulation?" Mr Westaway raised his eyebrows.

Mrs Cannington simpered. "Our American benefactress has a playful turn of mind. Indeed, at ten o'clock on the morning of the first day when painting is to begin, a messenger will arrive with the canvas, paints, and a bag of props, together with additional stipulations. Each of the three painters will receive exactly the same props and instructions and must complete the work by ten o'clock on the morning of the seventh day, at which time the messenger will arrive to collect the painting and take it back here for judging."

Her husband pulled at his whiskers and looked anxiously at Mr Westaway. "Seven days, Mr Westaway. What is seven days in a lifetime? Seven days which, in fact, may *change* your life infinitely for the better?"

CHAPTER 13

Change his life but *not* for the better. Faith was uncomfortably aware of this, sitting opposite Lady Vernon as the train pulled into the small country station and she saw Mr Westaway on the platform, scanning the opening carriage doors.

He'd invited them to be his guests and stay in his house rather than at the inn so that was some small victory.

When he recognised Faith he looked pleased, which gave her a small jolt of pleasure that was quickly replaced by dread. What must *she* do? Seven days in which to turn Mr Westaway into putty. Why should Mrs Gedge hate him so much she'd go to such lengths to play this game?

And why should it worry her? Faith had hardly been nurtured during *her* lifetime while Mr Westaway had been born with a silver spoon. The transaction between her and this man would be brief—not enough time to do too much damage, surely. Once she'd generated sufficient intensity in their dealings with one another to pass Lady Vernon's scrutiny, Faith could collect on her transaction, buy her little cottage in the country, and put all of this behind her.

Still, she couldn't help asking as the train slowed, "Does Mr Westaway genuinely deserve what we are going to do to him?"

Piously, Lady Vernon responded, "Mrs Gedge is a mother avenging her daughter who was led to believe by Mr Westaway that holy matrimony would be forthcoming."

"Then why didn't the girl simply sue him for breach of promise? That would have embarrassed the family."

Instead, it was Lady Vernon who looked embarrassed. "Matters didn't proceed down that avenue."

"He seduced her?" Faith shrugged. And if he had? But then, it seemed out of character for the man she'd come to know, unless he'd already learned his lesson, in which case, Faith was going to have to work extra hard.

She sighed and slumped back into her seat muttering, "I really don't want to do this."

Lady Vernon's tone was snide. "Madame Chambon *will* be pleased. I hear she is eager to continue to further your career with no return from you and to accommodate you in her comfortable Soho lodgings free of charge as she has done these past three years." She opened the reticule on her lap and pulled out a letter which she handed to Faith. "Mrs Gedge's contract, though if you'd rather we returned to London..."

Faith took the envelope, unsettled by Lady Vernon's words as a horrifying image of Lord Harkom seared her mind. The only person invested in Faith's future, and *safety*, was herself. She needed to play her cards right with Mr Westaway.

"Miss Montague, I do appreciate you coming back at such short notice."

Mr Westaway was standing before the open door, his hand extended to help her out of the carriage while someone else attended to her bags.

Faith smiled as she took his hand. It was large and firm and felt surprisingly dependable. Surprising because she hadn't considered that about him. He was an artist, and they were notoriously unreliable, weren't they? She also wasn't used to the feel of a man's hand—not since the clouts she used to receive when her father returned home, drunk and peevish.

"If I'm to be honest, this is quite an adventure for me," she told him as they started to walk towards his waiting carriage, Lady Vernon bringing up the rear. "My surroundings tend to lack variety, though it'll be an adventure going so far north when the season comes to an end."

"North?"

"Yorkshire. Remember I told you that I'm to take up a post as a governess there when the season comes to an end?"

He looked uncomfortable. "Yes, of course. But there are still some weeks until that time, and I feel sure that…other options may present themselves in the meantime."

"You mean because your painting will make me the toast of the town?" Faith shrugged. "I hope that will be the case. Sadly, I'm no different from most young women in London for these few months, though I suppose it's vulgar to say so." She laughed when she saw him colour up. "But it's true, Mr Westaway. Oh, don't worry, you've made your position very clear, and I hope that we can be good friends. But I won't deny that if a suitable match presents itself, possibly on account of your efforts with a paintbrush, I will consider my time these few weeks very well spent. There are better ways to while away a lifetime than teaching recalcitrant children or serving ungrateful relatives."

"You're a plain speaker sometimes, Miss Montague." He helped her into the carriage, smiling at her as he tucked her trailing skirts out of the way of the door. "I keep forgetting that."

"But we're friends now. I feel comfortable speaking plainly to you." She held herself primly as she clasped her hands together. "We both know where we stand with one another."

He laughed again as he leapt up front and took the reins, and Faith thought she could detect a note of friendly relief in his tone as he said over his shoulder, "Indeed we are, Miss Montague. I'd go so far as to say that we understand one another. In which case, the week ahead should progress swimmingly."

~

It was too late to begin painting that evening. Faith was tired after her long journey, and it was genuinely pleasant to relax on the terrace after dinner, enjoying the long daylight hours. The country certainly was a grand place to be compared with cramped and grimy Soho and, of course, the damp, leaky cottage she'd grown up in.

Both were a world away from where she was now. This lovely, yet extensive country house owned by Mr Westaway's absent aunt and uncle exuded a simple, relaxed charm. French doors from the drawing room opened onto a wide terrace, and the comfortable wicker chairs in which they sat were surrounded by urns and tubs of orange trees and quince bushes.

Lady Vernon, bundled up in a blanket, looked like a small, dissatisfied rodent, Faith thought, amused, as she enjoyed some desultory conversation with Mr Westaway. In the lengthening shadows, his pleasant smile appeared more readily during this conversation than previously. Yes, they were getting to know one another without the tension that must result from any possibility of a long-term future between them.

He was soon to leave on official business, and it was acknowledged by both of them that Faith was not a candidate for the role of anything other than an artist's muse.

But...

How was Faith to execute her duty if they were now to become simply friends? She was surprised to hear him laugh and realised she'd said something amusing. The anecdote about a lady in the street whose wig had been knocked off by a performing monkey had simply tripped off her tongue. As if she were enjoying playful banter with a trusted companion. When had she been relaxed enough to say words that weren't carefully calculated?

A whisper of ice through her veins made her shiver. A foreshadowing of something truly frightful held her in its grip for one terrible moment when the words died in her throat, and she must have looked as shocked as she felt, for instantly Mr Westaway was on his feet.

"I thought you were about to faint clean away," he told her after she'd regained her equilibrium and waved aside his offers of sending for a warm blanket, though he hovered by her side.

"I have a few years yet before I'll have need of such cosseting in weather like this." She tried to sound light as she indicated Lady Vernon, huddled into her blanket and fast asleep. Indeed, Lady Vernon was smiling as if in the middle of a very pleasing dream and Faith wished she could feel similar contentment for just a small part of her life. Then she remembered that soon, when she was her own mistress and living a life of blissful seclusion in her own little cottage in the country, she would always feel as contented as Lady Vernon looked.

But that relied on making Mr Westaway fall in love with her.

Mr Westaway had just begun to return to his chair. Perhaps he felt the evening was becoming too intimate.

Faith was about to announce her intention to retire to bed too, remembering from her lessons that it was important to foster a sense of loss if one was to keep a gentleman longing for more, when footsteps sounded upon the stone steps at the end of the terrace.

Sampson, Mr Westaway's faithful wolfhound, rose warily, tensed, then bounded forward, and Faith heard the bluff, welcoming tones of the elegant, white-haired gentleman emerging from the dusk and coming towards them with outstretched hand.

"You're back again, Crispin! I thought I saw evidence it was you and not your aunt and uncle. Sorry I missed you last week but good to see you now, my boy. And how did things go with your painting?"

It was as Lady Vernon stirred that Mr Westaway's friend and, apparently, neighbour, realised Crispin was not alone, for instantly he was all apologies as he rectified his omission and introductions were made.

"And tell me something of the composition of this painting?" asked their new arrival, Lord Delmore, relaxing into another wicker chair that was brought into the cosy grouping on the terrace while the fading light was supplemented by a bracket of candles. "I saw the first one Crispin painted, and I'm not surprised it garnered such acclaim. Though, of course, Crispin's talent is not alone responsible."

He smiled at Faith, but when she merely nodded her head, returned his attention to Crispin while Faith looked on. She was tired and wished she'd seized her opportunity to leave earlier. Still, it was pleasant to fade out of the conversation and observe the way Mr Westaway conducted himself when in the company of someone with whom he could obviously relax.

It was clear the two men had known each other a long time. Perhaps a little short of ten years, for she'd heard that was when Lord Delmore had bought the house next door. Yes, Lord Delmore knew Crispin's father from his London club and now made some comment about the man's ambitions for his only son.

"My week of painting here is perhaps a little more clandestine that I'd have liked, and I'm in two minds as to whether I want to win," Faith's host admitted.

Faith could tell he'd considered her to have dropped out of the conversation. She pretended to be as sleepy as Lady Vernon whose head had lolled to one side and who was gently snoring.

"Clandestine? To slip away and paint? You're in the wrong profession, Crispin. Foreign diplomacy is *all* cloak and dagger, and I know you hate subterfuge. Your father should have taken your character into consideration before he pushed you into following his footsteps."

"And yet, I can't think what else I would prefer. I have the necessary contacts, the enthusiastic backing of a father who's spent his life in the thick of it, and I won't deny there are aspects of what lies ahead that I relish." Crispin sighed. "Ah, to be of independent means but who am I to complain?" He grinned self-deprecatingly as he swept his surroundings with a languid arm.

After a few more minutes when Faith really was beginning to nod off and had decided there was nothing further to learn, she made a move to rise.

The two men stood and Lord Delmore, after acknowledging Lady Vernon, said indulgently, "I'm sure you'll be all the inspiration Mr Westaway needs under the circumstances. I admired the first picture he did last week, and as our esteemed painter says, the composition of the painting won't be known until ten o' clock tomorrow morning when the props are delivered, my curiosity is aroused. You'll not mind if I put my head in at some stage to see the work in progress? I know nothing of how art is made, but I'm a great admirer of it when it's good. What about you, Miss Montague?"

"All I know is that I must remain still and quiet, which is really my most important function, Lord Delmore."

He laughed. "How beautifully mannered you are. A credit to your parents with such sentiments tripping off your tongue, though I confess that I'm not averse to a lady speaking what is really on her mind. But you are young. That will come in time."

Faith liked his initial sentiments but felt a frisson of irritation at the paternalistic tone he adopted when referring to her suitably meek manner. Well, neither of them would ever know what went on in her mind, and what she did treat them to would be uttered with all the calculation of the most supreme diplomat.

But that was not for these men to know. Far better, right now, to simply blush prettily, bow her head, and say quietly, "I'm sure it will, Lord Delmore. Good night, gentlemen."

~

CRISPIN POURED LORD DELMORE AND HIMSELF A BRANDY when the ladies retired. There was something cathartic about a balmy evening with non-demanding company—namely not having his father present. Something that invited an ease of speech to which Crispin was unaccustomed.

Lord Delmore had been absent at his Scottish estate the last time Crispin had inhabited the cottage, and he was glad of the company now.

"I read a snippet in more than one newspaper that your painting was lauded a grand success. You're sure you won't mind if I wander over and see you at work in the morning? I shan't frighten the girl?"

"She's less of a shrinking violet than she looks. I think she was very tired tonight. Her conversation is usually more diverting." Crispin found himself defending Miss Montague even when he knew there was no need.

"She doesn't need to be capable of diverting conversation. She's an angel merely to feast one's eyes upon. Where did you find her? And how did you entice her up here when there's so much going on in London?"

Crispin shifted in his chair as he drained his glass. "Poor thing is penniless and jumped at the opportunity for a bit of publicity, to use the modern American jargon."

"Husband hunting. Naturally." Lord Delmore smiled. "She'll be snapped up before two months, I don't doubt. That's if *you* can resist her." He looked thoughtful. "Though I'd imagine you'd prefer your company a little livelier."

"Oh, she's sharp when she's well rested. Sadly, she's not in my scope. It'll be at least two years before I'm in the market for a wife. If I'm to be swept away by any romantic inclinations earlier than that, the young lady will need to bring a good deal more to the transaction than Miss Montague, I'm sorry to say." And he truly was sorry. Fortunately, matters had not yet got out of hand.

"Ah, the dictates of the pocketbook. Perhaps your father has someone in mind? An exacting man. Well, my advice would be to follow your own path, not the one laid out by your father if it's not what you want to do." He pursed his lips as if contemplating something unpleasant. "It can lead to a lifetime of unhappiness—for both of you."

Crispin was surprised by his candour.

At Crispin's look of enquiry, he went on, "Yes, I speak from experience because I was pressured into a path not of my choosing. Oh, it's not that I had great objections, but perhaps it was my passivity as a young man that caused a lifetime of regret. I agreed to my father's proposal when, had I been older and wiser and in control of my future path, I'd have steered well clear of it."

"You were pushed into a profession you disliked?" Crispin felt somewhat doltish saying the words, but the long silence unnerved him. Surely, Lord Delmore wasn't speaking of more intimate matters.

"My marriage, dear boy. No, I had no profession to speak of. Not a good state of affairs, either." Lord Delmore smiled ruefully. "I was pushed into a corner so that I had no choice but to make a declaration and then an offer that required me to follow through. It made neither of us happy. Poor Elsie has been gone these fifteen years, but it is to my eternal regret that I had not the strength of character to resist my father's pressure that I make her an offer when I was so inadequately equipped to make her happy. Neither of us brought the other happiness. And what sort of a marriage is that?"

"But you have two sons who have done you credit, and a daughter." Crispin spoke weakly.

"Indeed. A blessing and the greatest gift. Elsie said the same on her deathbed as she sought for something worthwhile to come out of being bound to someone so patently incompatible for nearly two decades. And two decades could be five in your case. Do not pledge your troth unless your heart is truly engaged. Don't let your father be the one to dictate what will or won't make you happy."

"Pleasing my father is satisfaction enough." Crispin was unable to meet Lord Delmore's eye. His father had always dominated him; he knew it. But now Crispin was leaving the country. In Germany, he could be his own man. He'd find fulfilment in his work and rise in the world through his own endeavours.

"Perhaps for now." Lord Delmore rose. "But your father

won't be around forever and then who will you have to please? A wife whom you don't understand? Whom you don't love?" He touched his breast. "Painting is your passion; I know that. I'm glad you have a week to indulge it. I hope it'll be a reminder of how much else there is to indulge, and that indulgence is not a sin."

CHAPTER 14

Faith rose the next morning with a sense of excitement and expectation. It was so unusual to feel something that wasn't dull resignation, that she leapt out of bed and was smiling as she wrapped herself in her peignoir and threw open the casement window.

The fresh morning air was a welcome and exhilarating slap in the face. Today was the start of a new chapter in her life. Today, Mr Westaway would begin the painting that would be the catalyst for so much. It could make him famous. He would be venerated; his ambition cemented, and Faith could slip away into her new life with the funds to exist in the modest, quiet fashion she desired.

She went to her wardrobe and began to dress, pulling on the modest, swathed skirt that was fashionable but only just, due to the paucity of trimmings.

"What do you think you're doing?" Lady Vernon stood in the doorway, her gaze critical and her nostrils twitching.

"What does it look like?" Faith hadn't meant to sound impertinent, but honestly!

"The morning is fresh, and you want to pick some flowers

in your nightdress. Put your peignoir back on and go outside. Mr Westaway will be watching from the casement; I assure you."

Faith rolled her eyes, but Lady Vernon was quick to snap. "You seem not to have the faintest idea as to how to wrap a gentleman around your little finger, girl! Do you want to succeed, or not?"

Sighing, Faith did as she was bid. As she tied the loose, flimsy garment about her, she muttered, "I can't imagine why you think you are better equipped to know how to entice a man. Have you ever received a letter purporting to a gentleman's passionately beating heart or, better still, a marriage proposal? That is what Mrs Gedge requires, and it's what I am *always* thinking of."

"I have received both, my girl, so I know very well how it is to be achieved. You have already thrown away your first opportunity, but you have been granted a reprieve. You have seven days. Seven days to achieve that letter or that marriage proposal. Otherwise, you are going back to Madame Chambon's and to many gentlemen far less tolerant and thoughtful than Lord Harkom if you're to continue to have a roof over your head. Where is your sense of urgency?"

Faith ignored her, of course.

A short while later, gathering a bunch of wildflowers that grew by the lake—in full view of Mr Westaway's bedchamber window—Faith reflected on her chaperone's chilling words. Seven days to achieve so much? Had she allowed herself to be carried away by confidence, again? Or was it fear, during the first week when she'd achieved precisely nothing?

She'd sensed she couldn't go too fast with Mr Westaway, but Mrs Gedge had always appeared so obliging during their afternoon tea sessions at Claridges, and Faith had been lulled into thinking she had all the time in the world to achieve what she had to. Not a paltry few days.

Lord Harkom had disabused her of that notion.

She rose slowly, enjoying the feel of the dew underfoot and the light breeze on her skin. As she turned back towards the house, a butterfly fluttered up from a nearby rose bush. She put her hand out and the delicate blue-winged insect hovered above it, finally landing on the flowers she held.

Suddenly, she was five years old again, enjoying a bank holiday with her parents in the days when her father still smiled and there were not so many mouths to feed. She and her two sisters had their parents' full attention as they picnicked with many other families enjoying a rare day off. The grass was soft and green; the sandwiches had never tasted so good, and nature was butterflies and blooming flowers—not vermin in the kitchen and mud underfoot picking stunted vegetables in the soggy garden.

She closed her eyes against the pain of memories unbidden. She didn't want to dredge up thoughts of her past. She had no past to call her own anymore. Her parents would have forgotten her long since. Perhaps the sisters closest in age, older and younger, would wonder what had happened to her, but it was best they never knew the truth—that Faith was a thief, according to her employer, who lived in a house of ill repute.

Her sadness was momentary. She was stronger than that. She had to be if she were to crawl out of the mire and be something more. Something more than what others would paint her—a thief and a prostitute.

But she *had* never been a thief, and she never *would* be a prostitute.

Forcing her thoughts to the painting she headed towards the house, glancing briefly at the casement windows and wondering how Lady Vernon could claim to know so much about the way gentlemen's minds worked.

~

CRISPIN STARED OUT THROUGH THE CASEMENT WINDOW towards the small lake at the bottom of the field. A light mist rose above it, and wildflowers littered the soft green grass. The scene was enticing and even more so when a movement caught his eye.

His breath caught. Miss Montague was gathering flowers still wearing her nightclothes. At least, only a light peignoir covered her nightdress, a thought which made him unexpectedly aroused.

He quashed his feelings quickly. Inconvenient and impossible to act upon.

Yet that didn't mean he wouldn't enjoy her company in the spirit of accommodation they'd tacitly agreed upon.

In seven days, he would create a masterpiece, and he'd need her compliance. Nothing more than that. A pleasurable whiling away of the time could be anticipated. He knew already she was good company. Easy on the eye, as Lord Delmore had pointed out, but that didn't imply Crispin would be unable to rein in the rampant impulses of a young man who hadn't had a woman in his life for a very long time.

His future was in Germany, and while his artistic temperament might suggest a romantic and spontaneous nature, he intended to be exacting when it came to choosing the right woman to spend the rest of his life with. He'd need to spend a great deal of time with her to ensure their minds were of one accord.

He'd not act with reckless abandon and allow infatuation to have any bearing on his decision.

Indeed, as his father counselled, it was far better to consolidate his career. In another year, perhaps, he might be better placed to put the necessary search for a wife near the top of his agenda. Not that Miss Montague was a contender, as he'd made clear to both the young lady and to Lord Delmore.

So why did he have to keep reiterating it? He hesitated before he dragged his eyes away from the scene by the lake. She'd stopped as if a thought, compelling, but not pleasant judging by her stance, made her hesitate.

He quashed the desire to quiz her when she returned. It was unwise to invite confidences. The less they delved into anything of a personal nature the better.

But he must think like a painter, and a good painter had a sense of the essence of his subject matter.

No point in wondering how he would paint her. The delivery of the props in an hour or so would determine that. For a moment, he cast his mind over to the brief. An eccentric American was behind the competition. Rockefeller? Rosenstein?

Imagine painting a canvas that would hang upon one of the walls of their homes. The idea sent a thrill of excitement through him.

Just as the sight of Miss Montague turning her lovely face up to the sun, smiling for a moment, sent a spear of foreboding through him.

Her fate lay in his hands. He could craft a future for her that was more than being a wife to a no doubt appreciative, but almost assuredly impecunious, young clerk, or as an unpaid servant to aged parents or small children.

He was roused by the sounds of gasps and oohs and aahs downstairs. So, the delivery was early. Not that he minded being put out of his anticipation. His mind couldn't settle until he knew how he would stage the young woman.

He hurried into the drawing room where a canvas bag lay upon the table. Around it stood Miss Montague, Lady Vernon, and the parlourmaid; all three of whom looked expectantly at him as he entered the room.

So much for being the aloof master of this temporary household. But then, there had never been any secret that this moment was the beginning of everything.

"I suppose there's only one thing for me to do," he said with a resigned grin at the company before he began to undo the ties.

A piece of paper with neatly written instructions lay upon a set of paintbrushes he unwrapped from its canvas covering, and a bag of something whose contents he couldn't quite identify.

"Completely unnecessary. I have my own," he muttered, but Lady Vernon was holding up one of the sable brushes and saying, "Perhaps this mystery person is signifying their knowledge of what is considered good quality in the art world. Or is that not true, Mr Westaway?"

Crispin had to concede that the materials were of the finest quality and now that the entire set was laid out, his earlier scepticism had been replaced by a definite itching of the fingers to get started. As he bent to pick up a brush, he intercepted Miss Montague's smile. She looked as excited as he felt. Yes, as if she relished what lay ahead as much as he wished she would if it were to be good.

The painting. It was about the painting, of course, and she'd shown interest in art and culture, so they were on level ground in this instance.

"Roses?" He picked up a handful of crimson petals that must have been picked within the last twenty-four hours, then looked at Miss Montague. "You're more a wildflower girl, with your delicate colouring, I'd have said, but perhaps I'm mistaken and the richness of these deep-hued petals will bring out something I'd overlooked." He was considering her as the inanimate subject of his talent, not the vibrant flesh and blood creature who fed his inspiration, but Crispin needed some distance.

"And the title? What is the title of this painting?" Lady Vernon asked, picking up the paper with its instructions. *The Lady of the Lake?*" She looked from Faith to Mr Westaway. "I suppose you can interpret that any way you like, is that correct, Mr Westaway? Yet I am sure I've heard the title used before. However, you must use the props supplied, the instructions say. Water and red rose petals. It could be charming provided it doesn't resemble a scene of carnage."

"What do you mean?" Miss Montague frowned at her chaperone who gave a theatrical shiver, replying in a whisper, "Blood!"

Revulsion swept over Crispin, and he gripped the table edge to steady himself. These were not memories he could entertain if he were to do justice to the brief.

Miss Montague raised her brows before remarking, "I'm sure I've heard about a painting called *The Lady and the Lake.* Do you know it, Mr Westaway?"

The oil painting that featured a naked woman reclining on a rock had garnered a great deal of critical acclaim, and now Crispin found it was impossible not to look at Miss Montague and imagine what she looked like with no clothes on, reclining on a rock or, in this case, floating in a lake. He swallowed and stepped behind the table, saying, "Perhaps you're mistaking it for John Waterhouse's *The Lady of Shalott.*" Before she could contradict this with some incisive remark that she was sure she was *not* thinking about that painting, because Miss Montague's mind was as sharp as a needle, he found himself taking her by the wrist and pulling her into the light by the window saying, in a contemplative, artist's manner, "So many possibilities, but what would be best in this instance? A lake? I hadn't thought there might be logistical difficulties."

Lady Vernon's nose crinkled as she stared through the window at the body of water in the distance. "Not especially appropriate with the reeds and ducks and mud and approaching storm clouds. I hope you don't mean to drown poor Miss Montague for the sake of your art. Can she even swim?"

"I can't swim." Miss Montague shook her head. "But I can lie in a bath, and you could paint in a background afterwards."

Faith had been told by Lady Vernon that this is what she must suggest. She supposed Lady Vernon thought that having Faith wearing diaphanous wet clothing might somehow entice Mr Westaway more thoroughly than otherwise. An outside body of water would have done just as well, but it was true that the weather was deteriorating while a bath would be heated. Not that Lady Vernon would have been thinking of Faith's comfort.

Regardless of the motive, Faith was now experiencing her first pangs of self-doubt. Mr Westaway still didn't look at her as if he couldn't live without her. His scrutiny was decidedly painterly in an objective, distanced way. He had enough self-control that he'd buried his initial admiration beneath a veneer, possibly something much thicker than that even, of objectivity.

But he was a diplomat, after all. He needed to hide his emotions, so perhaps his real feelings were very different.

She continued to study him as he looked into her face, while she tried to read behind the mild interest in his expression. His interest seemed to be motivated by nothing more than where she should be posed and in what clothes.

"I daresay that would work," he said as the first raindrops hit the windows. He smiled. "No, this weather is hardly conducive to outdoors painting, after all."

"A bath," announced Lady Vernon. "A heated bath for we don't want Miss Montague to catch her death of cold." Faith could read very clearly the gleam in Lady Vernon's eye. No, her concern was far from Faith's comfort. She wanted to control the situation as best she could. She had something planned; Faith was sure of it. Especially when the old woman said, "I have an idea, if you'll permit me, Mr Westaway. May I be so bold as to prepare my young charge in what surely must be the only fashion that can be suggested by the props provided?"

What could Mr Westaway do? Faith smiled at the pained look that crossed his face. As she turned to follow in her chaperone's wake, she quirked her mouth in a rueful smile, whispering as she passed him, "See what I have to put up with every day, Mr Westaway! If you let her have her way today, you can paint me however you choose later."

When he winked at her, Faith felt a ridiculous jolt of pleasure. For a brief moment they were in collusion, and Lady Vernon was the common enemy.

Once inside the large bathroom, Lady Vernon closed the door and pointed to the clothing she'd laid out on the chair by the window. "Dress yourself in that while Kitty fetches the bathwater," she said, directing the young undermaid who had followed them in.

In the city, the modern plumbing that Lady Vernon decried was a luxury unknown in this part of the world so, a dozen pails later, Faith lay submerged in a warm bath, her white gown floating about her, a simple posy of white flowers in her hands.

"Close your eyes, Faith, while I call Mr Westaway. But first…we'll add the finishing touch."

CHAPTER 15

Crispin trod the steps with mixed feelings, though he had to admit he was more than intrigued by Miss Westaway's impish parting. She was not so pliable as she seemed. Previously, she'd been not as vacuous as she'd seemed. What would the next surprise be? The truth was, he knew he was going to enjoy the next few days more than he ought.

The next surprise, when he opened the bathroom door at Lady Vernon's command, was not something for which he was prepared.

With the pleasure and anticipation of his parting from Miss Montague still fresh in his mind, the last thing he expected to find was the manner in which she'd been…prepared.

Good God, but the grey drizzle outside the small bathroom window was a good deal more comforting and easy on the eye than the horror that met him in the bath.

A girl dressed in white; her reddish-gold hair spread about her, holding a posy of flowers. And the bathwater. Red.

Only, of course, these were red rose petals. He had to remember that.

He had to remember that he must *never* revisit this part of his past if he were to stay sane. Turning away to look through the window, he tried to regain control of his emotions.

"Striking, don't you think, Mr Westaway?" Lady Vernon was smiling at him. "You can paint in the reeds and the river afterwards. Or had you thought to create an entirely different effect?"

He took a seat, pretending consideration while he attempted to push away the nightmare.

But would it be catharsis to face his memories head on and, in painting them, exorcise them from his mind?

Then again, was there something deeper at play? Why red rose petals? Why a girl in a white dress floating in water?

He had to rid his mind of what could only be ridiculous, unfounded conspiracies. Each of the other two painters would be doing the same painting, and they'd not be reacting as he was. Only if he could ground himself in common sense and allow his professionalism to dominate would he turn something good out of something bad.

"You've done well, Lady Vernon," he said. "And since Miss Westaway is already in position, I shall have my paints brought in and begin while there is still light."

A great weariness had cast its pall over the horror and fear. He was a survivor. At least, his reputation had survived, if not his soul.

"It's a strange question, I know, Miss Montague, but are you comfortable?"

She opened her eyes. "Unconventional, to say the least, but this seems innocuous compared to the stories I've heard from other artist's models."

"Who?"

"I spoke to several at the unveiling."

Of course, she would have. She was a young lady who didn't make up things. She liked to have her facts straight. Well, if he were going to be closeted with her in close confines for the next seven days, it would help to have some diverting conversation. Lady Vernon promised little enough of that.

He set up his easel and mixed his paints in the poor light, augmented by a sconce of candles and a lamp. For now, he was glad Lady Vernon stood stiffly by, or rather, had seated herself on a wooden chair at right angles to him. She'd better stay the entire time too, he thought, if he were not to be distracted.

Distracted? He had his work to keep him focused.

Time passed in a blur but he was jolted into the present by the sound of a loud clapping, and looked up to see Lady Vernon in the act of rising, her command accompanied by, "Mr Westaway, my charge might be in no danger of drowning in a bath, but she certainly is in danger of getting pneumonia."

"My apologies! Please, you must get dry." Without thinking, he put out his hand to help Miss Montague to rise, and she stood up, dripping before him, her gown clinging to her curves, entirely transparent though she appeared not to realise this as she asked with just a trace of coyness, "Wasn't I as still as the dead, Mr Westaway? That was what you wanted, wasn't it?"

Crispin wasn't sure what he wanted. He didn't want to paint her dead, and he certainly didn't want her standing in front of him now leaving so little to the imagination. Because the bath was elevated a foot or so off the ground, he found himself almost eye level with her breasts. And, of course, the effect of the cold was to highlight her nipples through the thin fabric.

Crispin didn't know where to look. Lady Vernon appeared to be occupied with arranging her bustle into the correct folds as she stood while Miss Montague was smiling happily at Crispin, taking the hand he offered her and leaning heavily on him to avoid slipping as she stepped over the side.

"You were perfect, Miss Montague," he managed, desperately conscious of the brief contact when one soft breast was slightly indented by his hand in the final movement.

Still, she did not seem to notice, chattering happily, though with chattering teeth, as the maid draped her in a towel and began to squeeze out the water from her skirts over the bath.

"The perfect drowned damsel, and now I no doubt resemble a water rat." She took a hank of her glorious hair and twisted it over her shoulder.

"You must sit in front of the fire and get yourself thoroughly dry." Lady Vernon managed to make a no doubt well-intentioned suggestion sound like a threat.

"I'll be down in a minute," said the young girl heading towards the door before she was halted by her chaperone's voice, "You'll dry your hair in your bedchamber and not disturb Mr Westaway with your foolish talk when now is the time for him to relax after his hard work."

Crispin hadn't realised he'd even said the words that encouraged them to join him in his drawing room before Lady Vernon was accepting and Miss Montague was clapping her hands and saying, "I've been dying to ask Mr Westaway his thoughts on Alsace-Lorraine. You will indulge me, won't you, Mr Westaway?"

What could he do except nod, even though Crispin knew that it was dangerous to exchange political views with anyone, and especially not a wide-eyed ingénue whom he'd now seen, firsthand, combined the most desirable curves with a mind like a whip and a face like an angel.

~

THE CRACKLING FIRE PROVIDED VERY WELCOME AND MUCH-needed warmth, for the cold had seeped through Faith's bones. Lady Vernon's command had come in the nick of time, and now, to Faith's delight, Lady Vernon was rubbing her eyes and declaring she could not remain a moment longer in the heated drawing room without falling fast asleep.

"I should stay, of course, Faith, but your hair is not yet dry. Promise me you'll be up in the next five minutes."

Faith flashed a look at Mr Westaway and saw he looked uncertain in the wake of Lady Vernon's departure. Quickly, she said as the door closed behind the old lady, "I wonder if you wouldn't be so kind as to take over the brushing from Lady Vernon, otherwise my hair will be the most unmanageable tangle." She handed him the brush to detain him when she was certain he was about to excuse himself. "I'm sure you must be used to such requests from female cousins."

Mr Westaway shook his head but had no choice but to take the brush thrust into his hand. Obediently, he followed her to the chair vacated by Lady Vernon while Faith dropped down upon the footstool. "Lady Vernon doesn't like me," she confided on a sigh. "I fear that I am a sore trial to bear, and that she enjoyed wielding the brush like a prison warder. I trust you'll be gentler with me, Mr Westaway."

Faith had to force herself not to smile when she felt, rather than saw, the effect her words had on him. So, she *did* wield some power, after all. She was just congratulating herself on making if only marginal success when, without pausing in his steady, thorough, yet decidedly gentle brushing, he said in a low, deliberate tone, "Lady Vernon should be more vigilant in keeping watch over you. It would not do for word to get out that she'd been lax."

And, of course, that could mean only one thing—that he was keeping his distance from Faith and any possibility of entanglement as much as possible.

She twisted her head. "We've already discussed this, Mr Westaway. Of course you don't want to find yourself compromised with someone like me; I completely understand. And even if, despite the greatest care taken, it was suggested I was compromised, and it won't happen, I assure you, I would act with honour; you must know that."

"Those words sound so wrong coming from your pretty mouth." His tone was downcast. "Indeed, you do speak plainly." He spoke so softly she could barely hear.

"It was the only way in my household," Faith told him, trying to sound more cheerful. As if this wasn't the weighty conversation it was. "With so many of us, it was difficult to get our way at the best of times. So, I've grown accustomed to being grateful for whatever I can have."

"And what is it you want, Faith?"

She was surprised he asked the question but answered it with an admirable show of equanimity, adopting a more serious tone but, she hoped, with enough levity not to frighten him. "I want to be respectably married, have a husband who appreciates me and is kind to me, and I want children. I want what every woman wants. Surely you know it's the desire of each and every debutante in London with whom I'm competing."

He'd taken on the role of hair brusher with care and gentleness but he laughed, tugging a hank of hair which made her wince. Immediately he was full of apology, but Faith waved her hand in the air before resting it seemingly arbitrarily on...his hand.

She kept it there, saying, "I've borne a great deal worse pain than this. Please continue with the brushing, Mr Westaway. It's not often I get to enjoy such a gentle touch. Perhaps that's why I'm so competitive. Not very attractive in a woman which is why I try to keep quiet in company. Gentlemen much prefer a young woman to have no opinions."

She turned at the silence and the fact he'd stopped brushing and faced him. He looked nonplussed.

"I'm sorry if I've disappointed you with my revelations regarding my true character, Mr Westaway. I'm sure you'd have far preferred to uphold an image of me as mild-natured and demure. That's how Lady Vernon told me to behave when I first came to London. But as I've got to know you more, I can't hide my true nature. I'm so far from the perfect, demure debutante Lady Vernon thought she was going to be chaperoning about London."

"But your beauty makes up for that." He shook his head as if he'd not believed he'd said it. "I'm very sorry I said that. The sentiment was unseemly on both counts."

Faith swallowed. She was feeling her way in the dark, so to speak. Yes, part of her tutoring was to exchange banter with a range of gentlemen, and she'd enjoyed it. But one false step and she could lose everything for which she'd worked so hard.

She pushed to the back of her mind any thought that she might actually be wanting this for reasons to do with her own heart rather than as a means to an end. Faith had never had the luxury to think of anything other than survival. And her survival depended upon twisting this man around her little finger. Making him fall in love with her.

The way he was looking at her bolstered her confidence that she could do this.

"You think you shouldn't say I'm beautiful because it'll

turn my head?" she asked softly. "Or you think that an independent mind should be irrelevant in the face of beauty." Faith shifted a little on her footstool but held herself back from contact. His lithe, strong body was within easy touching. She could have put her hand on his knee or risen slowly and cupped his face. How would he have reacted? Would he have sunk into a kiss...only to berate himself afterwards? Yes, she sensed a steeliness in him that would enable him to put reason above his emotions.

But what if she couched it as a business proposition? A ladylike proposition?

She cleared her throat and lowered her eyes, keeping herself firmly glued to the footstool.

"Mr Westaway..."

She wasn't sure if her approach was damning any chances she had, but she'd decided the logical path was best.

"Yes, Miss Montague." It looked like he'd managed, with an effort, to regain his composure, and that he was grateful to her for reining him back in, for there was a warmth in his expression that was far more friendly than incendiary.

"You know how I hope this painting is going to help win me suitors? I mean, I've made no secret of that, and it's ridiculous for any debutante to pretend otherwise."

"Yes, we both have high hopes for this painting. Though I don't know what I shall say if I do win and it comes to my father's ears."

"You'll be in Germany doing just as he wishes. And you'll have the accolades you desire. It's the perfect outcome." She sighed deeply. "As for me, I could be married in six weeks and, right at this very moment, not even know my husband —the man I'll spend the rest of my life with. Isn't that strange to think?"

"Very strange." He looked decidedly uncomfortable.

"Mr Westaway, I want you to kiss me. You see, I've never

been kissed before, and I'm very curious and would like to have just a little practise for when I meet the man I will marry." She smiled at him. "A single kiss is all right, isn't it? I mean, it doesn't mean my reputation or yours is besmirched. I've read plenty of romances where it's quite normal for a man and a woman to kiss and nothing terribly awful happens afterwards."

She sat with her hands clasped in her lap and looked at him enquiringly.

He looked back at her and shook his head. "I'm sorry, Miss Montague. That's not how a kiss is conducted. And regardless of how it is or isn't conducted, I couldn't possibly kiss you."

She nodded, as if conceding a practical matter. "I understand. In the novels I've read there has to be a strong feeling happening here." She touched her heart. "I just thought that it would be interesting to experiment so I could see how my heart felt when you kissed me, which of course you're not going to do now. I thought it would be nice to have some level of comparison for when I'm kissed by a real suitor with whom I'd consider spending the rest of my life." She rolled her shoulders and turned away, offering him the back of her head, and within a few seconds was relieved to feel the steady tug of the hairbrush over her hair. "I hope I didn't embarrass you, Mr Westaway."

"Not at all. It's good to be able to speak frankly to one another. I like a young woman who doesn't resort to artifice and veiled lies to get what she wants."

A chill of foreboding rattled inside her and Mr Westaway asked with genuine concern, "Are you cold?"

"No, but I should go to bed soon, I think." She stretched her arms, yawning as she stood up. "Thank you for today." She smiled at him as he rose. "I can't tell you how much more enjoyable it is to be here and part of your artistic world; also talking to you about interesting topics than the usual deadly dull kind of day I generally endure."

"Miss Montague—"

She looked over her shoulder as she made for the door.

His expression was conflicted, his body tense as he rose and took a half step towards her. "Just one kiss. A quick one. So, you know what it feels like." He spoke rapidly. "And nothing other than that."

"All right," she said slowly. "Just tell me what to do."

He cleared his throat. "You just kiss me. That's all."

"And then it's done." She sighed, satisfied. Or at least sounding satisfied with the way it was presented as she returned to stand in front of him, twining her arms about his neck.

It was not the first time Faith had kissed a man. Her education had required this as a minimal point of contact and, thank God, she'd never found herself in the position of having to do more, as did all the other girls at Madame Chambon's. In fact, it was only when she had kissed men for whom she felt absolutely nothing did she realise how impossible it would be to have to give them her body too.

So, she twined her arms about his neck, tipped her head, and waited to feel nothing but the physical sensation of pressure applied upon her lips. A physical sensation with which she was reasonably familiar.

CRISPIN STOOD AND PREPARED HIMSELF. HE WAS DOING HER A favour. Lord, he was doing them both a favour by getting it over and done with, clearing the air, so to speak. It was reasonable that a curious mind and plain speaking would deem this no more than it would be. And Crispin had only gone along with the idea because he was confident she knew their respective positions. He liked to think he'd forged a friendship with the young woman. Friendship between the sexes was entirely possible, he already knew that. He had women friends who enjoyed probing him on matters political, and he gained great pleasure from their company.

Just as he did from Miss Montague's. Certainly, she was younger and prettier than his other friends but, by presenting herself as just as intelligent, and acute with respect to his need for no form of entanglement, he felt safe.

Yes, safe, was his last thought as he lowered his head and put his arms gently about her to seal the kiss. A chaste, brief kiss with a sweet but definite ending would be a fine way to show her his true feelings. He could imbue it with respect, the merest sensory illusion that there could be more, and as he withdrew with just the right expression, he'd leave her under no illusions that he was in any way affected by their connection.

Yet, as she moved closer, standing on tiptoe to twine her arms about his neck, he was taken aback by the rush of sensation that speared his body. Her mouth was still several inches away; her eyes were closed, and there was a smile of innocent expectation that was heartbreakingly endearing.

He felt trapped. It would be wrong to leave her with the sensation that a kiss couldn't be more. She was embarking on a big journey for an innocent debutante. She had no idea what to expect. Surely, he owed it to her to show her just what a real kiss could be like?

It was his last moment of rational thought before another rush of sensation speared his groin, pounded in his head, and turned his vision into a multifaceted plethora of pumping, pulsing need that sent him reeling as her mouth fused with his and her arms about him tightened.

His world seemed suddenly a different place. He'd not expected to be so affected. He'd not expected to feel such connection. He'd not expected to feel anything beyond the casual enjoyment he'd experienced with so many past kisses.

Yet he was conscious of every nuanced change as this one progressed from what was supposed to be fleeting—the softness of her lips pressed against his, tentative, then growing bolder, sending tendrils of fire right through his body. Her breasts pushing against his chest as she leaned into him. Enjoying herself. Throwing herself into this as if it were the greatest enjoyment to be savoured, losing herself just as he was losing himself.

He'd thought himself in love in the past. There had been moments of grand passion. Or so he'd thought. And yet…he couldn't remember them. His mind was cast into the void, for only the present existed. Only the here and now as he was swept into a maelstrom of intense, physically satisfying, and yet totally unsatisfied, desire.

And it was as this desire roared into the stratosphere, nearly out of control, that a single cognisant kernel of self-preservation brought him rapidly back to earth. His hand, unconsciously, had slid downward to cup her breast, and she seemed to be pressing against him, searching for satisfaction beyond what was being offered.

He registered the need to extricate it, yet it was squeezed fast, against the thin fabric between his chest and her heaving bosom. But as he removed it and his hand touched her heated skin, it took every ounce of willpower not to insinuate it beneath her bodice. With her encouragement.

Dear lord, she was losing control just as he was, and unless he brought this to an end, they'd both be engulfed by the fiery flames of hell.

Unless he took charge, Miss Montague was going to keep kissing him, and he *wanted* her to want it. Wanted her to continue.

And that could prove fatal.

Panting, breathless, he put his hands on her shoulders and stepped backwards. Our of danger.

With enormous effort he tried to maintain his composure, tried to be the bigger man, bigger than he was, by pretending it hadn't affected him as much as it had. Running one hand through his hair, he blinked and offered her what he hoped wasn't a totally sappish smile as he murmured, "My apologies, Miss Montague, if that wasn't what you were expecting." What else could he have said? The kiss certainly hadn't been what *he'd* been expecting. He could barely stand. His body was straining, still, to take this further, but she was as out of bounds as she'd ever be.

Miss Montague, he noticed, looked a little dazed. She wandered to the fireplace and put a supporting hand upon the mantelpiece. He'd thought she might look at him, dewy-eyed with affection, but she looked troubled as she raked her fingers through her own damp hair and said, "Oh, please don't apologise for you were very kind to indulge me. I'm sure it was…so much more than I was expecting, Mr Westaway."

~

FAITH MANAGED TO MAKE HER WAY BACK TO HER bedchamber. As she lowered herself onto her bed, she wasn't sure how she'd got there, her mind was in such disarray. That kiss. No, it wasn't at all what she'd been expecting. The consequences were nothing like she'd intended. The kiss had been supposed to shore up her power, but with her knees still trembling, she felt entirely powerless.

A knock on the door was followed by the beady-eyed scrutiny of Lady Vernon, who lowered herself into a chair by the window and said, "I hope you used the time I allowed you wisely, my girl. He likes you, admires you, but you'll get nowhere with just that. Did you get him to kiss you?"

Faith objected to the question with an inner ball of such impotent fury she thought she might explode under the need to keep her response muted.

"That's between Mr Westaway and myself." She rose from the bed and went to sit at her dressing table where she began to plait her hair. "I am aware of what I must do. Please do me the courtesy of allowing me the freedom to do it at my own pace and using my own intuition."

Lady Vernon moved to stand behind her and began to undo the buttons on the back of her dress. "Please do me the courtesy of remembering your manners, and your gratitude. It was thanks to me you were given any opportunity to achieve anything at all, young lady."

"Yes, of course. But please let me go about this my own way. I assure you that you will get your money. That is, after all, what is important to you." She hoped the reflection of her gimlet eye in the looking glass was as piercing as the older woman's.

"I think you're in love with him." Lady Vernon's smile looked more like a grimace of satisfaction. "Don't think you'll marry him." Her eyes narrowed, and in the gloom, she looked like a witch or a goblin. "You're cleverer than to daydream that, Faith. He won't marry you." After a pause, she added, "Everyone in Mr Westaway's orbit, and beyond, will ensure that he won't."

Faith's legs were still shaking after Lady Vernon had left and Faith was preparing for bed.

Of course, there were. Faith had a mission to fulfil and too many people stood to gain something as a result of Faith's success—herself included.

Though her success might just come at a cost she'd not factored into the equation.

She stepped out of her skirt and peeled off her cuirass-bodice. Why was she so affected by Lady Vernon's unkind truth? It defied logic. Mr Westaway was a man who could do as he pleased and that alone put him out of her orbit. Faith was inured, so she thought, to entitled, self-absorbed gentlemen who took what they wanted and bargained for the rest.

The trouble was, Mr Westaway wasn't like that. If he were, her job would be so much easier.

She touched her lips. They still tingled from the memory of Mr Westaway's mouth, tender upon hers at first, before his hunger became so pronounced for that brief moment before he broke away. There really shouldn't have been time to have decided anything much about the quality of it. And yet, it had lasted long enough for her to realise that she was changed. Affected.

And that he had been, too.

But he was a man. Rich, entitled. If he were affected, he'd have forgotten it by morning.

She sat on the bed and rested her head in her hands, the silence of the room seeming to break into her thoughts.

Who was she trying to fool? That was only if he were the kind of gentleman who frequented Madame Chambon's. The kind who thought nothing of paying for their transitory pleasures.

Mr Westaway was not like that.

And Faith had been trained to entrap men like him. Good, decent men who, when embarking upon something like tonight's kiss, thought they were attracted to a good, decent woman.

She was the honey trap. His disappointed hopes and dreams would be all the more bitter for having realised the extent of his being duped.

Except that Faith had no intention of it going so far, and

nor did Madame Chambon. He would not know what Faith was because Faith came from Madame's establishment and Madame Chambon's was hallowed ground. Whatever devil's agreement made between Madame Chambon, Lady Vernon, and Mrs Gedge would protect the reputation of the highly lucrative Soho purveyor of beautiful and expensive women. Gentlemen of discernment and fat pocketbooks must always know they would be safe when selecting a girl from London's most highly regarded brothel.

Faith crawled into bed.

No, not a hint of scandal would link Faith with Madame Chambon's though Faith had no doubt Lady Vernon was as ruthless as her cohorts. She had no love of Faith, but as long as Faith delivered what was promised, Faith would be free to make her own way in the world.

Pulling the covers over her head, she thought of the days ahead—the escalation of searing passion, then a promise extracted from Mr Westaway so that the sting of rejection, timed just right, might be all the bitter.

It seemed too simple but, of course, there must be more at play than that for Mrs Gedge to have spent three years grooming Faith to be the means of breaking this young man's heart.

Perhaps there'd been a failed love affair between herself and Lord Maxwell, Mr Westaway's father?

Or was Mrs Gedge avenging the death of her daughter. Had the girl died of a broken heart after he'd spurned her?

Was money, not love, involved?

There was no point in quizzing Lady Vernon or even digging for the truth in her most artful and subtle manner. Lady Vernon conversed with Faith only upon her conduct.

And that conduct was required to become as scandalous as it was possible for a young, supposedly innocent virgin to be.

The night pressed in on her, her mind churning with questions but knowing only one thing— that tomorrow or the next, she must do whatever possible to compromise Mr Westaway in order to extract an offer of marriage, or at least an ardent declaration of love.

And, for the first time, the knowledge that this might mean sacrificing her virginity didn't trouble her in the least.

The fact that it might involve breaking hearts along the way, did.

CHAPTER 16

A beautiful, sunny day meant that the washroom wasn't the only alternative for creating a setting whereby Faith must recline amongst the water lilies.

At breakfast, when she went down and found Lady Vernon and Mr Westaway in the parlour, Faith was immediately besieged by conflicting suggestions. Lady Vernon thought the bath was the better alternative; Mr Westaway was keen on the lake.

Only the arrival of Lord Delmore stirred enough conviction one way or another.

"To the lake," he announced, and Faith wasn't unhappy about it. The surprisingly balmy feel in the air combined with her hopefulness was a good combination, so that she was unusually unconstrained and forthcoming as Lord Delmore quizzed her on her time in London during the walk through the gardens and along the lakeside, before they arrived at a small copse which Mr Westaway had spied out as a likely location.

The older gentleman seemed fascinated by Faith's impressions on the capital. He asked her about her family and her father, and she answered truthfully, for even though they were lost to her, she could imbue the reality of a poverty-stricken cottager with the high hopes of an equally poverty-stricken, though fictional, family intent on bettering their most promising progeny.

Surprisingly, Faith found she suffered no pangs of guilt for lying, or even sadness for letting her family believe her dead. There simply had been too many of them and her father too brutal and economical with words for her to have understood him. She genuinely had no desire to ever see him again. The others, too, were so different in the way they thought of life or conducted themselves that she'd have been happy to have called herself an only child.

Her future was here. In her hands. In Mr Westaway's hands. Meanwhile, Lord Delmore served a useful purpose in acting as a conduit for the questioning she'd have liked to have come from Mr Westaway, who appeared too absorbed in his painting to notice her or anyone else.

For the first half an hour, Mr Westaway occupied himself with setting up his easel, then sketching the backdrop so that Faith could enjoy being dry as she sat in one of the wicker chairs her host had a servant arrange for her, Lady Vernon, and Lord Delmore.

The last thing Faith felt like doing was going near water again but knew what was required. So, when Lord Delmore asked, "And does the idea of floating among the trailing water lilies horrify you, Miss Montague?" she just lifted one shoulder slightly and said, "This is a very pleasant country sojourn and being somewhat impecunious, which I've made no secret about, I shall pay my dues uncomplainingly when the time comes."

He seemed to like her answer enormously for he laughingly responded, "Not so demure, if you don't mind my saying so, Miss Montague. Most young ladies would not advertise such facts."

"I would rather no potential suitor was under any illusions, Lord Delmore." Faith decided she liked the candour in his twinkling blue eyes. He seemed far easier than the buttoned-up personages she was more likely to meet in London. And when he added, "I'll have to introduce you to my daughter-in-law. She could take a leaf out of your book when it comes to being candid and not putting herself above others," she decided he was quite fatherly in the kind of endearing way she liked to imagine her own father might have been had he not been cursed with ten children, no money, and a drinking problem. All of which, she supposed, meant that there could never be two men more different than Lord Delmore and her own father.

"It's time, I'm afraid." Mr Westaway cleared his throat, and they all turned. He'd not said a word in a good twenty minutes.

Faith was sure he'd even blushed when he'd nodded a greeting, earlier, before quite studiously avoiding any further direct contact.

Was he regretting last night? She certainly wasn't. An unbidden memory of the searing passion in that one short kiss sent the blood rushing to her cheeks. She was surprised that she'd blushed but also rather pleased that she'd managed it so artlessly. It served her purpose rather well.

Faith took a deep, audible breath, rose from her chair and glanced about at the company as she picked up her skirts and turned towards the water. Then she stopped and sat down again. "My shoes. I can't go in wearing these, naturally." She pressed her lips together and sent a rather imploring glance at Lady Vernon, who grunted as she moved forward in her chair before muttering, "I can't take them off for you, my girl. Not with my arthritis. Gentlemen, would it be so shocking if one of you were to do the honours." She put her nose in the air as if pretending great delicacy when Faith knew any pretence at anything remotely refined or delicate was a complete sham. "I'm sure you know that a lady is somewhat restricted when it comes to bending at the waist."

They'd know it, of course. Lord Delmore was a widower, and Mr Westaway must have had some experience with women, surely, to know that they always put on their footwear before donning their corset. And Faith was wearing a corset today, as directed by Lady Vernon for just this reason.

The two men exchanged long looks. Faith could tell they both wanted to offer but were reluctant to be the first. Finally, Lord Delmore conceded to the younger man, saying, "I'm not as agile as I once was, either, Crispin. Miss Montague, apologies for embarrassing you like this."

"I shall be more embarrassed when you see how poorly I manage in water. I presume you want me to float, but the truth is, I've never tried. I only know that if it can be learned, I'm sure I'll learn quickly. I don't want to delay you, Mr Westaway, when time is of the essence."

Faith stretched out her leg and pointed her foot while Mr Westaway went down on bended knee on the grass and rested it in the palm of his hand. She liked his touch. He seemed gentle and respectful, unlike many of the gentlemen who came to Madame Chambon's fuelled by rampant sexual desire.

But how surprising that she was enjoying her mission.

When Mr Westaway had removed her shoes, he took her hands and helped her to rise.

"Will you be all right getting to the water?"

"If I may lean upon your shoulder as I negotiate the mud. I'm not sure how deep it might be." She made the most of the contact, and when they were at the water's edge with the others a few yards behind them, he said, "I took unconscionable liberties, Miss Montague."

"And I do not hold you to account for any of them." She giggled happily. Silly, but it was no act. "It was too marvellously unexpected, Mr Westaway. And so comforting to know that I shall be able to enjoy these mysteries if I'm ever granted the opportunity." She patted his shoulder. "Don't trouble yourself anymore over it. It's in the past. Now I just have to lie amongst the water lilies and stare vacantly at the sky. I can do that. I can do whatever is required. Oooh!" She gave a squeal as the water reached mid-calf and then, because she knew when the dramatic would serve her well, plunged headlong into the depths with an even greater cry.

"I did it!" she squealed, emerging a second later. At home, the boys had sometimes bathed in the river, but Faith had never been tempted by the discoloured water from the tannery upstream. Her mother had always come down hard upon the girls for trying to emulate the boys who were so carefree in their nakedness.

Faith couldn't imagine what her mother would think of her daughter, now. But as Faith had never had the slightest respect for her mother, and truly felt her life was better for being free of her sanctimonious piety and propensity to lash out, like Faith's father, the reflection did not dampen this morning's proceedings.

All of which were progressing swimmingly if the admiration and mutual enjoyment on both Lord Delmore and Mr Westaway's faces were anything to go by.

"Just be careful amongst the reeds," Lord Delmore cautioned, "and keep well within your depth. This is a smart new set of clothes I'm wearing."

"You'd actually consider getting them wet and muddy on my account?" She sent him an impish smile. "I think that's the most gallant thing a gentleman has ever said to me." She could afford to feel lighthearted, for this morning was all about playacting, setting up the gentlemen to think of her as she wanted them to, not as she was.

"I think you'd inspire such chivalry from anyone who met you, Miss Montague."

Faith caught the surprised look Lord Delmore's words received from Mr Westaway and was emboldened. "What about you, Mr Westaway? I've heard that the focus of the true artist would not be torn away by anything."

"Except losing the very thing that keeps him focused." He grinned as he looked up from the canvas. "I suppose I'd have no choice but to rescue you if I wanted to finish my painting."

"Well, I prefer Lord Delmore's response, even though it's a relief to know I'd be saved in both instances. Am I floating artistically enough?"

Faith had adjusted to the water temperature and made sure her hair fanned out about her and the folds of her dress looked suitably artistic.

"It's perfect." Mr Westaway nodded.

"Will she have to go into the lake every day, Mr Westaway?" Lady Vernon asked. "There are logistical concerns with seeing her dress is dry when she puts it on each day only to then have to float in it for as long as it pleases you."

"Today will suffice, Lady Vernon." Mr Westaway barely looked at the old woman, but he smiled at Faith. "I promise not to sacrifice you, Miss Montague, to my artistic pursuits. Today I only need to sketch in the background and get a general composition."

Faith, who'd been floating for as long as she could manage, stood up. The water reached mid-thigh, and as she glanced down, she could see the outline of her corset beneath the fabric of her gown. She decided to remain standing for a while and pretend to be unaware.

"Perhaps she'll need a new dress," Lady Vernon went on. "Faith, get back in the water this instant!"

"Only if Mr Westaway says I must," Faith countered. "He's the artist."

She saw the way his eyes lingered on her just a moment too long before he agreed with Lady Vernon, the pause and the obvious reluctance in his tone music to her ears.

Faith lay back down in the water, but after another few minutes, her task really was becoming difficult. The chill was starting to seep into her bones.

When she could take it no more, she rose suddenly, but her feet stuck fast in the mud and she stumbled and fell to her knees. Her hands went out in front of her, and now her knees were sinking in sludge while the water was too high for her head to remain above. Her corset cut into her, and she couldn't move properly. Panic was swift. She truly was trapped. With her clothing too constricting, she could neither rise to her feet, yet nor was she agile enough to roll onto her back so that she was again floating with her face to the sky.

By the time a pair of hands gripped her elbows and hauled her to her feet, she was choking on the water she'd taken in, shaking with nerves and on the edge of tears.

"I have you, Miss Montague. A nasty fright, that's all." Lord Delmore led her to his chair, his tone fatherly, his concern making her want to cry even more. There'd been precious few people in her world that had ever spoken to her like that. "There, there, Miss Montague," he soothed, patting her shoulder. "Open your eyes, here's my handkerchief."

Mr Westaway had barely registered until it was all over, it seemed, for he was blinking at her over the top of the easel, and she seethed inside at the injustice of losing such an opportunity to play to his concern.

"I won't cry," she said between gritted teeth, and it was as if she were six years old again and her father was berating her for letting the cow run away, bringing the willow switch across her shoulders in a series of violent outbursts. Little matter that *he* had left the gate unlatched plenty of times and that the cow had always either returned home for milking or been brought back by one of the neighbours. "I won't cry. I won't cry."

She'd said those words so often as a child and she never did cry. Nor did she cry, now, but clearly the combination of hunched shoulders, stiff jaw, and defiant mantra was not the usual reaction of damsels in distress.

"You're very brave." Mr Westaway was on one side and Lord Delmore, standing on her other, was wrapping a towel about her shoulders. Lady Vernon was blinking dispassionately at her, not having bothered to rise from her chair, but she didn't count. Faith could bask in the attention from two handsome men and believe for a few minutes they genuinely did care she'd been frightened.

She relaxed her shoulders and smiled suddenly. "I won't do that again." Mr Westaway's brow was creased as if he didn't know what to say, so she saved him the trouble. "I'm sorry I spoiled things, Mr Westaway. I hope I was there long enough for you to get the sketch you needed at least. But I'm ready to go back again, if you'd like."

"Of course not!" Lord Delmore was quite vocal in defence of Faith having a reprieve. "Ten minutes is more than enough time for a gently nurtured young lady to float in a swamp. I wouldn't hear of it, and I'm sure Mr Westaway wouldn't, either."

"GAD, BUT SHE'S A RARE JEWEL," LORD DELMORE DECLARED AS he accepted the brandy Crispin handed him before taking a seat opposite him in the library. The long balmy evenings of sitting outside were gone since the summer days had given way to a dreary grey, with a decided chill in the air. "I wonder what her plans are when this is all over. Don't suppose she has her eye on you, do you think?"

"It's something that has already been aired between us," Crispin said, stretching his long legs towards the fire. She's very aware of my situation as I am of hers."

"And that is? Yes, yes, I know you told me she's penniless and looking to make a marriage." Lord Delmore seemed surprisingly agitated, which was uncharacteristic.

Crispin put down his empty glass and stared at the long-time friend of his aunt and uncle. A man of another generation. One he admired, certainly, but whose life and future seemed settled and predictable. "Are you suggesting you might make her an offer, Lord Delmore?"

Crispin had heard his uncle's old neighbour voice his disinclination to change his widowed status on many occasions.

So when Lord Delmore responded, "If you're not going to, I just might follow her to London and see how matters progress," Crispin couldn't have been more astonished. He was also astonished at the lurch of dismay that lodged in his chest cavity and hardened into a feeling he was quite loath to identify. For he really had been on his guard not to let the beautiful and engaging Miss Faith Montague get under his defences.

Perhaps Crispin's expression betrayed him for immediately Lord Delmore said, "Naturally, you have the superior suit, Crispin. You and Miss Montague make a good match, to my mind, and if I were standing here as your father, I'd be encouraging you to consider the merits of aligning yourself with a young woman with a lively intelligence and sharp wit, not to mention a good solid backbone. They're few and far between in my experience. Lord, don't I know it having been married more than thirty years and rearing a daughter frighteningly similar to my wife, God rest her soul."

"You think I should make her an offer?" Crispin was incredulous.

"You won't, of course." Lord Delmore stared at the hearthrug, his expression wistful. "She'd make you a good wife, but if you loved her like she deserves, then you'd disregard your father's strictures entirely. But I know you, Crispin. Ever the dutiful son and you couldn't be happy if you'd displeased your pater, as I see it." He hesitated, raised his head and said very seriously, "Give it another few days, my boy, and if you haven't fallen head over heels, then I hope you'll agree that all's fair in love and all that. In which case, if Miss Montague is indeed prepared to marry without love on her side, then I'm sure I could make a good case for her considering me a good prospect."

Faith? Lady Delmore? Living as neighbour to Crispin's aunt and uncle? He tried not to grimace. To keep a cool head. What Lord Delmore said about Crispin's reverence for his father's word made him sound more like a kowtowing schoolboy than a young man of integrity who was of one mind when his pater spoke only common sense regarding Crispin's need to prioritise his career over his marital concerns.

"I'm sure she'd consider you very favourably, Lord Delmore," he said carefully, hating the way the words sounded yet knowing he could never make the young lady a similar offer. And wasn't it just as well he'd kept his distance and not allowed free rein to the feelings inside him that might have escalated beyond his control?

"You think so?" Now it was Lord Delmore who sounded like the schoolboy.

Crispin nodded and smiled weakly.

~

"Not so clever, Faith." Lady Vernon sucked on her gums as she took a turn about the gravel path that surrounded the house. Her head was lowered and her sharp nose, in silhouette, looked like a miniature scythe. Faith knew Lady Vernon would not hesitate to stab her in the back if it profited the old woman. In truth, her own desperation was rising for Lady Vernon was right. Yet again, Faith had failed to strike the right note.

Yesterday's episode by the lake had elicited Lord Delmore's chivalry, but left Mr Westaway unmoved. He'd barely registered what had occurred though he'd been all solicitude in the drawing room, later. However, he'd deferred all evening to Lord Delmore, who'd paid Faith all manner of compliments and engaged her in light conversation. His attention had been enough to convince both Faith and Lady Vernon that the older man was interested.

"And don't think you can set yourself up with a peer and not have to account to the rest of us," Lady Vernon now muttered, echoing Faith's innermost thoughts. For what if Lord Delmore did surprisingly pursue her and offer her the respectability that would secure her future, and ensure she didn't ever land up in a gutter selling herself for a few pennies? She knew of enough girls who shared that fate, and she'd always considered she was clever enough for it not to happen to her.

No, Faith had believed she could secure her heart in a completely ironclad box so that the decisions she made to safeguard her future were entirely quarantined from any fanciful notions of romance. Love was not going to make a fool out of her.

So why was her disappointment that Mr Westaway seemed happy enough to let Lord Delmore pay court to her so acute? She was piqued from a distinctly personal point of view that had nothing to do with the greatest conundrum that must be faced—unless she carried out Mrs Gedge's orders she'd be out on her ear. Lady Vernon would see to that at the very least.

"I'm not going to encourage Lord Delmore, if that's what you're concerned about," she muttered, head bent against the brisk breeze, feeling on the back of her neck a spattering of raindrops from the branches of a monkey puzzle tree they passed under during their walk.

"Because you're in love with Mr Westaway?" the older woman asked. "It's been fascinating to watch, and I can't make up my mind whether you actually are a better actress than I'd given you credit for, or whether you've allowed yourself to be moonstruck by impossibilities."

"What does it matter?" Faith raised her head. "You'll get your cut, Lady Vernon."

"I will." There was a distinct smugness to her satisfaction, which made Faith wonder if Lady Vernon in fact had more belief in Faith's eventual success than Faith had. After a pause, the old woman said, "Tomorrow is the day you'll win him. I know what needs doing."

"Do you, Lady Vernon?"

She nodded.

Faith wasn't sure what to think. Lady Vernon had proved in the past that she could provide the impetus to get Mr Westaway to act in a more tender manner towards Faith. Even if he did withdraw immediately afterwards.

Lady Vernon had stopped and regarded Faith carefully.

"For such a well-tutored professional, you really don't know what to do when you're in love, do you?"

"I'm not in love."

"No?" Lady Vernon's look was ugly in its assessment. She shrugged. "Well, that's neither here nor there, is it, when you won't be able to claim him. But tomorrow he will realise he loves you and he has to have you. After that, there's no going back. Not for him, anyway. As for you, well, my girl, you have no choice but to do what you were engaged to do."

Faith turned towards the house and caught a glimpse of a face looking down at her from through the diamond-paned windows on the second story. Mr Westaway's bedchamber? Was that where she'd find herself tomorrow night?

She wanted to be there.

And because she wanted to be there, so much...with him...she realised that perhaps the only way to avoid disaster was to scupper Lady Vernon's plans.

Because, now she suspected there was more to this than simply making Mr Westaway fall in love with her only to break his heart.

No, there was something far deeper at play than she'd given credence to, and unless she ended this charade right now, she'd be the one paying the penalty for the rest of her life.

She was sure of it.

CHAPTER 17

Faith woke to the sound of rain beating against the windowpane. She opened one heavy eyelid and stared out into a grey sky. The tree branches scraped and scratched at the glass, and the wind sighed through the branches.

She sat up and reached for her poor, worse-for-wear cuirass-bodice and skirt that she'd worn the past two days for the painting and which Lady Vernon had arranged to be dried by morning.

But as her hands closed about the fabric, she encountered something light and unfamiliar.

These were not her clothes.

She put her feet to the floor and stood up, holding up the frothy, flimsy gown that was the right length for her but was not hers. She recognised it as something semifamiliar, an alternative fashion that eschewed the heavy corsetry, flounces, and swathing of the traditionally upholstered gowns of today's fashion.

As she held it up against her, a piece of paper fluttered to the floor.

Dear Miss Montague – she read – Perhaps this will be easier to wear for the remaining days you are required to work for me. I certainly believe it will suit you, and so anticipate the pleasure I will have of brandishing my brushes to do justice to your beauty."

Mr Westaway had bought her a dress. A light, flowing, delicious confection in white voile with flounces and furbelows that required no corsetry. A dress she could put on herself without the help of a dresser or lady's maid.

She stepped into it, wishing her heart did not beat so, and that her hands didn't tremble as she fastened the hooks and eyes.

Surveying herself in the mirror, she saw that the effect would be eminently desirable from a painterly point of view. She put her hands around her waist and smoothed the fabric over her hips. A perfect hourglass figure precluded the necessity of an undergarment that would impinge upon rapid undressing. She would be the creature in the medieval gown floating in the stream that was the stuff of Mr Westaway's imagination.

But she would not entice him.

No, her plans had changed. She would no longer play the temptress in the knowledge that her actions would lead an innocent man to his downfall.

Regardless of the contract she had with Mrs Gedge, she couldn't condemn the man she was afraid she'd grown too fond of to a future filled with dangers unknown.

"Miss Montague, you didn't sleep well?"

Faith shook her head and offered Mr Westaway a rueful smile while wishing Lord Delmore was on hand in the small bathing room. The piercing, soulful eyes of handsome Mr

Westway plucked at her heartstrings in a way they had no right to.

He smiled sympathetically when she shook her head. "If it's any consolation, I didn't either."

He positioned himself behind the easel but put his head around to ask, "And what do you think of the gown? I know Lady Vernon's arthritic fingers make it difficult to help you with your ordinary dress. Besides which, this will create the effect I'm after." He seemed to falter. "I hope you don't consider me too forward in choosing your wardrobe."

"You're the artist, Mr Westaway. I would wear a hessian sack if you required it."

"You would?" He ducked back in front of his easel to grin at her. "I should like that."

"I shouldn't like it, though. However, you're paying me."

His smile vanished. The dampening effect of her response had created the desired effect, but it hadn't made Faith happy to see him so effectively checked.

With a sigh, she shrugged her shoulders. "Forgive my being so out of sorts, Mr Westaway. You're right; I had an abominable night's sleep, and I'm not an angel when I'm not well rested."

"Despite looking like one. I'm glad you're wearing the dress. I think it will free both of us."

He was back in professional mode, not thinking of the double meaning of his words. In the tiny bathroom, Lady Vernon sat on a chair by the window, silent like a bird of prey, the great tub of steaming water beckoning Faith to submerge herself. Such a contrast to the dreary outdoors. On the water's surface floated rose petals while beneath, the flame from a dozen candles kept the water at a pleasant temperature.

"This is somewhat more enticing than yesterday's

escapade into the icy, murky depths of your local fishpond," she said, and he laughed.

"Yesterday, I sketched the reeds and the clouds above and the billowing folds of your gown, Miss Montague. It was the beautiful outdoors that will be writ large when the painting is exhibited and there was nothing wasted." He craned his head forward as if to study the planes and angles of her face.

"Now, I just need to render the perfection of my subject at close quarters," he seemed to stumble over his last few words, "so that the painting's viewers will appreciate the exquisite definition of my *Lady of the Lake*."

The air between them seemed thick with unspoken meaning. And promise. Faith swallowed and put her hand to her throat as if her lace collar were suddenly too tight.

His admiration was too much. But he'd not act on it. She strained to see the sincerity in his eyes and was rewarded with it a hundred-fold. Why did he not see the need to hide his feelings as she did?

"I'm sorry, Miss Montague, but it's time to submerge yourself, once again."

Faith put her hand in his palm as he helped her into the bath. It was a curiously intimate gesture, and she imagined herself suddenly stepping into a bath as most ladies did, without clothing. Did he, also? Is that why he blushed?

She hadn't meant to immerse herself so quickly that her skirts skimmed up to her thighs before she was able to smooth them.

Lady Vernon would have been pleased to have caught the flare of desire in his bright, blue eyes, but it was not what Faith sought right now. Not now that she'd sworn off the plan.

The plan.

What should she do? What *could* she do? She caught Lady Vernon's eagle eyes upon her and said, "Is this the effect you were hoping to achieve, Mr Westaway? Will you want me to wear this dress tomorrow?" She smiled up at him. "Did *you* choose it?"

"There was a certain stiffness to your previous attire that did not accord with the vision I had in mind."

"So, you did choose it!" She sounded as delighted as she felt, even though she knew it was unwise.

"I went into the village and sought the offices of a dressmaker who knew exactly what I was talking about. She also happens to be a proponent of the Arts and Crafts movement, and she had a loose-flowing gown she'd made for herself that just fitted the bill. I'm delighted it suits you so well."

"And I'm delighted you have such a good eye, Mr Westaway."

He smiled warmly. "I've always spied out quality, Miss Montague."

"And where is Lord Delmore today?" she asked as Mr Westaway slid behind his easel and picked up his paintbrushes.

"Do you miss him?"

She gave an embarrassed laugh. "Should I? I thought he was being instructed by you in the art of painting; that he was thinking of dabbling in painting himself and that was why he was always with you."

"I think you misunderstand his motives, Miss Montague. Now, if you could stretch your neck a little. Yes, that's right, you have a very beautiful neck, and the dress shows that to perfection."

"Does that mean you'll have to start the painting again?"

"Only in the close-up of you and it won't take too long to alter. I'll be finished by the deadline in three days." He paused. "I will need you to suffer spending a little longer in the bath today, though. I hope you won't be too cramped. I promise I'll work as quickly as I can."

"Of course." Faith stretched her limbs and pointed her toes. The iron tub was enormous, and she could float freely. It was quite liberating, though she'd have enjoyed it more if the water were a little warmer.

"Lady Vernon, are the candles lit beneath? It's a little cold."

Lady Vernon did not seem impressed. "There are five candles burning, Faith. Please don't complain. Mr Westaway has work to do, and you mustn't keep interrupting." She rose. "This is no place for an old woman with arthritic limbs. I shall fetch Molly to sit in."

Mr Westaway didn't try to fill the silence when she'd gone. Nor did he seem to notice that Molly had not come to take Lady Vernon's place. He seemed intent on his painting, the brush moving rapidly now, his face with a mask of concentration.

The minutes ticked by leaden and slow for Faith, who was feeling the cold seep into her bones and feared asking Mr Westaway to relight the candles which had gone out some time ago.

She shivered, and her teeth chattered.

Surely, he'd notice and come to her rescue.

The light began to fade outside casting long, gloomy shadows across the room.

Still Mr Westaway worked, completely absorbed. In fact, never had Faith seen him so animated as his brush flew across the canvas. She dared not interrupt.

In the depths of the house, the grandfather clock struck seven o' clock. Faith had been in the bath for two hours. She tried to breathe, but was shivering too much.

She tried to speak, but the words wouldn't come.

If was as if her body were caving in on itself suddenly. It had happened so gradually, but now the impact was swift.

She didn't know if she had the strength to ever move again. She was going to drown all over again but on the inside.

Perhaps she gave a soft moan for Mr Westaway looked up suddenly, and as his eyes locked with hers, it was as if he were only seeing her, the person, for the first time in all his frenzied painting, for he dropped his brush and strode forward, crouching by the side of the bath.

"Miss Montague?" He didn't wait for her to acknowledge him. Perhaps he saw that she was incapable. Certainly, the speed with which he rose and whisked her out of the bath and against him belonged to a man motivated by urgency.

She was shivering so hard now she couldn't speak. Her teeth chattered, and her body convulsed.

"Dear God, what have I done to you?" Seizing a towel, he wrapped her in it, squeezing the water out of her skirts so that it puddled on the floor and down his trouser legs. He paused, cradling her against him. She had her eyes shut, so she didn't see what expressions crossed his face, but the next moment, he'd hoisted her into his arms and was striding out of the bathroom and along the corridor to the servants' stairs, his footsteps echoing on the bare boards. This was not a part of the house frequented by the likes of Mr Westaway, yet it appeared they met no one. Not that Faith cared too much.

She was going to die of cold. Her bones ached to the very marrow, and her head ached. How had it happened so fast? Why had she let it happen? Her thoughts had wandered so very far away. Away to what freedom might feel like if she ever got out of the prison of her making. Of Mrs Gedge's making.

She felt his hand on her as he lay her on something that yielded slightly. A bed.

The ceiling was dark and unfamiliar. Not her room. Not a

room a gentleman would inhabit, she realised vaguely. The servants' attics or a musty room somewhere else.

"It was the closest." She felt his warm breath against her forehead.

The bathroom was tacked onto a little-used part of the house; she knew that. Knew also that he was not going to strip her naked and have his way with her when she was vulnerable. Yes, cold she might be, but she was not insensible. A girl who traded on her wits and who didn't intend landing in the gutter couldn't afford not to have a semblance of consciousness of what was going on around her.

But she was so cold. The spasm that tore through her and his hesitancy following the light hand on her chest, not her breasts for he was a gentleman and would remain one, she was certain of that, banished his diffidence.

He began to work the row of tiny buttons at the front of her gown quickly, stripping her dress over her shoulders and down to her waist while she wriggled to help him. For the gown was like an icy mantle, and she was desperate to get warm. Desperate to feel warmth against her frozen skin.

His warmth.

Reaching out, she closed her hands about his wrists, and he stopped.

"Make me warm." Her hands found his thighs, the rough fabric of his trousers. Wet. Like the rest of him as he'd held her, dripping against him.

It was only reasonable he get warm and dry too. She didn't say it, but her seeking hands and the expression she levelled at him made her thoughts clear.

She reached out her arms for him, and one glance at her face was enough, for then he was tearing at his necktie, unbuttoning his jacket and waistcoat, stripping off his trousers.

All with the urgency and attention to what came next that

she required.

The thought of skin to skin contact was like a burning obsession, although only conceived of in the minutes she'd spent conjuring them up while lying on the bed.

Before, it had been a necessary precursor to her freedom.

Now it was a raging want, and as he lowered himself into her arms and his hard, naked chest pressed against her breasts, she thought she would die of desire.

Warmth sizzled between them, his heated skin instantly communicating to her everything she needed, whipping up sensations she had no idea were possible in her carefully controlled human sphere.

"Hold me," she whispered, wrapping her arms and legs about him and pulling him tight. "Please."

He was as naked as she, and the searing contact lit a fire within her belly.

Desire? Is this what it felt like? She, who'd imagined she was immune was now as desperate as any common doxy to fuel the fires of the man in her embrace for her own ends. She wanted love; she wanted passion; she wanted human connection.

Sliding beneath the covers, they curled into each other, his warmth heating her all over, his erection pressing into her belly; strengthening her from within. Powerful. She felt it of her own accord and because of his worship, for that's what it felt like. As if he were imbuing her with a strength she could only experience through honouring this connection between them.

His lips found hers, lighting her up from inside, thrilling her with sensations she'd not thought possible.

She rolled on top of him, straddling him as she cupped his face, kissing him back with passion. What did it matter that the motion came naturally, observed during her time at Madame Chambon's though never acted upon until now. It gave her power and negated any gentlemanly requirement to question her desire to proceed.

She could no more have halted the escalation of raging need to take this to its culmination than tell him she never wanted to see him again.

For she wanted to see him…be with him…now…forever.

In all her life, Faith had never craved physical contact with another person for any length of time. Her body had never reacted to another human being as it did now. Conscious thought disappeared; instinct took over, and it was the most fulfilling, liberating moment of her life when he rolled her beneath him, and his mouth found her breast.

"Oh!" she cried, desperate for what she did not know. Only that the suckling of her nipple was the most delicious torment she'd ever experienced. Meanwhile, her seeking hands liked what they found. His young body was strong, hard and…responsive.

She pushed back the hair that flopped over his forehead, and her eyes caught his as he positioned himself at her entrance.

Oh, she was more than ready. She was more than wanting.

She sucked in a breath, and a small smile was all he needed to continue with what could never have been stopped with all the will in the world.

He slid into her, eliciting a brief jerk of surprised pain that was quickly subsumed by all the delicious sensations that followed.

This was nothing like she'd expected. And so much more than she'd ever hoped for, when hope was something that seemed reserved for other people.

She clung to him and moved with him, loving the knowledge that he was in another sphere, and that she'd taken him to pleasures unknown. That's what it felt like, with his breathing fast and shallow and his sighs responsive to her slightest movement.

His body spoke to hers as if they were made for one another. Sweat slicked her once-icy skin. Sizzling sensation tore across her nerve endings. Inside, her body was experiencing a firestorm of its own; a raging conflagration divorced from the pleasure that flooded her mind.

With a cry, he thrust into her one final time, flinging his arm about her and pulling her tightly against his chest before, panting, he lay on his back, eyes closed, face raised to the ceiling.

Faith curled into him; her free hand stroking his chest, lingering over his nipples, making him jerk and smile as she toyed with him.

"My darling," he muttered, opening one eye and staring down at her.

She didn't pretend to be coy or shy away from him. She had bled, and thank God he need have no doubts that he had indeed taken a virgin.

But that was academic. Faith wasn't going to let him go.

Not now, not ever.

CRISPIN WAS INFUSED WITH NEW GENIUS. HIS PAINTBRUSH HAD acquired magical powers. A life of its own. In the early morning, with the light as sharp as could be achieved on another gloomy day, he painted the glorious creature who floated in the bath and who gazed up at him through lazy, half-lidded eyes.

The water was comfortably warm, and the candles would continue to be refreshed. He wasn't about to lose her to some foolish preoccupation with his art though, lord, he wasn't sorry by what had precipitated this descent into madness.

It was madness, but he wasn't about to call it out for what it was and deny the possibilities that lay before them.

Them. He was not a young man to downplay what was real. Denial had been hard won during the drawn-out process accepting her as the helpmate of his future.

She'd arrived too early in his life, but he recognised her for what she was—the wife he'd spend his life looking for if he didn't claim her now.

And he'd claimed her as surely and effectively as a man of his moral code could.

"Are you comfortable, Miss Montague?" he said above the clicking of Lady Vernon's knitting needles.

"Quite, thank you, Mr Westaway." She flicked a covert, meaning-laden smile at him, managed through half an open eye, and he was satisfied. Their communication was as subtle as needed to be with a chaperone on standby, and as satisfying as any lust-craven gentleman could want.

Having sinned once, there would be no impediments to strengthening the precious, fragile bond through further sinning.

He would wed her, there was no doubt of that, and in the process, restore her immortal soul.

The precious enigma that she was would be in no doubt that his intentions, when all was said and done, were honourable. And by making that clear, she'd dispense with the inhibitions that, extraordinarily, had not been in evidence when they'd sinned the first time.

No, she was pure, that was not in doubt, yet he'd unleashed in her a primal desire that surely every man would ache to have as the essential makeup of the woman to whom God had joined and no man must put asunder.

"The water is not too cool for you, Miss Montague?"

"Slightly, Mr Westaway, but your painting must come first before I warm myself."

And that, you will not do without my help, Miss Montague, he thought, though his glance made that clear enough for she slanted a secret smile at him, instantly regaining her former gravitas when Lady Vernon dropped her knitting and stared for a long moment between the two of them.

But the old woman did not suspect. How could she? She was a dried-up husk of a creature with no understanding of human passion.

Miss Montague reared up before him, water dripping from her hair and dress, spattering the floor as she reached for linen with which to dry herself.

"Forgive me, I suddenly couldn't stay there a moment longer."

"Faith, you were not given permission!" Her chaperone was angry, and Crispin enjoyed seeing the flint in his beloved's eye as she stood her ground, pretending she didn't care that her actions compromised Crispin's ability to paint the picture that would earn him his place in the world.

There was no doubt this was a masterpiece in the making. She was his inspiration, his muse, and another night in her arms would solidify the power of creation, of genius, that would elevate this painting above the rest.

"The cold has a habit of seizing one suddenly. Taking one captive, Lady Vernon," he soothed. "Let Faith leave now if she must."

The old lady was not pleased, it amused him to see. It amused him even more to see how well Faith played the pliant schoolgirl with the invisible armour that suddenly sprouted metal spikes when her ire was aroused. He wondered what words were exchanged when the two of them were alone and Miss Westaway was defending her need to break what Lady Vernon surmised was the contract between them.

The contract that had been rewritten.

CHAPTER 18

he words that were in fact exchanged between Faith and her chaperone of course bore no resemblance to any he might have surmised.

"You can't behave like a prima donna or you'll never get his measure."

"You think I haven't already?" Faith glared, wanting to taunt Lady Vernon and keep her wondering, yet wanting her to know that Faith had succeeded so beautifully already.

But caution and the long game stilled her tongue, so she merely looked enigmatic when Lady Vernon demanded to know what she meant.

"You have three days, Faith. Three days to enslave him, torture him." Lady Vernon's nostrils flared. "Ruin him." The old lady stared out of the window as she toyed with the brush she was about to use on Faith's tangled tresses. "And then it will be time to live your own dreams." She looked so enraptured by this thought that Faith could have imagined she was living Faith's life in her own mind.

Faith sat down on a wooden chair in the centre of the room and held her head erect, waiting for Lady Vernon to play servant. How she did enjoy that. The old woman was a parasite; a cosseted creature born to a life of leisure, but too unattractive to snare the attention of a protector, so that as she aged, she had nothing but her own resources to draw upon.

Faith didn't need a protector. She was too clever. And, unlike Lady Vernon, she had multiple resources to draw upon: youth, beauty, wit, intellect, education.

Mrs Gedge had equipped her with the tools to exact the other woman's evil revenge, but Faith would turn the tables with a pure heart.

It strengthened Faith to know that her vitriol had a pure edge. She wasn't truly bad, as she'd once believed. Love had freed her, cleansed her. Her words and actions towards Mr Westaway were motivated now by truth and honesty; honesty in that she feigned nothing of her feelings.

If that meant her dealings with Lady Vernon were tainted, so be it. If she needed to play a role in order to emerge like a chrysalis, reincarnated from evil into good, it was transitory, necessary. That was all.

Lady Vernon was out of sorts as she tugged the brush through Faith's hair. Faith was playing her cards close to her chest with nothing to support the old lady's suspicions one way or the other. And there was nothing Lady Vernon disliked more than not being in control.

Faith knew this, and it delighted her to keep her guessing while she dreamed away the moments before she could throw a cloak over her nightclothes and slip away up the back stairs to the room they'd occupied the night before.

He was waiting there for her as she knew he would be, his impatience clear, his delight at the fact she'd come as gratifying as anything could be when he strode across the floorboards to greet her.

The sun coming in through the window behind him

highlighted his slender but athletic physique but it wasn't before she was in his arms that she could see how his eyes glowed with raw desire.

"My love, you've no idea how impatiently I've waited for this moment." He held her close, his breath hot against her ear as he murmured, "I painted you as you lay in the bath, with the sun burnishing your hair like a halo, dreaming of a time when I could see you just like that with no one but the two of us."

"And that moment has come." She twined her arms behind his neck and nuzzled him, breathing in the scent of him with rapture before he scooped her up and lay her on the bed. He joined her, holding her against his side while he kissed her eyes, her nose, her mouth, pausing to whisper, "You know what this means, don't you?"

She didn't, and her breath hitched, every sense suspended as she waited tensely. What would he say? He couldn't live without her and would she be his mistress? Or that she was the most intoxicating woman he knew, but this must be a secret between them? He loved her, but his father would never allow their union?

Silence stretched between them as a myriad of possibilities jostled for primacy. Faith couldn't be disappointed by what she knew was coming. She simply had to work with what she was offered.

"I want to marry you. I *will* marry you." He was above her now, his chest bare, his eyes boring into her with a fervour she could not believe was feigned.

Shocked, she couldn't answer but he went on, "You wouldn't be here if you didn't feel the same way about me. You're not one to give away your affections lightly, Faith. I've observed every nuance of you...the way your skin flushes when you're happy to see me, or irritated by your chaperone, or pleased with the way you see the painting taking shape. You're the perfect muse, but that's only part of why I need you." He was speaking faster now, the words tumbling out as if he had to persuade her to reciprocate his feelings. "Yes, I *need* you, Faith, because I think you are my perfect foil. My helpmate. We would be good together. A union in perfect symmetry. I am better with you by my side. Less selfish, more careful. I *need* to be careful with a painstaking eye to detail to be good at my job."

"Painting?"

"When I am a diplomat."

"But how can I be a diplomat's wife?" For the first time, she felt truly panicked. The thrill at hearing him put into words the depth of his feelings for her had given way to the practicalities. Little matter that she'd come to the country for the single purpose of receiving just such a declaration only to throw it back in his face, claim her reward from Mrs Gedge, and thus be free.

She would no more be free than a slave from Africa if she were forced to give up his love.

"I love you, Faith. My commitment is not in doubt." He stroked her cheek and gently kissed her mouth, his words more important than his desire, which was apparent as his body pressed against hers. "Is yours?"

She shook her head, and in a fresh burst of ardour pulled him down, her hands sliding to his trousers, indicating her impatience that he divest himself of all impediments to furthering the intimacy between them.

"I love *you*."

"Say my name."

"I love you, Crispin." The words came out on a sigh of happiness, made wonderful and magical...and pure...by the fact they were spoken in truth. And she was pure, wasn't she?

Pure in the Biblical sense. She'd not lain with another; she'd given her virginity to this man, and she had every right to claim his love and whatever else he offered.

That she was a creature bred for revenge need not enter into it. Faith had lived by her wits, and the prize was freedom. Never had she doubted she'd get what she wanted for she was cleverer than Mrs Gedge, cleverer than Madame Chambon, and cleverer than Lady Vernon. If Mr Westaway… Crispin…wanted to marry her, she could make a plan that would enable it to happen.

"You are not the shy creature I thought you at first," he whispered, rising above her to unfasten the front of her dress and sliding his hands inside. "But you're a great deal more buttoned up than you were yesterday," he added, referring to the fact she wore a corset and underclothing beneath her ensemble.

"You'll have to make me less buttoned up," she giggled, rolling onto her side so he could slide off her skirt, then onto her back so he could unlace her corset, and finally, giving him unfettered access to her combinations. "If romance can survive all that, I am completely yours."

"My darling, I relish the challenge." He kissed her on the nose. "And your humour. Lady Vernon doesn't know the half of you, does she?"

"Lady Vernon thinks she does." Naked at last, Faith revelled in the way his eyes feasted on her breasts. She breathed deeply, causing them to rise and laughing when the invitation was so implicit, he lowered his head to take one nipple in his mouth.

"Too divine," she whispered as sensation snaked through her limbs and coalesced at the juncture of her legs. The weight of him on top of her was unbearably wonderful, and she felt all powerful at the feel of his erection pressing against her. She'd seen naked men aroused before and been disgusted. But Crispin was too beautiful for words. Tender and kindhearted, masculine but conscious of her needs, she was not going to let him go.

To be joined with him again was to reinforce their bond. Unbreakable. That's what it would be. Faith had never loved before this. It's how she knew what it was. She'd observed him with the same intensity he'd observed her. She knew his moods, understood what drove him, sympathised with the obstacles placed in his path.

Well, there would be obstacles they both must face, but face them they must. If this truly were love, as each believed, then they would overcome.

Arching her back, she guided his hand to her mound, as if by accident, gasping at the pressure so that he blinked in surprise for just a second before he did exactly as she'd hoped he would.

Dear lord, but he was good. Her legs went slack and she was aching for him before at last he was inside her. With a gentle sigh, she grasped his buttocks and moved with him in glorious harmony.

Until both could take it no more and came together in a shuddering climax.

"We shall marry as soon as possible." His voice was urgent as he held her close, both still breathless from their love-making. "I can't bear the thought of being parted from you a moment longer than necessary."

"Your father will object. We need to be careful." Except that it was Faith who needed to be careful. Mr Westaway's father was less of a danger than Mrs Gedge.

Crispin seemed reluctant to accept this, and Faith was relieved when he finally agreed not to make any immediate announcement.

She'd been about to slip to the floor and start dressing but she needed to secure his promise and a promise was more easily extracted with skin to skin contact.

Madame had taught her that.

"Promise me you won't say anything until I say tell you it's all right to do so, Crispin? *Please?*" Playing for time was of the essence. She needed a few days in which to plan, to set in motion a means by which Faith could extricate herself from the tentacles with which Mrs Gedge intended to bind her.

She did not feel she was abusing Crispin's faith in her. If he loved her and could be confident the girl he wanted to make his wife was a virgin when he first made love to her, and if he still wanted to marry her, knowing she was penniless, and despite his father's anticipated opposition, what did the rest matter?

She put her finger to his lips as she rolled on top of him, then stroked his face. "Let this be our secret, Crispin, until the painting is finished." She kissed his chest. "Don't signal to Lady Vernon your feelings just yet. Can you do that?" Playfully, she added, "Though if you want to write me love letters to make up for what you don't say to me in person, that would be very acceptable."

~

"My most beloved Faith,

You are the moon, the sun, and the stars. When I conjure up your image, it's imbued with a magical glow for you have lit up my life. In just a few days, I know that everything worth having is invested in you. I do not write these words lightly. I have lived, and I have loved, but I've never known what love was until I met you."

With hope and faith that you return the love I feel for you, and excitement for our future as husband and wife, I'll end with a reminder that surely must not be necessary—only two more hours until we can meet again...no one but the two of us."

FAITH KISSED THE ENVELOPE AND LEANED BACK ON HER window seat, gazing at the sky and the distant green verdant hills, bathed in evening light as if they were imbued with everything Crispin, she believed, seemed to feel right now— hope and...faith.

Yes, he had faith in her and in a shared future. And Faith had every expectation that her own cleverness would trump anything Mrs Gedge or Lady Vernon might conjure up to shackle her.

Life had never been so thrilling.

She closed her eyes and hugged the envelope to her chest. Crispin had written words that had found their way right to her heart. He loved her with the intensity she loved him. He'd put into words the very feelings she felt when she imagined him here with her and their life together.

She'd have to make a copy of his words to keep. The letter itself would be her ticket to freedom in the eyes of Mrs Gedge. This would be proof Mr Westaway had lost his heart to her, and all Faith had to do in return was pretend to break his heart. Having spent the last three years of her life living a lie, it would be easy to execute this final, simple task.

Yes, Faith was clever at the best of times. But when her heart was engaged, there was nothing she couldn't do.

LORD DELMORE CLEARLY COULD NOT KEEP AWAY AND HAD been reluctant to discharge the previous day's business which had him visiting his solicitor rather than seated at Crispin's right elbow and watching proceedings.

A lot could happen in twenty-four hours, revealed his lordship a touch wistfully to Crispin, elaborating later that evening after Miss Montague had gone to her room to change into dry clothes.

"There's no point in my making a visit to the capital before the end of the season."

The two men sat in front of the fire with replenished brandy glasses as they waited for the return of the ladies and the edge in his friend's tone had Crispin pricking up his ears although he suspected what Lord Delmore was about to say.

"It's quite clear you're as smitten with the young lady as she is with you." Lord Delmore paused and looked long and hard into the fireplace, while Crispin waited for what would come next as clearly his lordship was pondering something deep and hard. Finally, he looked Crispin in the eye. "Your father won't like it."

Crispin wasn't sure how to take this. His friendship with Lord Delmore was not deep though it had grown over the years. The older man clearly lacked society since the loss of his wife after their two sons had gone to the colonies. Was Crispin being spoken to like an errant schoolboy for losing his heart unwisely?

Carefully he said, "I am twenty-six years old—"

"Oh, you have a wise head on young shoulders and I'm not about to persuade you out of your infatuation or your one true love. Just be sure you know what sacrifices you will have to make before you act too rashly."

Crispin was well aware of the obstacles ahead. His father would be intractable. In fact, he could possibly prove insurmountable, which was why Crispin had been toying with other measures to spirit Faith away—elopement being one.

"Lord Delmore, I am not a greenhorn, and I have known Miss Montague for some time now." He hoped he did not sound too defensive.

"Three weeks, I believe. I hope Miss Montague knows what she's taking on. It won't be easy for her, married to a man whose father exercises such fierce opposition as yours undoubtedly will."

Crispin felt the weight on his shoulders. If he'd had brothers, the burden of marrying well would have been shared. But Crispin was required to be everything to Lord Maxwell, and to fulfil his father's expectations both in the diplomatic arena as well as the marital.

"Initially, Miss Montague and I were very aware that a union between us would not be sanctioned by my father. We spoke about it openly at…the beginning." He hesitated over this. *The beginning* was only a few days ago, and yet a meteoric shift had occurred within him. And her? She seemed prosaic about a match between them. She was husband hunting; she'd made no secret of that. But her feelings had undergone the same metamorphosis his had done. They must have, otherwise she'd not have given herself to him with the intensity she had. No well-brought-up young lady would take such risks unless her hearts was inflamed. For her, this truly had to be love. Passion. Crispin was an artist. He knew what fire in the veins made one do.

"I cannot allow my father's disappointment to stand in the way of my future."

"Happiness?" Lord Delmore asked at his hesitation, and Crispin said quickly, "My happiness is not the only factor here. I believe that I will make the kind of impression on the world and progress as my father desires far more effectively if I have by my side the woman I believe will complement me and make me proud."

For a long time, Lord Delmore considered him. Then he sighed and returned his gaze to the fire. "How can I offer an opinion when I've never known what you describe?" His shoulders were slumped, and the sounds of crackling wood and the ticking clock were very loud. "My marriage was one of convenience. It brought me two fine, prosperous sons and a beautiful daughter, and I had every reason to admire my wife. I know nothing of the fires of which you speak." He touched his heart briefly. "Though having observed Miss Montague these past few days I can understand a little of what you mean. But you must do what you will, my boy, and accept the consequences."

"Do I have your support?"

Lord Delmore raised his eyebrows. "Of course! She is a fine young lady and you a fine young man. You are clearly an excellent pairing. Whatever support is required of me, I will offer it."

Crispin was relieved despite the faint acid in his lordship's tone. So, he truly had believed in a future with Miss Montague, for himself. Well, didn't that, in its own way, support the match? "Thank you, Lord Delmore. I'm much obliged. One request." Crispin smiled. "Please don't make this public before I do. Miss Montague is as aware as I am of the likely opposition. I will need to choose my moment carefully."

"Perhaps when you carry off the art prize of the decade. When the public sees for themselves the qualities, not least beauty, of your muse, it will be entirely understandable why you've let your impulses get the better of you."

"That is how it will be regarded? When the public cannot base their judgement on her fine intellect? Indeed, *that* is what swayed me. Her beauty attracted me, but her beauty alone was not, to my mind, sufficient for me to gainsay my father. I believe Miss Montague has a mind that will be an asset to both of us."

"I hope your father will be so forward thinking." Grudgingly, Lord Delmore added, "Though truth be told, it was the same with me. She does have a remarkable mind and a sharp wit. An intoxicating combination." He raised his glass. "I hear the ladies returning now. Good luck, old fellow. May you navigate the potential pitfalls ahead with the greatest of ease. She will win your father over; I have no doubt. And that's all you need to see this thing through as you would like."

CHAPTER 19

*O*nly a day left before they were to return to London. For nearly one whole blissful week Faith and Crispin had spent almost all day together and, latterly, much of the night.

Her beloved worked at a feverish pace in front of his easel, sending her loving looks when he thought no one else was looking, and passing her notes and love gifts at every other opportunity. Faith had no shortage of tokens in both kind and in writing to attest to the intensity of Mr Westaway's love. It thrilled her, and it filled her with a deep and satisfied sense of completeness. No one had loved her before. Not her mother or her father or any of the gentlemen she had ever met.

Crispin had his own reasons for keeping their relationship secret, and it suited Faith just fine. As she lay on the small iron bed they shared in the servant's attic far from anyone else, she went over her best course of action. Crispin had briefly mentioned elopement. It was, in Faith's mind, the best way forward. To be married in secret would guarantee her a passport to a trouble-free future. That she loved him with equal intensity was irrelevant in one respect; yet it was only for this reason she wanted to be certain of spending the rest of her life with him.

Mrs Gedge wanted to ruin him. Wanted to see his heart broken. Well, what could she do after Faith and he were bound together in the eyes of god and the law?

If she worried that Mrs Gedge would be vindictive, she tried to put those fears aside. Mrs Gedge had supported Faith for three years. Their monthly tea meetings had suggested a woman who was interested in furthering the prospects of her little protegee. Faith need only persuade Mrs Gedge that vengeance would hurt Faith in this regard more than it would Mr Westaway. Mrs Gedge had been a mother. She was a woman who knew how to love.

She would understand.

And if she didn't, Faith would be in Germany before Mrs Gedge ever learned the truth.

Now, as Faith sat at the dinner table opposite Crispin, Lady Vernon at her side, she couldn't wait for the old woman to withdraw for the evening and so give the young people complete freedom. Faith didn't care that the servants could not be unaware of what was happening. But this was a borrowed cottage. These were not Crispin's servants.

"I expect you are anxious for the next few days to be over." Lady Vernon's nasal tones cut into the silence as the parlourmaid removed the main course and brought in dessert. "What will you do with your winnings if you are indeed the chosen one, Mr Westaway?"

"I dare not hope to think I will be."

"No need to be so modest. Everyone agreed that your skills were far superior to your two competitors. If you win, you will be a rich man." She looked meaningfully between Faith and Crispin. "You will be free to do as you choose, surely?"

Faith blushed at the lack of subtlety, and also the fact that Lady Vernon was fishing for words Faith did not wish Crispin to offer. The last person she wanted to know that she already had a marriage offer was Lady Vernon.

"My father is always my first consideration, Lady Vernon."

Faith let out a slow breath. That was the answer she'd hoped for.

And she told him so when they met each other in their attic room.

"We will get married in secret, darling," she whispered as she stepped into his arms. "Like you suggested. I don't want my parents knowing beforehand and coming to you for handouts. They will, you know. Far better that we slip away quietly to Germany with no one the wiser. We can tell them when…."

He tapped her on the nose, then kissed her on the lips as he tightened his hold on her in the centre of the small room.

"I want my father to be there to bless us and to congratulate us with true joy," said Crispin.

Faith stepped out of his embrace and looked at him, puzzled. "You've changed your mind? Why?"

The need for Crispin to proceed in secrecy struck her anew. She'd realised, with frightening clarity, that the love letters and the marriage proposal she had in writing must never fall into Mrs Gedge's hands. Faith must appear to her to have failed. Lady Vernon had no idea to what extent it had progressed. She'd witnessed the occasional longing look, that was all.

She tried not to appear as anxious as she was.

Faith's bargain was predicated on the exchange of such evidence for a fee of five hundred pounds. Well, she would forgo the money. Of course, she would have to if she were to gain the loving future that was more important now than anything.

Crispin stroked her cheek. "My father's approval is important to me. I want him to love you as I do."

Faith sent him a wry look and he smiled back, adding, "Perhaps not quite as I do, but I know he'll appreciate the qualities I've recognised in you. I do believe he would come to see that your intelligence is an attribute that trumps the fact you have no dowry."

"Or illustrious connections. Your father will not want you allying yourself with a nobody, no matter how quick-witted she might be, or indeed how independent you might become through winning an illustrious art prize. No Crispin, there's not enough time. Please, my darling. We must marry quickly. And in secret."

Still, he demurred. "Faith, sweeting, we can have it all— the society wedding that gives you the acceptance you need and deserve. I would far rather that than have us sneaking away with whispers and innuendo."

"Oh Crispin, we may *have* to get married in a hurry."

Faith put a hand to her belly, though she was reasonably confident the precautions she'd been taught precluded any possibility that she might have conceived during their week of passionate couplings. Ten times. And now she was about to initiate another. Her body was on fire, and although she was disquieted by his talk, she was also confident she could persuade him of what was required.

She rested her cheek against his chest and raised her hand upwards to cup his cheek. "Tomorrow your painting will be delivered, and the following night it will be judged. You will win, Crispin, for it is a rare show of true talent. It's not because I'm biased that I say it."

And it wasn't. She truly was proud of his talent. He was a gifted painter, and it was wrong that his father didn't recognise how far his son could go in this direction if he didn't force Crispin to follow the diplomatic path to the exclusion of his art.

But Crispin wasn't attending to any talk of talent. Understanding, and now full of remorse, he kissed her full on the mouth then regarded her with an intent look. "I'm a fool for not taking more account of the lack of time we may have," he murmured. "I thought of it at the beginning when I was determined to marry you, and any consequence was a boon. But since your acceptance of my proposal, I've thought only of how to make this marriage one in which you are given the respect and public acknowledgement you deserve. An elopement is a shabby, shameful thing, and I'd do anything to prevent you enduring the disgrace of it."

"And I would do anything to be married to you at the earliest possibility. There'll be a whole lifetime to prove the naysayers wrong."

Trailing a line of kisses across her brow, he murmured, "You want to make your family proud, I know you do, despite you warning me they'll be at the gates looking for handouts. I want my father to be proud. Let me look after this, Faith." He kissed her nose. "Trust me, Faith. I'll make sure our future is wonderful; gilded with hope and possibility."

His words filled her with foreboding as his lips found hers, and when she shivered at the dangers he knew nothing about, he thought she was angling for a closer connection.

So he whisked her into his arms and lay her on the bed, joining her there where they quickly divested each other of their clothes.

And Faith put all thoughts of what might go wrong out of her mind, because for too long she'd been weighed down by fears of the future, and for just for these wonderful few days, she wanted to believe that the man who returned her love would be able to navigate the terrain.

Of course, with the clear light of a new day, she was again mistress of her own destiny, and the only person who could possibly know the extent of the perils that lay ahead. Faith knew only one course was possible—elopement.

Crispin was nervous as he oversaw the loading of his painting paraphernalia in the trunk that was strapped to the back of the carriage that would take it to the train station. Faith wanted to squeeze his hand in comfort, but Lady Vernon's brooding presence precluded that. Faith was not relishing the thought of being confined with the old woman for the journey to London. Crispin would follow an hour later, as suggested by Faith, to preclude the possibility of their feelings for one another becoming too apparent.

Tonight, they'd see one another amidst the throng of artists and an eager and appreciative public. Faith hoped she'd be well received as the innocent muse, and to secure a modicum of respect and acceptance in advance of a marriage announcement.

So, Crispin accompanied them in the carriage only as far as the station for his intention was to proceed into town where he maintained he had business with a solicitor.

When they reached the station, Lady Vernon boarded first and found an empty carriage while the footman loaded their trunk. As Faith prepared to join her, the steam rising about her in such a fog tempted her to take the risk of a quick kiss, though of course such fancies were swept away by common sense. Faith had lost her heart, but she'd not lost the clear-sightedness that ensured her wits were undimmed by emotion when it was necessary.

"In a few hours, you may be declared the winner of a prestigious prize and find yourself in possession of a fortune, Crispin. Will you still want me?"

"All aboard!" The station porter walked down the plat-form, slamming doors. He'd reach Faith in a moment, and she hung on his answer.

"This is no infatuation, if that's what you fear," he told her. His eyes were warm. "I want to shout out to the world that I am so very proud to make you my wife. We *will* do this properly, Faith."

"I'm afraid," she said, admitting the truth. "I want us to be married soon and quietly. If you truly love me, you'll forget about the fanfare, Crispin."

The previous night she had tossed and turned fearing for the consequences of doing things the way Crispin would have them done.

"Please, Crispin. I love you; I adore you." Again, she touched her belly. "What if you are caught up by the conse-quences of tonight, and our wedding can only take place six weeks hence. Or, what if your father tells you he'll give us your blessing only if you wait six *months*. Yes, it may be with all the acceptance and pomp and ceremony *you* would like, but what about me? Think of the shame I would bear if I were to bear a child less than eight months after our wedding day?"

The guard was nearly upon them. She gripped his hand, her expression pleading.

Finally, he nodded. "All right, we will marry secretly, and we will plan a second ceremony as if we'd never contracted the first. Does that satisfy you?"

"Train's leaving, Miss. Please board now."

Faith smiled her relief at him. She'd not thought of such a possibility, but it was eminently pleasing—clearly, to both of them. She stepped inside the train, and Crispin gripped her hand briefly through the door that was about to be slammed shut. "I'll organise a special licence. We shall marry in secret tomorrow, or if it can't be managed, the day after. Does that satisfy you? We will marry at the earliest because I love you and I want to prove it."

Faith exhaled on a sigh of relief. "You've proved that a thousand-fold. Thank you, Crispin," she whispered, reaching forward to touch his shoulder before the conductor slammed the door. "I look forward to seeing you tonight. I think it will be a night to remember."

~

"Lover's parting?" Lady Vernon asked as Faith seated herself.

Faith sent her an ingenuous look. "Mr Westaway and I have become friends, as is to be expected under such unusual circumstances. He cannot marry me, Lady Vernon; I explained that before."

"We all knew that from the beginning. Your job was to entice him into changing his mind. What progress on that front? Mrs Gedge will want to know. She's parting with a lot of money to ensure matters progress as she would have them."

"Mrs Gedge must have a very cold heart if she's spent three years plotting vengeance against the poor man." Faith couldn't help herself. "But *I've* not exactly been steeped in softness thanks to my less than tender upbringing. I want my freedom too. And I shall have it." She sent Lady Vernon a level look. "You are my minder, not my confessor. Nevertheless, you may rest assured we will all get what we want; you included."

~

A beautiful gown beyond Faith's imagination lay upon her bed when she returned to her lodgings at Lady Vernon's, for it had been deemed too risky to return to Madame Chambon's while she was in the public eye.

"Courtesy of Madame Gedge. She says it's her parting gift...on top of the five hundred pounds she anticipates handing over before too long."

Faith liked the fact Lady Vernon seemed uncertain about the undercurrents between Faith and Mr Westaway. Well, she'd not enlighten her. The old cow could claim her reward, and Faith hoped never to hear from her again once she and Crispin had left the country.

All they needed to do was slip away to marry in secret, and then they'd be in Germany before anyone thought to look for them. There, Faith had no doubt she could cement her new husband's affections to make up for the untruths he believed about her.

"It's beautiful." And it was. Made of midnight-blue silk with a froth of a train decorated with pink bows and an abundance of velvet flowers, it showed off her hourglass figure to perfection. Once she'd bathed, Lady Vernon's personal dresser helped Faith step into the skirt that was held close to the front of her body by tapes, pushing the fullness all to the back. Low cut with a décolletage trimmed with tiny pink silk roses it was a fairytale dress.

Little wonder she garnered so much attention when she was admitted to the Royal Society of Artists' gala.

Her painting was already on display together with the others, but Crispin's superior talent was apparent. Faith could hear it in the whispers around her. Whispers that included reference to her bountiful assets, also. Tonight was the culmination, almost, of her greatest desires, and her heart felt very full. Crispin would be honoured, as was his due, but she, too, was worthy of honour in her own right. Even if it were only for her beauty, Faith was still proud to claim it. The penniless daughter of a violent, alcoholic farm worker had come far indeed.

But how much further she intended to go. She would extirpate her roots; her past. The time would come when Crispin would ask more about her family, but she would navigate that difficulty as she was navigating tonight. Nothing was insurmountable. If necessary, she could pretend a different family. She'd find the right help. She'd claim her parents wanted nothing to do with her. That she'd been unable to admit such a thing when she first met him, for how could any man marry a girl disowned by her parents?

"Miss Montague, Sir Albion is asking for you." There was Crispin, smiling, encircled by admirers, and now drawing her and Lady Vernon into a gathering that included the patron of the society and his wife. They welcomed her warmly, reiterating their earlier words.

"You have succeeded very nicely in unleashing brilliance from this gentleman's brush, Miss Montague," said Lady McKinley. "There is no doubt about tonight's winner." She waved her hand at the three paintings lined up side by side on the dais. "Perhaps you will not go to Germany after all, Mr Westaway."

Faith glanced at her husband-to-be. Much as she wanted him to have the opportunity to devote his career to his art, Germany factored importantly in her plans.

"A shame your father is not here to see this." Sir Albion's nod encompassed the gathering as a whole. "He would understand that the public admires an artist in the same way they appreciate their need for a clever diplomat."

"I hope my father will come to understand that, too. But alas, he is not here, and I have not yet won the prize."

It was only a matter of time, of course. Only a matter of time before a hush fell upon the crowd as Sir Albion ascended to the dais and made his pronouncement.

It was about to become real. All that Crispin had dreamed of would come to pass. All that Faith had ever dreamed of would come to pass also. She had to cling to that belief, or she'd have nothing. Crispin loved her, and she loved him. They were young, good for each other, and free to marry.

Her thoughts had been running over this like a mantra, when she became conscious of the buzz that swept through the room. She felt a surreptitious squeeze of her bare arm, above her long gloves and below the puff of her silk and chiffon sleeve as Crispin passed her, signalling his excitement, his connection with her before cutting a swathe through the room on his way towards the stage.

Dear lord, he'd been declared the winner.

People congratulated him, and Faith felt an empathetic surge of excitement to see him so recognised. As she stared at the scene from the centre of the room, amidst strangers and well-wishers, the lovers and scions of the art world, and society as a whole, a feeling of the most intense desire swept over her. She wanted to belong.

She wanted Crispin more, but to belong to Crispin, to have his heart truly and completely, she *needed* to belong and be accepted by this world.

Crispin addressed a hushed crowd. Proudly, Faith heard him convey his thanks for the support he'd received; his pleasure at the fact the crowd endorsed the judge's choice and finally, with the room erupting into polite but enthusiastic congratulations, she intercepted his look from over the top of the heads of the throng.

Brief, but intense. Yes, they would marry in secret tomorrow. Nothing could stand in the way of their love. And when he boarded the packet for the first leg of his journey to Germany, she would be there too. Unobtrusive and veiled, certainly, but discretion was essential if they were not to be hounded by those who believed a penniless debutante was not good enough for him. No, nothing would part her from his side.

"I couldn't have done it without you, Miss Montague." Once back at her side, he bowed over her gloved hand and kissed the back of it. Sensation speared her like a physical lance.

"I just did my job, Mr Westaway." She smiled and was about to say more when they were interrupted by a familiar American accent, mid-Atlantic, as Faith had heard it described. "Please tell me how you would define that, Miss Montague. Your job, I mean."

Miss Eaves arrived in their midst, her expression eager as she held a pencil poised above a notebook. Her gown was plain but expensive; however, she clearly had a penchant for incorporating birds in her headwear for tonight six ostrich plumes waved in her coiffure as she moved.

"I hope you don't mind my interrupting, but my uncle has tasked me with writing up the story of tonight's win for Artist's Magazine."

Faith glanced at Crispin who seemed unperturbed, still buoyed up by his success. "Of course not. It's a great honour and a great surprise, both to receive the prize and to be mentioned in such an illustrious publication. But your question was directed at Miss Montague."

Having been given licence to speak freely, Faith said, "I perfected the art of stillness sufficiently for Mr Westaway to recreate the fiction that I was floating, drowned, in a lake. Other than getting a little cold and bored at times, I really didn't do anything."

Miss Eaves scoffed at this. "No need to be so self-effacing, Miss Montague. I'm sure the physical trials caused more irritation than cold and boredom. I'm here to write the *real* story. Once I've heard from you exactly how cold and bored and filled with discomfort you were, and then added how elated, or otherwise, you must feel now, I shall turn my full attention to Mr Westaway."

The young woman rolled her shoulders as if she couldn't wait to start scribbling, and Faith and Crispin shared a smile over her bent head once she'd scratched a few notes.

"Is this your first piece, Miss Eaves?"

Miss Eaves shook her head. "I've found a variety of pieces with which to fill the magazine over the past three weeks. But this is my first important piece. The size of the prize and the secrecy surrounding its benefactor has had the art world agog. Is that a word you English use in polite society?" She looked unperturbed, rushing on without waiting for an answer. "My uncle calls me brash and likes to edit my stories himself, but I'm the reporter on the ground. There aren't too many of us. Women, I mean, doing this kind of work, but the world is changing, and whereas a few years ago I'd have been a curiosity, now that is not the case. At least, not where I come from."

"I think things are slower to change in England," Faith murmured. "Traditions are strongly adhered to, including a woman's place." She stared at her toes. "A woman's respectability counts for more than her intelligence," she added, more to herself, though Miss Eaves picked up on this immediately.

"Oh, in America too, but there is much greater license and freedom from where I hail." Her pencil paused, and two blackbird-like eyes regarded Faith. "I've been fascinated by the difference in the way people think here, how people get ahead, what is accepted. Lord, but I wouldn't like to live my whole life in this country as the unmarried woman I am, keeping my head down, not being allowed to work. Anyway, I'm not here to talk about me. Mr Westaway, please tell me what inspired you to choose the type of painting you did? I believe you received a bag of props and had to create something from that. What did you have to incorporate? Each painting is significantly different though yours stands out, naturally."

"Rose petals, Miss Eaves."

Faith saw his clouded brow, and recalled his discomfort when he'd been confronted with the crimson flowers. His discomfort had clearly grown when Lady Vernon had made her suggestions, but with water as an essential medium, it was only natural that the petals had been arranged to float about Faith's prone form.

When they were alone together later tonight, if it could be managed in secret, she'd quiz him about it. There was so much they each had to learn about the other. But she'd observed a multitude of men during her years at Madame Chambon's, and there was a sincerity about Crispin that was lacking in the many braggarts and pumped-up blades who'd crossed that threshold.

Crispin's warm smile enforced every hope she had for the success of their marriage. When Miss Eaves departed having written her piece, and Lady Vernon was occupied in conversation with Sir Albion and his acolytes, he trailed her to the alcove where she'd sought a modicum of privacy.

"I hoped you'd not be waylaid," she said. "Or, at least, want to talk to me enough that you'd fob off everyone else."

"No one else is important right now." His eyes looked black and full of wanting. Turning, he plucked a full glass of champagne from a passing waiter and replaced Faith's empty one. "Only you, Faith darling." His low murmur was like melted chocolate, and it filled Faith with an inner glow.

"Tell me how important I am," she whispered, taking a small sip of her drink and fixing him with a sly, challenging look over the rim of her glass. She'd angled herself so that she faced the window and her flirtatious manner would not be observed. They'd not have long to be alone together.

"I need you like the earth needs the rain, like the birds need the nectar, like...a blank canvas needs a story. You're mine, Faith. My story, my sustenance, my inspiration."

"Inspiration?" She cocked her head, loving his willingness to elaborate, conscious that too much longer alone together might be dangerous. But then, she'd been crucial to him carrying off the prize. People would understand their solidarity for now. They were a team.

They'd always be a team.

"You are good and pure and honest. That's what inspires me. You're unlike any woman I've ever met."

"I'm sure you've met many women just as good and pure and honest." That was true enough.

He shook his head. "You're different. You are without guile. I love that about you. I look at you, and I see someone who would defend principle to the end."

Faith held up her hand, uncomfortable now. "Crispin, it's easy to believe the best when you're—"

"In love?" He took her hand and kissed the back of it before Faith pulled it back quickly. She tried to speak but he said, "You think I've had too much to drink perhaps? You're afraid that people will observe us? Why? Because you're afraid of the future? We are destined to be together, Faith. And we will be."

"You sound confident. I hope you're right." Her heart felt very full, but also very heavy suddenly.

"We shall be married as soon as I can organise a special licence." Now that she considered it, his eyes did seem unusually bright.

"A special licence is what's needed to elope?" she queried. Three weeks was the earliest they could be married in the usual way after having the banns put up in their respective parishes. For Faith, this was entirely impractical, so she was relieved Crispin had not even considered that idea.

"When I leave for Germany in two weeks, it will be with you as my wife."

"But it would still be a secret?"

"Are you certain you don't want your parents to attend? Not even one of your sisters?"

Faith shook her head. "They'll petition you for money. Oh Crispin, you don't know my family. They're impoverished, and the only reason I was given a few weeks in London was because Papa had ideas I could snare a duke."

"So, you think he'd be disappointed you snared only me?"

Faith coloured. "His excitement would be mortifying. If you love me, you won't bring my family into it. Please, Crispin."

"I do love you and I'm marrying you, not your family. You're right; it would be best if my father knew nothing of it until time had passed and I'd cemented my reputation doing what's required in Germany."

"Ah, Mr Westaway, there you are! Lord Athlone is anxious to meet you. Miss Montague." The new arrival offered Faith a cursory nod before drawing Crispin away, but not before Faith had recognised the curiosity and assessment in his eyes.

Of course, everyone would be wondering what Faith was to Crispin, and any more time spent alone in corners would have tongues wagging, which she could do without when it came to exciting the undesired curiosity of Crispin's father, should it get back to him.

But in terms of reinforcing to Lady Vernon that Faith was making inroads into her task of winning Crispin's heart for Mrs Gedge's evil plans, it was ideal.

"Mr Westaway seemed reluctant to relinquish you in order to meet Lord Athlone."

"He loves me." Faith paused in the midst of pulling the pins from her hair and viewed Lady Vernon with interest in the reflection of the looking glass. "Madly, deeply, unreasonably." She smiled. "I have him," she added slowly. "Are you pleased? After all, you'll get your money now."

"My loyalty is towards Mrs Gedge. I was more concerned that her three-year investment in you should be adequately repaid. Her desire to see justice done through you is more important to me than the pin money I shall receive to compensate me for the dreary time I've had chaperoning you about the place." Lady Vernon smoothed her black skirts over her knees. "You have to break his heart now, of course. That is, once you've proved beyond a doubt that you do have his heart."

"A pile of letters. You didn't guess, did you?" Faith hugged herself. She wanted to pretend ingenuousness. It would be her defence. Lady Vernon mustn't know that Faith was secretly plotting to forgo her own payment in order to disappear from the country without trace.

Lady Vernon sent her a glance laced with suspicion. "And how will you break his heart? You never actually discussed that part, did you?"

Faith shrugged. "He wants to run away with me. I shall disappear. With my money. With the money Mrs Gedge has promised me, and that is my payment for working for her for three years with the end agreement being all or nothing." Faith shook her hair free and wandered to the window. She stared out at the sun. "Mrs Gedge will have all the evidence she needs. Mr Westaway is a very passionate correspondent." She sighed. "And I shall have my freedom. At last."

"You speak as if you've been under ball and chain, when most girls in your position could only dream of what you've had: a roof over your head, an education, fine clothes, an introduction to society, all so that you might know how to behave."

"Oh yes, and I'm very grateful. I've made the most of all that she has insisted it suits her to bestow upon me...*as her slave.*"

She took a few steps into the centre of the room and presented her back to Lady Vernon so that she could help unlace her. It was good to treat the old termagant like a servant; the way she looked upon Faith.

"So, you have no gratitude for Mrs Gedge? None for taking you out of poverty and giving you the tools to prosper?"

"I'm grateful that I now have manners and know how to use a knife and fork properly. But not for the years I languished in a brothel where I was surrounded by nothing but misery." She closed her eyes. "Each night it was like listening to my potential punishment. The moans of the gentlemen; the pretended cries of ecstasy of the girls—my friends—before they'd weep their eyes out and tell me everything the next morning. It was a constant reminder that that was my fate if I should fail at my task. And now I am about to fulfil it; fulfil my destiny. It is a joyous moment."

Lady Vernon stared at Faith as she moved around to help her remove her gown.

"And you have no regrets?"

Faith raised her eyebrows. "Regrets? For gaining my freedom? Why, I am fashioned in your own image, Lady Vernon. My heart is made of stone."

Lady Vernon turned her with a light hand on her shoulders and smiled her first real smile. At least, that's what Faith thought it was until the woman said, "And so tonight I shall help you disappear, Faith, for of course that is the only way to fulfil Mrs Gedge's decree, which is what you've just told me you're in the process of doing."

Faith managed to smile. With every ounce of willpower, she kept her mouth steady and her voice even as she replied, "You'd really do that? Help me? Though, of course, when I have the money I'm owed, I can get as far away as I want."

"But he would find you, and that would not be pleasant for you. It would not further Mrs Gedge's aims. No, have no fear, Mrs Gedge knew you would succeed, and she has everything in hand. You will be spirited away to a safe house, just for a short time because, as you say, you've earned your freedom. But it will be necessary; I'm sure you'll agree. For everyone concerned."

Faith blinked, smiled, and blinked again. She took a few steps to the bed and sat down with as much grace as she could before Lady Vernon said, "Now, where are those love letters you've received from Mr Westaway?" She held out her hand. "Mrs Gedge will naturally want to see evidence though I could vouch for the truth. You don't think I've been as blind as I've pretended, do you?"

"I have them in my escritoire. I'll...fetch them for you in the morning. I'm very tired, you know. It has been an awfully big day."

"I think we should well get it over and done with, Faith. Give them to me now so that you might sleep in longer without troubling yourself over it in the morning." Lady Vernon's bright tone was so false Faith felt like calling her out on it, but she could not afford to unleash even a suggestion of anger; not even a hint that she was feeling suddenly beleaguered and frightened and as far from being in control as she ever had.

She knew when she was beaten, so she forced herself to rise and go to the small writing desk in the corner of the room. They were in a bundle, tied up with red ribbon, and the very sight of them made her heart sing before it dropped like a stone to the pit of her stomach.

What did Mrs Gedge intend doing with her? Where would she take her? No, Faith had to be prepared. She wasn't going to go with anyone, anywhere. Except Crispin. She'd pledged her love to him, and to him she would be faithful until the end.

When she turned, having picked up the bundle with all the reverence that such true and honest sentiment deserved, Lady Vernon was standing right behind her, hand outstretched, a speculative look in her eye.

"Ah, just imagine…" Her own attitude was reverential as she took possession of the only testament to loving feeling Faith had ever been shown. But Faith couldn't snatch them back. She had to be so very careful to hide her feelings. And she managed, for it's what she'd been trained to do her entire life.

Lady Vernon scanned the pages. She chuckled. "So, he really did fall hard for you, Faith. You were so sly I wasn't quite sure what was happening behind my back. And behind closed bedchamber doors. I'm sure you put into practice, admirably, everything you've learned from all the harlots with whom you've associated these past years." She fingered the letters, stroking them as she spoke, while Faith battled the urge to fly at her, whisk them from her and scrape her across the face with catlike claws, if only she had them. Instead, she whispered, "That was unnecessary, Lady Vernon. It makes me wonder who, here, is the real lady."

"You've done well, Faith."

Mrs Gedge smiled at Faith from across the table. Pots overflowing with luxuriant foliage and crystal chandeliers endowed the room with an opulence Faith found slightly overwhelming, in much the same way she'd been overwhelmed the first time Mrs Gedge had brought her to Claridges a little more than three years before.

"Not only have you blossomed into the great beauty I suspected you would become, but you also had the intelligence and cunning I saw in you when we made our acquaintance."

Faith smiled dutifully.

"Furthermore, you have conducted yourself with the grace and sophistication of the most well-brought-up debutante. And yet you've not allowed your fancies to get the better of you. No, you have shown that you have a will and determination as rigid as mine, and a heart that is just as hard." She leaned back in her chair and put the tips of her gloved hands together as she contemplated Faith. "So, are you excited to receive your reward?"

A little part of Faith's heart leaped at the prospect of an independent fortune. Five hundred pounds was beyond imaginable. She could set herself up for life with careful maintenance of such a sum. And then she could find Crispin, and this would be her dowry.

But that would not work anymore.

She'd chosen love over independence, and for that, she could afford no delays.

"Men hold the purse strings, and despite modern advances, a woman is still beholden to the males in her life for everything. Yet you, Faith, will call the shots, as they say in my country. I don't wonder you're excited. So very ready to break this man's heart and claim your reward? I wonder how you plan to do that, Faith? Lady Vernon says you've been playing your cards very close to your chest. Well, we shall talk about it in the morning. It's late." She pushed back her chair, signifying that their tête-à-tête was at an end.

"And Lady Vernon is waiting for you. She has a special surprise, too. After all, tomorrow is the beginning of a new chapter in all our lives.

Faith had no choice but to rise when Mrs Gedge did. She was aware of the flickering interest of the other diners, for there was undeniably something arresting about the wealthy American woman that went beyond her sumptuous dress. Her auburn hair, streaked with grey, gleamed beneath the bright lights of the restaurant, like the diamonds of her choker. Her ageing skin was lustrous, and her teeth were small and sharp and very white for a woman in her fifth decade.

"Mr Westaway is basking in the glory of his sudden notori-ety. He is being recognised for what he's always wanted—his talent. If only his father would appreciate him for it, too, the young man could be no happier. But you are his compensation for the lack of family support. In you, he has found something to love that loves him back. He thinks you are his rock; his salvation." Mrs Gedge chuckled as they wandered towards the double doors. "My Constancia could have been all that and more to him, if only he had let her. If only he'd been prepared to accept her as one of his set. But men like Mr Westaway are leery of outsiders, Faith. Outsiders like my Constancia. Outsiders like you, although he doesn't know it yet."

Faith glanced from a table of diners staring at them to Mrs Gedge's granite-like eyes. The pieces were starting to fall into place. "You sponsored the prize so he had a greater height from which to fall?"

Mrs Gedge looked satisfied. "I did indeed, Faith. But surely you guessed that long ago. Just as you guessed at my motive."

"To punish Mr Westaway for not falling in love with Miss Constancia? Your daughter..." She remembered the head-strong, beautiful, often rude and thoughtless young woman she'd been employed to serve three years ago.

"I did, Faith. Mr Westaway and Constancia were the perfect couple. But he spurned her, you know. Belittled her because she was not of his set. Oh, on first appearances he's every young woman's dream: handsome and charming, in line for a title and a fortune, earnest and ardent, intelligent and artistic. But at heart, he's like all the young men of his kind—completely unwilling to accept an outsider like my Constancia, even with a grand fortune."

She hooked Faith's hand in her arm and patted it in a motherly fashion as they wove their way through the restaurant. The doors opened, and the evening breeze blew in to greet them. A conveyance would soon arrive for Mrs Gedge. She would have made arrangements for Faith too, and no doubt that meant being conveyed back to Lady Vernon's.

But Mrs Gedge's unkind assessment hung heavily in the air. This was not how Mr Westaway was. Faith knew that, yet how much did Mrs Gedge really know him?

"So, Faith, tomorrow you will attend the ceremony to publicly honour Mr Westaway. You will be the shining star at his right hand, and you will be fêted and lauded. But that is not the path to freedom, Faith. You're clever enough to know that. Only you have the power to chart your own course. And, Mr Westaway's affections will be transient. You know that, also. He will not forgive your past and your lie. No love is that strong." She looked fondly at Faith as her carriage drew up. "So that is why I am confident you're going to visit me for that very large cheque I am looking forward to giving you."

Mrs Gedge raised her chin and adjusted the fur stole about her neck, no doubt as much to block out the cold as to hide the crepey neck which gave away her age. She squeezed the tips of Faith's fingers lightly.

"Enjoy your last evening together with this young man. Make him wring every last drop of joy from it, too. I shall think of you both…and the happiness that my Constancia might have enjoyed had she not died."

A vision of the crimson-red rose petals drifted across Faith's mind. It was Mrs Gedge's way of calling forth the last image Mr Westaway would have had of her. She realised that now. In a bath filled with the blood that pumped from the wrists Miss Constancia had sliced.

On the top step outside the hotel as the wind ruffled her hair, Faith finally understood why Mrs Gedge wished for vengeance against Mr Westaway and why she'd chosen Faith.

It had been Faith who'd shown Miss Constancia Gedge the secret entrance to the guest room that Mr Westaway would be occupying that weekend. Faith's reward would be Miss Constancia's gold and garnet bracelet. Miss Constancia had promised.

Faith had known nothing of any of the guests that were spending the weekend with the Gedge's, though she'd suspected Miss Constancia had lost her heart to someone on the invitation list. Why else would she ask Faith to help her to slip into a gentleman's bedchamber wearing nothing but a diaphanous, cream silk peignoir?

Faith was unaware of the extent to which her mistress was unhinged by her romantic entanglement—her unrequited feelings.

But when Miss Constancia had been rejected, she'd killed herself in Mr Westaway's own bathtub.

Mrs Gedge was already heading towards the carriage, the doors of which had been opened by the footman standing at the bottom of the stairs.

"Come along now, Faith," Mrs Gedge exhorted her, and Faith moved forward reluctantly, realising the older woman wished her to take a seat inside the carriage beside her.

Patting Faith's hand as they rounded the street corner, and the horses set off at a more even trot, the older woman said upon a sigh, "You must have guessed by now the association between my daughter, Constancia, and Mr Westaway. That I have sought to use you to avenge his poor treatment of her that led to her death."

Faith said nothing as she stared into the darkness, turning her head slightly to observe Mrs Gedge's sharp-featured profile as she listened to the crackling of a piece of parchment the American drew out of her reticule and held up as they passed the glow of a street lamp.

"I do not need to see to read the last words he penned to her." Her tone had grown tighter, and there was a bitterness in the delivery that had been absent in her former breezy manner towards Faith.

"I know your daughter's death was a great blow, Mrs Gedge." Faith chose her words with difficulty. "But she died by her own hand." It was not the moment to declare that Mr Westaway was blameless. Mrs Gedge's trust in Faith depended upon her belief that Faith would follow through with the long-held agreement between them.

"My daughter believed she could do nothing else when her honour had been compromised to such a degree, that public shame and humiliation were inevitable after Mr Westaway reneged on the pledge made between them."

Mrs Gedge held out the letter for Faith to take while she began to relay its contents.

"First, he told Constancia that she was charming, every man's dream, but that he had intended marrying his childhood sweetheart upon her twenty-first birthday, which was four years hence. That is, a few months from now, Faith."

Faith tensed at the sympathetic hand Mrs Gedge placed briefly on her thigh before she went on. "When Constancia and Mr Westaway first met, it was like a flame was ignited in both of their hearts. I never wanted Constancia to marry an Englishman. At least, not one who had relatively few expectations and no title, when I knew that with Constancia's fortune, she could have married a Rockefeller back in America or an earl at the very least."

She sent Faith a scornful look. "But Constancia was not one to listen to reason. No, not my beautiful, wilful girl. The two lovers had become far too inflamed by their feelings for one another and their intention to run away together before…I don't know what happened." Mrs Gedge's face was a mask of derision now. "Perhaps his ardour actually did cool overnight. Perhaps he was contacted by his childhood sweetheart and persuaded to adhere to a previous, more compelling promise which prompted this letter." Snatching it back from Faith, she tapped it with a gloved finger. "But his words scored grooves of the deepest despair in my Constancia, and she, who obviously knew how to gain secret entrance to his chamber, and you will attest to that, Faith, I know! went there to persuade him otherwise. When he remained unmoved, she did what a young woman will do who is compromised, embarrassed…ruined." The word was a whisper, a half hiss, a half choke, while Mrs Gedge's face was a mask of malice. "She slit her wrists in his bathtub. Yes, Mr Westaway returned to find his former lover dead…by *his* hand."

Faith didn't know what to say to this. She remembered that night as if it were written in indelible ink upon her brain. Mrs Gedge had come upon Faith picking up Miss Constancia's bracelet in the young lady's bedchamber and gazing at it with indecision. Miss Constancia had promised it to fifteen-year-old Faith in a hurried whisper if Faith could help her gain admittance to a young man's bedchamber. There had been several young men staying at the house for that particular Friday to Saturday. Faith had not seen Mr Westaway, for she surely would have remembered him.

Now, Mrs Gedge was declaring, not only that Mr Westaway had once been a faithless lover to her daughter, but that Mr Westaway had all but forced the young woman's hand in taking her own life.

"Why did you not tell me this before you instructed me on what I must do with regard to Mr Westaway?" she asked.

"I felt that if you held him in such aversion, the naturally occurring mutual interest might be inhibited. You knew, of course, that he must be sacrificed, and you were a willing accomplice in this."

Faith hated knowing this was true. As much as she hated being so receptive to the woman's words, right now. A fire was raging in her breast. Had Mr Westaway really seduced and then abandoned an innocent young woman?

"So, Faith, I cannot have a similar fate befalling you, can I?" Her tone was concerned. "Not the girl I've nurtured all these years. My own proxy daughter."

Faith blinked. This was hardly what she supposed Mrs Gedge considered her. Mrs Gedge might have paid for an education, a wardrobe of fine clothes, and a roof over her head, but that had all been for her own self-interest. She'd never made a secret, from the beginning, that Faith was nothing more to her than a means to an end—a method of betrayal.

The way Mrs Gedge now laid out the supposed facts was far more disturbing than Faith might ever have thought.

If she'd truly thought about it at all.

THEY WERE OUTSIDE LADY VERNON'S LODGINGS NOW, AND THE door to the old dowager's house was being opened by a servant. Light spilled over the portico as Faith was helped to disembark, swishing her pink and black swathed skirts behind her.

She wondered what she'd wear when, tomorrow, Faith stepped out on Mr Westaway's arm to a no-doubt rapturous welcome from an adoring public.

Would she quiz him about the letter? About everything Mrs Gedge had told her surrounding his relationship with Miss Constancia? Or would she follow through with their own escape plan, trusting that this time Crispin really was in love with her, and that he would be waiting when it was time for them to slip away? What of this childhood sweetheart? Was she still lurking in the wings? Or was she a figure of Mrs Gedge's imagination?

Yet, she had seen the letter briefly, when there was

enough light to persuade her that it was Crispin's handwriting. And she had read the sentence that mentioned Constancia.

Faith's heart was heavy, and her mind was in turmoil as she climbed under the covers of her bed that night.

But as she drifted off to sleep, she was comforted to recall the light in Crispin's eyes when he had bid her farewell. And all the other times when he'd gazed upon her with a look that was so real and so intense, she could not entertain a shadow of doubt that he truly loved her and meant every promise he'd ever made.

Well, tomorrow he would have to make one final pledge for her to believe him. If he truly loved her, he would not promise to run away with her only to then leave her in the lurch.

If he agreed to run away with her in order to be secretly married before he departed for Germany, she'd know his heart was true.

CHAPTER 21

"**M**rs Gedge organised for me to wear this?" Faith stared at the exquisite white and silver gown laid out on the bed in her chamber in Lady Vernon's house, adorned with swathes of white velvet bows, and compared it to the plain finery she'd worn previously. Wondered, also, if she'd have to give it back.

But Lady Vernon, who was smiling for a change, said, "Mrs Gedge recognises when a job has been well done. This is your reward. To step out in style so you can compete with the most well-endowed heiresses. Mr Westaway won't be able to keep his eyes off you. Or his hands." She sent Faith a beady look. "No doubt he'll find a way to spirit you away into a back room for a short while. And no doubt you'll relish the opportunity."

Lady Vernon's mind was like a gutter, Faith decided, though refrained from saying so.

"It's your chance to entrench what he'll miss for the rest of his life. For you will leave him shortly afterwards, and he will forever wonder why. You will break his heart."

"While I go on to enjoy the happiness that is my reward,

bolstered by a handsome cheque from Mrs Gedge? It's a fair exchange." Faith tried to summon enthusiasm as her mind whirled over how she might make her own escape.

"After tonight, when he is happily thinking of your glorious years ahead together, you will be spirited away to somewhere he can't find you." Lady Vernon chuckled at Faith's blank look and traced a fingertip reverentially down the front of the gown upon the bed. "Ah, I wore a gown such as this, once. Many years ago." Her expression softened. "It earned me a marriage proposal, too." She looked up at Faith. "You surely didn't think we'd simply abandon you, my dear girl. After all you've done for us and knowing that Mr Westaway has no intention of keeping true to any pledges he might have made you. He would not have followed through. Indeed, he would not. We are looking after you, as you deserve, and we have a place for you to hide while poor Mr Westaway wonders what has become of you." She straightened and clapped her hands. In an instant, her dresser had materialised, and Lady Vernon put her hand on the doorknob.

"You will be a sight for sore eyes, my dear. Tonight will be a special night, indeed."

❧

"ONE COULD TELL SHE WAS A BEAUTY WHEN SHE WAS FLOATING in that lake wearing what might be mistaken for a nightdress, but look at her now."

The chuckle that followed the young reporter's comment was the first distinct piece of conversation Faith heard as she passed in a seeming daze through the packed reception hall.

Crispin disengaged himself from his conversation with Miss Eaves and Sir Albion, intercepting Faith a few feet away.

For a second, they halted and stared at one another while the crowd pulsed around them.

"I have never seen a woman as stunning as you look tonight," he whispered, his eyes raking her with unbridled admiration. "And all too soon I have to give you up to all the other people who want to similarly compliment you and be seen with the latest toast to London town."

Faith glanced about her and saw they were garnering a good deal of interest and that his words were true. If they were ever to succeed in slipping away together, she'd better not allow him to be too singular in his attentions.

"People are looking," she whispered. "Oh Crispin, we won't have a moment to ourselves this evening, and I'd so wanted to talk to you." Her chest tightened, and the knot of worry grew.

"And I to you, my dearest. We must get married before I leave for Germany. You are so right, and I've been caught up in this…frenzy, fielding probing questions from father who is hardly delighted, I'm afraid. He threatens to come down to London before I depart for Germany when that had not been the plan." He glanced about him, his frown creased. The reception hall was a sumptuous location for an event like this, but there were no antechambers where they might be private.

Faith saw Sir Albion's wife turn from her conversation with her husband. She was bearing down on her, when Crispin said in a rushed whisper, "Your chaperone seemed only too happy to give us licence to be alone together, before. Is it possible?"

His words trailed off and Faith tugged his sleeve, urging him to finish his sentence. The suggestion had to come from Crispin. Faith could not be seen to be too desperate.

He raked back his hair, smiled at the advancing woman and whispered, "There is an inn not far from here that I know can be accessed from a side street so that you might be completely unobserved in entering. The Green Whistle. Could you possibly meet me there when tonight's proceedings are finished?"

"Do you mean…we'd run away together, tonight, Crispin?" She was fairly certain he didn't mean this, but he needed to give her some idea of his plans on the timing of their elopement.

"I'm not in a position to do that yet, my darling. One more day, and everything will be organised to my satisfaction."

"What is so important to organise tomorrow?"

"I have interviews; my photograph will be taken, and there are many wonderful things that will happen to entrench my reputation as an artist that have been planned for tomorrow. Oh Faith, you have no idea." His voice caught with emotion, and Faith understood the enormity of achieving one's life's ambition. Wasn't she within a hair's breadth of achieving hers?

Yet…

"I'm sorry, but we can't do it tonight, Faith." Concern wiped away his ebullience, and he leaned forward slightly. "It's too soon, though you surely can't imagine I'm prevaricating because I'm not sincere."

She shook her head, though she wasn't sure what to think. "I shall be at The Green Whistle later tonight. Somehow, I'll contrive it."

"Tell the servant who lets you in that you have room bespoken in the name of Mrs Emily Hardwicke." He glanced at her hands as if he would whisk them up and kiss them with an ardour to match that that was in his voice.

And then Lady Vernon was upon them; her gushing praise of Crispin's prodigious talent bringing their conversation to an end.

~

THE SOIREE SEEMED TO LAST FOREVER, WHILE FAITH DID HER best to conduct herself appropriately. She was a shy debutante with a modicum of intelligence, as far as the rest of the world was concerned, and her efforts to project that image were aided by Lady Vernon, who made an apparent attempt to draw Faith out of her shyness.

"Answer Miss Eaves's question, Faith dearest," she said with contrived gentleness on one occasion when Faith was faced with a volley of queries on her impressions of London.

"It can feel overwhelming to a country girl," Faith said, glancing at Crispin on the other side of the room, in earnest discussion with a group of gentlemen. Her body throbbed at the thought of being alone with him in just a couple of short hours.

"And you have brothers and sisters, I gather. A few of them. What do they think of your success? What a shame they could not be here." Miss Eaves's pencil sped across the page.

"Everything happened so fast with the announcement of Mr Westaway winning such a grand prize they did not have time to make the journey." Faith was careful to avoid mentioning anything that might indicate even the location of her family. They were sunk in rusticity and never heard the London news until the greatest events were at least a month old. They certainly would make no connection between their Faith and the glorious creature she'd become.

The gathering began to disperse towards midnight, and Lady Vernon took Faith's arm, drawing her towards the door after they'd said their farewells.

"You have arranged a final assignation? The moment to cement what you are to him? To exact the greatest revenge when you are whisked away forever tomorrow?" Her beady eyes roamed over Faith's expression as if she were looking for guile. She gave Faith's wrist a squeeze. "Ah, but I'm sorry that it had to end this way though there really was no other, was there? The young man is enjoying his greatest moment of glory, and your secret visit to him will fill his heart with triumphant joy. He thinks he is on the cusp of life, the pinnacle of attainment, but that is how Mrs Gedge planned it. There is no more acute suffering than to have reached such dizzy heights before such a crushing fall."

Foreboding sliced through Faith. Was this really all Mrs Gedge had planned for Crispin? Was the extent of her loathing for him so great that destroying his happiness was her only plan? Or did she intend Crispin's descent to be an even greater one?

She forced a smile. "He will be distraught," she murmured. "For he loves me greatly. I have done everything Mrs Gedge would have me do. He is enslaved."

She had to believe that.

For if she couldn't count on the security of his love, she had nothing.

But in the private room at The Green Whistle, Crispin's ardour and sincerity could not be in doubt. Instead of swooping upon her with words of enthusiasm as to the astonishing reception he'd received that evening, his words were all for her.

"I couldn't have done it without you, Faith! You were the most glittering star in the firmament, my exquisite girl." He swept her into his embrace and covered her face and neck in kisses. "Because of you, I'm where I've always wanted to be in life. My work…my painting has been more important to me than anything. That is, until I met you." He cupped her face and stared into her eyes. "You think I'm not sincere about running away with you?" He dropped his voice. "We both have good reason to marry in secret, though I believe mine is greater." Then a smile tugged at his mouth. "I don't care about your family hounding me for what I can do for them, financially or otherwise, for I would gladly do it. I would do anything that would please you, Faith. But my father would put everything in my way to prevent me marrying you, Faith, and that's the truth. He's always wanted me to marry the daughter of his best friend, our neighbour, and there was a time when I thought I could do it. But my heart was not engaged."

"And the young lady? Is she in expectation of a marriage proposal?"

"No. We've known one another since we were children, and a match between us was once considered desirable by our parents. I'm sure she's as relieved as I am that the idea has not been mentioned for several years."

"So, there've been no other young ladies who've... entranced you?"

Crispin laughed and set her at arm's length. "I suppose you need to get the full measure of me before you make your final commitment to becoming my wife. All right—the truth..." His expression was suddenly serious. It was as if all the joy had drained out of him.

"Oh Crispin, there has!" Faith cried, but he pulled her back into his arms, shaking his head, fiercely.

"There was a young lady with whom you might say I was unwillingly involved a few years ago." He hesitated.

Lord, was he referring to Miss Gedge? Faith froze in his arms and willed him to go on without prompting questions that might seem odd to him.

But he seemed inclined to talk.

"She was a lovely girl. Bright, golden hair, a little like yours though she had not your serenity, your beauty. In fact, there was nothing serene about her. She was determined to make a catch, and she was...what is the term? Brash?"

"So, not a shy and sweet young thing from the provinces."

"Oh no, she was an American heiress looking for a title. She could have done better than me. Her mother hoped she would. But she fell for me, and it took very little on my part to make her believe we were destined to be together forever."

"So, you gave her hope?"

"Oh Faith, you know I'm not like that. I never believed I did at the time. But then she started writing me passionate love letters. I didn't know what to do. I told her that I was going to marry my childhood sweetheart. That my father had arranged it years ago, and this is how matters went in our world. I tried to make it less wounding and put the blame on me, but she was persistent."

Faith felt him shrinking away from her until he gently extricated himself from their embrace and went to the window. Softly, he said, "She killed herself because of me. You need to know that, Faith."

Faith ran to him and wrapped her arms around him, more joyful than she could show, for she believed he was nothing but truthful in his portrayal of the affair with Miss Constancia Gedge. It all made complete sense, now.

"If it's so painful to you, please, say nothing more, Crispin." She squeezed him tight and Crispin kissed the top of her head, tilting up her face to say with concern, "You're crying, Faith. What is it?"

"I haven't been entirely truthful with you, Crispin, and if you truly love me enough to want to run away with me, then I need to tell you something."

She felt him freeze, before the inevitable thaw, because of course he loved her, and that meant he trusted her…

Only, would he still love her when she had come to the end of her confession?

"What is it you want to tell me, Faith?"

The tone was encouraging, loving still, but for how much longer?

She took a breath, struggling for the truth she owed him. "I'm more than just a penniless debutante looking to make a good match."

He registered this with a squeeze and a murmur. "No, you're so much more than that, Faith. Of course, I know it."

She heard the rattle of a wagon on the cobbled street below the window and waited for silence. "My family origins are obscure. Far more obscure than I've led you to believe. Yes, I have nine brothers and sisters, and parents who will indeed touch you for every penny you might have and that's because they have nothing. They're yeoman, country stock. Some would call them peasants, and I would be one of them had it not been for a rich benefactress who gave me an education when I was in service."

She pulled away and looked at him, tortured by the extent of what she'd divulged to no one else. What would he think, not only in view of the fact he'd been lied to, but that she was so very humble?

He looked surprised. His frown and the way he was chewing his bottom lip were not signs she liked.

"You lied to me, Faith? About this? About your family?"

Faith twisted her hands together. Oh lord, if he were upset about her lying about this, how would he react to everything else?

Trying not to cry, she whispered, "When I got the opportunity to be your model; when Lady Vernon persuaded you to paint me, I never thought it would lead to this. I had the right credentials for that. For an artist's model. I could be silent; I could be enigmatic. What did it matter what else I was or wasn't? You'd made it so very clear that even if I'd had the slightly more elevated background I'd told you I had, I still could not be considered suitable in your father's eyes, and therefore not in yours." She pulled her cloak about her shoulders and began to pace. Would he send her away? She thought she'd die of a broken heart if he did. Quietly, she went on, "I didn't trouble myself about telling you the truth, because I imagined that if I were to be given more work for other painters my real background would play against me. But then I fell in love with you, Crispin, and you loved me back. I pressed you into showing your real feelings, and then pressed you even more to run away with me."

Leaning against the wall, she dropped her head. "I don't expect that, now. I'm not here to beg you to run away with me because the truth changes everything. I've lied to you, and I am not the woman you thought me."

A barking dog outside; a quarrel between a couple on the pavement, and the crackling fire were the only sounds as Faith waited for Crispin's response. When she glanced at him, his sloped shoulders and bent head as she stared into the flames suggested he was as deeply aggrieved as any man could be.

But when he turned suddenly to face her, there was a glow in his expression that was so at odds with the dire scenario Faith had conjured up, that her heart leapt with hope.

"Do you love me, Faith?"

She clenched her fists. "More than I love anything on this earth." And it was the truth.

"And you would marry me if *I* had nothing? Nothing, that is, other than prospects. I mean, would you love me if I were disowned, for example? If my father cut me out of his will?"

Faith hadn't considered this possibility, but it honestly didn't matter for the fact was, she would. She'd grown up with nothing, and while her expectations had been altered by the events of the past three years, she didn't suppose Crispin meant that living in a hovel was a likely outcome.

Nevertheless, she'd do even that, if she had to.

But she said, "As long as you had enough to feed me…and our family, it would be enough for me."

Tensely, she waited.

Then in two long strides, Crispin was holding her tightly in his arms, and his mouth was on hers as he communicated so very thoroughly the extent of his love.

CHAPTER 22

He had nearly everything for which he'd ever dreamed. His hard work, conducted for so long in secret, then put on hold while he obeyed his father's strictures, had now made him a sensation.

And his love for the woman who inspired his creative impulses, and filled him with joy and the greatest desire to protect her from anything at all unpleasant in the world, was returned.

So, when he received news that his father intended travelling to London the following day, Crispin should have felt in a strong position to defend his decision to pick up a brush and paint.

Unfortunately, he had every fear that his father would question at what cost to his real career this ten-day hiatus had taken.

As he directed his valet on what to pack in the trunk that would go ahead to Germany, his chief fear was that his father was about to burst into his townhouse in his usual bombastic manner and do his best to destroy his hopes and dreams.

He would not succeed. No, Lord Maxwell would not

destroy Crispin's future happiness. Crispin's future was his own to decide.

Which was all the more reason to make tonight the night he whisked Faith off, so they could be secretly married in advance of whatever objections Lord Maxwell might have to his son's choice of wife.

It would not be a marriage that could be publicly disclosed.

Well, they were both in agreement on this point. They'd travel on the same packet, but not as husband and wife. Crispin would take up his posting, and in the weeks that followed, they'd contrive an excuse whereby she could be introduced as a suitable contender for his suit.

He'd been dismayed by her revelation; there was no doubt about that. She'd portrayed herself as someone she wasn't, and yet the essence of her was pure and true, and that's all that mattered to Crispin right now.

Now that he thought about it, perhaps it was better that she had divorced herself so completely from her peasant roots. She could pass as the finest lady in the land, and that's what was required if she were to be accepted by society as a diplomat's wife.

Besides, having such a fine actress might very well suit Crispin's purposes, he thought as he nodded for the first trunk to be sealed shut. It was pushed against the wall of his bedchamber and, like a dozen others currently stored in a spare bedchamber, it would travel ahead and be in situ when he reached the handsome dwelling in Leipzig that had been bespoken on his behalf.

Crispin moved about his room, staring at the familiar objects that made it so masculine. He imagined a lady's dressing table by the window; its mahogany surface littered with feminine objects. A silver-backed hairbrush like the one Crispin had already bought for Faith. A row of little bottles whose contents he couldn't begin to imagine though he could imagine the setting. He'd like to paint the beautiful Faith seated at her dressing table, having her hair done, perhaps.

A surge of great affection edged with desire made him straighten and try to cast his mind back to what he must do. The fact that Faith's apparent shyness concealed a sharp intelligence and keen observation powers might indeed make her the perfect helpmate.

He certainly had no doubts about the wisdom of marrying her. However, with so much to do in so little time, he had to put aside his desire to spend every moment possible in her arms.

"Benson, do you suppose my father will go riding before he gets in his carriage to come down to London and give me a verbal whipping?"

"That would depend if he wants to take the edge off his mood, sir."

Benson could be relied upon to be honest.

"And do you suppose this mood you speak of will be predominantly prideful or…not?"

Benson rose having secured the strap buckle. He gave the wooden trunk a firm pat for good measure.

"Knowing his lordship, sir, I'd say the latter were more likely. Not that it'll be of consequence, for soon you'll be departing for foreign shores, so there'll be little more that your father has to say that will greatly impact you, sir." He gave a short bow. "If that'll be all, sir."

"No, that is not all, Benson. I need your opinion on whether I will cut a more sartorial figure in the green or burgundy striped waistcoat."

"If you wish to impress the gentlemen, I would suggest the burgundy."

"And if it is not the gentlemen I wish to impress?"

Benson smiled a little. "Then I shall lay out the green waistcoat for you this evening, sir. What time will you be going out?"

This time it was Crispin's turn to smile. How could he not as he contemplated the happy outcome of this evening's wilful escapade—certainly wilful in his father's eyes. For the first time in a long while, he felt ridiculously confident that Faith would win over Lord Maxwell.

When the time was right.

"I shall leave here at eight this evening. Don't wait up for me." No, he and Faith would want a leisurely time to consummate the marriage-to-be that he had absolutely no qualms about contracting now.

"Very good, sir." Benson bowed and backed up a few steps to the doorway where Crispin was surprised to see Carter, the butler, hovering in the passageway before the older man moved on. Crispin moved back to the trunk, turning to glance back through the open door, for the two servants remained outside, apparently conferring with each other. He was on the point of returning to his work when his attention was caught by the expression on Carter's face.

Carter was the archetypal impassive retainer while Benson, the younger man, enjoyed a bit of levity.

There was no sign of levity on Benson's face now, however, as Carter whispered in his ear. In fact, in terms of disgust and horror, it very much resembled Carter's.

And that's when he noticed what had occasioned such altered behaviour as he straightened and took a few steps towards the door.

The two men had their heads bent over a newspaper.

"I think, sir, you ought to see this." Benson cleared his throat as he stalked past Crispin and placed the newspaper upon his writing desk.

The man couldn't seem to meet Crispin's eye and as

Crispin moved forward, a great premonition sweeping away his initial perplexity as he glanced at the headline—*The Elaborate Ruse of the Painter's Muse.*

Dear God, someone had discovered the fact that Faith was not the penniless debutante society believed her to be. The truth was out, and now those well-upholstered society matrons who decided who was acceptable, would be conferring right now as to whether to allow a former servant into their rarefied domains.

He felt sick. Faith had so perfected her role as a well-brought-up lady, that she could have been accepted, without question, anyway.

And now this.

He put his hand over the newspaper article and looked at Benson. "I don't need to read it for she has told me of her past," he said gravely. "Nevertheless, I refuse to hold it against the lady, or to judge her harshly, though I've no doubt my father will."

Benson blinked. In fact, his mobile face betrayed such surprise at Crispin's words that Crispin was angered. He'd not thought the young Benson would be so easily shocked.

"I see you have your own opinion," he said, drawing back his shoulders. "Yet I would suggest you judge her over harshly when she is guilty of no more than your own sister."

This brought a sound of such apoplexy from both Benson and Carter that Crispin's ire was fairly whipped up, but before Crispin could speak, the young servant burst out, "With all due respect, my sister does not even know that... such establishments exist, and if she did, she'd hardly be one to step across the threshold—with all due respect, sir." Benson's nostrils flared and his colour heightened. "And considering your father's long-established enmity with Lord Harkom...well, I can't imagine what he's going to say!"

"What on earth are you talking about, Benson?" Crispin

was more confused than angered by the young man's feisty response. "And what's Lord Harkom got to do with any of this?"

Crispin had no doubt Benson's sister had stepped across the threshold of many a dwelling as humble as the one in which Faith had been brought up.

And yet even as this thought registered, so too did a kernel of fear that he had missed a fundamental piece of what was under discussion.

Carter cleared his throat and tapped the newspaper. His bald pate was sweating. "I think, sir, that as you clearly have not read in its entirety the published facts, it is not my place to acquaint you with what will come as a great shock and perhaps disappointment." His Adam's apple bobbed up and down, and his breathing was laboured. He looked nervously at Benson who said, in halting tones, "Given the fact, sir, that I surmise the green waistcoat was to have been worn to impress the lady in question." His elegant finger tapped the newspaper article that Crispin now pulled more closely towards him, while he considered whether to reprimand Benson on such an appalling impudence as Benson went on, "I think we should perhaps retire and allow you to...digest what has recently come to light.

Clearly, Benson was outraged by the fact that Miss Montague had insinuated herself so thoroughly with the rich and titled.

But Lord Harkom?

Crispin had little liking for Harkom, whom he considered a devious, self-serving creature, and the fact that Faith's name had obviously become mixed up with his to the extent that it had made it into print, was deepening his concern.

"Like my sister I, myself, *naturally* have not stepped over the threshold of this...this..." his colour heightened "... Madame Chambon's, and nor am I suggesting that you know anyone who has, sir." He sent a pointed look at Crispin. "But that a…creature…who has been indentured to the woman who owns such an establishment, who has carried out her evil designs in order to entrap a good man such as yourself… should have insinuated herself into your good offices and become your muse, well, sir, I cannot bring myself to utter the extent of my horror and outrage." His shoulders rose and fell as he struggled to control his feelings while Crispin stared at the two men, confounded, as Benson went on, "But she has been exposed. She and Harkom will no longer be able to carry out the devious plan they no doubt were hatching to cause you ill. Yes, I would go so far as to suggest that you were her quarry from the very beginning, sir. In fact, it is Mr Carter's opinion that this was her very plan, hatched in concert with this…Madame Chambon *and* Lord Harkom, no less. Why, the photograph of the two of them together in that very house says all that needs to be said."

And indeed, after Crispin had pushed away Benson's hand in order to properly make out the photograph that went with the text so damningly summed up by his valet, a great pounding in his ears left him with a feeling akin to being shaken by a monstrously large and glossy cat whose meows of self-satisfied relish indicated his lowliness in the great order of things.

There was his Faith, wearing the simple gown she'd worn when he'd first met her those few short weeks ago, in the arms of a gentleman who looked as if he would like to devour her on the spot. It was little consolation that Faith was looking serious. As if she wanted to be elsewhere. Lord Harkom, as Crispin could now distinguish him, was leering, proprietorial. Like he'd come to the house—yes, Madame Chambon's nunnery—in expectation of securing a great conquest.

And he'd secured Faith.

"You may go now, Benson," Crispin said, tracing the picture with his forefinger, lingering on the damning title of the article which had been penned, he now saw, by Miss Eaves.

Meddling, interfering Miss Eaves, who'd come to London to establish her future at the expense of Crispin's.

The fact that Faith had been ruined in the process was, at this very moment, immaterial. For, in the intensity of this moment of discovery, the enormity of her crimes was laid so bare as to reveal the fact she could have had no real feelings for Crispin.

And that she probably never had.

THERE WAS ROOM FOR ONE MORE DRESS IN HER CARPETBAG. Not that Faith had many that would be appropriate for the life she'd soon be living. How would the wife of a diplomat, a future British envoy, be expected to dress? Something modest would be appropriate in the interim, but after that?

Well, Faith was excellent at research. She'd researched everything that would make her beguiling and differently exciting in Mr Westaway's eyes. Fortunately, it hadn't been hard to find herself excited over international politics while she'd had to stop herself from overdosing on intrigue. The relationship between Germany and Great Britain at the moment was volatile, to say the least, and she was confident she could be a great asset to Crispin.

She could hear Lady Vernon issuing orders to a servant in the passage. Faith dropped in her tooth powder and brush, a thrill of excitement rippling through her. Lady Vernon planned to whisk Faith away later this evening, but by then, Faith would have been whisked away by someone far more exciting. Yes, Crispin had accepted the truth of her altered situation in his eyes. She'd told him the truth of her humble beginnings, and he had still accepted her.

"Mrs Gedge is looking forward to handing over the cheque you so deserve, Faith." Lady Vernon stood in the doorway looking like a smudge of something unpleasant, thought Faith as she glanced from the grey-pallored creature with her yellowing teeth, to the smooth line of her own fashionable princess-line pelisse.

"I'm sure she is. I've done her bidding thoroughly. Mr Westaway will be bereft." Faith's gaze didn't linger on Lady Vernon's face. She returned to her packing and wondered why Lady Vernon still lingered in the doorway. Was she Faith's gaoler now? Faith tried to keep her face impassive. If Lady Vernon wasn't going to let her out of her sight, then Faith would have to climb out of her bedchamber window in the middle of the night to escape. She would do whatever she had to.

"I believe you still have a few gowns and pieces to collect from Madame Chambon's."

Surprised, Faith looked up to see Lady Vernon studying her with interest. "I would be careful of crossing that threshold in daylight. Or any time, for that matter. Perhaps you should send for your possessions."

Faith pretended to consider the option. The term possessions really encompassed only a few trinkets and a ring given her by her grandmother. In total, they were worth very little, but they were all she had to remind her…of a past she wanted to forget.

The only reason she'd especially want to visit would be to say farewell to Charity. The only other real connection she'd made in her life was with Crispin.

He'd opened her heart and poured music into it. She'd become the person she'd always wanted to be: alive, interested, allowing her intelligence free rein.

However, if she were being allowed to leave the house alone to go to Madame Chambon's, it was greater good fortune than she could have hoped for.

"Yes, of course I'll be careful," she said. She glanced through the window at the sun dipping in the blue sky. Before nightfall, Faith would be out of here. Away from Lady Vernon and her life of pretence and subterfuge.

Soon she'd be with Crispin and, if he entertained any doubts, she'd prove to her new husband that a girl brought up in poverty truly could be worthy of a respected diplomat and a celebrated painter. She relished the challenge. She would be the best, most devoted, most educated wife he could wish for.

A little later, Faith stood up from her chair and faced Lady Vernon across the three feet of Aubusson carpet that separated them in the old lady's spartan townhouse.

"It's growing late. Perhaps I should make a quick visit to Madame Chambon's now." Her trunk was packed in her bedchamber, ready to be carried into the carriage that would be called later this evening to take her to Mrs Gedge's, and thence on to an unknown location for an unspecified waiting period. Faith hadn't asked too many questions for she'd never intended travelling that route.

Lady Vernon's change in plans, in that she was no longer visiting a friend and was now going to remain indoors, meant Faith would have to arrange to have her trunk collected later. She had a brush, a change of linen, and a few necessities in a small carpetbag so this would have to suffice.

"Send my regards to Madame Chambon." Lady Vernon looked up from her tatting. "And don't be too long, my girl."

Faith shook her head. This would be the last time she'd see Lady Vernon. And what a relief that was.

"Oh, do give her this now that I've finished with it. It might entertain her." Lady Vernon brandished a newspaper as Faith passed her chair. "Don't stay talking too long. Half an hour is the limit. You're to come right back, for at eleven o' clock tonight you're going on a different journey."

"Yes, Lady Vernon." Faith took the newspaper and hurried out of the room and up the stairs, snatching her carpetbag from her bed and shoving in the newspaper as she pushed aside the curtains and saw her hackney waiting in the cobbled street below.

Freedom.

It was exhilarating. Crispin would be pacing the floorboards at The Green Whistle at nine o' clock, as agreed. They'd parted with regret but excitement too, eager for the new adventure that awaited them both.

With the coins Lady Vernon had given her, Faith paid the driver and pulled her veil down over her face as she entered the premises through the back entrance. Her heart clutched as she remembered the last time she'd come here less than 48 hours before. The night of loving she and Crispin had shared had helped her survive the impatience to be with him.

"Crispin," she whispered, as she slipped through the open door and into what turned out to be an empty parlour.

She was too impatient to sit, so she went to the window and stared down at the traffic below. London had overwhelmed her when Mrs Gedge had brought her here as little more than a child. She'd grown used to it, though, and come to like the anonymity.

What would Germany be like? She couldn't wait to explore it with Crispin.

Catching sight of her reflection in the mirror above the mantelpiece, she saw the tenseness in her eyes. Little wonder. She'd put her future in Crispin's hands, and given up her opportunity to find independence through what Mrs Gedge would have been willing to pay her had she chosen a path of revenge rather than love.

The clock on the landing struck the half hour.

Where was Crispin?

Worry niggled at her as she walked restlessly to the window and back. She'd seek occupation in tidying her hair perhaps. Scrabbling in her carpetbag for the ivory comb, she encountered instead the newspaper she'd forgotten she'd taken to give to Madame Chambon. That would divert her.

She pulled it out and lowered herself on a spindly chair at the round table by the window where she could supplement the fading light by lighting the reading lamp.

It was a respectable newspaper, but as Faith glanced at the front page, she decided it must be filled with enough scandal to entertain Madame Chambon.

The old bawd would be titillated by such salacious pickings as the story behind the scandalous young woman who'd clearly been featured on the front page for parading herself as something pure when her heart was full of sin, if the headline was anything to go by. Faith did not even consider a parallel until Crispin's name caught her eye.

She put her hand over her mouth and gasped. Crispin? What connection did Crispin have to a woman clearly reviled in the press as someone shameless?

And then, as a sensation of stepping into an icy bath passed over her, Faith realised that it was she, herself, who was the subject of the article.

Faith Montague, named and shamed, by a major newspaper. Not only that, photographed in the arms of none other than Lord Harkom. The photograph had been lined up beside a photograph of Crispin's painting of Faith.

She thought she was going to be sick.

It was the picture taken just before Lord Harkom had tried to force himself on her. Just before Faith had been all but forsaken by Lady Vernon for her failure to win Crispin's affections before Mrs Gedge had given Faith her reprieve.

Regardless of what Faith might have been, there was no mistaking the kind of company she kept. The revealing costumes of the other prostitutes at Madame Chambon's proclaimed it brazenly to the world.

Hunched over, she read the article more closely in all its tawdry detail. It detailed her supposed life in scathing detail. Faith had come to London as a penniless country girl; beautiful and cunning. She had fallen quickly into vice, but her exceptional looks and talent for mimicry had earned her the interest of Lord Harkom, who had made her his mistress and, when he'd given her her congè, seen her taken under the wing of a female benefactress who'd set about equipping her with the skills needed to insinuate her way into Mr Westaway's heart.

And all for what?

For revenge.

Revenge for the loss of a daughter whose death this so-called benefactress laid squarely at Mr Westway's door.

So close to the truth, in fact, but so far in its most essential details—Faith had never intended to follow through with a plan that would destroy Crispin.

And Faith had never taken up with anyone before she'd met Crispin. Her beloved Crispin had won her entire loyalty. She'd given up her only chance of independence to be with him.

Panic swirled about her as she digested the implications.

She placed her palms down on the newspaper as if to obliterate the pictures and the content while she stared about the room that would remain empty—but for her.

Crispin had read this. Lady Vernon had given it to her as a sign.

What could Faith do now? She was exposed.

She rose quickly and shoved the newspaper into her

carpetbag, hurrying to the door and pulling down her veil once again.

Where could she go? She couldn't return to Lady Vernon's. The woman had had a part in all this. She'd betrayed Faith. But what about Mrs Gedge? She'd invested heavily in Faith's education for three years. What would she think to know that her minion, Lady Vernon, had betrayed her too?

Only, Faith had no idea how to contact Mrs Gedge directly. They'd only ever met at Claridges Hotel for tea once a month.

She glanced up at the star-studded sky and shivered in the chilly night air.

She was about to hail a hackney but realised she'd not have the funds to pay for it. She'd used the only coins she had, the ones Lady Vernon had given her, to get here.

So, with heavy footsteps, she began to walk.

In the direction of the place she'd called home for three years, and which she'd sold her soul to leave.

～

"Faith, what's brought yer back 'ere," squealed the tweeny, Lizabet, who opened the door to her. At least one person didn't know, she was glad to note.

"Just here to pick up a few belongings and see a few friends. And Madame Chambon."

"You really want to see 'er?" Lizabet grimaced as she led Faith through the gloomy passageway to the salon at the back of the house.

It was early for business, but a handful of the girls lounged about in varying states of dress and undress.

A couple whispered as Faith entered, but Charity

straightened with a smile of genuine pleasure as Faith caught her eye.

Faith crossed the room and lowered herself onto the seat beside where Charity was pulling on a stocking seated in the informal sitting room.

"What have the girls been saying about me?" she asked her friend in a whisper. "Tell me the truth."

Charity shook her head as she glanced about, perhaps to see that Madame was nowhere about. "Oh Faith, it's a bad business, and I don't know how much is fiction, but the fact is, the photograph is damning enough. What will you do? Will you come back here to live? I'm sure Madame Chambon would take you in. She'd probably consider the notoriety would make you more valuable. And it would, don't you think? See, there's always a silver lining."

"I hardly call that a silver lining and no, I have no intention of—" She broke off at the honeyed tones of her former mistress.

"Ah, Faith, what a pleasant surprise, though I always knew you'd return."

Madame Chambon loomed over them, a frightening and imposing figure in a gown of lavender and lace, the russet hairpiece intricately interwoven with coils of fake and real hair, her beady eyes gazing at Faith through wire-rimmed spectacles.

"A short visit only," Faith said, her throat so dry she felt lightheaded. Her legs felt lacking the substance needed to stand up. And yet she needed to leave this place as fast as she could.

"Oh?" Madame's look of enquiry was tinged with scepticism. "And where could you possibly be going at this time of night? Oh yes, Lady Vernon's, am I not correct? She had plans to whisk you away in order to complete the terms of Mrs Gedge's arrangement with her."

Madame Chambon straightened, patting her large bosom and emitting a waft of cloying patchouli perfume. "But a great deal has changed in the last couple of hours, Faith." Her brow creased. "Events have fairly run out of control, and…I think you must come to my office in order for me to acquaint you with everything to do with Mrs Gedge and Lady Vernon, whose authority is superior to mine where you are concerned, my dear. Charity, please excuse us."

Charity's concerned look made it plain that she understood the menace behind Madame Chambon's words.

"And please, Charity, do make a little more effort with your appearance tonight. I know you're tired, but if you can't attract the gentlemen like you used to, you will have to find somewhere else to lodge. I'm not a charity." She gave a sudden, short laugh as if only then realising the play on words.

What could Faith do but follow Madame Chambon along the gloomy passage and step into the opulently decorated office, where the brothel madam entertained a range of business associates from her fellow bawds to young gentlemen negotiating a contract to relieve Madame Chambon of one of her girls.

Or a woman like Mrs Gedge, though Faith was certain Mrs Gedge had never set foot in these Soho premises.

"Now, sit down and tell me what has brought you here when I was almost certain you'd run off to be with your lover; the charming Mr Westaway." Madame's nostrils flared. "You thought Lady Vernon very credulous if you truly believed you could hide from her the state of your heart. You are a strong-willed young woman, Faith, and Lady Vernon is a sharp-eyed—"

"Gaoler and snitch!" Faith spat.

"Those are singularly unkind terms for a noblewoman who has fallen on hard times and is simply using whatever resources she can to keep a roof over her head." Madame Chambon twisted in her chair in order to locate a decanter of sherry on a shelf behind her. "When nerves are being tested, I think a little fortification is in order. Faith, a glass?"

"And risk being drugged?" Faith shook her head, and Madame raised one eyebrow.

"I'd be careful of making unfounded accusations, Faith, since I think you have precious few options but to come back here." Madame settled herself in front of Faith and shook her head slowly, her look one of great tragedy. "I never thought it would come to this when Mrs Gedge brought you here, a wide-eyed country girl, though of course the fact that a bit of stealing wasn't beneath you augured well. I don't like it when my girls enter my doors with too many scruples. They are the difficult cases, I will admit. But you, Faith, were just perfect for what I had in mind, and to be sure, you have not disappointed me. It has all come to pass exactly as I had hoped." Her smile stretched to encompass her sharp, yellow eyeteeth. "Mrs Gedge had scruples, though." She shrugged. "To begin with, that is. And then she met Lady Vernon during the depths of her grief. A fortuitous meeting, indeed."

"I have never stolen in my life, nor will I," Faith said softly. "And I will *never* sleep with a man I do not love. So, I will profit you nothing if you force me to remain here for even one night."

She rose. "Mrs Gedge might have believed I stole her daughter's bracelet, and she might be filled with bitterness over losing Miss Constancia, but she cannot blame me for that." She shook her head. "No, she cannot be so evil that she'd see me sold into slavery because of what happened three years ago. Because I chanced to be holding up the bracelet that Miss Constancia promised would be mine if I helped her enter Mr Westaway's bedchamber. I was barely fifteen years old. I'd never seen something so valuable. I'd never ever laid eyes on Mr Westaway. I only discovered that Mr Westaway was the man Miss Constancia had killed herself over when he told me so himself." Faith shook her head again, her desperation rising. "It makes no sense. It's out of all proportion for a woman like her to do something like this."

"Like what, Faith? You're looking around my office in a very disdainful manner. Almost as if you felt yourself my superior. Or were the wife of a diplomat. A person who would never deign to step over my threshold. In fact, who may not know what comforts a house like this offers a husband like the one she'd surely neglect if he failed to give satisfaction. Very easy to do when one has such high expectations."

Faith struggled to breathe. "Mrs Gedge would not have paid for my education for three years, and a roof over my head, and food and clothes…all very great expenses…merely to see me forced to work in a…brothel!"

"What a terribly unsavoury term to use for my high-class establishment. However, you're quite right, Faith. Of course, Mrs Gedge never embarked upon a singular scheme against a blameless country girl. And nor did she. She was very willing to hand you a handsome cheque seeing Mr Westaway so unhappy, but matters took a surprising turn. Indeed, we were all taken aback: Lady Vernon, myself, Mrs Gedge who, as a token of her goodwill, insisted that I give you this."

Faith was halfway to the door when she turned, and her horrified gaze fell upon the glittering bauble Madame Chambon was holding out to her.

"You'd realise, of course, that the stones are really not worth much, though no doubt at fifteen you imagined the piece a king's ransom." Madame dangled the pretty piece of jewellery enticingly in front of her as she looked from Faith's mutinous expression to the bracelet that Miss Constancia had promised her three years before.

"You can keep it," Faith muttered, her hand upon the doorknob.

"Oh, my dear, that's very kind of you, but I would hate to fall foul of Mrs Gedge…or Lady Vernon, for that matter. And they have insisted it be a memento for you to keep…to remind you of their generosity towards you these past years."

"I'm not staying here, and I don't want it."

"Well, that's your decision, of course, Faith. You are perfectly at liberty to leave." She smiled sweetly. "So, you're going to seek refuge with your young man, are you? Or with one of your many friends? Perhaps your family, though I'd gained the impression there was little love lost between you. Nevertheless, your room is made up for you, and there are a few fine gowns hanging in the wardrobe that I anticipated you'd need. And I'll give this to Charity for safekeeping until you change your mind." She rose. "Good night, Faith. It's been a lovely little chat, and I'll be sure to pass on any messages that come for you."

CHAPTER 23

"Some may call it talent, but look where your intransigence has led you?" Lord Maxwell sent a derisive look at the half-finished painting upon the easel in Crispin's study. At this time of day in the city, the location offered the best light.

The fact that the painting was a study of Faith in languid repose, her resplendent hair framing her exquisite face, only shored up his father's argument. Unsurprisingly, no sooner than the news had broken back in his home village, Crispin's redoubtable pater had leapt upon his horse in order to cover the distance to London in a fraction of the time it would have taken him by carriage.

Thus, Crispin had had no warning of his lordship's arrival, which too quickly followed his own discovery of the day's damning news splashed across the newspaper which Lord Maxwell now brandished.

"You have been made to look a credulous fool!" his father now shouted, when Crispin made no reply to a statement that could not be refuted. "You were set up from the start, my boy. The cunning plan of a procuress and her sidekicks is providing society with unimaginable titillation. Just as you're about to step onto the world stage supposedly as a diplomat, a figure synonymous with tact, cunning, and strategy. Christ, boy, but you've disappointed me!"

He slammed down the newspaper and began to pace, while Crispin remained in the chair behind his desk where his father had found him contemplating a world that had quite literally shattered about his ears.

"I've always disappointed you, Father," he muttered. Strangely, uttering this particular truth was not nearly as painful as learning the extent of just how greatly he had been set up by Faith and Lady Vernon; two seemingly artless women he'd invited into his house. Women to whom he'd offered friendship and...

Love.

He'd offered Faith his heart, and he'd honestly believed in her sincerity when she'd claimed to have reciprocated. Maybe she *had* grown fond of him, and maybe she *was* saddened at the way matters had gone. That was the best he could hope for since there was nothing anyone could say or do to refute the cold, hard, indisputable facts. Faith had been one of Madame Chambon's girls, and Lord Harkom, his father's arch nemesis, had been her protector.

His father ignored him. He was muttering as he paced the floor, and for the moment, he looked entirely absorbed in his own thoughts until he swung around and ground out, "I'm damned if I know how we can paint this in a way that doesn't make you appear a complete idiot, boy! Yes, an idiot! I wouldn't be surprised if the position for which you've worked so hard all these years is withdrawn, and you never set foot in Germany to make the mark that—"

"That *you* have so longed for, Father," Crispin interrupted him with more energy as he raised his head. "Yes, you! This has always been what *you* wanted. My desire to paint was nothing as far as you were concerned, and yet I've just won a prestigious art prize, and my talents have been recognised—as I have always wanted them to be."

"Ha! What value is that when you were set up to win! Yes, I know that part is not yet confirmed, but who is this mysterious benefactor, eh?" He nodded fiercely to corroborate his theme. "No one knows, do they? Suggesting that this was the very means by which you have been made a laughing-stock. Yes, a laughing-stock on all counts. Why, you've succumbed to every lure cast your way. And yet, you are to be a diplomat! Yes, and you will be!" His father went on, hastily, "Because there is nothing else you can do. Your art certainly won't bring you the financial rewards you need to live the life of a gentleman. I don't know of any suitably connected, well-dowered young lady who would want anything to do with you for a few years. No, my boy; the only thing for you is to go quietly off to Germany with your tail between your legs, and pray that the press isn't having a field day in Leipzig as they are over here!"

A knock on the door interrupted his angry tirade, and Carter put his head around the door.

"Young lady here to see you, Mr Westaway."

"Unaccompanied?" Lord Maxwell barked before throwing back his head with a laugh. "My, my, what a brazen little piece your jezebel is. Persistent, too."

"Please leave, Father."

"Certainly not! I shall stay quietly here in this chair in the shadows by the window, and you can introduce me when it's timely. Carter, bring the young lady in."

Before Crispin could move out into the passage, Carter was ushering Faith through the door, and Crispin's heart was in a tumult he could not begin to explain. He'd thought rage and disappointment would be his chief emotions, but longing trumped them all.

A waft of lavender heralded her entrance, and he longed to clasp her to him.

"Crispin, I'm so sorry! Not everything is the way it's been portrayed in the newspapers!" She hurried forward like a breath of spring sunshine and gripped his hands, and he couldn't help holding them as he ground out, "Faith, how can you refute the fact that you lied? You targeted me in order to set me up. Isn't that the truth?"

Tears glistened on the edge of her lashes as she tipped her face up to his.

"I lied to you at first, but I confessed. Crispin, I never meant to hurt you. I certainly never meant to humiliate you or damage your career."

"But that's what you've done." He dropped her hands and turned his head away, acutely conscious of his father in the corner whose expression communicated his disgust. Faith, who had her back to him and so had not noticed they were not alone, went on, "Crispin, I have never been one of Madame Chambon's 'girls' as the newspaper claims. Nor have I ever been…kept! Not by Lord Harkom, not by any man! I was a…a virgin when I gave myself to you."

Perhaps she could see that he was not as moved as she'd wish. As he might have been had his father not been present.

Her voice took on a greater note of desperation. "Crispin, you must at least believe the truth of that! Why, the evidence was there. Whatever my sins might be, the fact is that I swore I would never give myself to a man I did not love. And then I met you. Yes, I fell in love with you, even though it was against my better judgement. Even though it was not as others would have wished it. I would confess all, if you would only say you still love me. That you want to still love me. I can prove the lies that are in that newspaper. Please, Crispin!"

There was nothing Crispin wanted more than to hold

Faith against his chest and at least hear what she had to say. But a movement from his father suggested this would not be wise. Lord Maxwell would make the situation so much nastier if he made his presence known and Crispin had to protect Faith from that, at least. He'd hear her out when they were alone.

But for now, he'd have to show his father that he was not susceptible to her pleas. Perhaps there really was some explanation that could paint her in a less damning light, though, God help him, the picture of her in Harkom's arms surrounded by a group of harlots could hardly be explained away.

Still, she deserved an audience.

Alone.

"Faith, you've said all you need to." Putting his hand upon her shoulders, he turned her towards the door, careful to block any view she might have of his father. "I'm sorry." He lowered his eyes, careful not to look at her trembling mouth for fear he might lose control and just kiss her with all the disappointed passion that still burned within him. "Goodnight, my dear. I'm sorry it's come to this. I wish you well for your future."

A soft chuckle from Lord Maxwell was his reward when the door had closed behind Miss Faith Montague—the only woman he'd ever loved.

"Hardly masterful, my boy, but I'm glad to see you're not a complete slave to that soft heart of yours, which was always going to be your downfall." He rose and pointed to the desk with its pile of papers. "Now, read this latest report on the situation in the Black Forest. Meanwhile, I shall go and see what I can do to minimise the damage your foolish exploits have done to your reputation."

❀

"No passionate leave taking? Or did you decide not to stay with Mr Westaway, after all.? Why Faith, it's barely eleven o'clock." Madame Chambon was waiting in the shadows when Faith returned to the house in Soho. She couldn't look at the woman; her defeat was so enormous. A great sob threatened to reduce her to a quivering wreck at Madame Chambon's feet, unless she could make her escape and throw herself onto her bed in the privacy of her room.

Her old, hated iron bed with its aged, dusty quilt. It represented so much that was wrong with her life, but right now, she had nowhere else to go. Lady Vernon would not be welcoming her back in a hurry. No, Faith had outlived her usefulness to the old termagant; Madame Chambon had made that clear.

She was about to pass Madame Chambon on her way to the stairs when she hesitated. It had taken her a long time to untangle the few facts she could about her altered situation.

"Mrs Gedge didn't hate Crispin Westaway as much as she hated me, did she?" She swallowed painfully. "Why? I never hurt her? I never stole from her? And yet...yet everything she's orchestrated has resulted in *my* ruin. Granted, Mr Westaway's reputation has suffered, but I...*I* have been ruined so much more effectively."

Madame Chambon put her hand on Faith's shoulder and walked her to the bottom of the stairs. For just a moment, she sounded as if she sympathised.

"There's no room for sentiment in this business, Faith," she said. "Money is the only currency, and everyone has to pay their way. I don't think Mrs Gedge set out to destroy you, Faith." She brightened. "And, when all is said and done, she has endowed you with so much you would never have had as an ignorant servant."

"As I stand, I am in her debt." Faith began to tremble. "But after tonight? What happens to me then? Would...would she take me back as a servant? Would that satisfy her? For I would do anything rather than stay here with all that entails."

The pressure of Madame Chambon's fingers increased, and her smile became cloying as she steered Faith along the corridor. "I suspect Mrs Gedge would be unmoved by your loyalty, Faith. To have you under her roof would only remind her of everything she has lost. Do you not think that, perhaps, her feelings for you changed as she saw you grow into the beauty you have become…while her daughter lies mouldering in her grave?"

Faith suddenly understood. Jerking herself from Madame Chambon's grasp, she picked up her skirts and was about to take to the closest flight of stairs, when a masculine chuckle by the door of the drawing room made her whip her head around.

"It's been too long, Miss Montague." Faith recognised the voice before the face. Panicked, she searched for escape, but Madame effectively blocked her way to the stairs or the door to the street.

"Come, Faith, no need to be churlish." Madame's fingers dug into her arm as she propelled her towards one of the private entertaining rooms. She opened the door and pushed her in, Lord Harkom following close behind.

Now, Faith was standing opposite his lordship was turning the key in the lock. He stood facing Faith, arms akimbo, a speculative smile upon his thin lips.

"Let's get down to business, Miss Montague. My intelligence has it that you're all alone without husband *or* protector." He closed the distance between them and took both her hands in his, raising them to his lips. "So, I am here to offer you a solution."

Faith felt like a trapped canary. No one would come running to her aid if she screamed, but violence might be the result if she offered resistance.

Forcing herself not to reveal her terror or revulsion, she regarded him steadily.

"It is true; you have caught me at a disadvantage," she admitted, gently extracting her hands and making her way leisurely to the sofa in front of the fire. "Perhaps you'd pour us both a drink," she suggested, indicating the decanter on the sideboard as she sank against the cushions. "I do not come cheaply."

"You are not actually in a position to make too many demands, my dear," he reminded her as he poured them both a brandy before seating himself beside her, so close that his thigh was pressed against hers.

Faith managed not to flinch. "Thank you, Lord Harkom," she murmured, taking the brandy from him while she sought desperately for a means to play her cards so that she was not his victim—his plaything. At his mercy in any way. "Mr Westaway knows that to his cost."

Lord Harkom let out a bark of laughter. "Who played who for a fool? No, don't even try to make me think that you ever had the upper hand in that little affair, Miss Montague. Faith." He stilled and, with his eyes fixed on her face, ran the forefinger of his right hand gently around the edge of her décolletage. It was such a bold, proprietorial, and insulting action but Faith dared not move. She could not risk insulting him when she had no idea how to play this game. Lord Harkom was dangerous. One misstep on her part and he'd tumble her here and now. He'd force himself on her, and not a single person would come to her aid. Not only that; the whole world would consider she deserved it. That was perhaps the most painful reflection of all. She had not a single person she could depend upon. No friend. No lover. No family. No one would defend her honour. Everyone believed she was a liar and a whore.

"Mr Westaway paid a high price to enjoy me." She stared

back at him, steadily, trying to still her breathing and keep her bosom from rising against his wandering fingers. "What price are you offering me, Lord Harkom? I do not work on a one-night, rotational basis. And while I have always brought value, I don't come cheaply. As I said."

Two small lines appeared between his eyes as he seemed to weigh up her words. Perhaps see her in a new light? As less of the victim than he'd come here believing?

"I don't know what Madame Chambon has told you, but this plan to humiliate Mr Westaway has been three years in the making. Do you know what care and consideration goes into achieving such a public fall from grace? Yes, two days ago he was society's darling for the talent that saw him carrying off the greatest prize money ever offered in an art competition. Now it's been revealed he was set up from the start. Brought down by the beautiful muse he fell in love with and was going to run away with. And that the art competition was rigged!" A tremor of self-disgust ran through her to even utter the words, but he seemed to be paying attention.

Good. She needed him to redress the power balance, even just a little. She needed all her wiles and cunning; all that intelligence about strategy and human behaviour that she'd honed over the past three years, to come to her aid.

"Why are you here, Lord Harkom? Surely not for a quick rutting to enjoy the spoils for just one night only. I thought you were playing the longer game. Given the enmity between your two families, I thought you'd come here to offer me something that I would consider attractive, and that would strike at the heart of Mr Westaway and his father's ability to enjoy peaceful nights."

Oh, Faith was sure Lord Harkom had considered both and that the longer-term proposition would follow naturally upon the immediate gratification of his carnal desires right here and now. But Faith had to show herself as a woman of business.

She drew her shoulders back and increased the space between them, just a little. Thank God he'd removed his hand as he clearly contemplated what she was saying.

She smiled at him, her confidence growing. "Have you made an agreement with Madame Chambon? I need it in writing, Lord Harkom. A six-month contract with an exclusive residence for me. If I am to be kept, it will be by a rich man who does not stint when it comes to showering largesse upon his most treasured possession—the woman who brought down his enemy."

Yes, she'd sown the seed. He'd probably had something in mind that would involve keeping her as his mistress in order to rub the noses of Crispin and his father more thoroughly into how they'd been played. But Faith's plan suggested she'd come more willingly, and play her part more convincingly, if he met her part way. And that could only be to his benefit.

When he didn't speak, she rose. "Well, perhaps you and Madame Chambon should speak together right now, Lord Harkom." She sent him another sweet smile and offered him her hand before indicating the door with a nod of her head. "Lady Chambon's office is just down the corridor, as I'm sure you know. Meanwhile, I need to change into something a little more...appropriate." She glanced down at her gown then moved towards the door, pausing with her hand on the doorknob. "When an arrangement is in writing, you know where to find me."

He did not stop her. Clearly, he took her at her word and would, most likely, follow through with a meeting with Madame Chambon to nut out the details, knowing, as Madame Chambon had probably told him, that she had nowhere in the world to go.

For she didn't.

Unless…

It was a forlorn hope but there had been someone who had treated Faith kindly.

~

THE STREET WAS DESERTED WHEN FAITH ARRIVED AT THE small cottage by the river where she'd been conveyed so many times during the past three years. She'd been utterly terrified going by foot, carrying a carpetbag with one simple, old gown she'd snatched from her wardrobe together with the few possessions she had that might be worth anything.

It took several bouts of knocking before there was any response, and she nearly wept with relief when it was opened by a frightened-looking scullery maid.

"Mary, can you tell your master that he has a visitor," Faith exhorted her as she pushed her way past the child and into the familiar space.

The girl blinked open sleep-laden eyes. Faith suspected she'd been sleeping in front of the kitchen fire. Indeed, that's exactly where Faith hoped she might find some rest for the few hours that remained of tonight.

"Master's been long abed," the girl protested mildly though she didn't look as if she'd outright deny Faith. She was too young for that. And not as desperate as Faith to have her way, for the master was not an unkind man.

Faith waited nervously in the small back parlour where she'd spent so many hours at her lessons during the past three years.

Her first thought was that Professor Monk *must* receive her. Well, she was certain of that, at least. But what if he was part of Madame Chambon and Mrs Gedge's evil plan?

No, surely not. Not the kindly professor who took such pride in Faith's intelligent answers when he quizzed her on world diplomacy and the historical relations between countries.

But if he was not part of the evil plan, he must surely know what had happened to her since all of London could talk about nothing else, it would seem.

What would he say when she told him she had nowhere to go? That it was her own fault she'd fallen the way she had? Would he say that he was a man of learning and moral rectitude and their past association meant nothing to him?

Everyone else in Faith's life had forsaken her. The few friends she had were in no position to help her. Professor Monk would be like the rest of them—filled with moral outrage that would require her to pay for her sins.

Instead, his greeting was fatherly, and his first words suggested he'd not even heard what all London had been talking about.

"My dear Faith! Has your carriage broken down? Is Lady Vernon injured? Oh, dear me, I can't think why else you'd be on my doorstep all alone at this hour of the evening."

He was such an innocent guileless old man Faith knew he honestly did believe only the options that would put her in the most favourable light. Being faced with kindness and concern was so at odds with everything else she'd encountered this last terrible day, that she let out a great sob.

"My poor girl, come closer to the fire. You're in shock, surely? Oh, I do hope nothing terrible has happened. Truly, I wouldn't know what to do. Indeed, all I can think to do right now is to offer you some brandy."

"And a bed for the night?" Faith looked up at him, pleadingly, warmed by the light pressure of his hand on her shoulder. So different from the menace communicated by both Madame Chambon and Lord Harkom.

He blinked in surprise as he turned back from ushering

Mary out of the room to fetch Faith a small draft of something "strong and medicinal".

"Please, Professor. I've been turned out of the house where I lodge. There was…an argument."

His kind eyes grew a little sterner, but before he could say anything Faith hurried on, "I was pressured to…accept the offer of a man whom I know to be unkind and…*bad*. Yes, bad."

"Forced to wed against your will?"

Faith nodded as she covered up the lie with the words, "I was told I had to accept this man's offer, or I would have nowhere else to go."

"What man? What man would force you into such a bargain, Faith?" The professor looked truly concerned, and with a sigh, Faith whispered, "Lord Harkom." For if she offered part of the truth, it was something, surely.

To Faith's surprise, the professor's eyebrows shot up. "Dear me, Faith. Was Lord Harkom proposing *marriage* or…" He stopped abruptly."

Sadly, Faith shook her head. "No, Professor, that's why I came here. When I refused him, I had nowhere else to go."

"You have a benefactress who has paid my fees for three years, and yet I've never met her. Would she not offer you lodging?"

"Mrs Gedge." Faith shook her head. "No, I cannot go there either, for she too was insistent that I…" She finished on a sob.

"What about your chaperone? I briefly met Lady Vernon on one or two occasions. Why are you not staying with her?"

"I told you. They wanted me to accept an offer from Lord Harkom." She hung her head. "I'm not that sort of girl."

He blinked, owlishly, and stared at her as if she were suddenly a different creature.

Faith stood up. "Please don't condemn me for what has

been out of my control. I want only to do what's right, but I have nowhere to go. No one to turn to. I only wanted shelter for the next few hours until the dawn. That's all I ask of you. Please, Professor. I'll sleep in the kitchen and leave before light. Just let me stay here where it's safe. Just for tonight."

"What then, Faith? What will you do then?"

"I'll find work. Anything. I'll be a servant. I could work for you, Professor. Could I?"

She stared hopefully at him, but he shook his head. "You can't waste your talents, my girl, and I won't employ you to scrub floors when I cannot have you under my roof in any other capacity. Let me think."

He rose and began to pace, scratching his whiskered chin as he began to mutter, for he always did this when deep in thought. As if he had to verbalise every possibility.

"You say you have been used, girl. Educated to be the intellectual match of any man when it comes to diplomacy, strategy. For that's what I did when I was instructed to give you a rudimentary understanding of the relations of the world stage. To make that the key focus of what I taught you. Why, I find this very difficult to understand."

"It was not because of Lord Harkom but an enemy of his. A man who is going to be British Envoy in Germany. I was used to make him look a fool, and then suddenly Lord Harkom was paying his addresses in a most alarming manner, and I had to escape. Perhaps…perhaps you know of a position where I could go. A place I could act as governess?"

"It was the very line of thought I was following." He gave a decisive nod. "But where? What family do I know?"

"I don't care. Any will do. Anywhere I can do an honest day's work and have food and a roof over my head. I don't require much. I just have to get away from London."

"My poor Faith." He regarded her sadly. "I never expected

this when I agreed to teach you all those years ago. You are my most gifted student. A great beauty, indeed, now that I perceive you in a better light. And I fear a great evil has been perpetrated against you, though I cannot begin to fathom why. Of course, I will help you. Mary will make up a bed in the spare room, and tomorrow I will send you on your way, but not alone and friendless. I promise I will do what I can to help you, little though it may be."

CHAPTER 24

One Year Later

"And all that pink means it belongs to the British Empire." Faith put her finger on the map on the table in front of them and traced the borders, while her two charges stared dutifully with downcast heads, though their eyes kept straying to the trees and sunshine outside the schoolroom window.

Little wonder now that the sunshine had swept away two days of rain and the swathes of beautifully scythed lawn beckoned for a game of cricket.

"Is it teatime yet?" asked George, the eldest, sighing and wiping his nose with the back of his hand.

"I want a butter sandwich," said seven-year-old James, George's younger brother by two years.

Faith pushed back her chair and stood up. She could hardly blame them. The weather was glorious, and the little boys had been angels. They were good children for the most part; sweet and obedient, and they loved her. It warmed her heart to know that.

Which surprised Faith for she was not used to being

loved. Not in such an innocent, overt manner by two little boys who spontaneously hugged her and did not even have to be exhorted to say goodnight every evening at seven—whereupon she'd receive a freely given kiss on the cheek by each.

Even after all this time, it brought a lump to her throat for she hadn't realised there were people in the world who did things for others without expecting payment of some kind.

Faith patted each boy on the head. "Enough geography. Time to stretch your arms high, boys, and take deep breaths," she said, leading the way. Like them, she didn't want to think about the British Empire and have to trace the borders of Germany one more time today.

"Close your eyes. Arms up high." She stood on tiptoe and thought, as she often did, of Crispin. He'd been one of these types of children once. A rare breed who acted out of the pureness of his heart which might, perhaps, account for why she'd lost hers so thoroughly.

And why her heart remained ever loyal, for she understood that, in the end, there'd simply been too much evidence circulating to blacken her name in his eyes.

"Ah, Miss Montague, I wondered if you could ask Ellen to have George and James in their pyjamas a little earlier tonight." Pretty Mrs Heathcote, the boys' mother, stood in the doorway smiling fondly at her boys, both of whom showed more delight than was warranted when she asked them if they'd enjoyed their afternoon lessons.

Having a mother as kind and maternal and interested as Mrs Heathcote was a great part of why George and James had such open hearts, Faith surmised. Did kindness and thoughtfulness to others really breed a child who would in turn grow into a kind and thoughtful man or woman?

It didn't necessarily follow, of course, that a child

followed in their parents' footsteps. Crispin's father was cold and demanding, while he'd lost his mother young.

Yet he was sensitive, kind, artistic, thoughtful.

Faith liked to think she fell into the category of those who could change into someone better once they had good reason to, or were shown how.

"Of course, Mrs Heathcote." Faith smiled back. It would mean she had an extra half an hour to herself this evening, too. Not that she had much with which to occupy herself. She'd have dinner with the rest of the servants, but she'd not stay to sew and talk beyond half an hour after that. While the servants were decent enough people, they liked their own chatter and Faith's presence constrained them. She'd over-heard the cook, once, saying something along those lines, and while Faith felt accepted as one of the household, and certainly suffered no unkindness at the hands of anyone, she simply wasn't 'one of them'. Not one of the family of four who lived upstairs in their very elegant country manor house, or one of the seven servants who toiled below stairs.

Duly, at half past six, Faith had the boys ready for bed and brought them down to say goodnight to their parents, who were entertaining a small number of people for their regular Friday-to-Monday.

The party was assembled in the drawing room, the three gentlemen and Mrs Heathcote sitting in front of the fire, while one of the female guests sat at the piano and the other stood at her right-hand side, turning the pages and singing in a sweet soprano.

Faith stood in the doorway, holding the hand of each boy, and gazing at the companionable grouping while she waited for the women to finish providing the entertainment.

The two ladies, fashionably dressed in low-cut evening gowns with elaborate bustles, looked to be in their early thirties; their husbands, or so she could only assume, handsome men sporting impressive moustaches. Turning a little, she noticed a third gentleman she'd not seen before, half hidden behind a large urn. His face was turned, but what she could see of his expression bore the signs of a pleasant disposition and a fair amount of appreciation as he listened.

She was about to sweep forward with the boys, when the gentleman swung around to face her, and a shocked breath caught in her throat; just as her own recognition must have registered on her face, for he raised his eyebrows and his eyes widened.

Mrs Heathcote stood up in a rustle of silk, now that the music had just come to an end, and swept towards her children, saying over her shoulder, "Lord Delmore, here are the boys, come to say goodnight."

The other two gentlemen were busily complimenting the ladies on their fine rendition, and Faith stood, frozen, barely able to force her mouth into the requisite smile, as Lord Delmore patted the boys on their heads and said he'd heard many good things about their attention to their studies.

Beyond a short, sharp look at Faith, and a murmured good evening, he said nothing, and after Faith had returned to her bedchamber, after handing George and James over to their nursemaid, she sat, trembling on her bed, and wondered how soon she would be exposed.

And yet, Lord Delmore had been a kind man she reflected, as she took a shawl from her wardrobe and wrapped herself in it to stave off the shaking. Would he really reveal her identity?

He might, if he believed she'd contaminate the children of his friends. A whore could be accepted nowhere in society.

Only, she wasn't a whore. She'd just happened to live amongst a house full of them.

She rose and went to the window, staring out at the

moonlit lawns and neat gravelled pathways that wound amongst the trees.

A masculine cough sounded by the shrubbery beneath, and to Faith's surprise, she saw that Lord Delmore had gone outside to smoke a pipe, and that he was walking very deliberately around the terrace, coughing at various intervals.

Several times he glanced up, but of course he'd be unable to see which was Faith's room—Faith was certain he was trying to communicate with her—before he finally set off on the path towards the river.

Faith ran to her wardrobe and put on her one dark, serviceable coat, which might be considered acceptable wear for a walk in the gardens on a moonlit night without occasioning comment.

There was no question about the fact that she needed to be able to speak to him in private. She needed to find out what Lord Delmore intended to tell the Heathcotes. He might condemn her and expose her, but she suspected he'd tell her, first.

The light crunch of gravel beneath her hasty footsteps made her arrival to within his orbit known.

"Rather a surprise to see you here, Miss Montague." He didn't turn from his contemplation of a curious nodule on a trunk of willow tree when she came up to him by a small inlet half hidden by bulrushes, out of sight of the house.

Her insides quivered as she waited tensely for his next words. They would reveal something of his intentions, surely. Just running the short distance between the house and the river, Faith had thought only of how important it was for her to keep this job.

If she were dismissed, she'd have to return to Madame Chambon's.

And if she had to return to Madame Chambon's, she'd rather die. Yes, death would be preferable than having to give herself to a man, or men, in a transaction that took no account of the heart.

"Your name was on everyone's lips a year ago, Miss Montague…and then you disappeared."

Faith shifted position as she stared at his back before he turned to face her. "My old tutor arranged for me to work for the Heathcotes when I had nowhere else to go." She swallowed. "If you tell them what the newspapers printed about me, I'll lose my job."

"And do you like working here? Looking after two little boys? I imagine it's very different from what you are used to."

Faith shrugged. "I had nine brothers and sisters growing up. That was not a lie. And then I was strenuously educated for three years. So, what I do now is not so different from my realm of experience. Loving what I do is what's different."

"Ah, Miss Montague." He shook his head, his look sorrowful. "I am placed in a difficult position. My loyalty is towards the Heathcotes. They are old friends of mine. Good people."

"And I am not?" Faith bristled. "But of course, that's what the papers printed, isn't it? And there was a photograph."

"Of you and Lord Harkom, yes; a man who is no friend to Mr Westaway." Lord Delmore took out a handkerchief and mopped his brow. He looked a little older, but his eyes were still kind beneath their bushy brows. "I'm sorry, Faith. I want to believe that you've been ill done by and indeed, I do see that you have taken the path of redemption. Otherwise, no doubt, you'd still be…"

He hesitated, awkward suddenly, and Faith ground out, "Not with Lord Harkom! I've met him only twice, and that was two times more than I would have liked. He is not a good man. I never had any association with him other than accidental. It's nothing like the newspapers printed."

Lord Delmore frowned. "Yet you have a letter from him.

Did you know that? Yes, it was delivered to my house after one of your…friends…came in search of you and found the residence where you'd spent last summer empty."

For a moment, Faith had no words. Finally, she whispered, "Lord Harkom wrote to *me*?" The thundering in her chest was almost painful. "Why, it makes no sense at all. Who brought the letter? Where is it?"

"I can't remember the young lady's name. Only that she couldn't write, so she dictated some words to my maid, Sarah, when she delivered the letter. The young woman was in the district, visiting a family member who, by coincidence, lived nearby, she said."

"When was this?"

"Only a few weeks ago. And, my dear, I'm not sure if I tucked the letter into my portable writing desk or left it in my bureau at home. But naturally, I shall forward it." His eyes raked her with a look of the old appreciation with which she'd become familiar. "I simply had never expected our paths to cross again."

"I don't want it if it comes from Lord Harkom." Faith sighed. "And it sounds as if I shall have to start looking for another job if your conscience will smite you for not telling Mr and Mrs Heathcote who I really am." She clasped her hands together. "And yet, I may still hold out hope for they are decent people. They, at least, would give me a hearing to decide whether I was a good person on balance, rather than condemn me for what five inches of editorial declares is the truth with no refutation from me."

Lord Delmore stepped forward and touched her arm. "I shall keep my silence for now, Faith. But only if I am assured that nothing you do will harm or embarrass this family."

The censure in the man's normally kind face cut Faith to the quick. How easily people judged on the basis of nothing more than hearsay printed in a periodical. What about the presumption of innocence? She was just a woman, she supposed. A woman from a poor background with too many enemies.

"Of course, Lord Delmore." She inclined her head and turned.

There was no more to be said.

EXCEPT THAT LORD DELMORE HAD INDEED TUCKED THE letter he'd received all those weeks ago into his portable writing desk, and when he found it the next morning, he delivered it straight to Faith as she was walking the boys along the gravel path by the river.

"It's not from Lord Harkom," she told him in relief after she'd ripped open the envelope before scanning its contents.

But her relief was short-lived, and by the time she'd come to the bottom, she was breathing heavily and wished she could sit down.

"What is it, Faith?"

She shook her head and glanced between the man standing opposite in a copse of trees by the river, then up to the house. "It's not from Lord Harkom, but it's *about* Lord Harkom, and it only confirms his evil reputation. Poor Mr Westaway."

Lord Delmore straightened his tie as he smiled. "That's the first time you've mentioned his name. I wasn't sure if you ever spared our talented painter, or should I say, diplomat, a thought."

Faith stared at the man before her and shook her head, unable to fathom the insinuation that Faith felt so little for him. "My lord, he is *all* I ever think about. That is, when I choose to dwell on the few good things in my life."

"And what does the letter say about Lord Harkom? What does your friend know that the rest of society does not? Oh,

Faith." He looked profoundly saddened. "What got you into such a calling? Perhaps I should never have given you a letter if it re-establishes your connection to this dreadful life you once lived."

Faith knew she couldn't expect him to understand. Defending herself would be beyond useless, also. "My lord, we all have to survive, somehow." She glanced behind her. George was calling her, and he was too close to the river to make her easy. She began to walk towards the boy, saying over her shoulder, "And sometimes we don't have very many choices. But what we choose to believe about *other* people—provided we have done our due diligence—certainly is up to us."

⁓

THE LETTER HAD BEEN PROFOUNDLY DISTURBING. CHARITY HAD spoken of vague ramblings and claims Lord Harkom had made after he'd consumed a great deal of whisky and was sufficiently pleased with the way Charity had performed in bed.

Faith wondered whom Charity had corralled to write such things, for although Charity was intelligent, she'd never been able to form her letters in the right order to make into words anyone could understand.

Clearly, Charity had been sufficiently alarmed by Lord Harkom's claims to want to tell Faith, even though she did not know the specific nature of the correspondence Lord Harkom claimed had unexpectedly come into his hands, and that would ruin Crispin Westaway if it were made public.

The letter, Charity was certain, was contained in an unlocked chest in his bedchamber, but Charity had had no opportunity to look for herself. She'd simply been told the litany that Mr Westaway would never continue in his current diplomatic role after this letter was made public, and all that stood between Westaway and ruin was Lord Harkom's good nature.

Charity wrote that his mood had turned ugly, and he'd told her that if she knew where Faith was, she should pass on the message that Crispin Westaway's future was entirely in her hands. Yes, Lord Harkom demanded a warm welcome from the woman who'd shown so little gratitude towards him for his generosity the last time they'd met; that Faith had an opportunity to rewrite their history, and in return, Lord Harkom would ensure Westaway's dark and ruinous secret never came to light.

Of course, in the months since their separation, Faith had followed Crispin's progress like the girl in love she was. It delighted her when she heard news that he'd impressed his superiors. When the newspapers had finally stopped making reference of his humiliation over the art prize that had been shown to be a ruse in order to entrap him with a common prostitute, a great weight had fallen from her shoulders. At last that was considered old news, and now, both of them had new lives to forge.

Except that Crispin's was filled with promise, while Faith felt that hers was like a dull continuum, punctuated by terror that she'd lose even that through exposure.

All she wanted was security, food, and shelter without having to sell her soul for it.

She hoped to remain with the Heathcotes until George went to school at Eton, like his father, after which Faith would find another position. Indeed, that was the best a governess in her position could hope for.

And Faith no longer had high hopes for anything.

But the letter had jarred her out of the quiet life of acceptance she'd been living. It reintroduced danger into her life, and reminded her painfully of the future she'd thought was within reach. The one that had been based on honesty and trust and hope.

In her bedchamber, she scoured every line for a hint from Charity as to what she thought Faith should do. Did Charity believe Lord Harkom? It would be easy to manufacture falsehoods in order to lure Faith back to him.

Yet, why would Charity go to the extremes of travelling hours into the country, if she didn't think Lord Harkom really did possess dangerous information that he'd not scruple to use against Crispin? Perhaps his information was not dangerous to Crispin, personally, but the policies Crispin endorsed. The policies that ensured Britain keep the peace amidst the turbulence of world politics.

Just a few words were all it had taken, but Charity apparently knew when a boast contained more than the kernel of truth that threatened to blow up a man's career like a powder keg.

Pillow talk. How many men had been brought undone by pillow talk? Perhaps without even knowing it, for they were all too liable to underrate the intelligence of the females they used for their pleasure.

Nervously, Faith addressed Mrs Heathcote after the boys had had their breakfast the next morning. The guests had left, and her mistress seemed in a particularly satisfied mood for all had gone well and now peace reigned again.

"My poor Faith. I'm so sorry to hear your mother is dangerously ill. Yes, of course you must go to her." The young matron looked up from the bench where she was making preserves with one of the maids in a small dark room in the back of the house. Her expression was genuinely sympathetic, and Faith wished she'd not had to lie in order to gain a few days. Yet what could she do if Crispin were in danger? If she could have avoided ever seeing Lord Harkom again, she would have.

"I'm sure we'll manage for five days without you. My mother can pay us a visit and spend all the time she wants to with the boys without worrying that she's interrupting their education. There! The matter is settled, and you must think only of what you can do for your family. Family is everything, I know."

Mrs Heathcote looked so pretty and so innocent as she stood above the marble countertop, spouting what she knew based on her own fortunate experience of life.

Faith bobbed a curtsey and thanked her, relieved to have got over the first hurdle so easily.

What would follow surely had the potential to be diabolical.

CHAPTER 25

The road outside Madame Chambon's house was painfully familiar, but Faith wasn't going to step across the threshold, even via the kitchen, so she waited nervously in the narrow side lane. Fortunately, Charity was soon out to greet her, having been sent a message by the bootboy.

"Faith! I never expected to see you again! You got my letter, didn't you? I hope I didn't alarm you, only I thought you might find it important considering what Mr Westaway was to you." Charity looked striking in crimson, her red-gold hair gleaming as it rippled down her back. Her evening gown was of the finest silk. Yes, Charity had become the reigning favourite during the year Faith had been away, and Madame Chambon saw the advantages in dealing well by those who brought in the greatest names, titles, and, of course, money.

"I'm so glad I was free to come," she went on, after a quick hug and a nervous look over her shoulder. "Though I have to meet Lord Stanford in five minutes." Her mouth curved up and Faith stared, incredulous as she asked, "You don't mind?"

Charity shook her head. "I mentioned him before. He's a

regular, and I truly believe he's going to speak with Madame to release me."

"And make you his mistress in your own establishment?"

"Well, he's hardly going to offer to marry me!" Charity laughed before her expression grew serious, and she returned to the matter which had brought Faith to London.

"Lord Harkom's speech alarmed me greatly. He mentioned enough specifics to make me believe he truly had something to use against Mr Westaway, and yet I have not the slightest idea what it could be. Only that all Lord Harkom's correspondence is contained in a small leather chest which he keeps under his bed." Charity touched Faith's shoulder. "I didn't want to put you in danger, but I knew you'd want to know."

Faith stared at Charity's gown, and asked, "May I borrow a dress, one of your finest, for just one night?"

"And a governess doesn't have such confections in her wardrobe?" Charity's smile was rueful. "If I had the learning, I once thought I'd prefer to be a governess, though whether that would satisfy me now, I don't know." She smiled again, clearly thinking of Lord Stanford. "Of course, I'm happy to offer you my finest gown for the night, but I would urge you to reconsider seeing Lord Harkom in person. He was very angry with you, and vengeance is his natural response. I only told you because I couldn't hold onto the information. It sounded dangerous."

"Lord Harkom will agree to see me, at least." Faith raised her eyebrows. "If vengeance is his first inclination, I shall be ready to meet him on equal grounds."

CRISPIN WASN'T EXPECTING TO BE INTERRUPTED. DURING HIS two short weeks back in England, he had a great deal to do.

Right now, he was preparing for a meeting with several ministers, so when he called "Come!" he was expecting the maid to announce Lord Grinwald with whom he would be conducting delicate negotiations.

Instead, he was surprised but pleased to find himself greeting his old friend and neighbour Lord Delmore. It had been a long time. More than a year, in fact, and as their acquaintanceship had been limited to the time Crispin spent at his aunt and uncle's home, and it was known that Lord Delmore's fondness for London was minimal, the gentleman's arrival was highly unusual.

"What brings you here? My short tenure here in London is not widely known." Crispin ushered Lord Delmore to a seat and called for tea, not liking to recall when they'd last been in company together.

Should he bring it up? It would only revive a time long past when Crispin had shown himself the foolish stripling he'd once been.

"I've heard good reports of your progress through the ranks, and not just from your father." Lord Delmore seated himself and glanced about the room: at the hunting scenes, the plaster busts, a suit of armour by the fireplace.

No flowers in vases. No lace doilies. No sign of any feminine touch.

He didn't ask the question though. Merely waited until the maid had placed the tray upon the table, poured them both a cup of Darljeeling, and retired.

"I saw Miss Montague last week."

Her name struck home like a well-placed blow to the solar plexus. Crispin hoped he didn't betray himself. Not by the fiery reddening of his face, which he tried to obscure by taking a judicious sip of his drink, nor by the clearing of his throat, which must surely denote discomfort to a keen observer.

There were a thousand questions he wanted to ask, but he didn't know where to start. Didn't know if he should ask anything, in fact.

He settled with, "Indeed."

"She looked very demure as one might expect. She's a governess, you know."

"Good lord!" This was unexpected.

"Yes, one would have imagined she'd have capitalised on her notoriety and made herself a fortune while she could. That was my initial thought, too."

Crispin put his cup down carefully. It was still too full to risk holding it when his hands were shaking. Strange. He'd found himself quite self-contained during these past months. His father's disgust, followed by the harsh tutoring he'd received at the hands of his pater had, he thought, cauterised all feeling.

Except shame.

And it was curious how that could be wrapped up and put away when hard work was all consuming.

"I wouldn't be surprised if she plans to see Lord Harkom. I don't know when, and that is why I'm here. I think you should stop her. Talk to her first, before she does something rash."

If everything that had gone before had been surprising, this was the most surprising of all. Crispin was glad he'd not been taking another sip of tea for even without, he still choked on his shock.

"Lord Delmore, I can't imagine why her…decisions and way of life should be your concern. They certainly are no longer mine."

"I thought you felt a *tendre* for the young lady. I thought she'd engaged your heart to the extent you were prepared to go so far as marriage, even when you believed her penniless."

Crispin shook his head and put up his hand, and Lord

Delmore went on, "But it's not because of your feelings that I sought you out to tell you this." He sighed heavily. "Lord knows, I'm a man who likes the simple life. The skulduggery that's your domain now that you're in the thick of delicate continental diplomacy is not for me. I'd far rather be mouldering away in the country with a good book than breathing in London smog for a good cause."

"I'm your good cause? Or Miss Montague? I'm sorry, Lord Delmore, but I fail to understand you at all. You know what Miss Montague was revealed to be. I can have nothing to do with her—*especially* now. Besides," he muttered, "I thought she was with Lord Harkom in a capacity that made visiting him hardly a reason for you to come rushing down to London to tell me about it."

"I'd have thought the same had it not been for a letter my maid took, or rather transcribed, on behalf of one of Miss Montague's friends. Yes, one of those ladies of disrepute who are so desirable to the likes of Lord Harkom. It seems he's been highly indiscreet with a little ladybird who is far more intelligent than he gave her credit for. Even if she's illiterate."

Crispin rose, more to alleviate the difficulty of sitting still when his agitation was so great he didn't know what to do with himself. He poured them both a brandy and, without asking, handed one to Lord Delmore.

"So, what does this little ladybird suggest Lord Harkom has that could be of such interest to Miss Montague?"

Lord Delmore took a thoughtful sip. "She mentioned something about a letter. Or a couple of letters. I don't know, exactly. Just that these letters were potentially damaging."

"Damaging? To whom?" Crispin shrugged. "I have nothing to hide, yet you obviously give credence to whatever matter of grave import these letters contained. Anyway, why should it concern me? Why should anything Miss Montague does concern me? You know what I risk should it be revealed I have any association with her."

Lord Delmore worried his lip as he sent a dark look towards his younger friend. "When I look back on my life, I have far more regrets about the things I *didn't* do than those I did. Now, it's true that I don't know what these letters contain. Nor would it appear, does the, er, fair Cyprian who made the journey to find Miss Montague. She was simply worried enough by the suggestion of damage Lord Harkom hinted they could do to you, that she felt the need to travel a great distance to alert Miss Montague."

"I'm sure there's nothing further about my private life that can be disseminated to the public that would further embarrass me or discredit me," Crispin ground out.

His painting career lay in tatters. His personal standing had taken a very great hit. Thank God, he'd been able to remove himself from London almost immediately afterwards while his father had worked hard to pass it off as less than it was.

Certainly, less than it was to Crispin. Yes, Lord Maxwell's boy had been caught up in a vile scam that was to have won him a bride from the ranks of the impure through means of a bogus art competition.

After the shock and outrage, the sniggers had followed. Crispin had left the country at this point.

Now he'd returned to commiserations and bolstering affirmations that he'd had a lucky escape. He'd been clever enough to have seen through the young lady in time.

So, Crispin's reputation was intact, and he'd recovered his social standing.

But the state of his heart and his sense of trust would never recover.

"But what if it's not about your private life, Crispin? What if it's more than that? Yes, I know that a year on you still are wounded by what you see as Miss Montague's betrayal. Nevertheless, she *was* in love with you."

"Everything about her was a lie."

"Except, as I've just said, her love for you, Crispin." Lord Delmore's tone was patient. Crispin eyed him suspiciously, staring into the fireplace as he said darkly, "You sound like my father might have sounded if he'd ever chosen persuasion before threats. You are not my father, you know."

"But I'm an older man with more experience of matters like these. I have two grown-up sons and a daughter, all of whom are, in fact, older than you. Forgive me if you think I'm patronising you. That certainly was not my intention. But I do sense something sinister at play. I'm not suggesting for a moment that you go in search of Miss Montague. But do, I urge you, find her friend and hear what she has to say. I believe that trouble is afoot. Lord Harkom has an axe to grind. And we both know he's no friend of yours or your father's."

CHAPTER 26

he busyness of the small newspaper office and the professional air of the two young women bent over their desks, writing, took Faith by surprise after she'd been led up two flights of stairs to this unconventional scene in the attic above a barrister's premises.

"Can I help you, miss?" The younger woman, who was sitting at a large wooden desk beneath the window, raised her head to look enquiringly at Faith. Clearly, she did not recognise Faith as she halted her work, her pen poised above the paper.

"You're a proper lady journalist, now, Miss Eaves? Isn't that what they call you?" Faith looked at the various newspapers and magazines that were strewn about the tabletops and which lined the walls, some framed. "You achieved your dreams, after all." She hesitated as her eye was caught by the glaring front page of an issue published on August 15th, 1878. She didn't need to go any further to confirm the date, for the headline alone clearly depicted Faith's spectacular fall from grace. Even from a distance, the grainy photograph of Lord Harkom holding Faith in a waltz hold, surrounded by a group of women who were clearly not ladies, made Faith shiver with revulsion. "You've achieved your life's ambition."

Two furrows appeared between Miss Eaves's eyes, but as her gaze followed Faith's to the newspaper before returning to Faith, it seemed she finally reconciled the demure governess before her with the woman whose life she'd turned upside down.

Miss Eaves squared her shoulders.

"Miss Montague, why did you not say you were coming?" She glanced at the older woman who was still working but who was clearly also listening, and said, "Mamie, please would you leave us alone for a few minutes."

When Mamie had left the room, Miss Eaves invited Faith to sit, and when Faith said she didn't have long and would rather stand, Miss Eaves stood too and regarded her, still frowning, from the other side of the room.

Faith straightened. "I was hardly assured of a warm welcome in view of what you'd said about me in the past, so I thought the element of surprise might play in my favour." She moved to the window embrasure and found that she was suddenly far more nervous than she'd expected to be. She fiddled with the curtain tassel but kept her eyes on Miss Eaves, who straightened and said calmly but with a note of defensiveness, "It's the job of the journalist to tell the truth. The facts. I'm sorry if my article revealed you for what you are, or were, Miss Montague. I was seeking the truth and I laid it out for the public, as they deserved. It was nothing personal."

"But for me, it *was* deeply personal, Miss Eaves. For me, it was the ruin of my life." She swallowed, finding this even harder with every word, which was strange when she'd spent so many of the last months existing in a state of semiconsciousness; unable to properly feel anything, really. "You fed my dreams and ambitions into the furnace to feed your own."

"Why, Miss Montague, what a lovely way you have with words. Surely, you are in the wrong calling." She glanced pointedly at Faith's demure clothing and said, "Or have you seen the error of your ways and turned to another means of earning your living."

This was not going the way Faith had hoped it would. Miss Eaves, for all her emancipation, knew nothing of the desperate choices a woman had to make, daily, when she had no resources.

"You are very fierce in your determination to forge your own way in the world, Miss Eaves. I see you have your own office. And a secretary, even." She nodded, approvingly. "You must be paid well for your writing to manage the rent and wages since I know your uncle was very much against his niece working."

Miss Eaves pushed back a lock of chestnut-brown hair and her pert nose twitched. "I do work hard, Miss Montague. And the provision of a bit of space in a building that my uncle has no use for accounts for very little, and is only temporary until such time as I can properly establish myself and be completely independent."

Faith nodded. "That is generous of your uncle to give you such patronage. You must have won him around with the excellent reporting you did on last year's art prize. I daresay, after your hard work at the office—in space supplied by your uncle—that you go home to sleep in a bed and eat food that is supplied purely through your own endeavours. Or, is your food and lodgings supplemented too?" Faith couldn't seem to stop fiddling with the curtain tassel, but she glanced up to see Miss Eaves's reaction as she added, "Well, at least, only until such time as you make sufficient earnings through your writing to completely support yourself."

Miss Eaves flushed, but she kept her composure. "I resent the criticism, Miss Montague, though I understand your feelings at having been exposed for living a lie. I am a fierce advocate for furthering the opportunities of the fairer sex, but women will only ever be taken seriously, especially as newspaper reporters, if we are not afraid to speak the truth, however unpalatable."

Faith closed her eyes. "I don't disagree with you. But I cannot begin to explain the risk you run in ruining reputations, not least your own, if the truth as *you* see it, is only the partial truth."

Miss Eaves leaned against the table, and her fingers drummed an agitated tattoo. "Photographs don't lie. There was the truth, Miss Montague, and I told it. I'm sorry if it destroyed your marital chances, but the whole of society can breathe a sigh of relief that you did not insinuate yourself into their ranks once you were shown to be—"

"To be…what, Miss Eaves? The mistress of Lord Harkom, because that's what was suggested by the photograph? To be a prostitute, because the camera showed me standing in a room surrounded by women who certainly weren't dressed like ladies and so that was the assumption?" Faith shook her head. "That photograph was taken minutes before Lord Harkom attacked me, wanting what I refused to give since I had never traded my body for money or anything else—and I never have or will, which is why I work as a governess." She indicated her clothing.

"Please, Miss Montague; it is very easy to don a garment and pretend to be what you are not."

"It is, Miss Eaves. And that is what I did for three years as I was groomed to entice Mr Westaway to fall in love with me once I became his muse for the art prize which a wealthy woman—also American—established in order to wreak her own warped vengeance. I lived at Madame Chambon's, but I was not one of her girls. And I have never traded my body for money or material gain. Not with Lord Harkom or anyone else."

"This is sounding more and more like a Penny Dreadful novel, Miss Montague." Miss Eaves swatted at a fly and began to pace. "You can't expect me to believe a word of what you say."

"Of course, because words can twist the truth, yet photographs can't? That photograph was staged. So much of what you *inferred* was untrue."

"My inferences were endorsed and expanded by someone who knew very well the lie you lived."

"Indeed? And who was that? A woman who was jealous? A man whom I'd refused? Whoever it was, was certainly no friend of mine, though I might begin to guess."

"Lady Vernon came to see me. Yes, the dowager duchess. She'd discovered your true identity, and was incensed that someone like you should become the darling of the town when she knew what you really were."

"And had done since the moment she deposited me at Madame Chambon's three years before, and on every occasion she escorted me to my tutor in Bethnal Green, or to take tea at the Claridges Hotel with Mrs Gedge who established the art prize with just this outcome in mind. Yes, the millionaire American woman who wanted to kill the joy in Mr Westaway, the man whom she held responsible for her daughter's suicide, but she wanted to destroy me in the process because she couldn't bear that I was alive and beautiful, while her daughter was cold in the ground. An eager, gullible female reporter played very nicely into her hands."

Miss Eaves raised her chin and looked squarely at Faith. "I'm sorry I'm unable to offer you tea, Miss Montague."

"No matter, since I would not have accepted." She sent a pointed look at the newspaper in its frame upon the wall that had dissected her life as its front-page story. "It's so easy to believe that what one sees constitutes the truth. So much more so when you choose to believe that higher rank constitutes a greater propensity for delivering the truth. I'm afraid I have to go now." She ran her hands down the sides of her serviceable gown. "It's time for me to change into something more appropriate for this evening."

"Well, I'm glad you still have such evenings to look forward to then, Miss Montague, though I daresay I won't be seeing you at Lady Ridgeway's Masked Ball tonight. You had quite convinced me that I was the architect of the ruin of your entire life." She sniffed.

Faith faced her proudly. "I would never lay that at anyone's door, Miss Eaves. And nor do I look forward to this evening in the slightest. I simply hope that the risk I take will advance the safety of those nearest and dearest to me." She narrowed her eyes. "Unlike you, I like to do a little more research to ensure that the facts disseminated to the world are based entirely on truth."

CHAPTER 27

The looking glass was very complimentary. Or perhaps it was the dim lighting. Or the pale pink ruffled gown that clung to Faith's curves, accentuating her slim hips, flat belly, and generous breasts. The fashions of the day could be most suggestive, and a young lady who wore them as well as Faith did, was sure to come in for a great deal of generous praise.

Which was why it was important that Faith make her exit from Madame Chambon's without having been noticed.

She'd dressed in Charity's room, helped by her friend who'd acted as lady's maid, pulling in her corset until Faith could barely breathe. Charity was slighter than she was, and Faith had not worn fashionable, constricting corsets for a year.

When her coiffure was complete, a riot of curls rippling down her back, secured by a braid that held her fringe back, and a pair of sapphire earrings dangling beneath her ears, Charity's gasp of admiration was the first step needed to bolster the confidence that was fast being eroded by fear.

She'd always feared Lord Harkom. Right from the

moment she'd noticed the wild gleam in his eyes when drinking with the other girls when she was a fifteen-year-old and made to peek from the top of the stairs to observe how the ladies used their attractions to lure a man into spending more. There was not a trick Madame Chambon missed and even though the gentlemen complained, they still tipped handsomely for their drinks as a prelude to the other pleasures they'd come to enjoy.

"I'm sorry you had to entertain Lord Harkom," Faith said, turning in a slow circle to ensure she'd not missed anything that could be improved upon. How different from the usual routine of dressing merely in order to bring a little learning to two little boys at the Heathcotes.

"There's far worse than him, but he isn't a…generous lover." Charity shrugged. "Still, he didn't hurt me as he's hurt some of the other girls. Maybe he wasn't as drunk—though he was drunk enough to be surprisingly free with his speech. Oh Faith, I hope I haven't done wrong in telling you something which now has the potential to see you in grave danger. I know I can't talk you out of this, but you will be careful, won't you? Don't let him…" Her words trailed off as if she didn't know what to say, ending finally, "You've never been one of us. I can't bear to think of you being used like a common—"

"Don't say it!" Faith turned upon her almost angrily. "You do what you have to do to save yourself from starving in the gutter. What man wouldn't do the same if the roles were reversed and women ruled the world?" Putting a hand to her forehead, she willed herself to be calm. She needed a clear head, and her corset was decidedly constricting when it came to growing emotional.

Drawing back her shoulders, she said quietly, "I will be careful. I have planned this well. I will never give myself to a man I do not love, and I would rather die than allow Lord

Harkom to take that which I would only willingly give." She tapped the pendant around her neck. Upon it hung a tiny silver vial, hollowed out with a tiny stopper. "When Lord Harkom invites me to drink champagne, half the contents in this will see him lose consciousness, while I help myself to the information I'm sure he can't help boasting about."

"But Faith, that is far too dangerous! If he catches you, he'll punish you dreadfully!" Charity looked like she was going to cry. "He'll torture you! He did that to Anastasia, and it took her three weeks before her face was healed. Imagine what he'll do to you!"

Coldly, Faith said, "I won't let him. The entire contents of this vial are enough to kill someone my size. I'm prepared to take my chances, Charity." She smiled suddenly. "But I *won't* fail. I won't let Lord Harkom be the cause of my destruction for a second time."

SHE DID NOT FEEL SO BOLD BY THE TIME SHE WAS ADMITTED TO Mistress Kate's dancing rooms later that evening. Faith had it on good authority that Lord Harkom was going to be in attendance, having spoken to the ageing courtesan earlier in the afternoon to ensure she'd be received.

Once she'd made it clear that she was not here to poach any of Mistress Kate's long-term, favoured Cyprians, there'd been no opposition.

"Lord Harkom, is it? You're welcome to him," Mistress Kate had said with a curl of her lip. "I should pay you for the service you'll be rendering me this evening if you take him off my hands."

Her words did nothing to increase Faith's enthusiasm in her venture, though it did firm her resolve. Lord Harkom was a man who'd traded with impunity on his lineage for far too long. The fact that Faith intended ruining his reputation in a professional rather than private capacity gave her far greater satisfaction.

Now, Faith arranged herself on a chaise longue beneath a window in one of the smaller reception rooms, with the agreement that Mistress Kate would ensure that Lord Harkom came upon her at some stage during the evening.

A chance meeting would be far more effective to her plan than otherwise.

Of course, she'd also be vulnerable to other visitors, but she'd have to navigate those complications as they arose.

The room was thick was the scent of perfume and powder, and overwarm from the fire and the many people who occupied it. Faith gazed around her and wondered at the fact that Mistress Kate's had remained so popular for so long. It had been established by Kate in her youth, but even as she'd aged, she'd retained the loyalty of the many gentlemen she'd pleased during her career while ensuring an eager turnover of girls.

No, not eager. What girl would wish for a life so uncertain?

Nervously, Faith ran her finger around her low neckline. Lord, but it was difficult to play a role so alien to her natural inclination, but she had no choice if she were to achieve anything of value in her short, worthless life.

The room was growing even warmer as it filled with more perfumed, heated bodies. Behind her fan, Faith recognised several regulars from Madame Chambon's. But they were men she'd only seen from afar. Other than the night she'd been photographed, she'd never been on display. And surely a grainy photograph in a newspaper, and a painting that had briefly titillated society a year ago, would not reveal her tonight.

Only Lord Harkom would recognise her sufficiently to stop.

But, of course, the effort to which she'd gone to shore up her natural assets attracted the attention of those on the prowl. And the fact that Faith was here, in this room, proclaimed her as the whore she'd sworn she'd never be.

Nor would she, though she inclined her head and answered demurely when a couple of young blades on the town lurched up to her.

"What blessed charms has Mistress Kate served up to us tonight," declared the darker one, swaying dangerously as he looked from Faith to his friend. "Why, perhaps you'd care to dance, miss. The orchestra has just tuned up, don't you hear?"

"I like my men to be steadier on their feet, though you are very kind, sir." Faith simpered at him from over her fan. "And taller. Yes, I like my men to be taller. And even darker than you."

The gentleman pushed back his shoulders. "Why, you do have a discerning eye, don't you?" He sounded aggrieved. "Perhaps you never do get up and dance if you set your standards so high."

Faith made a pretence of sighing deeply. "I've spent many an evening languishing here," she said. "Disappointed. Waiting." She fluttered her eyes and raised them to the ceiling and was in the process of returning her gaze to the disaffected young man before her, when she beheld the very reason she was here.

And her heart did a frantic lurch to the top of her ribcage before settling like a stone.

"For a gentleman like me," supplied Lord Harkom, easing himself into her orbit and elbowing Faith's original admirer and his friend out of the way. For a long moment, he stared at her; a calculating gleam in his eye.

As if he'd run her to ground.

Faith turned her head, a frisson of fear making her mouth tremble.

All to the good. Let him see her fear. It would make him believe all the more powerfully in his mastery over her. He'd think he'd caught her by surprise.

He took a step closer. "Well, well, well," he murmured. "Miss Faith Montague. Who would have thought to find you…here."

Faith raised one shoulder as if in defiance and part self-protectiveness. She saw his gaze brush over her bare flesh, and the desire leap and dance in his coal-black eyes.

Oh God, she did not want to do this. And yet, she had to go through with it. Had to make him believe in her fear, her reluctance. It would stoke the abusing monster within him to act.

"Lord Harkom." Her tone sounded husky and inviting. She swallowed. "Good evening." What else could she say?

He settled himself beside her, his thigh pressing against hers on the love seat as he called to a waiter to bring them both brandy.

She took the cut-glass tumbler she was offered without a word, but was forced to answer when he remarked, "It's been some time since we last met. Since you reneged on the agreement we had, in fact. I wondered where you'd gone. Yes, I've often wondered that." He looked at her enquiringly, a note of menace in his tone.

"I found a friend who was good to me. Very good to me." She took a sip of her brandy and allowed a note of sorrow to creep into her voice while her eyes rose heavenward. "Sadly, all good things come to an end."

"So, you were quick to find a replacement for young Westaway. And me. Glad to know you weren't broken-hearted all this time. But you're at a loose end tonight, I can see." He stood and put his hand on her shoulder, his fingers playing with the light fabric that edged her shoulder strap. Faith shivered, and he ran his hand down her arm and gently gripped her elbow, as if feeling its smoothness, its composition.

"Ah Faith, you and I have some unfinished business, don't we?" With both hands on her shoulders, he drew her up. The familiar notes of leather and sandalwood filled her senses. She'd been too close to the smell of him before. "Come home with me and I'll show you I'm not the man you thought you feared."

Faith stared up at him and shook her head. "I don't want to go home with you, Lord Harkom," she murmured. "You can offer me nothing that I want."

His lordship glanced about the room. "You think there's someone here who can? Perhaps those two striplings who were courting you earlier?" Drawing her closer, he dipped his head and whispered, "I'm a rich and powerful man, and I think you know that I want you. Let bygones be bygones and I'll show you how kind and…generous I can be."

Faith stood her ground. "No, Lord Harkom." She shook her head. "The first time I met you, you tried to take what I was unwilling to give. You would not take no for an answer."

"A mere misunderstanding." He gave a gentle laugh. "Your procuress sanctioned more than a little persuasion to break you in. Encouraged it, in fact, since she said you'd never learn what you had to do otherwise."

"You were not gentle with me, Lord Harkom." Faith's trembling was real. "I have been fortunate to have enjoyed the protection of a man who was nothing but kind."

"It was not kind to leave you, Faith." Lord Harkom encompassed their surroundings with a sweep of his arm.

"He died unexpectedly, Lord Harkom. And left me with but a little provision. Not enough to tide me into my old age.

I need to shore up my future while I can, while I am young and still—"

"Beautiful." He dipped his head to breathe in the scent of her hair and murmured it again. "So beautiful, Faith, and you have taught me the lesson of valuing that which I want so very much." Lightly, he placed both hands on her bare shoulders. "See how gentle I can be when it's worth my while? I want you, Faith. Not just for tonight. Come home with me, and I promise that I will treat you like a precious China doll."

Faith took a faltering step, her reluctance so from the heart, but at the same time furthering her purpose. Before they'd reached the doorway, she stopped. "You must woo me, take it slowly, treat me like a lady, if you are to enjoy me beyond tonight. If you think tonight is for settling old scores or teaching me a lesson, then that will not further your interests, Lord Harkom."

"My, my, Faith. You've learned how to negotiate and dish out threats. How very sweet." He laughed. "And intriguing."

"So, you promise you will deal with me kindly? Yes? Then I shall tell Mistress Kate who I am going with tonight. That will be my insurance, Lord Harkom."

She let him lead her through the throng, to stop to say a word to Mistress Kate, then out of the doors and into the street.

"Mind the step, Faith. I wonder if my offer of brandy was such a good idea. You want all your wits about you if you're to enjoy what I have in store for you."

"I hope you're not accusing me of overindulgence, my lord." Faith looked up at Lord Harkom, blinking as if to clear her head. "And I'm not sure I want what you have in store for me."

"Yet you're coming with me, aren't you, Faith?" He flagged down a hackney carriage and helped her in. "All the way to my beautiful home where I can make you feel like the princess you are. The princess I could make you. You are intrigued, aren't you? You want to know what kind of man I really am?"

Faith settled herself into the dark interior, sighing deeply as she dropped her head onto Lord Harkom's shoulder. At least feigning sleep for a few minutes would give her time to think and dispense with the need for conversation.

When the hackney halted outside his townhouse, she straightened, rubbing her eyes as she stared at him in the light of the gas lamp on the pavement.

He jumped out and opened the door, but she remained on the cushion.

"I'm really not sure this is such a good idea, Lord Harkom."

"Why, my dear? You considered it an excellent idea not so long ago."

She looked mutinous. "You helped ruin my reputation. And you and I have never been friends."

"But there is so much potential for us to be much more than that, eh Faith? Besides, I had nothing to do with the publication of the photograph, I assure you." He took her hand and helped her out, while she went unresistingly. Like a lamb to the slaughter. Except it wouldn't be hers. She was determined upon that.

When he put his arm about her, taking advantage of his close proximity to caress her breast, she slapped his hand away.

He laughed. "Oh yes, there are certain pretences to be kept up. I think that's part of your charm, Faith. Now, let me help you up the steps. That's a very tight skirt you're wearing. Very daring but very delectable. I shall enjoy seeing the mechanics of how you get it to cling so alluringly to that lovely body of yours. Yes, I'm quite the lover, but quite the engineer too. One is never just the one thing, don't you agree?"

"I don't promise I'll stay, Lord Harkom," she warned him as he led her through his sumptuously decorated townhouse. "You shall have to work hard to persuade me that there is any advantage in furthering our...acquaintance. If you do anything against my will, you will regret it; I promise you."

"Oh, I do love being threatened by a beautiful woman."

His chuckle chilled her to the bone. Faith sent him an arch look as they passed along a dim corridor lined with family portraits. "Don't think you can treat me as you treated me before when I was naïve and vulnerable."

She dismissed his inevitable scepticism at her words with another warning. "I'm neither of those things though, of course, I won't pretend I'm not looking for a protector. I doubt it will be you for more than this one night, but given time I shall find someone to my liking. Someone worthy of me, and someone who will punish you if you dare do wrong by me. Do you understand?"

Still chuckling as he nodded, he escorted her through the door, closing it behind them, catching Faith off balance as he pushed her against the wall, pinioning her like a butterfly as he covered her mouth with his.

Faith brought her knee up with enough pressure to break the contact without hurting him excessively, saying brightly, "Too soon, my lord. What did I tell you? A little wooing to break me in is required, I thought I'd made that clear. Perhaps some champagne? My head is starting to clear and, increasingly, I think that coming here was a very bad idea."

To her relief, amusement replaced the scowl that she'd feared was the precursor to greater menace.

He swept her an elaborate bow. "Of course, my dear, let's bring out the champagne before we get down to business, if that's what you want." He gripped her forearm and led her towards the dining room where he pulled out a chair for her, before ringing the bell for champagne.

Faith took the bottle as he was about to open it, her mind reeling with the risk of doing what she was about to suggest, rather than staying safely here.

As he sank into the chair beside her, she tickled his cheek with the feather in her headdress. "We don't *have* to drink it here, my lord." Her tone was teasing. "I only wanted to make clear that I don't expect to be hustled into any congress without the necessary preliminaries." Rising, she pointed to the glasses before them. "Why don't you take those, and I'll take this, and we can remove ourselves from the proximity of the servants. We can partake of a glass while you compare me to the stars and the moon and the sun, and if your words are pretty enough, and I've consumed enough to make me insensible to the terrible mistake I know in my heart of hearts this really is, then we can proceed from there. How does that please my lord?" She looked playfully at him, astonished to see the transformation. Charity was right. He truly did like being ordered about by a woman.

But, of course, he'd got ahead of himself, and Faith could only hope she was able to reel him in, for once in his bedchamber, he marched her to the bed and tossed her down upon the counterpane, looming over her to kiss her throat and the swell of her breasts. Faith wriggled out from beneath him and stood with her hands on her hips.

"Really, my lord; it's all or nothing with you, isn't it?" She moved unhurriedly towards the small sofa in the centre of the room where she settled herself, tucking her feet beneath her and waving the uncorked bottle towards him.

"Now you can do the honours. I need a drink, Lord Harkom. Probably two if I'm going to enjoy what you have in store for me."

"But not so much that you'll be in danger of not remembering such delights, my precious," he murmured.

Faith hiccupped as she took it, tossing back a long draft as he was in the process of sitting down.

"There's no danger of that, Lord Harkom, though I will need you to top me up." She waved her half-empty glass in the air while indicating the champagne bottle on the sideboard adding with a suggestive look, "I'm referring to my drink, as I'm sure you understand."

He hesitated then visibly relaxed. Perhaps he liked what her double entendre suggested—that she was growing drunk and malleable, and he'd soon have her where he wanted her.

"Well, well, you are in a delightfully pleasing mood tonight and very different from the last time we met, Faith," he remarked, his back turned to her for the few seconds she needed.

The less than two seconds it took for her to uncap the tiny vial around her neck and tip the contents into her glass.

"Having London's most beautiful woman in my bed was beyond my expectations when I set out this evening." He brought them both a glass of fizzing liquid before settling close beside her on the sofa, placing his free hand on her thigh.

She'd ignore it for now. The hand of a man on her person. A man she despised. It was intended as foreplay, but as God was her witness, Faith would do whatever was in her power to avert what Lord Harkom had in mind.

She studied him over the rim of her glass. Did he suspect anything? Or did he imagine that her desire for material goods could overcome the deep loathing that he'd whipped up in her when he'd manhandled her so roughly a year before?

It was a shock to realise that his experience must have

seen the return of women whom he'd abused so that Faith's behaviour tonight was not aberrant.

And yet, to her it was so very aberrant.

But then, wasn't she the consummate actress?

For a year, she'd played her role as demure governess so well she'd never been suspected for the fraud she was. For the woman of notoriety she was. For three years prior to that she'd been trained in the arts of seduction. She knew how to whip up a man's desire, how to spur him on when he might have second thoughts, how to pleasure him in bed. In an academic sense, only, of course.

And how to take control if a situation suggested danger. This was where her energies were being channelled now, for she had no intention of doing any of the former.

She'd rather die than have to practise those bedroom skills she'd silently sworn would be reserved for the man she loved.

Crispin.

But did she love him enough, after all this time, that he deserved the ultimate sacrifice?

Their love had been brief, passionate, and sincere. She still believed that.

But how quickly he had dismissed her.

Lord Harkom's hand crept further up her thigh as he bent to refill their glasses at Faith's mumbled direction.

"When we've finished the bottle, we can begin the grand finale!" she declared.

"Or the first act," he responded with a throaty chuckle.

Lord, neither if Faith's plan came to fruition.

But dutifully, and as her role required, she giggled, nibbling his ear as she leaned into him; distracting him with her pretence of embracing his overtures.

"Oh, but you are killing me with anticipation, my love," he muttered, twisting his large body so that he suddenly seemed in danger of crushing her as he trailed kisses along her jawbone.

"Let's drink to that!" she declared with a raucous laugh, raising her glass high, offering it to him with an impish look while she relieved him of his empty glass.

Obediently, he drained the contents of the glass before finding himself in possession of another glass filled with fizzing liquid while Faith declared with false joy, "Yes! Drink to tonight's wild congress."

And without questioning, Lord Harkom drained that glass, too.

CHAPTER 28

Crispin had never desired visiting Madame Chambon's when it was lauded amongst his set as a place of high revels.

And certainly not after he'd learned it was Faith's lodgings, for by then his heart had been eviscerated by her faithlessness, and Madame Chambon's represented everything he despised. It had hothoused a woman who'd learned tricks to trap and entice a man when he'd thought himself so clever in sniffing out artifice.

He'd thought Miss Montague so uniquely innocent and unaffected by the world around her; a fragile rose without thorns, and he was to have been the gallant who would rescue her and gently teach her the ways of the world.

Now, surrounded by the far-from-innocent young women from whom he presumed Faith had learned the tricks of the trade, he felt out of place and deeply uncomfortable.

Lord Delmore had placed him in an impossible position. Crispin had no wish to delve into the overinflated mysteries that an imaginative young Cyprian had been hinting at, for surely they did not endanger him, and surely she was merely fishing for Crispin's involvement for reasons unknown?

He suspected these reasons unknown had a very clear and calculating agenda.

"Charity?" he asked, when an elfin-faced creature sat on the arm of the sofa he was sitting on, her chestnut hair brushing his cheek as she leaned towards him.

"I heard you were looking for me, sir. Come along, shall we?" She took his hand and he rose, silent as she led him along a corridor and up a flight of stairs to a bedchamber on the first floor. "Now, where shall we begin?" Her smile was pleasant and helpful as she waved him towards the large iron bed that dominated the room. A lamp upon the side table bathed the room in a soft glow, and the red-velvet counterpane and plumped-up pillows filled his senses with unexpected desire.

Not for Charity, who'd dropped one shoulder of her evening gown and who seemed pretty and pleasing enough.

But for Faith.

For all he knew, she was still here, and this was just the prelude for finding himself in the right bed.

Her bed.

Yes, he'd weaken if he saw her again. He knew he would.

And he despised himself for it.

Taking a seat on the edge of the counterpane, he said, "I want you to tell me what you know about Faith Montague." He made no move to adjust his clothing, while Charity by this stage was hitching up her skirts to kneel on the bed beside him, one hand already insinuating itself inside his shirt.

She withdrew it as if stung. "Good lord, you're Mr Westaway, aren't you?"

With a scramble and a tugging of her clothing to appear

more decent, she took up position at the end of the bed and regarded him, curiously. "I never thought you'd come *here*?"

"Where else might I find her?" Amusement swept away his discomfort. She seemed horrified to be in the company of a gentleman he hoped Faith had painted as not using women in such a cavalier fashion.

"Certainly not here!"

"But this is the only address I have for her."

"She's not lived here for a year. And before that, she never lived as one of us. You do know that, of course."

Before he could make any remark to this, she indicated the bed. "Faith lived in the attic like one of the servants. She didn't have a bed for entertaining."

"But she lived here for…how long? Three years?" He didn't care what she made of his scepticism.

"Yes, Madame had instructions to teach her how to entice a gentleman, but Madame was instructed that she was to be kept pure." Charity sighed. "It was difficult for Faith. Some of the girls were resentful of her because she was so beautiful, and because she didn't have to do the things they had to do for money. They saw that she had lovely clothes, and that she was given learning from a tutor, and that she went to tea at Claridges once a month. She didn't have many friends."

Crispin held up his hand. "*Who* made these instructions concerning Faith?"

"Mrs Gedge. I remember the name only because Faith made up the saying that rhymed, "Working for Mrs Gedge was like living on a knife edge."

"Mrs Gedge." Crispin rolled the name over his tongue as a bitter taste filled his mouth. "What did she look like?"

Charity shrugged. "I never saw her. I only heard that she had bright-red hair. One of the girls saw her when she came in her carriage with Lady Vernon."

"Lady Vernon came *here*?"

"Often. Though she always came in disguise. Sometimes she'd bring girls to Madame Chambon."

"Good lord." He looked about him, horrified. "Lady Vernon brought girls here?" He couldn't begin to imagine the humpbacked dowager stepping foot in a place like this. "And one of these girls was Faith? When was this? When did Lady Vernon bring her here the first time?"

"About three years ago. I wasn't here, then."

"But *why* was Faith brought here?" Crispin stared at the counterpane which must have seen so much action, then through the windows at the church spire outside, and tried to assimilate his thoughts. "If she wasn't one of you, and if she lived in the attic, what possible reason did she have for being here?"

Charity settled herself more comfortably on the end of the bed, tucking her knees beneath her chin as she looked at him. "You do ask a lot of questions. I hope they're going to help Faith." She raised her eyebrows and went on, "Faith had been a servant for Mrs Gedge, who accused her of stealing. She hadn't, of course. Faith was always honest; I hope you know that. Always true to her word. But when a fine lady accuses a servant of something, whose word is going to be believed? So, after Mrs Gedge accused Faith of taking her daughter's bracelet, she brought Faith here because she said Faith had to work off her debt to her."

"What proof did this Mrs Gedge have against Faith?"

"None, of course. She simply found Faith holding her daughter's bracelet in her daughter's bedchamber, and when Mrs Gedge challenged her, Faith said the young lady had promised it to her for showing her a secret passage into a gentleman's bedchamber." Charity shrugged again. "Being here wasn't all bad, of course. Faith got a good education, and she loved her lessons in art and in history and politics. She used to teach some of us more interested girls, both because we liked to learn, but also because it helps pass the time with the gentlemen who don't always want to do things in bed. And, then Faith got to go to smart places. Like I said, sometimes she'd take tea at Claridges with Mrs Gedge."

"Did you say Mrs Gedge was American?"

Charity nodded. "It's hard not to miss an accent like that. I never heard her but Grace, one of the girls here, said she heard an American accent coming from the carriage the night Faith was brought here. And Faith said the lady she'd worked for was an American."

"Do you remember Faith ever talking about Mrs Gedge's daughter?" A tingle of apprehension ran all the way down Crispin's legs as he thought of the life of indenture Faith must have lived within these walls.

"Yes, but the girl died. Killed herself, Faith said. Not that she knew her well as Faith had only been working for Mrs Gedge, or rather, Miss Constancia, for a little while before this grand house party."

"So, Miss Constancia asked Faith about a secret doorway?" He'd always wondered how the young woman could have slipped into his room without him knowing it.

Then slipped into his bed.

Lord, he'd never forget his horror. He'd overreacted though. He saw that, now. But to find a young woman, naked in his bed in the middle of the night in her own house, had been beyond traumatic.

Charity sighed. "And then the young lady did herself in with the young gentleman's razor in his bathtub. They found her in the bath. Not a sight one would forget, I imagine."

No, it had not been. Crispin's stomach churned at the memory. But he'd hardly known the girl. Met her on only a few occasions before she'd set her cap at him.

Crispin rose. It was too difficult to have to think about, though the vision of a young woman floating dead in his bathtub, her red-gold hair spread out about her, her face serene and deathly white in contrast with the blood-red water, often returned to haunt him.

"Mrs Gedge was not only Faith's benefactress; she was the anonymous benefactress of the grand art prize."

The prize that was to place Faith under his roof with instructions that she must make him fall in love with her.

Why? So she could break his heart, of course.

And what choices other than to obey would be available to a vulnerable young girl with a threat of prosecution hanging over her head?

"Where will I find her?" he asked, and Charity cocked her head.

"She's gone to see Lord Harkom, of course. I thought you knew. But, I suppose you had to be told that Faith's not the girl you thought her, otherwise you'd not want to rush over there now. Which you really ought to do."

"She's with Harkom? By God, I ought to—!" He raked his fingers through his hair. "She's with him…*now*, you say? Why not tell me this earlier!?"

"I just told you, Mr Westaway. You came here believing Faith used you as an opportunity to better herself. You didn't believe she loved you, which I assure you, she does. Otherwise, she'd not risk herself with Lord Harkom in order to salvage those letters he says are so damaging to you."

Crispin shook his head. "I have nothing to hide. No love letters that I've ever written which run the risk of sullying my reputation. I can't imagine what Lord Harkom thinks he can hold over me. Unless…!" He moved quickly to the door. "Unless he was using it as a ruse in order to lure Faith to him. She refused him before so…"

Charity fidgeted with her necklace. "Lord Harkom doesn't like to be turned down; it's true. So maybe what you say is right. But nor would it have been right for me to say nothing if there really was something to those letters."

"But why wait so long? Why did you not write immediately, if that was your fear?"

"I'm not stupid, sir, but the letters do have a way of mixing themselves up before my eyes. And no, Faith was careful that no one knew where she was so as not to put me, or her friends, in danger. Besides, I was hoping I'd see you myself so I could tell you about Faith. Like I'm doing now."

"How unlucky I missed her if she was here earlier tonight!" He strode to the door. "Thank you, Charity. I shall go there now. I just hope to God I'm not too late."

FAITH LOOKED AT THE PRONE FORM OF LORD HARKOM WITH satisfaction. Sprawled on the sofa, arms outstretched, legs splayed, he did not look the kind of specimen she'd consider worthy of her, for all he was handsome in a cruel, effete kind of way. And rich.

He would have set her up, nicely.

If she were that kind of girl.

Carefully, she assessed her opportunities. She could only trust that Charity had been right.

She hurried to the large bed and went down on her knees to scrabble underneath. The light was too dim to see, so she rose and quickly carried the lamp to aid her search, going down on her belly to feel about in the dark.

Perhaps Charity had mistaken the chest for something else?

Perhaps Lord Harkom had moved it?

Lord Harkom made a loud snoring noise and his body convulsed, making Faith jump, too.

But as her arm swung wide, it found the handle of an

object which, drawing it towards her and into the light, turned out to be a small, neat chest.

With no lock.

Her hands were trembling so much, and her heart beating so fiercely she felt sick, but time was not on her side, so she set to her search with as clear a head as she could.

The letters were arranged in bundles, and the top few seemed to be correspondence from various women to Lord Harkom. Tied up in ribbon, they all seemed similar she decided as she slipped each from its envelope and read the first couple of sentences. Mistresses and spurned lovers. There seemed a lot of those.

As she neared the bottom, her spirits fell. Perhaps she was looking in the wrong chest for there was no sign of anything that suggested an interest in Mr Westaway.

Until she reached the very bottom and found the only envelope not addressed to Lord Harkom or from Lord Harkom.

Faith rolled back on her haunches and closed her eyes a moment. Could this be the letter she was after? Her fingers seemed not to work as they should, and it was difficult not to tear the cheap, single sheet of paper she pulled from its envelope before quickly scanning its contents.

Lord Harkom groaned in his sleep, and Faith's fingers went slack. She stared at the letter, its words a jumble in front of her face. This must be how Charity had felt every time Faith had tried to teach her the alphabet.

But it wasn't that Faith couldn't understand the contents. There was nothing ambiguous about the information, or about the demands for satisfaction or else public disclosure would follow.

Putting a hand to her bosom to try and still the rapid rise and fall, she closed her eyes. Her stomach churned. This wasn't what she'd expected to find. Not at all.

But it clearly was what Lord Harkom had alluded to when he'd told Charity he had correspondence that would damn Mr Westaway in the eyes of the public.

She was just tucking the envelope into her corset and about to close the lid of the chest and rise, when the last three letters of a very familiar name caught her eye.

"Christ, but my head hurts!"

Faith jerked her head up, snatching blindly at the letters and stuffing three, indiscriminately, down the front of her bodice before pushing the chest back into its hiding place and taking up the lamp as she rose to her feet.

"Faith, is that you? What are you doing?"

Faith waved the lamp. "Oh, Lord Harkom! I was so worried and about to fetch help. I…I thought perhaps you might have had a seizure."

When she saw the top of a letter poking out from her corset, she put her hand down her front to push it out of sight and gave her décolletage a little tug, as if righting her clothes.

She leaned over him and put her hand to his cheek. "Goodness, but you are dangerously hot to the touch. You need some water. Instantly!"

Before he could grip her dress with his grasping hand, Faith nimbly eluded him and glided to the door. "I'll be back with a servant and something to drink as soon as I can!" she lied.

When she'd finally escaped into the corridor, she picked up her skirts and ran for her life.

CHAPTER 29

"*L*ord Harkom, my apologies for intruding at this late hour!" Breathing heavily after his sprint from Soho to the more salubrious environs of Mayfair, Crispin stood in the doorway of his lordship's bedchamber and eyed with dispassion a clearly dissipated Lord Harkom, who was lying in an alarmingly abandoned state.

The two empty champagne glasses did not augur well. Not with the dishevelled state the other man was in, his evening clothes rumpled, though fortunately, the counterpane didn't look too disturbed.

Still, the chaise longue was a comfortable affair, and it was clear Harkom had been entertaining female guests. Crispin could tell by the lingering fragrance of peonies. Faith liked the scent of peonies, though he didn't care to think too much along those lines.

Had she really come here? Had she ventured into the lion's den in order to safeguard Crispin's reputation? How would he know if these were just more lies? Charity seemed sincere enough, but, like Faith, she'd been trained to act a part.

Harkom blinked and rose, stiffly, from the chaise, running his hands through his rumpled hair and gazing blearily about him before focusing on Crispin.

"Gad, but that was some sport, and I don't wonder you've elbowed your way in looking for your piece of the girl. I knew you'd come sniffing her out, but she's gone now." Harkom laughed and lurched to the cabinet where he kept his brandy.

Crispin eyed him beadily. He seemed addleheaded yet not drunk. Surely, he should have been more aggressive and demanding as to how and why Crispin had found his way to his room. A servant certainly wouldn't have led him there.

Indeed, Crispin had been very creative in gaining admittance to Lord Harkom's townhouse with none of the servants the wiser.

With an unsteady hand, Lord Harkom poured them both a measure and handed one to Crispin, who put it down on the nearest surface. He was not about to drink companionably with the possible violator of the woman he loved.

"What did you do to her? She didn't come here willingly." The anger started in his spine and was like a slow burn to his brain. He didn't know if he'd have the self-control to behave as he ought, for physical violence would get him nowhere. Finding Faith to ensure she was safe was his primary concern.

Harkom blinked, with difficulty it seemed, as he turned back to Crispin. "Oh yes, she hooked her little hand into the crook of my arm and all but begged me to look after her. I found her at Mistress Kate's." He smiled, nastily. "Terribly sad. Her previous protector had died, and she had no other offers of a roof over her head. Of course, it was music to my senses. It's rather well known in some circles that she's become my little obsession."

"But she's not here now." Crispin tried to hide his nervous

distraction as Lord Harkom leaned against the sideboard. The man was holding his hand to the side of his head and swaying.

He seemed to be having trouble concentrating on the matter at hand. "No, I can't imagine what I was thinking, letting her go like that. Still, she'll come back. And if she doesn't soon enough, I know how to make her."

"I'll get to her first." Crispin's voice was a dangerous growl.

Harkom blinked. For a moment he looked surprised, then his face took on its habitual sneer. "Oh, the fact you had her first was a great pity to me, but I intend to *keep* her. With your name about to be so sullied, you'll wonder how you never knew before now that you had no friends."

Crispin bit into his bottom lip. "I have done nothing of which I am ashamed."

Lord Harkom chuckled and began to count on his fingers. "No past dalliances with married women; no secret babies foisted on well-bred young ladies." His voice was becoming increasingly slurred, and he seemed to have difficulty standing straight. "It's true enough, what you say. Sadly, you had no say in this little matter, though if you ask your father if your mother was an innkeeper's daughter, you might be a little disappointed by his lack of conviction when he tries to deny it."

Crispin blinked stupidly at the other man. "What are you saying?"

Lord Harkom sent him a long look, though he blinked rapidly throughout, as if trying to keep Crispin in focus.

"Never wondered why you look nothing like your father?"

"I take after my maternal line."

"So that's what you've been told? By your fond pater? Or your anxious aunts?" The older man laughed. "Of course, it's what you'd want to believe, but what about if your mother was barren? Or believed she was barren after ten years being married to your father yielded no heir for poor desperate Lord Maxwell?"

"This is an outrageous claim. No one will believe it! On what basis can you even suggest such a thing."

Lord Harkom's lips stretched wide, and his nostrils flared. "Only from the woman who delivered you, asking me for money in return for a letter she'd kept between your father and the poor unmarried woman whom he paid to relieve her of her baby." He examined the half-moons of his right hand.

"Anyone could have made such a spurious claim, but where would it get them? It's a forgery, of course! What possible reason would she have to contact *you*?"

"Because she also found the love letters your mother and I exchanged before your mother was forced to marry your father, a much older man she could not bear, by the way."

"You lie! My mother would never—"

"How would you know? You were only an infant when she died. You don't even remember your mother."

It was true, but it did not bear up Harkom's claims. Crispin shook his head as if to clear it. Lies! And yet, an uncomfortable kernel of possibility had taken root. Not only did Crispin look nothing like his father, or indeed, the portrait of his mother that hung in the dining room, Crispin's temperament was as different from his father's as it was possible to be.

Harkom shrugged. "Your father married the woman I loved and blamed her for being barren when clearly the problem lay with him. But he needed a son, didn't he?" He chuckled. "You only have to read the letter to find out how he managed it. Why, your father *bought* you, believing you were his, when in fact the girl was already pregnant when she allowed Lord Maxwell to lie with her. Pregnant by a farm labourer!" He burst out laughing. "I can't imagine where you got your delicate hands from and your fine, painterly sensitivities. Anomalies arise where one least expects them to, don't they? But yet, it's all in the letter."

Crispin shook his head. "No, I don't believe it. Show me the letter. Or don't you have it? Perhaps Faith succeeded in retrieving it, after all. It's the reason she came here after she learned from her friend, Charity, whom you visited at Madame Chambon's, that you had information that was damaging to me?"

Lord Harkom jerked as if he'd been stung, and his eyes glanced to a location somewhere near the base of the bed. Regaining some composure, he said, "Your Faith proved most faith*less* when she aligned her star with mine. I promise you; she was not thinking of you, or retrieving letters, when we made love this afternoon. I've never been with a woman so eager!"

"How dare you!" Crispin clenched his fists and strode over to Lord Harkom, gripping the man's collar and forcing his head up. "You lie! Faith has a pure heart and pure motives. She would never have come to you and put herself in danger unless it was to help…me."

It was a sobering thought. Whether or not it would prove true, was another matter. But yet, it's what he wanted to believe.

To his surprise, Lord Harkom's head lolled, and he slumped even further down the wall. Crispin was not met with the aggression he'd expected.

As for the story he'd just told Crispin, it was so far-fetched Crispin couldn't begin to assimilate how there could be a grain of truth in it.

And yet, he'd never felt he belonged in the home he'd grown up in. His father had always seemed distant and alien, though wasn't that normal?

"Show me the letter," he demanded once more in a low voice. It couldn't be true. A father who was a country peasant, and a mother who was an innkeeper's daughter? Common yeoman stock?

Perhaps Lord Harkom acceded because he was concerned at Faith's reasons for coming to his room. He certainly would not have done it on Crispin's account. He took a couple of staggering steps towards the bed and dropped to his knees, pulling out a small wooden chest.

Two narrow furrows between his eyes grew deeper as he shuffled the papers and his breathing increased. He appeared not to see Crispin when he turned his head in his direction, his eyes glassy as he muttered, "By God, the wench has taken it." He thumped his hand on the lid. "The wench has stolen the letter. Why did I not think that might be a possibility?"

"One might not have thought it necessary to lock a cupboard or a chest containing incriminating documents if peddling lies is such a commonplace event." Crispin moved towards the door, then, on second thoughts, changed direction and took a few steps towards Lord Harkom. "I was going to leave like a gentleman, but in view of the fact that apparently I am a man of no breeding, let me give you this for your treatment of Faith and all those other poor women you treat like playthings."

Striking out with a sharp uppercut, he watched with satisfaction as Lord Harkom crumpled to the floor.

WITH THE LETTERS burning a hole in her bodice, FAITH made her way to Madame Chambon's as quickly as she could, entering through the back door and arriving in Charity's bedchamber to find it mercifully empty but for Charity.

"Oh, my dear friend, I was so worried for you," Charity

wept as she threw her arms about Faith. "Did Lord Harkom hurt you? Did Mr Westaway find you?"

"Mr Westaway?" A thrill of longing travelled through Faith at the sound of his name, but disappointment followed for the fact she'd not seen him. "He really went after me? I mean, he took the trouble...not through vengeance?"

"Lord, Faith, must you be so suspicious? I'm not and look at the life I lead." Charity indicated her room with a sweep of her arm. "So, you found what you wanted from Lord Harkom and he didn't hurt you?" The fact she was so anxious about Faith's well-being made Faith want to weep on the spot.

Also, what she'd learned upon reading them.

"He didn't hurt me, no. And I have the letters.

"So, now you know the truth? Or was Lord Harkom nothing but hot air?"

A tear forced its way out of Faith's eye as she put her hand to her bodice. "It wasn't what I wanted to be the truth, but I do have the incriminating letters—and Lord Harkom doesn't. That's the main thing." A spasm of fear made her reassess as she turned towards the door. "Please don't ask me about it now, Charity. Look, I really should go. I can't subject you to danger. Now I need to find Miss Eaves. Perhaps she can help me."

"Miss Eaves!" Charity scoffed, calling after her friend as Faith ran to the door, "Come back, Faith. I'm perfectly safe. You know Madame Chambon guards us like a wolfhound, and the only reason Anastasia got hurt was because Madame thought she needed teaching a lesson. Please tell me why you want to seek out Miss Eaves? She's no friend of yours. Unless you want her to print the letter you found!"

"Dear God, only one of them." Faith swung around, her jaw set. "I'll never breathe a word about the other letter, and so I'm not even going to tell you what was in it. But Charity, when Anastasia got hurt, didn't she leave shortly afterwards?"

Charity nodded.

"Do you know where she went?"

"No, I don't, Faith. She moved on to another life. That's how it is with girls like us. No need to look so concerned."

"She left with Lady Vernon, didn't she?"

"I don't remember exactly—"

"Please try." Faith gripped Charity by both forearms and looked into her friend's eyes. "Try and remember who took Anastasia away."

Charity looked puzzled, and then a look of understanding crept over her face.

"Yes, I don't have time to tell you more, Charity, but this is the reason I need to find Miss Eaves. She might not be the one who can reveal this to the world, and although she's been no friend of mine, she does have connections, both in the newspaper world and in society. And it's because of her belief that she really was telling a truth the world needed to know, that she printed what she did about me, that I think she's the person most likely to help me now."

"But Faith, you don't even know where she lives!"

"No, but I do know where she'll be tonight." Faith turned and hurried back, a thought occurring to her. "Charity, I need your masque. The one on a stick. Indeed, it's fortuitous that Miss Eaves will be attending Lady Ridgeway's Masquerade. I'm sure she'd not want to talk to me unless we were in disguise."

CHAPTER 30

Crispin didn't care that he was damp with evening mist by the time he'd walked to Madame Chambon's. He needed a bracing walk to clear his head, and he wasn't going anywhere afterwards. Not after he'd located Faith. What he'd say to her, he wasn't sure.

And how she'd react to seeing him after all this time, he had no idea.

Would she consider he'd let her down? He hadn't found her in a whole year though it wasn't for want of trying.

Was there any truth in Lord Harkom's claim, earlier, about what he'd done to Faith?

Not *with* Faith.

He couldn't believe that, and not after Charity's claims that Faith had gone to see him because of her concerns over Crispin.

Her *concerns* over him?

What? About the letter regarding his parentage? Or were they other concerns?

Had Faith read the claims espoused by Harkom? Were they indeed written down as allegations? Letters? Faith had the letters, he suspected, but could there be any truth in them?

His throat felt dry, and his head was sore. The street lamps looked hazy like his surroundings. Was his father's coldness predicated upon the fact that Crispin was not his natural-born son? Could he have suspected that he'd had someone else's bastard foisted on him?

By an innkeeper's daughter?

Crispin swallowed. No, this was Harkom's way of extracting the maximum from the situation. It couldn't be true.

By the time he reached Madame Chambon's, his outerwear was slick with wet, but he didn't care. He just wanted to find Faith and sink into her arms. If she could forgive him, it didn't matter if Harkom's allegations were true or not.

Of course, if Harkom's allegations were given credence, then that was a different matter. But he didn't want to go there yet. He just wanted Faith.

"Oh, Mr Westaway; you just missed her." Charity was lying on her front on her bed, when Crispin entered after knocking briefly and being invited in. She rose onto her knees, her face a picture of delight as her silk peignoir fell away revealing the mounds of her full white breasts over the top of her corset. "I'm so glad it's you though," she added, as she covered herself. "I mean, that *because* it's you, you don't want any of my pleasuring." She blushed, and Crispin could see the flare of colour was real. He was sure he blushed too, as she went on, "I mean, it would be so wrong to be pleasuring the young man whom my best friend is in love with."

Crispin felt a stab in his chest cavity and tried to ignore the words that resounded in his head...*the young man whom my best friend is in love with.* Could that really be true? "Please, Charity, I don't think I have much time and I need to find her!"

"She's gone to Lady Ridgeway's masquerade," Charity told him.

"I can't believe I was too late!" He raked his hands through his hair. "Was she…all right after her encounter with Lord Harkom?" He could barely push out the question, though it seemed odd that Faith would make her way to further revelry if she were not.

"She didn't say. She wanted to find Miss Eaves. She had an important letter to give her."

He blinked. "Miss Eaves? She's going to give the letter to Miss Eaves?"

Could she really have hated him so much?

All the hope and expectation he'd built up drained out of him.

Charity slipped to the floor and went to her dressing table where she began to pin up a curl. "Well, *one* of the letters. She wouldn't tell me about the other one. But the letter she was going to give Miss Eaves was the important one, she said."

"The one she found in Lord Harkom's chest?"

Charity nodded, looking at him in the mirror. "Well, she found them both there. But this one is the one she hopes is going to put things right."

"But…Miss Eaves destroyed Faith's reputation. Faith's not…planning revenge, is she?"

Charity turned as she let out a surprised laugh. "What a masculine thing to say. Revenge? Faith would never resort to revenge to harm anyone." Her forehead wrinkled as she reassessed this statement, looking more closely at Crispin as she added, "I mean, she never intended wreaking revenge on you, Mr Westaway. That was Mrs Gedge's idea, and you do know that Faith was entirely powerless in that woman's hands. Just as I'm powerless in Madame Chambon's. Do you think I like doing what I do to earn a living?" She shrugged. "I simply have no other choice open to me."

This was not the time for Crispin to delve further into these murky depths. When he found Faith, he intended asking her a good many questions about her motivations, but there was too much at stake now for him to tarry.

"Yes, make your way to Lady Ridgeway's, and I hope you find Faith. And that you'll be good to her, for I fear what she's found puts her in very grave danger."

"You know?" Crispin moved forward and gripped Charity's shoulders, forcing her to look at him.

Charity's large blue eyes suddenly filled with tears which she brushed away, saying with a shaky laugh, "I try to pretend there's nothing happening under this roof, and that we're all safe as long as Madame sees us as bringing in the money, but the truth is, a girl is never safe here. One wrong action and Faith could be next."

"Surely you can't mean it." He didn't know what to say. "Are you suggesting there is something more sinister at play than Mrs Gedge's plan for revenge against me?

Charity nodded. "It was in a letter Faith found. I think the letter was from Lady Vernon to Lord Harkom, but Faith wouldn't tell me. She said it would put me in danger to know."

"What do you think it's about, Charity? I need *something* to go on."

"I think it's about a girl who disappeared from here a few months ago. A girl called Anastasia. Lord Harkom was very cruel to her. He hurt her. And then she disappeared."

"And Lady Vernon's involved?"

Charity nodded, her lower lip trembling. "Please don't ask me anything more, Mr Westaway, because it would all be guesswork. It's only after Faith left that I really began to puzzle it all out. And this is my conclusion. I think Lady

Vernon and Lord Harkom are in some evil business together. And unless Faith is very careful, she could find herself in some extremely hot water."

~

FAITH'S ATTIRE WAS PERFECTLY SUITED TO THE EVENING'S entertainment, while Charity's demi-masque on a stick provided the necessary anonymity. Her identity would be discovered in due course, but initially, Faith might be able to mingle enough to search out Miss Eaves before she was asked to leave.

She found the young woman in the midst of a group of ladies all talking about hats.

Only Miss Eaves was not sufficiently interested, so her eyes were scouring the room in search of greater diversion when Faith dropped her demi-masque and caught her eye.

Miss Eaves's mouth fell open, but a subtle crook of her finger had Faith following her into the shadows.

"Well, well, Miss Montague. I see you are back at your trade." The young woman's eyes raked Faith's ensemble with obvious censure, for the figure-hugging ensemble, while fashionable, was risqué. "I just wonder how you have made your way inside without being recognised. You know you have no place here."

Faith had no time to defend herself or try to alter Miss Eaves's opinion. The young woman had clearly become a great deal more polished and sophisticated since the first time Faith had met her.

"Read this and tell me what you think." Faith thrust Lady Vernon's letter into Miss Eaves's gloved hand and waited impatiently as the other slowly began to read—with obvious reluctance.

Finally, she handed it back. "White women snatched from

a London brothel into slavery? Sold to a sultan in Constantinople? Really, Miss Montague? You expected everyone to believe you a fine lady when you were nothing but a yeoman's daughter caught for stealing. A very clever one, obviously, to have entrapped Mr Westaway as you did. But this?" She tapped the letter with her forefinger before handing it back to Faith. "A forgery! You want me to print this as a front-page story so I can be sued for libel?"

"Only if it were proved untrue."

She gave a brittle laugh. "I'm sorry, but I can't indulge your wild fancies, Miss Montague. Not tonight, or any other night." She turned, but Faith turned with her, gripping the sleeve of her expensive evening gown.

"Please, Miss Eaves, you're the only person I know of with connections that might be able to bring justice to Lady Vernon and Lord Harkom."

"How convenient. The very people you claim are the architects of your demise." Miss Eaves's smile dripped scepticism.

Stung, Faith dropped her hand. For a long moment, the two women stared at one another. Faith looked away first. She had no more time to waste.

"Then I'll find Lord Delmore. If you won't believe me, he will. I should have gone to him in the first place." Angrily, Faith swept past her, the crowd parting as she made her way to the double doors.

CHAPTER 31

The inclement weather did nothing to aid Crispin's evening. Although his evening clothes were damp, they were passable enough for him to excite little attention when he entered Lady Ridgeway's ballroom a little later that evening.

He managed to bow and nod with sufficient politeness, that his anxiety and hurry to find Miss Eaves and, hopefully Faith, were not too apparent.

A year had passed, and he'd given a good account of himself in Germany. Society tended to forget a young man's transgressions and, in time, regard with amusement the fact he might have been hoodwinked by a beautiful girl in order to paint her. If he'd distinguished himself in his consular post, and besides, was ensconced somewhere on the Continent where out of sight meant out of mind until the matter was more or less forgotten, then all to the good.

So, Crispin found himself nodding and forcing a smile and a greeting to all manner of unexpected past acquaintances of his father and himself as he pushed through the throng.

How long would that last? he wondered with a stab of discomfort, and then was surprised that the depth of his shock over his own possibly lowly origins didn't overwrite his fears over Faith to the extent he'd have imagined they would.

And wasn't this because, being on more of an equal footing, so to speak, she'd suddenly become so much more accessible to him?

Of course, it wasn't as easy to spot her when most people carried a mask on a stick, although in many cases, this was dropped due to the late hour and amount of champagne consumed.

A pink gown. That's what Charity had said she was wearing, but none of the women in pink gowns were Faith, and none could hold a candle to her, besides.

But there was Miss Eaves, her dark-brown hair and ruddy face instantly recognisable as he closed the distance between them, arriving right before her as she turned away from a group of ladies discussing, he could just make out, hats.

"Mr Westaway!" She seemed to lose her composure for a second before she added, "We have not seen you for some time, though I hear you have distinguished yourself. I hope your father is well."

"I'm flattered that you have followed my career and take a concern in the family." He genuinely had not intended it to sound so ironic, but rather than let it rest, Miss Eaves flushed and said, "I told only the facts as they presented themselves, Mr Westaway. I'd imagined you were thankful for your lucky escape. No one wants to be taken for a fool or enter into a lifetime contract against their will."

"Which is exactly what happened to Faith. Have you seen her, Miss Eaves?"

Miss Eaves sent a longing glance towards the circle in

which she'd earlier been ensconced before answering, with a shrug, "She was here earlier."

"Good lord, then she has given you the letter?" He felt his shoulders slump. "She came here with that express purpose."

"I heard an outlandish story of women being lured into some kind of unbelievable slavery to the Ottoman sultan. All the product of a disordered mind and only a forgery to substantiate it."

"Then you saw the letter?" Crispin felt himself come to life. "Faith was going to give you the correspondence between Lady Vernon and Lord Harkom to verify the truth of this. She's taken an enormous risk to uncover the truth, managing to extract it from Lord Harkom. I've just come from there."

Miss Eaves pressed her lips together. She seemed unable to answer.

Crispin could barely keep still. "Miss Eaves, you must tell me how long ago she left! Miss Montague is in great danger. I'd heard whispers that suggested such a thing was happening, but there was nothing to substantiate it until tonight. The letter is no forgery, Miss Eaves. Surely you could tell that for yourself!"

"Mr Westaway, I…" She bit her lip, her confusion apparent. "I don't know what to tell you except that she told me she was going to find Lord Delmore."

Crispin turned on his heel. "If you see her again, detain her," he said, over his shoulder, his tone urgent. "Persuade her not to go anywhere unless she is accompanied."

He was about to slip into the crowd when Miss Eaves detained him with a hand on his sleeve. When he looked into her frightened face he noticed her skin was very pale and there was a tremor in her voice as she said, "Miss Montague left the room about half an hour ago. I followed her, when my uncle called me over to meet a new arrival just as Miss

Montague was descending the front steps." She pressed her lips together and rolled one shoulder, and Crispin felt a stab of very real terror, justified as Miss Eaves finished, "Lady Vernon seemed to be waiting for her from just inside the carriage that had drawn up. I caught only a glimpse before Miss Montague was inside. And…" she hesitated "… in the glow of the lamplight, I believe I saw Lord Harkom. Certainly, at the time I believed it was Lord Harkom, for I returned thinking with such scepticism of her renewed defence that she'd ever had a willing association with him."

Crispin was already heading towards the door. "And nor has she, he said angrily. "Miss Eaves, if you see anything or hear anything that could help this case, please send a message directly to my lodgings. Dear God, I just hope and pray I find her in time."

CHAPTER 32

The blindfold was cutting into Faith's eyes painfully by the time she was released. When she stumbled, she realised it was as much due to the fact the flooring was unstable as that she was disoriented.

The cry of seagulls and the smell of brine and tar made it clear that she was on board a boat.

Or something larger, for the room was commodious with a large porthole that looked over the ocean. Dawn had broken, and the fact that her head hurt unconscionably compounded the realisation that she'd been drugged.

She swung around to confront her captors, and was not surprised to see Lord Harkom's golden hair lit by the late-afternoon sun that shone through the glass and, seated upon a chair at his side, the hunched, crow-like form of Lady Vernon.

"My, my, Lady Vernon; it's been a long night for you," Faith remarked drily. "You're not usually an early riser, so I'm sorry to put you through such discomfort."

Lady Vernon grimaced which Faith took to be a smile. "I was not going to be denied the pleasure of seeing you go where you deserved. My goodness, but you've caused us a great deal of trouble, Faith. Finally, you'll be getting your just desserts."

Faith looked towards the porthole where the choppy sea was partly obscured by the crew in striped jerseys leaping from the rigging onto the deck. She could hear voices. Shouts that at first she thought were in French, before she realised some of them spoke a language she didn't recognise. "You won't get away with this, Lady Vernon. Nor you, Lord Harkom. Your activities have been exposed."

"On what evidence, my dear Faith?" He looked satisfied as he paced back and forth across the room. "Whatever correspondence you found is now back in my possession. Besides, who might you have told who would actually believe you? A liar and a whore."

Faith shivered as she imagined the groping that must have been involved when she was unconscious. She swallowed, her fear obviously showing before Lord Harkom said, "I haven't violated you, if that's what you're worried about. There'd be little pleasure for either of us in doing that if you were not awake to enjoy it." With a glance at Lady Vernon, he added, "All good things must wait, and I have a special parting gift for you before the boat sets sail. I'd have liked to have kept you, my dear, in the style you could have enjoyed, had you been a little cleverer. In fact, I had thought you came to my residence to negotiate a special agreement with me." He sighed. "However, your quick mind and ability to master the politics of a situation will stand you in good stead when it comes to learning a new language. Turkish, in fact. Yes, you have an eager patron a few hundred miles north of Constantinople waiting for you. He's paid a king's ransom for a girl fitting just your description, and since I have decided you're more trouble than you're worth, I'm taking you there, myself."

"Or face capture, yourself, in England!" Faith shot back.

"Oh, the passage of time and the fact there is nothing to connect me with any wrongdoing will stand me in good stead."

She'd managed to keep her fear under control when she was speaking, but having to listen to him spout his evil, unleashed the shivering she'd kept in check until now. She clasped her arms about herself for she had no opera cloak or other means of warmth, and her evening dress was very bare about her bodice.

"So, Faith, have you anything to say for yourself?"

The light from the porthole spilled in a luminous circle in the centre of the room, and into this Lord Harkom stepped, as if he were a golden prince rather than the Prince of Darkness she now knew him to be.

"She's not going with you, Harkom."

Faith turned with a start; the familiar voice so unexpected and so welcome. A tall, brown-haired gentleman in evening clothes, with tired eyes, high cheekbones, and a sensitive mouth, locked eyes with her.

Crispin.

She'd thought of him so often during these past twelve months. Too often, in her imaginings, their welcome was curt and full of recrimination at the way each had failed the other. But now, as he stepped into the full beam of light to stand face to face with Lord Harkom, he looked every bit the handsome hero of her dreams.

"It's over, Harkom." He turned to Lady Vernon with an exaggerated bow, following a brief smile of encouragement for Faith before he went on, "Your activities have been revealed. Thanks to Lady Vernon's correspondence, we've been apprised of your involvement in the trade of friendless young women from English shores to the Ottomans. You will shortly be in custody, and Miss Montague will be leaving with me."

He took a step forward and, with hope and happiness flooding through her, Faith moved towards the hand he offered.

"A little peremptory, I think, Mr Westaway." As Lord Harkom spoke, the boat gave a shudder and a jolt which sent Faith stumbling briefly into Crispin's arms, before her nemesis snatched her against him, pressing her face against his shoulder with one cupped hand. "Well, well, this is unexpected. It would appear we've already set sail for foreign shores. Sorry, Lady Vernon; just a minor disturbance to our plans. I'm sure you'll find your sea legs soon enough."

Faith, after a brief struggle, realised it might not be a good time to vent her outrage. Lady Vernon, for her part, seemed equally outraged, for she drew her bony frame to its full height and sent a querulous look towards the door.

"I have hardly prepared for sea travel, Lord Harkom. Go and see what's happened! We can't have set sail yet."

"Oh, I very much fear we have, Lady Vernon." Lord Harkom shook his head with a look of feigned regret. "I didn't think it would come to this. I'd very much hoped it wouldn't. But I'm not a man to leave anything to chance."

"Except that your stupidity invited this whole debacle." Lady Vernon pointed at Faith before turning to Lord Harkom. "Lord only knows what you were doing when you invited this conniving creature into your bedchamber, and with an unlocked chest, too! That's what's behind all this." She began to shake as her fury mounted. "We have the letter back. The two letters back. Originals, and the only evidence of our involvement. We've been so careful. I've been so careful. This was not necessary. I want to go home now. Give the orders that we are to turn back." Her arm trembled as she pointed at the sea through the porthole.

Lord Harkom gave Faith a squeeze and lowered his face to put his cheek against hers. "All in good time, Lady Vernon; all in good time." He dropped a kiss upon Faith's brow. "I want to enjoy this one first. I want Westaway to feel the pain I felt when his father married the woman I loved."

"What do you want from me to guarantee that no harm comes to Faith? That she is granted her freedom." Crispin spoke softly but clearly, and Lord Harkom barked out a laugh.

"It's a bit late for that, don't you think? You've been resting on your laurels a whole year, and you clearly didn't give poor Faith here a second thought."

"Faith is very good at hiding her tracks," Crispin said pointedly. "I searched for you, you know." The fact he spoke directly to her made Faith's heart beat wildly as she held her breath and kept eye contact with the striking man before her. "I'll admit that after we were parted, I was angry and disappointed. My father told me it was what I deserved. What I should have expected."

"Just as we expected he would," Lady Vernon said, on a sniff. She'd walked to the porthole and stood staring dolefully out at the white-capped waves that surrounded them, turning to say over her shoulder, "A brothel is hardly the environment a gentleman such as he would like to think nurtured his son's intended."

"But more than he deserves," Lord Harkom ground out. "Did your father suffer to see his only child so horribly compromised? I hope he did. Has he been disappointed by what he was dealt? I'm sure he has. After all, what can one expect of the son of an innkeeper's faithless slut of a daughter and a country yokel."

"You've concocted this story without a shred of evidence." Crispin held himself proudly. "Meanwhile, the two of you are clearly guilty of a crime that would see you rot in prison.

You've been soliciting girls and selling them into slavery." He regarded Faith with a sad smile. "Faith was lured into doing what she never would have done of her own volition."

"And she has served our purposes well." Lady Vernon gave a short laugh. "The only fly in the ointment was Mrs Gedge. She wanted to be kept updated regarding Faith's progress at every juncture. She wanted reports that she actually was getting her lessons; that she was being turned into a lady. Yes, she wanted Faith to be every bit as accomplished and desirable as her own Constancia had been so that she could entice Mr Westaway with her charms."

"Not that that went very well, initially," Lord Harkom resumed. "I'll admit I was mightily taken by the girl's beauty when I spied her at Madame Chambon's, but it was only after I learned that there was any connection to Lord Maxwell that she became of such interest to me."

Faith gasped. "That's why you tried to take me, unwillingly! After I returned from being painted at the end of the first week. The first painting." She swung around to confront Lady Vernon. "You decided that I'd failed in my mission to Mrs Gedge, so you might as well make use of me by selling me to Lord Harkom."

Lady Vernon sniffed. "And then, all of a sudden Mrs Gedge was offering me more money to make a final onslaught for the second painting. Suddenly, she'd elevated the prize money, and my reward, and you, Faith, were becoming too interested, yourself, in the young man you'd initially intended to seduce and leave. Ah yes," she sighed. "It was becoming very interesting and filled with possibilities. I could collect from Mrs Gedge—spectacularly, I might add, after the newspapers obligingly ran their story—*and* claim a reward from Lord Harkom who had his own particular vendetta against Mr Westaway."

"So, Miss Eaves was part of this, too?" Faith couldn't

believe she'd been so gullible, but Lady Vernon dismissed this notion. "The silly little thing lives to tell the truth. Women who deceive and are otherwise immoral deserve to be revealed for who they are so that men can respect the rest of the fairer sex. Yes, she ran that story believing it was in the interests of advancing women's rights. And that such apparent transparency was needed in the interests of maintaining the integrity of the arts world. Oh, she was delightfully sincere and oh, so obliging."

Lord Harkom laughed. "An unexpected piece of largesse, that was. As was discovering that Westaway surely had fallen in love. With you, Faith! The woman who'd been recruited to break his heart. And, that not only had you broken his heart, you'd made him a laughing-stock, severely damaged his career prospects, and thoroughly damaged his relationship with his father. Why, you were just perfect. But then you disappeared. You were good, Faith. No one could find you, and I'd almost given up hope when suddenly, here you are." He turned. "And here Westaway is. Ready for the final reckoning." His nostrils flared, and he patted his pocket before drawing out a small pistol. "The crew are disinclined to tie you to the masthead, and the captain maintains the fact that this is a regular sailing. But just be aware of what you risk if you try to overcome me, Westaway. Your father killed the woman I loved, and I am more than happy to kill you."

Crispin shook his head. "You lie. What could my mother possibly have seen in a cruel and twisted madman?"

Lord Harkom ignored him. "Yes, he snatched her away from me and, not being satisfied with that, he broke her heart and then he killed her."

"My mother died of fever," Crispin countered.

"The woman you believed was your mother. The woman who agreed to travel to France, pretending to be in the early stages of pregnancy, so that there'd be no questions asked after she returned with the brat that was foisted on an innkeeper's daughter by Westaway senior. The bastard he thought was his, but who was cuckolded when the child—you—arrived a good month earlier than you should have done. Yes, your *real* mother, the innkeeper's daughter, was already a month gone to her country yokel lover when she agreed to be a broodmare to your father. It solved a very great problem for her, no doubt. Yes, she garnished her pocketbook and lived very comfortably, until the money ran out and she wrote to me informing me of the situation, after having been apprised of my vendetta against your father." He pointed the revolver at Crispin and shook his head. "Look at you, Westaway. Parading about in those clothes like a gentleman. It's a joke."

Crispin didn't seem to heed him. He neared Faith and held out his hand. "Let her come to me for now," he said, smiling at Faith. "You can torture us later. I've been waiting for this a long time."

To Faith's surprise, Lord Harkom released her and she ran into Crispin's arms. She barely registered Lord Harkom's desultory clap. "What sport the two of you will provide as we proceed to tear young love asunder. Yes. Hold her, kiss her, enjoy her for this short time, while my heart breaks to think of such a lovely thing being so tarnished by what I have in store. Yes, when we reach shore you'll be parted, never to see one another again." He looked through the heavy doors and then outside at the raging seas. "For the next two days, you are my captives and will be completely beholden to me. So, you may have a few minutes under my watch to remember the closeness that you once apparently enjoyed. After that, I shall enjoy tearing the two of you apart once more—just as your father did to me and your mother."

~

Faith lay on her back upon the covers of the large bed in the stateroom to which she'd been assigned and stared through the porthole at the choppy seas beyond. Her cheeks were damp from tears, but there was no point in wiping them away. More would simply join them.

It had been a long time since she'd wept. Her upbringing had made her strong. Her father punished softness. And that meant tears. Faith had never enjoyed closeness to either parent or, in fact, her siblings. They'd bickered and lashed out at each other, and she'd seen her removal from the family home to work in the big house as a reprieve from such pettiness.

She'd not even cried when she'd been falsely accused of stealing. Injustice was a natural part of her experience.

Her education at the hands of a man of kindness and ethics had given her a new realisation of life and human beings. Perhaps it had set her up for unhappiness by making her realise that even she had prospects for it. Professor Monk had given her enough examples of people from humble beginnings who had changed the world and received their just rewards to give her hope that she, too, might find a meaning for her life.

Now, as the boat was lifted and tossed upon the waves of the English Channel, Faith imagined the worst that Lord Harkom had in store for her. He might even make Crispin watch.

She shuddered, and a sob lodged in her throat.

"Faith."

Terrified, she half rose, ready to fight with everything she had at her disposal.

It was Lady Vernon, her gimlet eye trained on Faith.

"You're to get yourself ready to receive Lord Harkom this evening. I've brought you a change of clothes and a few other necessaries to clean yourself up. You're hardly looking your best."

"He can take me as I am," Faith muttered, but the prospect of clean water for washing and a change of linen and new gown was too enticing. She felt dirty and unkempt.

"So, Lord Harkom keeps women's clothing and ivory brushes on hand for such contingencies?" Faith asked Lady Vernon, as she'd worked on her coiffure and changed into the dark-blue confection with its ruffles and ribbons that was presented. It did not require a corset, and nor were there combinations. It was the perfect item for easy divestment, she thought cynically. Lord Harkom wouldn't need to do much work to have her where he wanted.

Lady Vernon didn't answer as she appeared to be on the point of leaving. Faith detained her. "I need to go outside for some fresh air. I shall be sick, otherwise, and Lord Harkom won't want that, I'm sure."

Fortunately, Lady Vernon didn't seem too troubled by the suggestion, saying, "I suppose there's not far you can go." So, Faith found herself on the forward deck with the wind ruining the smoothness of her newly brushed hair, hurrying towards the railing while Lady Vernon remained just inside the doorway, protected from the cold.

"Faith!"

It was Crispin. She turned, her hands shaking as they gripped the railing before Crispin covered them with his own.

"I am so sorry for putting you through this." His voice tickled her ear and sent tendrils of warmth through her.

"You aren't responsible," she returned, shocked he should even think it. "I was given the mission of breaking your heart. I accepted."

"Did you have a choice?"

Seaspray weighed down her eyelashes and dripped onto her cheeks as she raised her eyes to look at him.

"Oh Faith, you were young. A child, when you were taken by Mrs Gedge. You were slotted into a life for which you were completely unprepared, but you used everything you had to survive. Look at you!" There was admiration in his eyes. "Your beauty was an advantage. Of course, it was. But you had a mind that was agile, a clever wit, and a love of knowledge that was fed; however extraordinary those circumstances were."

"And now you are a captive at the hands of your father's arch nemesis; a man who is clearly mad, and who thinks that destroying you will punish your father in the way he wants to." Faith squeezed Crispin's hand. "You're here because of me, and for that I'm truly sorry."

Crispin smiled down at her. "I'm just as responsible for being here. I'm culpable for not having been able to better look after the woman I love. Don't think I haven't thought about that all these many hours I've had to suffer the rocking of this boat, and know that soon a time will come when Harkom exerts his vile power and makes us both suffer."

He glanced towards the doorway where Lady Vernon was sheltering. Perhaps she wasn't planning to intervene because of the discomfort and the cold. Perhaps it was under Lord Harkom's orders. After all, the greater the bond forged between Faith and Crispin now, the more they would suffer later, when Lord Harkom decided it was time.

"I'm afraid," Faith whispered, nestling against him. "I've only ever been with a man I love. When I saw Lord Harkom earlier this evening, I was fired up with zealous rage because I thought I had nothing to lose. I drugged him, and I succeeded in my mission. But now he has triumphed."

"Because I have failed you."

"Not you!" Faith twisted in the circle of his arms and

raised her own to cup his face. "Why would you have behaved otherwise? Miss Eaves printed a story that looked very credible. So credible that *she* believed it because, as we know, she is a young woman who is driven by principle—on the surface, at any rate. The photograph told a compelling story. The villains were people of standing in high society. I was revealed for what I am. And people like me are never believed above people like Lord Harkom and Lady Vernon and Mrs Gedge."

Crispin wrapped her more closely in his arms. "You know I will fight to the death to protect you from Harkom when he comes to you, this evening."

"Oh, don't waste a good life when I am what I am," Faith said, trying to smile. "It's what I was trained for. It's what Charity endures numerous times every day. I've been living in a cloud. Don't be foolish on my account, Crispin. We are very effectively Lord Harkom's prisoners, and I would be happier if you saved your energies for a surprise attack rather than when he is expecting it. For you know that is his plan."

"Lord, but you do know how to read a man."

"I've been trained in the science for years. I applied it very skilfully to you." She couldn't help smiling. "If I made you love me, though, it was at my expense. That was where I failed in my mission."

"Oh no, it wasn't. That was where Lady Vernon and Mrs Gedge must be congratulating themselves. They were able to destroy you at the same time as my reputation. A double win. Mrs Gedge couldn't bear the thought that her beautiful Constancia should be dead while you, a worthless creature in her eyes, should only grow more beautiful; accomplished. Everything she'd have wished for her daughter." He stopped, gripping her forearms as he asked, "But Faith, do you still love me? After all this time, and all the hours you must have run over in your mind how I'd failed you. Forsaken you."

"I thought about you every day, Crispin. I wondered how I could still love a man I knew thought the very worst of me. Because you did, didn't you?

He nodded. "There was no piece of evidence I could find to exonerate you. Not until yesterday and…" he looked up at the tall mast and rigging, the sails flapping loudly in the wind, "a lot has happened since then."

They were aware of Lady Vernon coming towards them.

"I suppose Lord Harkom would want you apart, now." She sounded distinctly out of sorts. "I wish to go to my cabin and I can't leave you here."

"Where is Lord Harkom? Not retching his guts out, I trust?"

Lady Harkom's nose twitched. "I gather that's exactly what he's doing, but I'm sure he'll recover soon enough. He has grand plans for you, Faith." Her mouth twisted.

"I never liked you, Lady Vernon, but I had no idea I had such good reason to trust my instincts." Faith stared her down. "Your evil knows no bounds, does it?"

"We all do what we must to survive. A title is no guarantee of a comfortable life. I've not wished for much, and I'm hardly extravagant. Not like his good lordship." She indicated the innards of the boat, and presumably, Lord Harkom, with a jerk of her head. "Without supplementing my meagre allowance, I too would have been placed in your situation, Faith. Only…I don't have quite your assets. So don't play the moral high ground with me."

"You and Lord Harkom make strange bedfellows," Faith countered. "I hope he makes this line of business worth your while. You do know what awaits you when you return to England."

Lady Vernon shrugged. "Don't threaten me, girl. You'll be

long gone, and I intend to be safely returned to England before too long. I hadn't factored in this trip across the channel, it's true, but Lord Harkom and I can come to some agreement over that. So, don't worry yourself over my future, Faith. Enjoy your nabob in the delightful harem seven hours' camel ride from Constantinople, or wherever Lord Harkom has arranged for you to go. There were several options. He may be planning to auction you, for all I know. And I don't care a jot. You were always more trouble than you were worth. I never understood Mrs Gedge's need to play so fairly by you."

"Indeed, I admire your trust in Lord Harkom," Crispin remarked. "He's hardly renowned for dealing honestly with anyone."

"Come on, Faith." Lady Vernon ignored him. "I'm going to lock you in your cabin now where you can expect a visit from Lord Harkom as soon as he's feeling up to you. As for you, Mr Westaway," she shot him a look as if unsure what to do, then shrugged. "I daresay I can't order you to your cabin, and these sailors apparently won't take orders from any but their captain, so enjoy your view of the high seas. I'll be glad when land is sighted. Like Lord Harkom, I was not made for boat travel."

THERE WAS ONLY SO LONG THAT CRISPIN COULD SPEND IN THE biting wind. When he went in, he tried Faith's door, but it was securely bolted. He tried Lord Harkom's door and found that similarly bolted from the inside. However, instead of the silence that had greeted him when he'd knocked lightly for Faith, he could hear retching and a drawn-out groan from the other side.

On the quarterdeck, he located the bosun, the only crew

member who could speak English it appeared, and asked him if Lord Harkom was in need of assistance.

"Like the ol' woman, the seas ain't the thing fer 'igh-born stomachs. All 'e needs is ter put 'is two flat feet on summat that doesn't move."

"Is Lord Harkom *so* seasick?"

The bosun sniggered. "Can't drag 'imself from 'is bunk."

"And how is the young lady who is locked in her room supposed to eat her dinner?"

"I'll take summat to 'er. The gennulman gave me orders ter see she were well attended."

"If his lordship is so indisposed, perhaps you'd allow her some fresh air at the same time she takes some refreshment."

"I can do that fer 'er if it's worth me while." The bosun offered him a gap-toothed grin, and Crispin obligingly dug into his pocket and withdrew a pound note. The bosun's eyes grew large. "She can 'ave all the time an' all the vittels she wants, sir," he said, taking the note with a shifty glance to ensure he'd not been observed by any of his fellows.

Crispin glanced about him. "Then let her go, now," he ordered but the bosun shook his head. "Not wiv others about wot'd see me disobeying orders." He sent Crispin a sly look. "Why don't you go and get yerself some rest. I'll let you know when the coast is clear."

Crispin went to his bunk and lay down.

He presumed they were not going to dock within the next few hours, perhaps longer. And it had been a very long day already. But how could he sleep after Lady Vernon's ominous words?

Lord Harkom was involved in the white slave trade, and Faith was his next victim.

He'd learned that she'd been ready to consume a vial of poison and kill herself only a few hours before. What might she contemplate doing now? The thought terrified him, but he was powerless to help her. Yet again, he'd failed her.

Despite his best efforts, sleep claimed him at last, and when he woke at the sound of his door being slowly opened, he was refreshed enough to have a weapon ready. The candlestick was clutched in his right fist, and Lord Harkom was going to receive the full force of a hefty blow until, in the darkness, he heard Faith's tentative voice.

"Crispin. Can I slide in next to you? There's not much room, is there?"

Her words sounded so ridiculous under the circumstances that he laughed as he drew aside the covers and brought her close against his side.

She rested her head on his shoulder, and he stroked her face, staring into the darkness.

"The bosun forgot to bolt the door when he took me my food." She laughed. "Can you believe that?"

"I can."

"Of course, it was you, wasn't it? And here I am." She snuggled in closer and hooked one thigh over his, partly to stop from falling out of bed, he supposed, while a tremor of longing shook him to the bone.

"And Lord Harkom is terribly indisposed. He hasn't left his stateroom since he spoke to us." She sighed. "Maybe he's afraid of being accosted by you, Crispin."

"A terrifying proposition." Crispin felt his inadequacy. "Harkom is a champion pugilist, and I'm hardly fighting material. No, he knows he holds the upper hand. As soon as his strength returns, he'll carry on as he pleases." He began to stroke her cheek. It was soft and smooth, but also hot to the touch. In the darkness, he imagined its flush of colour. He'd have liked to have been able to see her. He was a painter, after all. But simply touching her filled him with a deep peacefulness. "He may also choose to stay in his room because he realises he's miscalculated. He's on a boat that wasn't prearranged for nefarious dealings. The crew will answer only to the captain, and the captain has no interest in breaking the law. Harkom realises this, I think."

"Then we could enlist the captain's help?"

"I've tried. The captain says his orders are to take us to Rotterdam, and that's all he'll do. He's not taking sides."

"Will you kiss me, Crispin?"

"It might be dangerous."

"I like danger."

He found her lips easily in the dark. She'd been waiting for him, and she drew him into the kiss with a light hand upon his cheek.

He'd not been exaggerating when he'd voiced concern about the danger. The simple touch of his lips against hers ignited him from within. The feel of her breasts pressing against him, harder with each rising breath, became a conflagration that threatened to consume him.

"I love you, Crispin," she whispered, shifting over him so that her body covered his and his hand came in contact with her naked thigh when he sought to hold her as the ship pitched.

"And you, Faith. I love you, too."

She wriggled a little, and suddenly she was positioned directly above him, and he was straining to keep his basest impulses in check. But her hand was on him, her little fingers working the buttons of his trousers, and he was in no doubt what she wanted.

There were no words to be said. No doubts or fears to be allayed. Their time was limited and their need for one another all consuming.

He skimmed her smooth, moist thighs until his hand was on her heated mound. With a sigh, she cupped his cheek and kissed him more deeply.

The need to protect her was uppermost in his mind, but so was his need to communicate his real feelings for this brave and beautiful young woman.

She wanted him. She was ready for him. She made that clear enough as she felt for him.

Another pitch of the boat, and he was as one with the woman for whom he'd sacrifice everything.

~

THEIR SLEEP WAS SHORT, BUT DEEP AND REVIVING.

When Crispin awoke, it was to find Faith gazing down at him, her eyes luminous in the gloom.

"Lord Harkom will come for me soon, and you won't be able to stop him. I don't want you to die in some fruitless attempt to save me." Her voice was determined; her mouth clenched.

"And fail you a second time? Lord, Faith, we were so nearly man and wife. How different things would have been if the timing had been in our favour. We might not be bound before the law, but I feel as if we are."

"You didn't fail me before. Circumstances conspired to put us both in an impossible position." She hesitated. "I don't blame you for believing what everyone else did. And nor do I blame you for not following through on a marriage that would have bound you to a woman who would surely have ruined your career."

"Oh Faith, my career is not as a diplomat, I see that now." He stroked her cheek. "You made me see that. This last year has been anathema to me. I thought following the path that would make my father happy would earn me his approval. But, here with you…" It was difficult to put his feelings into words. "You're what's important, Faith."

"Because of that letter? Because you think that you're no

better than me after all?" She twisted within the circle of his arm and looked down at him. "How can it be proved?"

Already, Crispin's mind was turning on what the immediate future held for both of them. The question of his origins seemed almost unimportant when he very much feared he'd not ever make it home to England. If Harkom really planned to spirit Faith away using a distribution ring that had yielded success and financial rewards in the past, he'd not scruple at disposing of a man he not only hated for personal reasons, but who had the power to see him face the noose.

Faith seemed to grasp this at the same time for she gripped his arm tighter. "Crispin, what are you thinking? That it doesn't matter? But it does. It matters because you *will* escape. You will return to England, where you'll prove that you're every bit the son your father would be proud of. I'm sure he is very proud of you, even if he doesn't show it. I couldn't bear it if I were the reason you'd have to make a choice between your father's wishes and your own."

He held her tighter and felt a stab of pain for what she must have experienced to have been so belittled by a man Crispin felt less and less affiliation with, regardless of his true parentage.

What he had, now, was what he had to fight for. Faith was his responsibility; his true love. If they survived their ordeal, he'd sacrifice everything for her.

"As long as I have breath in my body, I will fight for you, Faith," he vowed.

"I will not be a burden." She pressed her lips together. "Love does not survive when it means sacrifice and duty at the cost of what's truly in your heart. I pushed for you to marry me—quickly—because I was afraid for my future. Yes, my future. I didn't think about yours, Crispin; only that I believed I could make everything up to you by making you happy…pleasing you during the years we had together as man and wife. I've been taught how to please men. Yes, listen to me and don't shy away from the awful truth. When I met you, it was by design. I'd spent three years groomed in how to entice *you*. You owe me nothing. You certainly don't owe me your life!"

He felt her tears raining down upon his chest, and tenderly brushed her wet cheek with his fingertip. "My dearest Faith. Because of you, I feel more alive in this moment than I ever have. I owe you everything!" He kissed her again. And then, because he was afraid of her wilfulness, he cupped her face as he angled himself over her, and said softly, "Your place is by my side. While you are here, I will do all in my power to protect you. I would give my life to see you safe, Faith. You need to know that."

AND FAITH WAS VERY MUCH AFRAID THAT THIS WOULD BE THE cost Lord Harkom would extract.

She also knew the time would come, sooner rather than later, when her nemesis would recover sufficiently to make his overtures.

When she was sure Crispin was sleeping, Faith quietly climbed out of their shared bunk and slipped out of the room.

Breathing in the fresh air on deck, she spied land and her heart sank. On board the ship, they had the protection of the crew who, although they'd offered little in the way of overt assistance, nevertheless refused to lock them up.

And, with Lord Harkom so indisposed, Lady Vernon had not enforced Faith's prisoner status. But soon matters would come to a head.

She tapped softly on the door. "Lord Harkom, it's me,

Faith. I'm alone, and I want to speak to you." The sound of footsteps made her cringe, and hurriedly she added, "I have a crew member with me so don't try to take advantage. I just need to speak to you." She glanced over her shoulder at the Frenchman who showed no understanding, but who stood implacably nearby, as she'd requested.

"I'll go with you willingly if you'll release Crispin," she said, leaping back with a squeal when he flung open the door.

He looked ill and haggard, his appearance not improved by the ironic curl of his lip. "Do you think that'll please me, Faith?" He laughed. "To have you submit to me, meek as a little lamb." This time he threw back his head and indulged in his mirth even more. "Why, what did Madame Chambon teach you? Certainly not how to tread carefully with men of my proclivities which, I daresay, is all to the good. Now, where's your Mr Westaway? I was feeling mightily indisposed a few minutes ago and certain I'd not have the strength to crawl from my bed, but your delightful little proposition has fired me up."

Faith darted back at his approach, but he gripped her shoulder to stop her fleeing and barked out the order, in French, to the seaman behind her, to fetch Mr Westaway.

"I'm already here," Crispin announced, arriving behind Faith and attempting to pull her to his side.

"The little wench has offered herself to me, Westaway, so hands off, thank you." Harkom waved a pistol in his face.

Tendrils of dismay curled around Faith's inards to see the expression on Crispin's face, and to realise how badly she'd compromised both their safety.

"Yes, she came here, of her own volition, and offered herself to me if I'd allow you to return home safely. Isn't that sweet? Especially considering the way you treated her all those months ago. Now—" With a jerk of his wrist, Faith found herself in the circle of Harkom's arm, before he'd pinned her by her neck, his other hand holding the revolver.

"How easy to claim self-defence for your death, Westaway," he snarled. "But that would be letting you off too easily. No, you can come in and watch your beloved debase herself at my command. And you will die, knowing that her fate is to do the same for the pleasure of the various Far Eastern nabobs who are willing to pay a high price for an English princess with the treasured golden hair and white skin."

Unable to move, Faith shuddered as he caressed her cheeks, sliding his hand the length of her neck to skim her décolletage.

"Stop!" Crispin lunged forward but was halted by a sharp crack as Harkom fired in the air.

"Yes, loaded, in case you thought otherwise. Now, would you kindly step inside, Miss Montague. I've been waiting for this a long time now."

Faith screamed and gripped the lintel as Lord Harkom proceeded to pull her inside, slamming the door in Crispin's face.

"You can listen to her wail and beg, Westaway!" he shouted. "Unfortunately, I can't do what I have to do *and* keep my pistol trained on you."

RAISING HIS LEG HIGH, CRISPIN KICKED AT THE DOOR, BUT IT held fast. He could hear Faith's whimpers within and the sound of Harkom's harsh laughter, before the thud of a body landing on the ground.

Again, he tried to kick in the door, but it was solid, and locked.

"Faith! Are you all right! Harkom! For God's sake! You

don't need to do this to have your revenge on me. You can shoot me now if it'll please you! Let her go!"

Another muffled cry from Faith was too much. With a howl of rage, Crispin hurled himself against the door, but still it would not yield.

"You might have more luck if you had a key, Mr Westaway."

Crispin turned at Lady Vernon's silken tones. She looked like a crow of ill portent as she hovered at the end of the corridor, her back to the light so Crispin could see only her illuminated form. And then he heard the clink of keys, and saw she held up the keyring upon which a dozen keys dangled.

"No! Don't, please don't!" Faith's cry from indoors was tortuous, but Lady Vernon seemed unaffected.

"Don't try to take it from me or I'll cast it overboard," she warned as he began to stride towards her. "I'll give it to you on one condition." The sea was only a few feet from her. She could throw it over her shoulder with ease, and he would never have it.

"What is your condition?" There wasn't much time, but if he could save Faith from Harkom's final assault he'd agree to anything.

"I fear we're being followed." With a jerk of her thumb she indicated a schooner much closer than Crispin would have believed. There was no time to investigate further, but it seemed to be heading straight for them. "If we are apprehended, you'd better swear on your life that you'll say Harkom took me captive, as Faith's chaperone. Do that, and not only will you have the key, you'll have my testimony as to what he's been doing. Otherwise," she shrugged, "I can't see there will be any case for Harkom to answer. Not to mention there's the matter with the letter from your fond, cash-strapped mother. Your real mother, that is."

"Give me the key and you have my word."

And then it was in his hand, and Crispin was striding back down the corridor, inserting the rusty key, and thrusting open the doorway upon a scene of vile degradation.

~

FAITH KNEW THERE WAS NO POINT IN STRUGGLING, AND YET she could not do otherwise. To submit without a fight went against any grain of survival instinct she had, while the hope she could cause Harkom damage made the penalty she'd pay worth it.

"You are more a fighter than I gave you credit for, Faith. I'm sorry I didn't try harder to break you in," he panted as he caged her body with his.

"I'll die fighting, Lord Harkom," she vowed, jerking her head upwards to try and bite his ear.

He slapped her then, and she yelped with the pain, her world hazing into red and black for a moment before her consciousness became refocused on what he was doing with his other hand.

She tried to wriggle free for it was now beneath her skirts, while his other was busy unbuttoning himself. She felt like a moth in the maw of a giant, deadly spider, and her efforts were futile.

Crispin was just on the other side of the door, but it was solid, and he was as helpless as she. If she could only lie still. Stop herself from reacting and it might be better for all of them. Harkom might lose the ability, even, if he were confronted by meek passivity.

It would certainly be better for Crispin who'd be tormented by what he was helpless to remedy.

"You'll die, any way I take you. You'll die in a Turkish

harem far away from here, unmourned by any, Faith, for you gave up your right to respect a long time ago."

"And you did not, Lord Harkom?"

"Ah Faith, but you are a fine sparring partner. Why did I not make you my mistress when I could have set you up so nicely after Westaway forsook you?"

"I never forsook her!"

Suddenly, the door was open and Crispin's tall, straight form was silhouetted in the doorway for a split second before he hurled himself onto Lord Harkom.

It was enough to knock him off her and, taking advantage of her reprieve, Faith rolled out from beneath him, finding sanctuary half under the bed.

Crispin's eyes were trained on Lord Harkom, while Lord Harkom's pistol was trained on Crispin.

"You'd die for her?" spat Harkom. "Gutter scum? You're more of a fool than I thought. A pretty face that will corrode soon enough, and then what will it all have been for? Well, it doesn't matter, does it, for you'll be dead!"

And then there was another commotion, outside, followed by the sound of splitting wood before the boat was jolted as if it had been sideswiped by a much larger vessel.

Faith screamed as Harkom's weapon discharged.

CHAPTER 33

Faith screamed and threw herself upon Crispin's body, just as the boat was boarded and newcomers had spilled into the room.

More evil was about to render her more helpless.

If Crispin were dead, she wanted to die too. What was left for her if she was dragged home and forced to fend for herself, yet again? Her only refuge was Madame Chambon's, and who knew how involved she was in the evil trade plied by Lady Vernon and Lord Harkom.

So, she simply buried her face in Crispin's neck, sobbing as she felt his weakened hand upon the back of her head; sobbing even more when she heard his whispered, "I'll make sure you're looked after, Faith."

How could he look after her? The bullet wound to his chest had caused a spreading stain that she'd tried to staunch with her skirts, but still the blood oozed. He'd die from loss of blood before he died from anything else, and Faith would be watching, unable to do anything.

Her mind was so focused on Crispin's needs, she gave no thought to Lord Harkom until she heard a masculine voice she could not place—although she was sure she'd heard it before—bark out a directive to someone else, and then the pounding of feet before a groan of pain.

"Harkom! That's enough!"

Turning her face only so she could observe what was happening out of the corner of her eye, she saw a stocky young man bending by the prone figure of Lord Harkom, who gave a yell of pain as he was rolled over and his arms were tied behind his back.

"Christ, I'm not going anywhere! Can't you see I've taken a bullet?"

And indeed, a spreading pool of blood near his shoulder bore testimony to the claim.

But he was not mortally wounded as Crispin was. If Faith wasn't focused so wholly on protecting Crispin from evil, she'd have hurled herself on her violator and clawed his eyes out.

"Faith? Faith, are you all right?"

With an effort, she turned her head, blinking dazedly to find herself staring right into Lord Delmore's eyes.

"Crispin's been shot," she wept, the tears starting to flow. "Lord Harkom shot him." With the emotion unleashed, she found she could not stop, and as Lord Delmore put his arms about her to draw her to her feet, she still could not stop. "He's dying," she whimpered as she pressed her face against Lord Delmore's chest.

"We're going to do everything we can to help him; make sure that doesn't happen," soothed Lord Delmore standing above them. A light salt-tinged breeze ruffled his overcoat. He smiled encouragingly before gently pushing her away in order to kneel beside Crispin.

"I've seen men worse than that come off the battlefield, and live. Come with me, Faith. The boat's waiting." He beckoned to someone just out of sight and, shocked, Faith locked eyes with the last person she expected to see on a boat so far from home.

But as she allowed herself to be led by the woman she blamed for causing her downfall, she realised too that Miss Eaves must have acted swiftly and boldly to have effected the rescue that had just taken place.

Miss Eaves sent her a level look as an array of emotions flitted across her face. "I had access to a much faster vessel than the one Lord Harkom enlisted to take you away," she said as she helped Faith across the deck and to the railing, where a sleek schooner was moored beside the leaky tub they inhabited.

"It's my father's. He's sailing around the world and happened to have come into port just two days ago, so was available to take us on this little jaunt when I woke him last night having enlisted Lord Delmore's help." Her smile broadened as she released her grip on Faith's arm so that Faith could take the hand offered by a waiting crewman who stood on the rocking deck of the *Clever Amy*. "Yes, I do want to make it as a newspaper reporter and a woman on my own terms, but it does help to have well-placed connections; I admit it."

"Your father?" Faith gaped as she took in Miss Eaves's words before a strident American voice made her turn, and she was confronted by a tall blonde man built like a wrestler wearing a crisp, cream suit. He was shouting orders to the crew to bring the wounded and bound Lord Harkom down the ladder, but at the same time there was an air of life about him that suggested he was enjoying himself enormously.

"Miss Montague?" Coming out of a barked command to one of his crewmen, he offered Faith a deep bow. "I'm Ellison Eaves; pleased to meet you. My daughter didn't do you justice when she described you, my dear girl. What an ordeal you've been through! Amy gave me the barest of details so you'll have to fill me in on the return journey. I look forward to it, though I promise you, it'll take half the time that old leaky sieve took to get you this far."

Faith was saved having to answer by the arrival of the captain of their vessel with whom Mr Eaves dealt very cordially, before Amy's father pulled out a fist full of notes, which he proffered to the captain with the instruction that if he were called upon to supply further details, he'd be sure to remember who the real villain of the piece was, indicating pointedly the form of Lord Harkom who was being carried, groaning, along the gangplank.

Faith stood forlornly at the railing, as she watched Crispin being carried with a great deal more tenderness than his lordship, out of the cabin and across the deck. Gripping his hand as he passed, she was relieved to feel the gentle pressure in return, and she released it to follow the group into one of the commodious cabins where, to her surprise, Miss Eaves appeared, saying, "Stay here with him, if you like. We're about to set course for England, so make your appearance in the dining room whenever you're ready. There'll be a good dinner laid on, and I'm sure you could do with a fortifying brandy." She ran the back of her hand across her forehead. "I certainly could after the events of tonight, though I'll have to keep a clear head in order to write my story." Then, to Faith's surprise, she took her hand and shook it energetically. "I can't thank you enough, Miss Montague, for providing me with the copy I need to keep my name front and centre. This time, though, I hope I can go some way towards making up for the last article."

Faith clenched her jaw. "I really don't care what you print, Miss Eaves. All I care about is Crispin." Despite starting so strong, her voice dissolved as she added, "I don't think I could bear to lose him a second time."

"Nor will you!" came Ellis Eaves's robust tones as he

appeared behind his daughter like a well-dressed hulking giant. "Can't you tell the difference between a mortal wound to the heart and when a feller's only been winged? Sure, there's lots of blood to make the women squeal and despair, but it's hardly mortal. Lord Harkom, though. Well, it's touch and go with him, I'd say."

"And Lady Vernon?" Faith swung around and searched for her amongst those milling about the deck of both boats. She'd not seen her since glimpsing her through the doorway after Crispin had hurtled in and torn her from Harkom's suffocating onslaught.

"Lady who? Lady Vernon? Ah yes, I remember the name, but can't say I've seen other ladies about the place other than you and Amy."

CHAPTER 34

"**A** deep breath for courage…all right, Faith?" In the corridor outside his father's study, Crispin took Faith's hand and gave it a squeeze. "Remember, nothing he says can make a jot of difference to the fact that you and I *are* going to be married."

He'd thought he'd suffer nerves in the lead-up to this historic confrontation, but for the first time, he felt a lightness of being he'd never experienced before.

And when his father issued the command to enter in his usual stentorian tones, he did not quake or wish himself a hundred miles away. Instead, he sauntered in and said, "Father, I want you to meet my future wife, Miss Faith Montague. We're getting married at St Margaret's on Saturday next and hope you'll do us the honour of attending with your blessing."

"Miss Montague…" Lord Maxwell drew out the pause. "I'm pleased to meet you." He rose from his chair at his desk and indicated the cluster of seats by the fireplace. "You seem to enjoy the bright lights though I can see they might seek you out."

Crispin was surprised to see the flare of admiration in his father's eye.

"You and your compatriots made quite a sensation in bringing to justice one of London's most surprising villains. Yes, involved in a grubby scheme we shall not mention for delicacy's sake."

"Faith's actions were heroic."

"I heard yours were too, Crispin. But I wonder…" He came out from behind his desk, and although he smiled at Faith, the furrow between his eyes didn't augur well. "Have you truly considered the ramifications of this hasty marriage? Marrying between the stations, no matter how distinguished the behaviour of each party, is bound to lead to unhappiness."

"So you truly believe one's status should be shackled by one's origins? One's birth?" Crispin watched his father carefully as he went on, "Lord Harkom received a letter from…let us say that she was not a lady but a woman who purported to be my real mother. Outrageous, of course! Unless you believe it invites investigation rather than condemnation?"

Lord Maxwell blanched and held his son's look for a long moment until Crispin broke the silence. "Or do you think it's the *learned* behaviour and ability to conduct oneself appropriately in the social sphere to which one is to be elevated that defines a true lady or gentleman?"

He smiled to see his father's internal battle. Crispin's own shock at the discovery of his likely parentage had been replaced by acceptance. So much had happened between learning the information, and now.

"For if that's the case, then Faith and I were made for each other. Don't you see, Father. Each of us has been elevated from our humble origins. Each of us has been taught how to behave in the sphere our benefactors intended for us—as one of the top ten thousand."

Lord Maxwell had recovered himself. He did not even refute Crispin's insinuations that he might believe his parentage was more humble than he'd believed. He began to pace, his hands behind his back.

"You've proved yourself a finer diplomat than anyone expected." His voice was gruff. "You need a wife who can adapt to the restrictions and the expectations…the loneliness of being in a foreign country, even. I see that. I see how loneliness for you, my boy, can be a danger."

"So, this is the basis on which you would sanction my marriage to Faith?" Crispin was careful to spell it out. "Because she knows how to behave, she's decorative, she'll keep me occupied and, in Germany, she'll be out of the glare of inevitable interest."

Lord Maxwell stopped and inclined his head. "These are not inconsequential considerations."

"But you are not disposed towards withholding your endorsement?"

"I am not…on condition you continue in your current position."

"You know of my love of painting."

"Of course, I do, boy, but there's a time for everything. You need to put food on the table. So, have your wedding, leave the country and, in a year or so, if you still wish to paint, then I shall give you my support."

This was more than Crispin had expected. But would Faith understand just how momentous this was? He swallowed. The kernel of doubt that had been initially motivated by fear of his father's reaction turned to doubt that Faith would consider this an acceptable compromise.

He turned to find her gazing up at him, a faint smile about her lips, her beautiful eyes filled with understanding.

"I think what your father proposes is very wise," she said, putting her hand on his arm.

"You do?"

She nodded. "Sometimes we need to make sacrifices simply to keep a roof over our heads or to satisfy those upon whom we depend."

Her understood her meaning. It was the only way she'd survived.

But there was more.

She gave his arm a gentle squeeze. "Your father has only your best interests at heart. He wants to see you succeed. No parent wants to see their children make a mistake that can destroy their lives and that can never be undone."

"I won't give up…" He'd nearly said 'my painting' but then he'd long ago realised that his painting was not the most important thing in his life. "You, Faith. I won't give you up." The words sounded impassioned, even to his own ears but he didn't care.

Faith smiled. "Your father's not asking you to do that and, besides, even if he did I'd ensure I was too forceful for that to happen."

"It would not be necessary, I assure you," he murmured, longing to kiss her.

"No, I think I'm confident on that score," she replied with a soft, happy laugh. "But your father is right. You need a profession until you are established as a painter." She paused, "And if what I've heard from Miss Eaves is true, her uncle is very keen to offer you all the patronage you need from that quarter."

Crispin looked from his father to Faith and could hardly believe his good fortune. He had the backing and the love of both. He had the loyalty of the woman he adored while a promising career as a painter beckoned.

"I think I have everything I could wish for," he said, feeling bemused, quite suddenly. "What about you, Faith? Is this what you want?"

. . .

Faith gazed up at the man who promised her more than she could ever have dreamed of.

It was almost too much to take in. Within seemingly a few heart beats she suddenly had security. She had freedom and respect.

And she had love.

The love of a man who had proved he had the courage of his convictions. Crispin had set out to protect her when he still believed the worst of her. But his loyalty to what they had once shared had driven him on. What else would account for his actions of the recent past?

"You are what I want, Crispin," she said, softly, so only he could hear. "I don't care if you're a diplomat or a painter, I just want us to be happy together."

"I think she'll be good for you, my boy." Lord Harkom must have heard for he looked approvingly at both of them. "Just make sure you really are the man she thinks you are."

Faith recognised how his gruff words might be interpreted by a sensitive young man as doubt edged with criticism. She'd rarely encountered a kind word, herself, until she'd met Crispin.

"Have no fear on that score, Lord Maxwell," she said, gripping Crispin's hand, tightly. "If you could have seen the heroic way he faced down Lord Harkom who was holding a gun, you'd be agitating that he receive a medal of valour." But as she tipped her face to Crispin's, her words were only for him.

"We will be good for each other, Crispin. And I promise I shall never let you down."

"I know you won't, just as I know my own mind, Faith." His eyes glowed with feeling as he took both her hands in his, ignoring his father behind them. "I didn't realise how much I wanted to keep painting until I met you. But with you as my wife, I know I'll spend the rest of my life trying to do justice to your beauty and your goodness with more than just a paintbrush."

Still holding her hand he gave a sharp tug so that she had no choice but to stumble after him, through the open door and into the passage where he pinioned her against the wall and kissed her soundly.

"And that's just the beginning," he promised, cupping her face, his expression adoring.

Faith sank against him as she twined her arms around his neck and closed her eyes.

"The beginning of a grand new life," she whispered as a great weight lifted from her shoulders. The secrets and lies had been exposed and Crispin still wanted her. But the kiss had unleashed something hard to control and her body ached for him. Spirals of desire were shooting up her spine. She tightened her grip around his neck and pressed herself against him, her voice hoarse as she whispered, "If you really want to show me that your father has no hold over you, then kiss me again." She laughed softly. "Prove that this really is a new beginning."

THE END

Keep reading the series to find out what happens next!
Get Wedding Violet here.

WEDDING VIOLET (Book 4)

Abandoned at the altar, Max, Lord Belvedere believes he's evaded family obligation in favour of a life of adventuring in Africa. But his ailing Aunt Euphemia has other ideas.

When Max finds himself in the delightfully diverting arms of Violet Lilywhite while visiting London's most prestigious House of Assignation, he happens upon the perfect plan. A sham wedding to a 'penniless shop girl' should fulfil Aunt Euphemia's romantic dreams without losing him his newfound liberty.

Violet agrees to the deception with no hesitation. Lord Belvedere is certainly the most charming and surprising of all her male consorts but she has no illusions about a shared future. She wants only to escape the clutches of infamous Madame Chambon.

The plan appears perfect until Max and Violet find themselves falling in love.

Can Max give up his plans for freedom in an exciting new land? Or is freedom to be found in the arms of the woman he loves?

~

What kindle readers say about Wedding Violet:

"Very well written and entertaining, to me, this is the best in this series so far! This is such a heartwarming story. I love Violet's spirit, she is smart, upfront and makes the best of her situation."

"The ending of this story took me completely by surprise! A wonderful surprise with a happy ending for Max, Violet, and Aunt Euphemia."

"…entertaining, well developed and moves smoothly, the ending will surprise you."

OTHER BOOKS BY BEVERLEY OAKLEY

HEARTS IN HIDING Series
The Duchess and the Highwayman
The Bluestocking and the Rake
Duchess of Seduction

SCANDALOUS MISS BRIGHTWELLS Series
Rake's Honour
Rake's Redemption
Rogue's Kiss
The Wedding Wager
The Accidental Elopement

DAUGHTERS OF SIN Series
Her Gilded Prison
Dangerous Gentlemen
The Mysterious Governess
Beyond Rubies
Lady Unveiled: The Cuckold's Conspiracy

GEORGIAN MYSTERY ROMANCE Series

OTHER BOOKS BY BEVERLEY OAKLEY

Wicked Wager
Her Valentine's Secret

FAIR CYPRIANS OF LONDON Series
Saving Grace
Forsaking Hope
Keeping Faith
Wedding Violet
Christmas Charity

GET A FREE BOOK

Would you like to know when I have new releases as well as get the romantic start to my Regency-set 'Dynasty'-inspired *Daughters of Sin* series?

Yes, please send me my Free Copy of Her Gilded Prison!

Just visit: https://www.subscribepage.com/n5n5o9

Beverley was seventeen when she bundled up her first 500+ page romance and sent it to a publisher. Rejection followed swiftly. Drowning one's heroine on the last page, she was informed, was not in line with the expectations of romance readers.

So Beverley became a journalist.

After a whirlwind romance with a handsome Norwegian bush pilot she met in Botswana's beautiful Okavango Delta, Beverley discovered what real romance was all about, saved her heroine from a watery grave in her next manuscript and published her first romance in 2009.

Since then, she's written more than twenty sizzling historical romances laced with mystery and intrigue under the name Beverley Oakley.

She also writes psychological historical mysteries, and Colonial-Africa-set romantic suspense, as Beverley Eikli.

With an inspiring view of a Gothic nineteenth-century insane asylum across the road, Beverley lives north of Melbourne with her gorgeous husband, two lovely daughters and a rambunctious Rhodesian Ridgeback called Mombo, named after the safari lodge where she and her husband met.

You can also:

- Sign up to my newsletter and get a free book here. https://www.subscribepage.com/n5n5o9
- Like me on Facebook here: https://www.facebook.com/AuthorBeverleyOakley/
- Follow me on BookBub here: https://www.bookbub.com/profile/beverley-oakley
- Visit my Website here.
- http://www.beverleyoakley.com/
- Visit my Amazon Page
- https://www.amazon.com/Beverley-Oakley/e/B01HOFCS8K/ref=dp_byline_cont_ebooks_1

Thank you and happy reading!
Beverley Oakley

www.beverleyoakley.com/
beverley.oakley@gmail.com

www.ingramcontent.com/pod-product-compliance
Lightning Source LLC
Chambersburg PA
CBHW030231120726
47903CB00005B/1443